Love this cover sketch...
but could we please try
something where Connor
isn't SUCH a focus?
Maybe he can be
smaller this time.

# EVERY TIME
# I GO ON
# VACATION,
# SOMEONE DIES

# EVERY TIME I GO ON VACATION, SOMEONE DIES

A NOVEL

CATHERINE MACK

MINOTAUR
BOOKS
NEW YORK

First published in the United States by Minotaur Books, an imprint of St. Martin's Publishing Group

EVERY TIME I GO ON VACATION, SOMEONE DIES. Copyright © 2024 by Catherine Mack. All rights reserved. Printed in the United States of America. For information, address St. Martin's Publishing Group, 120 Broadway, New York, NY 10271.

www.minotaurbooks.com

Designed by Omar Chapa
Endpaper design by David Baldeosingh Rotstein
Front and back endpaper art: book cover sketches by Monika Roe;
wine stain © BERNATSKAIA OKSANA/Shutterstock.com;
doodles of sun, cocktails, sailboat, ice cream, soda, lounge chair © Drawlab19/
Shutterstock.com; doodles of sunglasses and sandals © Rawpixel.com/
Shutterstock.com; folded paper texture © hely/Shutterstock.com

Library of Congress Cataloging-in-Publication Data

Names: Mack, Catherine, author.
Title: Every time I go on vacation, someone dies / Catherine Mack.
Description: First U.S. edition. | New York : Minotaur Books, 2024. |
Series: The vacation series ; 1
Identifiers: LCCN 2023056221 | ISBN 9781250325853 (hardcover) |
ISBN 9781250359018 (international edition) | ISBN 9781250325860 (ebook)
Subjects: LCGFT: Detective and mystery fiction. | Novels.
Classification: LCC PS3613.A272544 E94 2024 |
DDC 813/.6—dc23/eng/20231207
LC record available at https://lccn.loc.gov/2023056221

Our books may be purchased in bulk for promotional, educational, or business use. Please contact your local bookseller or the Macmillan Corporate and Premium Sales Department at 1-800-221-7945, extension 5442, or by email at MacmillanSpecialMarkets@macmillan.com.

First U.S. Edition: 2024
First International Edition: 2024

10  9  8  7  6  5  4  3  2  1

*To Stephanie Kip Rostan and Liz Fenton—*
*for always believing in me and encouraging me to swing for the fences*

The beginning is rarely the beginning. It's the middle, or it's near the end, or it's on its way to being that way. Death might be the inciting incident, but death doesn't just happen. There's a beginning, middle, and end to that, too.

—ELEANOR DASH, *WHEN IN ROME*
(THE VACATION MYSTERIES #1)

One doesn't recognize the really important moments in one's life until it's too late.

—AGATHA CHRISTIE

# EVERY TIME
# I GO ON
# VACATION,
# SOMEONE DIES

# ABOUT THE AUTHOR

Eleanor Dash is the author of the Vacation Mysteries series, which began with *When in Rome*, a runaway bestseller that was on the *New York Times* bestseller list for six months. Eleanor studied marketing at the University of Southern California but ended up skipping out on her first day of work with a big advertising company because she was deep into writing. Oops! That probably wouldn't have worked out anyway.

Eleanor lives in Venice Beach, California, with her sister, Harper. One day she hopes to work up the courage to jump out of an airplane, but since she gets vertigo in tall buildings, that's highly unlikely.

You can follow her on all the usual places on social, but why would you want to?

# CHAPTER 1

## I'm Going to Kill Him

**Rome**

Bless me, Father, for I have sinned.

I want to commit a homicide.

Why, you ask? Bear with me for a second, and I'll explain.

I write books for a living. But the thing is, I never meant to write a book in the first place. I know that sounds nuts—who writes an entire *novel* by accident?—but that's what happened. Ten years ago, after a life-changing trip to Italy during a crisp January, I wrote a book.

And okay, I know what you're thinking. Didn't Elizabeth Gilbert do that already? Was it some kind of *Eat, Pray, Love* knockoff?

I want to say no, but the truth is—kind of?

I mean, there were thefts, detective work, and even a murder. But there was also lots of travel, a love story, and pasta.

I'll get to all of that.

What you need to know right now is that when I got home after a whirlwind month of adventure, I had an overwhelming urge to write down what had happened, and it spilled out of me in a feverish rush. How I met Connor Smith, how we got embroiled in solving a series of robberies that ended in a murder, how we fell in love—I sifted through everything we'd experienced and out came *When in Rome*.

And the things that happened in the months after that—getting an agent, selling the book at auction, being flown to New York to meet my publishing team—felt like a continuation of a dream I couldn't seem to wake up from.

My wake-up call came six weeks before the book was scheduled to launch that November.

Because I'd forgotten one *tiny* detail.

I never told Connor I was writing about *him*. I just invited him to meet me in New York and didn't tell him why.

If I'm being honest—and that's what this is about, right? *Confession*—I thought that when I told him, he'd pick me up and twirl me around like in a scene from a movie.

That's not what happened.

Instead, I got, well, not *blackmailed* exactly, but something blackmail adjacent.

Because once Connor understood that he was soon to be the star of a true-crime novel—that I'd changed everyone else's names, including my own, to protect the guilty, but not his—he wanted 10 percent of my advance. It was that or—he told the publisher with an élan I had to admire—he'd *see us in court*.

Even though he didn't have a legal leg to stand on,[1] my publisher didn't want to take the chance.[2] And there was a clause in my contract that said if we went to court, *I'd* be on the hook for the legal fees.[3]

I didn't remember even *seeing* that clause.

---

[1] I've always wanted to use footnotes in a manuscript, but my editor would never let me. Anyway, if you care about the legalities, you can use another person's <u>real</u> name, likeness, etc., in a book so long as they're presented in a neutral or positive way. Since Connor was the hero of *When in Rome*, it wasn't defamation.

[2] I should note that I'm not a lawyer, and you shouldn't construe anything I write in here as legal advice.

[3] You can skip these, by the way. But if you're interested, it's called an indemnification clause. Google it.

I mean, does anyone read twenty-page single-spaced contracts?

I was going to from now on, obviously. But in the meantime, what if I gave him the cut of my advance he wanted, my publisher asked. That would make it so much simpler for everyone.

So I paid.

One book, I thought. One book, and then I'd be rid of him.

Everyone who's ever been blackmailed in the history of blackmail probably thinks that. I'll pay *once*, and that'll be enough. Spoiler alert: It's never enough.

Not for Connor.

Because *When in Rome* sold beyond everyone's wildest expectations, and Connor was there for all of it. Slipping his arm around my waist in countless photos. Showing up *everywhere*. Basking in the fucking glow. And then my publisher offered me an enormous amount of money to write a sequel. Maybe I could write something else someday, but for now, more Connor, please! And could you be a darling and get it done in six months so you publish a book a year? Of course you can.

Anyway, when Connor got wind of the offer, he insisted I take it. I wouldn't want *certain information about me* to go public, would I? No, he didn't think so.

He took 20 percent of my advance that time.[4] And when *Murder in Nice* was almost as successful as the first book, my publisher wanted another. And another. And another.

I tried pitching something else, but all they wanted was Connor. With his blue eyes and charming smile—"like Captain America with a smirk," I'd written, because I was twenty-five and an idiot.

And now it's ten years later, and I feel like I'm stuck with him forever, like Agatha Christie was with Poirot or Sir Arthur Conan Doyle

---

[4] No, I'm not going to tell you how much they paid me. Talking about money is gross.

was with Sherlock. They eventually killed off their main characters, and that's what I'm going to do.

I'm going to kill him.

I just need to find a way to get away with it.

"... Ma'am? This is all very interesting, but I can't absolve you of a crime you haven't committed."

Oh, shit. Did I say all of that out loud? To an actual priest? Looks like it.

I lean back in the confession box, resting my back against the worn wooden frame. Though my thick, dark hair is up in a topknot, the tendrils that have escaped are hot against my neck, and this seat is murder on my back.

"So," I say to the small screen in the wall, "if I ask for forgiveness *after* the fact, you can give it, but not before?"

"That's right, ma'am."

"Shouldn't it be 'signorina'?"

"I'm visiting the parish from America, ma'am."

The one church I visit in Rome, and I get an *American* priest?

"Oh, yeah? Where from?"

"We're not supposed to talk about ourselves."

"It's Texas, right?"

"... I'm from Dallas."

I smile in satisfaction. I've always been good at accents. "I knew it."

"Ma'am?"

"It's Eleanor, I told you."

"Do you want to pray on your thoughts about ..."

"Connor Smith?"

"I've found it helpful to pray on my anger. It soothes the soul."

Praying isn't going to help me get rid of Connor, though, which I knew when I came in here. But it was very hot out, and the worn marble church sitting on the corner of the piazza looked so cool and inviting, I couldn't help myself.

Once I was inside, I gazed around the incense-infused space and the mahogany-paneled walls. I was drawn to the small booth tucked into a corner. The confessional, I realized when I stepped past the bloodred velvet curtain. I'd always wondered what they were like. Turns out: small and stuffy. But before I could leave, there was a cough through the wall and a soothing voice suggested I unburden myself. Seemed like a good idea at the time. Now I don't know how to get out of this conversation.

"Eleanor? Are you in here?"

Oh, thank God.

Oh, um, I mean, thank you, God.

I pull back the curtain. My younger sister,[5] Harper, is scuttling down the aisle with a worried expression on her beautiful face. She's wearing a white poplin dress that shows off her long, tanned limbs and complements her chestnut hair, which, like so many things, is one shade better than mine.[6] She's wearing it braided and wound around her head, a look that suits her but would make me look like Princess Leia's less attractive sister.[7, 8]

"I'm here!" I wave my hand so she sees me.

Her face relaxes. Her eyes are a shade better than mine, too—a perfect cornflower blue framed with heavy, dark lashes. Mine are washed out, and my lashes are almost invisible without mascara.

"What are you doing in here, El?"

I step out of the booth. "Confessing my sins?"

"You haven't been gone long enough for that."

"Ha ha."

---

[5] She's a little over two years younger than me, which makes me thirty-five. Joy.

[6] Think Evangeline Lilly in her *Lost* days, not with that terrible haircut she had in the first *Ant-Man* or *Quantumania*.

[7] Or Evangeline Lilly's less attractive sister—ha!

[8] Okay, okay, I shouldn't be so hard on myself. Sometimes people say I look like Rachel Brosnahan when she's a brunette, but her *Mrs. Maisel* wardrobe is much more fabulous than anything I could pull off.

She plucks a piece of lint from my navy dress. It's made of the same material as hers, light as a feather. She found it for me on a shopping trip to New York. Besides being my sister, she's the best personal assistant anyone could ask for.

I wish she didn't resent me for it so much, and I'm terrified she's going to leave me at the end of this trip. She hasn't said it explicitly, but she's dropped enough hints about me doing more stuff *on my own* that it's clear where she's headed.

Away from me.

"You don't need to do that," I say, catching her hand.

Do I even need to tell you that her manicure is a perfect ballet pink, while I've long stopped bothering with getting my nails done? No, right? You've got the picture.

"We need to get going," Harper says.

"What's next?"

"The Colosseum."

"Must we?"

"They want us to get some shots there to start hyping *Roman Holiday Gone Wrong.*"

"I haven't agreed to that title."

"Regardless."

"Okay, fine. But I need ice cream if I'm going to be back out in that heat."

"It's called *gelato.*"

"I'm doing it again, aren't I? Being the stupid American tourist?"

"Kinda."

"Sorry, sis." I rope my arm around her neck and pull her close. She smells like lemons and home to me, a slight variation on my own scent.

"I saw a gelato shop around the corner," Harper says.

"You're a lifesaver."

"You get any insight in there?" She points over my shoulder.

Oh, crap, I left Mr. Texas alone without saying goodbye. "Hold on."

I step to the confessional and pull the curtain back. "Are you still there?"

"Yes, ma'am."

"I've got to go."

"Go with God."

"Okay, thanks." Okay? *Okay?* Do I go directly to hell now, or do I at least get to plead my case at the pearly gates? "Thank you for listening."

"You can leave an offering in one of the boxes."

"Oh, right, sure. Will do."

But wait. Wasn't he supposed to give me rosaries to say? A penance? Something that will wash away the sin of wanting Connor Smith dead, even if it's just on paper?

I search around for the offering box. Harper's standing with her hands clasped behind her, staring at the huge stained glass window above the altar of Madonna and Child. The sunlight is filtering through it, throwing out a pinwheel of colors. She looks angelic, and I almost don't want to disturb her. But I also badly want a gelato, and she's carrying my wallet.

Yeah, yeah, I *know*. I'm working on being less dependent, I promise. But the truth is that my life would be a mess without her.

"Harper?"

She brings her head down and turns. She looks disappointed, like I've woken her out of a particularly good dream. "Yeah?"

"We're not Catholic, right?"

"How could you not know that?"

"I remember church at Christmas, and didn't we go at Easter sometimes? Am I making that up?"

"I'm not your memory palace."

"Aren't you?"

"Ha."

"So?"

"Yeah, we went at Christmas. Mom loved the carols."

"Right. And Dad loved the Easter egg roll!"

She touches her nose with one finger and points the other at me. "We have a winner."

"I wish I remembered them more."

Our parents died when I was eighteen. Which should be more than old enough for me to remember them, but instead, having to immediately become Harper's parent seems to have erased most of my memories.

The good ones, anyway.

Harper smiles sadly. "Me too."

"Anyways . . . Should we jet?"

"You wouldn't happen to know where Connor is, would you?"

"Isn't it your job to keep tabs on him?"

"I was too busy looking for you."

"How did you find me, anyway?"

She waves her iPhone. It's in a cherry red case to distinguish it from mine, which is a deep candied blue.

"What's that supposed to mean?"

"For a person who writes mysteries, you are weak in the ways of stalking."

"You're tracking me through your phone? Did I authorize this?"

"I run all of your passwords, social media, banking . . ."

"So, you could defraud me in a hot minute."

"If you didn't pay me amazingly."

"Which I do."

"Which you do."

"Harper . . ."

She turns away. "Not now, okay? After."

"After what?"

"When we get home. Then we'll talk."

Shit, shit, *shit*. I was right. She's leaving me.

"Why wait?"

"Let's enjoy the trip."

"Connor and all?"

She bursts out laughing, then stops herself so quickly I can almost hear the record scratch. "About that . . ."

"What's he done now?"

She meets my eyes, and there's a terrible mix of heartbreak and resignation in hers that hurts my heart.

"Harper?"

Her eyes fill. She wipes a tear away with the back of her hand, and my own throat tightens in response. A wave of violence floods through me. And even though I'm in church, even though I was *just* seeking forgiveness, I have only one thought now.

I'm going to fucking kill him.

"Eleanor?" Connor's voice shatters my murderous thoughts about, well, *him*. "Ah, there you are."

I turn around slowly. Connor's standing with his hands on his hips, devastatingly handsome in a seersucker suit and a matching fedora. His face is tanned, and his dark blond hair is short on the sides and brushed back from his forehead. His eyes are the most striking thing about him—a deep sea blue, like the Mediterranean on a calm day.[9]

"Where the hell have you been?" I say with an edge to my voice I can't seem to bury.

"Oh, ho, ho, she's angry." His accent is half British and half the flat accent of a Canadian. He's never given me a clear answer about where he grew up.

Juvenile detention, I suggested once, and he hadn't denied it.

"I've told you not to talk about me in the third person."

He leans forward like he's bowing to the Queen.

Oh, wait. She died, right?

---

[9] He's a dead ringer for Chris Evans, but without that Midwestern wholesomeness. If anything, that edge of danger makes him <u>more</u> appealing. I know, right? Connor knows that, too.

The King, then. Hmmm, that sounds weird.

"Whatever my lady wishes."

"She wishes you'd disappear," I mutter.

"What's that?"

"Nothing. We're late. *You're* late."

He looks past me at Harper, and I realize she hasn't said a word.

"Harper," he says, using his most charming smile.[10] "You're looking well."

I can feel the blush spreading up Harper's cheeks even though I can't see it. It's that way with people you know too well sometimes. Their reactions become yours.

"We should go," I say.

"I need to speak to you, El," Connor says.

"What about?"

He steps closer as Harper takes a step back, trying to fade into the background like I wish I could.

No such luck.

"I need your help," Connor says.

"Why?"

He lets out a long, slow breath. "Someone's trying to kill me."

Wait, *what?*

---

[10] And it's extra fucking charming, let me tell you.

# WHEN IN ROME

[JACKET FLAP COPY]

TO CATCH A THIEF...

When Cecilia Crane goes to Rome for a one-month holiday before she starts her first job after college, she isn't looking for anything other than good wine, pasta, and someone to teach her Italian. But then she meets the dashing Connor Smith, an American expat with an air of mystery who's all too happy to show her around Rome and teach her everything he knows about his favorite city.

They fall quickly into a whirlwind romance, but there's more to Rome, and Connor, than meets the eye. The city is gripped by a series of daring, unsolved bank robberies, and Connor's been tasked by an insurance company to investigate them. Cecilia and Connor join forces to solve the case, but the more they dig, the deeper the secrets they start to uncover.

And then a body turns up at one of the robberies... Will Cecilia and Connor crack the case before it's too late? Or will this Roman holiday be her last?

# CHAPTER 2

## Justifiable Homicide

"Someone's trying to kill me," Connor repeats when I don't say anything for longer than is normal for me.

"Are you joking?"

"I most definitely am *not* joking."

My brain is whirring. *I* was just thinking about killing him and someone's beaten me to the punch? Is this God answering my prayers? No, no. I'm going to hell for even thinking that. And Connor's still here, alive. So my prayers haven't been answered.

Not yet.

"Why would someone want to kill you?"

"I would've thought that would be obvious," Harper says under her breath, but, you know, not *that* quietly.

Connor ignores her, intent on me. "I don't know why."

"So why do you think someone's trying to kill you, then?"

"It started a couple of weeks ago. At first, I thought it was an isolated incident, but now . . ."

"What isolated incident?"

"The brakes on my car gave out when I was driving in the Hills."

He means the Hollywood Hills. He has a house up there paid for by yours truly.[11] It's nicer than my house, even though I'd never want to live that far away from the beach. He claims it was mostly paid for with his finder's fee money,[12] but he blew most of *that* at the baccarat tables in Monaco soon after he got it, so . . .

"The Citroën?"

And yes, he drives a baby blue Citroën from the 1960s because of course he does.

"Yes." He takes off his fedora and runs his hand through his hair. Usually, he does that to draw attention to its thickness (his hair *is* pretty awesome), but today it comes across as a genuine nervous tic. "Thankfully, I realized the brakes were out when I was going uphill, so nothing bad happened. I was able to turn into a driveway and call Triple-A. The car's old; I chalked it up to bad maintenance."

"That sounds scary," Harper says.

"It was."

His voice is steady, but I recognize the tone—genuine fear.

Goddamn it.

"What did the garage say?" I ask.

"The brake-fluid hose clamp failed, which they said was likely due to the age of the car."

I sigh slowly. "Is that it?"

"No. Yesterday, after the tour of the Vatican, someone pushed me into traffic. If it hadn't been for a passerby who yanked me back at the last

---

[11] He continues to take 20 percent of my advances, plus any royalties I make after that. My publisher had to create a new column on my royalty statements because usually the only deduction is for the agent's 15 percent. His column is called "consultant." I suggested "extortion," but the lawyers nixed that because they thought it might be "tortious." That's a fancy word for "I might get sued for calling what Connor's done by its real name."

[12] More about this later.

moment, I would've ended up under the wheels of one of those hop-on, hop-off buses full of bleeding tourists."

I know it's wrong, but I can't help but smother a laugh. The image of impeccably dressed Connor being flattened under the wheels of a bus full of sightseers in fanny packs using selfie sticks, well . . . it's not *quite* a cartoon, but it is cartoon *adjacent*.

"Where did this happen?"

"That main road into Vatican City."

Harper and I had been on that road yesterday, too. The Via della Conciliazione is a beautiful cobblestoned boulevard lined with sandstone buildings that connects Vatican City with Rome. But it was also so thick with tourists that it was hard to breathe. I'd been jostled more times than I could count.

"Hmmm." I click my tongue against the roof of my mouth. "Harper, let's go."

"Wait, I—"

But I don't wait for him to say anything more. Instead, I grab Harper and haul her outside. Connor has some good qualities—even I can admit that—but his tendency to think everything is about him isn't one of them.

I mean, who thinks being elbowed in a crowd equates to attempted murder? Connor Smith, that's who.

And yes, I agree with Harper that if he *were* murdered, there'd be a long list of suspects. But just because someone's a master at creating antipathy doesn't mean that every almost-accident is a cover for something nefarious.

All this to say, I doubt very highly anyone's trying to assassinate him.

Except for me, that is.

And that's our little secret.

We step out of the church, and I immediately feel like I'm drowning in heat. Whoever thought it was a good idea to book a tour in Italy in July is a lunatic.[13] But I'd said yes to it, hadn't I? So maybe I'm the lunatic.

I mean, obviously.

"Can we get gelato now?" I ask Harper, clinging to the shadow cast by the church as I cover my eyes with a pair of oversized sunglasses.

"Don't you want to find out what's going on with Connor?"

I glance over my shoulder as he exits the church. He's put his fedora back on, but his shoulders are still slumped like he has a slow leak.

"Do you?"

Harper shakes her head. "I vote for ice cream."

"This is why I love you."

"Also genetics."

"True."

She links her arm through mine and we march away from Connor. I don't care if he follows us. I need to shake off the cognitive dissonance of the last five minutes.

Because what if someone *did* kill Connor?

That would be amazingly convenient.

Which is why it can't be happening. Or maybe I'm magic. I've sometimes suspected as much. I know it sounds crazy, but sometimes I think something and then it happens. Okay, well, once.[14] But still . . . [15]

Sigh. *This* is all just magical thinking—the idea that I can make what I know needs to happen come true with my thoughts. It's going to take more than that. A whole book, in fact. Can I do it? Incur the wrath

---

[13] Like many things you'll read in the next 350 pages or so (but not all), this is a clue.

[14] I was home sick once and flipping through channels and the logo for Warner Bros. came up on the screen, and I thought, it's going to be *The Lake House,* and it *was.* I love that movie. Don't judge.

[15] Okay, I know that's a lame example. But sometimes when I'm speaking to people, they pause, and I know the word they're going to say before they say it. That's a kind of magic, right?

of my "public" and my agent and my publisher and let him die in the next book?

If I *did* do it, I could kill him off in the first third, and then use the rest of the novel to introduce my new hero. No, *heroine.*

Yes. Good. My new main character will be a competent, trained *woman.* A police officer, maybe. *The* police officer brought in to solve Connor's murder—

"El?" Harper says, tugging on my arm.

"Yeah?"

"You okay?"

"Hot, but why do you ask?"

"Because you were talking to yourself. It sounded like you said, 'One quick blow to the head.'"

"Oh, sorry. Plotting."

"I'll never understand how you do that."

"What?"

"Figure out plots when you can't even pay your electric bill on time."

I pull her closer. "Don't be silly. You could do it if you wanted to."

She stiffens. Shit. That wasn't the right thing to say.

Harper was supposed to be the writer in the family, something she'd been planning since she was eight. Instead, I got a book deal, and she agreed to be my assistant for a six-month stint that never ended. Now her life is too much about me and she barely writes anymore.

I don't know what to do about it. But the unspoken agreement between us is that we don't speak about her writing, or her *not* writing.

We struck that bargain when I'd pushed her finally finished manuscript on my editor a couple of years ago and she'd politely declined to publish it. When I asked her why, she'd asked me if I'd read it. The truth was, I hadn't. I was so certain Harper's novel would be as brilliant as Harper, I hadn't stopped to check.[16]

---

[16] Proof positive that I can't actually foresee the future.

"I'm sorry, Harper, I didn't—"

"It's fine."

"No, it isn't."

She pulls away. "It doesn't matter."

"We can ditch this stupid tour and go somewhere and talk."

"Nope. Remember? After."

"Okay, after."

"Come on, it's just over here."

We round the corner onto a short, narrow street full of tiny shops and tourists. There are old cobblestones under our feet, and the storefronts are a colorful mix of reds and blues. It's a nice respite from the busy street behind us, and whatever bullshit Connor's spinning.

The gelato shop is, miraculously, free of the usual long line, and we step inside. The young, hot guy behind the counter coos over Harper, like all men do, and I try not to let it bother me.[17] It's no coincidence, though, that the two men I've been in love with met me without her present.

Anyway, she doesn't give the gelato guy her number when he asks for it, just picks up our order—lemon for me and chocolate for her.

I want to linger in the cool air and stare at the vibrant colors of the massive vats of gelato, but Harper pulls me outside because we need to meet our tour guide in ten minutes.

Once we're on the street again, I take a slow bite of lemon-flavored creaminess while the hot wind blows on my face. I close my eyes in pleasure, savoring the cool feeling in my mouth.

By the time I leave this trip, I'm going to be equal parts gelato and Aperol spritz.[18]

Speaking of which: "Is there time for a drink before the tour?"

"Absolutely not."

---

[17] Okay, it <u>obviously</u> bothers me. But I'm trying to bury it in a footnote.

[18] OMG, I just found an Aperol spritz sorbet recipe! I'm doomed.

"Damn it."

Harper grins at me before a storm cloud passes over her face. I sense Connor's presence behind me, like how the air changes before it rains.

"I need your help, Eleanor," Connor says.

I turn around slowly, but not slowly enough. He's standing so close to me that my elbow catches on his arm and my cup of gelato pops out of my hand and falls to the ground. Its contents spread across the cobblestones, immediately melting like butter in a hot frying pan.

If I murder Connor in revenge for killing my ice cream, would that be considered justifiable homicide?

"Sorry about that, El." Something in his tone is different—less sure of himself, less cocky. Like his voice in the church, it reminds me of the Connor I used to know.

"Suppose it's true. What do you want me to do about it?"

"Help me figure out what's happening. Like the old days. You remember."

I shudder despite the heat. That's the problem. I *do* remember. Too much of it.

"Your brakes failed on an old car, and you got jostled in traffic. That's a pretty thin plot."

He nods slowly. "It's all true, though."

"What aren't you telling me?"

He takes his fedora off and holds it between his hands. "I'm not certain I can say." His voice is full of emotion and—

Oh good God, no. No, no, *no.* I am *not* going to feel sorry for Connor Smith.

"If you want my help, you're going to have to tell me everything."

He glances at Harper. She stares back, eating her gelato slowly.

"Harper's part of the equation," I say. "You tell me, you tell her."

"And I have your promise that you'll keep whatever I say confidential?"

"If someone *is* trying to kill you, we might have to involve the police—"

"No. No police."

This is what I get for plotting a murder in a church. And *shit*. I forgot to put money in the offering box. I'm being punished—this is the penance Mr. Texas Priest forgot to mete out.[19]

"Okay, no police for now," I say. "Spill."

He works his jaw and then opens his mouth to speak, but before he can get the words out, the air is filled with a *Pop! Pop! Pop!*

"Get down!" he shouts, dragging me to the ground with him. He covers my body with his, half suffocating me into the cobblestones.

And now I know I'm not just being punished; I'm in hell.

Because only the devil could come up with an ending for me like this.

---

[19] I had to look this one up. He was supposed to tell me to say the rosary, which means saying "Our Father" on the first bead, then "Hail Mary" on the next three beads, then something called the "Mystery," which goes on for five <u>decades</u>. No, thank you. I can wrap up a mystery <u>way</u> faster than that.

# THE VACATION MYSTERIES SERIES ORDER

*When in Rome* (Book 1)

*Murder in Nice* (Book 2)

*Death on the Thames* (Book 3)

*Gibraltar Is for Dying* (Book 4)

*Highland Killing* (Book 5)

*Loch-ed Away* (Book 6)

*Suspect in Seville* (Book 7)

*Passed Away in Paris* (Book 8)

*Drowned in Porto* (Book 9)

~~Roman Holiday Gone Wrong~~[20]

~~Lost in Amalfi~~

~~Escape to Amalfi~~

~~Escape from Amalfi~~

*Amalfi Made Me Do It*

---

[20] This title sucks. They probably won't let me keep <u>my</u> title, but a girl can dream.

# CHAPTER 3

## Was This on the Itinerary?

Those shots in the air aren't the end. I don't die. None of us do.

Instead, after a moment of silence where Connor's fully on top of me like we're about to get busy, he pushes himself up on his elbows and looks down. "Now do you believe me?"

"Get off me!" I say as I give him a push.

He rolls sideways, landing on his back, a satisfying *oof!* escaping from his mouth.

It was satisfying to me, anyway. It probably hurt for him.

I check around me. Harper's still casually eating her ice cream as if nothing unusual happened. I sit up slowly. My back feels wet and sticky. I landed in my melted gelato. Because of course I did.

"Why did you do that?"

"I was saving your life, thank you very much." Connor pushes himself up and looks around quickly. There's a small circle of people staring at us with curiosity while the rest of the tourists go about their day.

"It was a car backfiring, you dumbass." I stand up and glare at Harper. "You enjoying this?"

Harper gives a small shrug. "Kind of?"

I reach around my back to the wet patch. It's right between my shoulder blades. "Can you hand me a Kleenex?"

Harper makes a spinning motion with her finger and I turn around. She pats at me with a Kleenex for a moment, then stops. "That will have to do."

"No time to go back to the hotel?"

"Sorry, no."

"But I'm all sticky."

"You want to switch dresses?"

"It's fine."

I mean, I *do*, but there's a schedule to keep. I can suck it up.

"Is Connor still on the ground?" I ask.

Harper checks over my shoulder. "He's standing now."

"Which way to the Colosseum?"

"Hey! You can't just ignore me," Connor says.

I roll my eyes as I turn to face him. He doesn't look any worse for wear from our tumble. I'm the only one suffering the consequences of his actions, as per usual.

"You said you were going to help me," he says.

"Did I?"

"It was implied."

"This is how you repay me? Throwing me to the ground and jumping on top of me?"

"I thought someone was shooting at us."

I put my hands on my hips. "In the middle of a crowd? In the middle of the day? In the middle of Rome?"

"You think assassinations don't happen in daylight?"

"No one's trying to kill you."

Connor stoops and picks up his fedora. He puts it on his head at a rakish angle. "You think this is all in my head? That I'm just some massive narcissist?"

"If the shoe fits."

"I'm telling the truth."

"Fine. But if you want me to believe that, you're going to have to give me more to go on."

He works his jaw for a moment, then gives in. "I think I know who it is."

I *knew* it.

"Who?"

He checks our surroundings. No one's paying attention to us anymore. "Someone's been blackmailing me."

Oh, the *irony*.

"You're joking. About what?"

He glances at Harper again and a nervous knot forms in my stomach. Connor has a million secrets, but I have just the *one*.[21] If this has something to do with that, then I truly am going to end him.

"I got involved in something financial last year," Connor says.

"Something shady," I guess.

"It was a good opportunity. But then it went south, and, well, I . . ."

"You covered it up?" Harper says.

Connor cocks his head to the side. "In a manner of speaking."

"But someone found out?" I say. "And that person started blackmailing you?"

"Yes."

"That doesn't make sense."

Connor's eyes flash with annoyance. "People do get blackmailed, El."

"You think *I* don't know that?"

We stare at each other, a contest of wills, which I win for once because it's Connor who speaks first. "Why did you say it doesn't make sense, then?"

"You paid this money?"

"Yes."

"How much?"

"I wouldn't want to say."

I grit my teeth, but I'll circle back to that later. Who cares how much

---

[21] I'm not telling you what that is <u>now</u>. Keep reading.

it is? Only there would be *some* poetic justice in him losing everything he took from me.

"Why would the blackmailer kill you, then?"

"He told them he wouldn't pay anymore," Harper guesses because she's always been the smart one. "Right?"

"Yes," Connor says.

"How did they react to that?" I ask.[22]

"They said something about making me pay for it."

Good Lord, who's writing this person's dialogue? Were they twirling their black mustache at the same time?

"When was this?"

"A couple of days before the car accident."

"So, your brakes failed right after someone threatened you, and you didn't think the two were related?"

He doesn't say anything, just scowls for an answer.

"Did they contact you afterward?"

"No."

"Hmmm." I touch the back of my dress. The gelato is half dried and has hardened into some new substance. "And what about after yesterday?"

"I haven't heard anything from them since that last message."

"Which you received how?"

"Through encrypted text."

"Unsigned, I assume?" He nods. "Do you still have them?"

"They disappear after you read them."

"No screenshots?"

"No."

I put my hands on my hips. "Didn't you used to be a private detective?"

---

[22] I'd tried to stop paying Connor when I renewed my last contract three years ago. It would be a fresh start, I said, for both of us. He didn't even say anything. He just gave me this <u>look</u>, which was enough to let me know that nothing had changed and nothing was going to change. His "consultant" fees remained.

"No need to mock me."

"Right, sorry. I'm just . . . surprised."

"At?"

"All of it, frankly. I wouldn't have thought you'd cave to blackmail."

His face changes to that vulnerable look again.

He's going to have to stop doing that.

"I don't want to go to prison. You understand that, surely."

Oh, I understand. "How long would you get?"

A fantasy montage is running through my mind. Connor in an orange jumpsuit holding some scratchy towel and those slipper shoes they make prisoners wear. His thick hair growing lank and gray.

No one's ever said I lack imagination.

Connor grimaces. "I understand the sentence for being an accessory is lengthy."

We lock eyes again and we're having two conversations. The things we say out loud and the things that are simply understood between us.

"As interesting as this is, we need to go," Harper says. "We're already late."

"To be continued," I say to Connor.

He puts his hands on his hips. "Is this not more important?"

"There's nothing we can do about it now. Let's do the tour, and we'll discuss it afterward."

He doesn't like it, but he doesn't have much choice. "All right. And, um, thank you."

This stops me. I've never heard Connor thank anyone before. Certainly not me.

"Tick tock," Harper says, tapping her foot.

"Yes, coming."

I link my arm through Harper's, and we walk down the street with Connor following behind. We're only a few minutes from the Colosseum, so we won't be too late. It's something Harper's always bugging me about—my tardiness. Harper's never late for anything.

"What do you make of that?" Harper says once we've turned off the side street and are in the middle of a crowd on the Piazza del Colosseo. The sky is a perfect, icy blue above the Arch of Constantine—a tall marble structure with three arches in it.

"I don't know yet."

"I bet he knows who's blackmailing him."

"Agreed. Or a list of suspects at least."

"Wonder why he didn't tell you?"

"That's how Connor operates. On a need-to-know basis."

"True. This way."

We cross the street to the courtyard outside the Colosseum. Doing this in Rome always feels like taking your life into your hands,[23] and today is no exception. Pushing someone into traffic *would* be a good way to get rid of someone. People must get run over by cars in this city all the time.[24]

We make it safely across, and now we're directly in front of the Colosseum. Its faded marble contours rise above us, looming over the throngs of tourists wearing small yellow transmitters on black lanyards, and tour guides yelling out the prices of their tours.

I did this tour ten years ago with Connor. He'd dazzled me with his knowledge of Roman history. Then he'd taken me out for one of the best meals I've ever had at this little tucked-away restaurant and kissed me until my knees were weak on the Ponte Fabricio.[25] Early the next morning, a bank was burglarized while half the city was at the Festa de'

---

[23] The symbol on the traffic signs for when it's the pedestrian's turn to cross shows a person <u>running</u>. Enough said.

[24] Turns out they do! More than 1,300 people were hit by cars in Rome a couple of years ago, and more than forty people <u>died</u>.

[25] The oldest standing bridge in Rome, apparently, constructed in 62 BC. "Imagine all of the people who've kissed here," Connor had said, then we'd done just that. I think I actually <u>swooned</u>.

Noantri.[26] I'd been instantly fascinated with the robberies, and Connor was, too. Soon after, he was hired to investigate them and we figured out that we made a good team.[27] It felt like a confirmation of the feelings I had for him, but then . . .

I push away the dark thoughts trying to crowd their way in. All this talk of murder—real and imagined—coupled with being back in this city with Connor has left me feeling unsettled. The day may be sunny, but there's a shadow across it.[28]

"Where are we supposed to be meeting the guide?" I ask.

"Over there, I think." Harper points to a group of twenty middle-aged women standing in a tight-knit circle. They're all wearing the same T-shirt, and it takes me a minute to realize the design on the front is *When in Rome*'s book cover.

My heart sinks. "This is a fan event?"

"Did you not read the itinerary?"

I didn't read the itinerary. I never do. Reading about the details of travel exhausts me. Instead, I'd opened the email so it was marked as "read" and forgot about it.

"Some of it?"

"You're the worst."

I glance over my shoulder. Connor's looking at the pack of fans with mild amusement, his distress from a few minutes ago erased. "Pretty sure I'm not."

---

[26] A super religious festival where Romans carry a Madonna statue through the streets. Connor held me close to him in the crowd and whispered facts about it in my ear the whole time, and I could actually feel myself falling in love.

[27] That was the first time I realized that I had the right kind of brain to puzzle out mysteries. Before then, I thought my skill at figuring out escape rooms was useless.

[28] Let's just say that there's a reason I'm telling you about the details of our romance in the <u>footnotes</u>.

"Yes," Harper says. "It's a fan event."

"And these fans are?"

"The BookFace Ladies."

"The what now?"

"You know, BookFace? That thing they do on Instagram where they hold up the book to their face to match the image?"

The cover for *When in Rome* is half a woman's face with the Roman skyline in silhouette behind it. The women's T-shirts all have some variation of a woman holding the book to one side of their face so the face on the book makes up the other half.

BookFace. I get it.

"Why's it on their T-shirts?"

"That's how they got here. The contest? Please do not tell me you forgot the contest."

"Of course not."

Only I have. Because there's no way in hell I'd agree to do a book tour with Connor *and* a bunch of fans. I love my fans, I do, but some of them are nuts.

Why else would they want to sleep with Connor and make "jokes" in endless emails to me about how they're going to "take me out" so they have a chance with him?[29]

Oh! Maybe it's a fan who's trying to kill Connor?

Only, wait, that doesn't work. It's *me* they want to kill, not him.

"Remind me of the details again?" I say to Harper.

"They posted their BookFaces on Instagram, and twenty of them won an all-expenses-paid ticket to Rome."

"Right, right."

"There were twenty thousand entries."

---

[29] I keep these emails in a folder labeled "crazy people." If I die suddenly, Harper knows to turn this folder over to the police.

"Wow . . ." I clear my throat. "And the parts of the tour that are with me?"

"Today at the Colosseum and then the lunch tomorrow in Pompeii. Some stuff later."

"The *lunch*."

"There will be alcohol."

"There better be. Any other surprises in store for me?"

She gives me a sideways grin. "Shoulda read the itinerary!"

# INVITATION TO THE *WHEN IN ROME* TENTH ANNIVERSARY TOUR

Please join

**ELEANOR DASH**
**CONNOR SMITH**
**GUY CHARLES**
**OLIVER FORREST**

and the entire Vacation Mysteries Extended Universe
on this once-in-a-lifetime Italian vacation!

With stops in

**ROME**
**SORRENTO**
**AMALFI COAST**

including day trips to Pompeii and Capri.

Watch Eleanor as she researches her next book
and get exclusive behind-the-scenes access to her process.
Then attend the biggest mystery convention in Europe in Salerno!

Featured guests include

**EMILY MA**
**ALLISON SMITH**

and

**ABISHEK BOTHA**

**JULY 1–11**
Don't miss out!

# CHAPTER 4

## If You Touch Her Again, I'll Kill You

"Oh my God, it's Connor Smith!" The BookFace Ladies rush us, pushing past me and Harper with books in hand and Sharpies at the ready.

"Can you sign this, Connor?"

"When's the next book coming?"

"You and Eleanor are still together, right?"

"Is it true you guys are having a baby?"

Um, *what?*

"Deep breaths," Harper says.

"Did you hear that?"

"You know there's always crazy rumors about you guys in the Vacation-verse."

"I hate it when you call it that."

"At least I didn't call you Connel."

I shudder. That's our mash-up name in the fandom, though sometimes it's Elcon. Both are on the long list of reasons I want out of this relationship.

I mean, would *you* want to be called something that sounds like it came from the planet Krypton? Especially if it was a constant reminder of the first guy to break your heart?

"You'd be on the hit list if you did," I say to Harper.

"Ha ha."

We watch Connor as he interacts with the fans. He *is* good at it, signing every book and smiling at each of the women like he might consider taking them to bed if they asked. Something I'm sure he's done more times than I know about.

Then the selfies start, and he does his trademark move—cocking a finger gun at the camera while he makes a *queek-queek* sound with the side of his mouth—and the moment's over.

"Can you sign this, Eleanor?" One of the BookFace Ladies pushes her book toward Harper.

Uh-oh.

"I'm not Eleanor," Harper says, her voice tight.

"That's me," I say, stepping forward.

"Oh, um . . ." She glances between me and Harper. "Are you sure?"

"Pretty sure."

"What happened to you?"

I reach up to smooth down my hair. "Oh, I fell into some ice cream."

"Gelato," Harper amends.

"Right. Anyway, you wanted me to sign?"

"Yes, please."

I take the book and flip it open to the signature page. This isn't the first time Harper and I have been confused for each other, and I get it. She *looks* like the kind of person who'd have adventures on the French Riviera and write about them. Next to her, I look like who I am: a woman who spends most of her days in stretchy pants with her hair in a messy bun.

On the other hand, my photo *is* right there on the back cover, and they're supposed to be uber-fans. Would it be so hard to get it right?

Ugh. I sound awful, even to myself. In my defense, incidents like this play right into my imposter syndrome. Any normal person with my level of success would question whether they deserve it, but when it happened by accident?[30] When it was never the plan? When it *was* the life plan of your best friend and sister?

Hell yeah, I have trouble looking at myself in the mirror sometimes.

"What's your name?" I ask the woman. She's in her fifties, and her face is already sunburned.

"Susan."

I sign the book to her as Harper takes a few photos with her phone, then hand it back.

I wait to see if anyone else wants my signature, but apparently not.

Whatever. *My* ego doesn't depend on the number of books I sign at an event.[31]

Susan clutches the book to her chest, then walks back to another woman in her forties who's snapping pictures on her phone.

Oh, no.

"What's *she* doing here?"

"Who?"

"Her." I start to point, then lower my finger. "Crazy Cathy."[32]

Harper follows my gaze. Cathy's bleached-blond hair is in a topknot on her head. She's wearing a BookFace shirt, white shorts, sturdy walking sandals, and long dangly earrings that I'm pretty sure have my face on them. She started showing up at my events six or seven years ago, and it got weird, fast.

"I don't remember seeing her on the list. Maybe she was one of the last-minute replacements?"

---

[30] More on this later. I keep saying that, don't I? Bygones. As I said, the footnotes are <u>optional</u>.

[31] It's not like I keep a spreadsheet or anything. Harper does that for me.

[32] Remember those comments I made a chapter ago about nutty fans and my crazy file? Well, it's 50 percent Cathy related.

"Isn't she supposed to be banned?"[33]

"Not sure it's legally enforceable here."

"So, you're telling me I'm on a tour with Connor, nineteen fans, *and* my stalker?"

Harper takes out her phone. "I'll call Marta, the publicist, and find out how this happened." She steps away and I take a moment to collect my thoughts.

It'll be fine. It's not like she's ever threatened me. Well, just the one time. But she's been quiet for the last year. And we'll never be alone together. She hasn't even talked to me yet.

Harper comes back.

"Well?"

"Couldn't reach her. I'll try again later."

"Keep an eye on Cathy." I check the time, wishing I'd insisted on that drink. "Is this tour starting or what?"

"I think this is our guide." She points to a blowsy woman in her fifties with tawny, windblown hair and loose clothing that makes it difficult to determine her exact shape.

"Hello, hello! Are you Harper?" the woman says as she approaches us. She talks in a singsong voice with a slight accent.

"Sylvie?"

"Nice to meet you." Sylvie looks around. "Is this our group?"

"Yes. These twenty, plus Connor and us two."

Sylvie smiles in Connor's direction. He's talking to Susan and Cathy like he doesn't have a care in the world.

Is this the guy who was cowering on the ground twenty minutes ago?

He probably made that whole thing up for some stupid reason of his own. But what if he didn't? Am I going to help him *stop* someone from killing him?

---

[33] I put the ban in place after she'd shown up at our house three times in one week. And by "ban," I mean restraining order.

"He is handsome, no?" Sylvie says.

I give her a fake smile. "Yes. Very handsome."

"Too bad about the personality," Harper mutters.

Sylvie frowns. "Shall we begin?"

Harper calls the BookFace Ladies over, and Sylvie starts the tour, giving us some background facts about the Colosseum. It quickly becomes apparent that Sylvie has a tenuous grasp of history.

I'm pretty sure, for example, that they did *not* film the *Gladiator* movie here, despite Russell Crowe's tongue-in-cheek tweet about taking the family to the "old office" when he was visiting Rome. But this is the proof she offers that it happened. After she says that Spartacus fought in the Colosseum's inaugural gladiatorial bout,[34] I decide to tune her out.

I have a murder to plot, after all, an attempted murder to solve, and a stalker to avoid.

More than enough to keep me occupied.

Harper, on the other hand, is not so lucky.

"That's not true," she says ten minutes later after Sylvie says that there weren't any women gladiators. Harper's first degree was in literature with a minor in history. "There's evidence that women did fight here."

"Evidence?" Sylvie says.

"The frieze on the arena floor? The one that shows Amazon and Athena fighting?"

Sylvie's forehead creases like she's trying to remember. "Oh, yes. But that is just decoration. Roman men, they liked their strong women, no?"

Harper's horrified, but Connor starts to laugh. "Harper always knows better, Sylvie. You'll see."

Harper shoots Connor a look that could, well, *kill*, but Connor simply winks it off, then takes the arm of the youngest fan. She's pretty but probably forty, fifteen years above his usual age bracket.

---

[34] He died a hundred years earlier.

This *is* the man who told me once that he was the "Leonardo DiCaprio of private detectives."[35, 36]

Gross, right?

I should put that in the next novel. Then everyone will understand when he turns up dead.

"Now," Sylvie says, "let us examine the friezes on the west portico."

We follow Sylvie down a hall, and I try to go back to my plot, but I've lost it.

Not for the first time.

The tour winds on, up and down stairs, around corners, and through the crowds, and I'm tired and thirsty, and the sun is touching my skin like it wants to kiss it.

Please, God, let this be over soon.

Jesus. Rome is making me religious.

"And now, because you are an A-one special guest, I have gotten you a tour of the catacombs." She points to the floor of the Colosseum, where the structure for a series of underground rooms still exists.

Sylvie leads us down a long set of stone steps until we get to a velvet rope that's being manned by a burly older man with a fierce expression. "You may take as many pictures as you like. Please do not use flash."

The BookFace Ladies twitter in excitement and I sigh internally. It was like this yesterday at the Vatican, where I found myself being pulled into a private tour of the Sistine Chapel while a massive line wound its way through the stone courtyard in the full sun. I don't like getting things because of my celebrity; I can wait in line with

---

[35] For those of you who don't read People.com obsessively, Leonardo hasn't dated a woman past the age of twenty-five for most of his adult life. He gets older, and his girlfriends stay the same age, with an expiration date on their twenty-fifth birthday. Charming.

[36] Connor's forty-five, by the way. So this BookFace Lady would be a perfectly appropriate age for him if the world wasn't skewed for successful men.

everyone else. But I've learned over the years that you often aren't given a choice.

It's always made me wonder, though, about the celebrities who came before me.

Had they demanded these private audiences with art?

"El?" Harper says.

"Yeah?"

"You're up in the clouds today."

"You should be used to it by now."

"We just need to do a quick tour around the Forum after this, and then you're free."

"To drink a million Aperol spritzes?"

"At least two."

"Sounds like heaven."

We follow the group into a tunnel made entirely of sandstone. I reach out to touch the thick stone walls. I try to picture it. How terrified the gladiators must've been while the lions roared overhead and the crowds screamed for blood.

"No touching of the cave!"

I pull my hand back like a scolded child, and we shuffle through the tunnel until we're back out in the hot sunlight on the stadium floor. We're on a metal walkway, the walls rising up on both sides. Above us, in the rostrums that surround the floor, a crowd looks down on us like they must've done to the gladiators centuries ago.

It's beautiful and overwhelming, and I experience that feeling of transference I get sometimes when I'm writing. Like I'm one of the people waiting to do battle, the crowd howling its pleasure and delight. Like I can smell the blood and sweat and fear of those expecting the same fate.

Like my death is waiting for me.

I shiver, a shadow passing over my grave.

This would make an excellent setting for a murder.

But how?

I've committed so many literary murders that the possibilities cycle through my mind quickly. If Connor tripped and fell onto the grate, would the blow to his head be enough? Or if one of the stones was loose, and just a bit of pressure could drop it on him . . .

"I do need your help," Connor says, coming up next to me.

"Why?"

"Because I've tried to figure this out on my own and I almost died yesterday."

"I already gave you a solution. Go to the police."

"You know why I can't do that. Come on," he says, smiling down at me. "We work well together. You're *good* at this. Think about the Giuseppe case. You figured all that out on your own."

Ugh. I hate it when he's nice to me.

"I'm not some naive twenty-five-year-old anymore, Connor. If this is some scam, I'm not going to go along with it."

"It isn't a scam, it's my life."

"Is there a difference?"

"Okay, then. Forget it." He strides away, pushing past the BookFace Ladies.

I feel a moment of regret, but it's quickly replaced by relief.

Whatever game Connor's playing, he's let me off the hook.

I should take the win.

The tour comes to an end as Sylvie leads us to the exit. "And now, Miss Author, you enjoyed the tour, yes?"

"Yes, Sylvie, thank you."

Harper steps in to tip her, and Sylvie smiles, then bustles away with a mention over her shoulder that she'll see us tomorrow.

I shudder at the thought of what her mix of fake and real history will do to Pompeii.

But that's a problem for another day.[37, 38]

We walk back into the courtyard full of tourists, and Harper tells the BookFace Ladies we'll see them tomorrow, then leads me toward the Forum to get some photos. I make sure that Cathy isn't following us, then exhale and try to focus on the real history in front of me.

This part of Rome still looks like an archeological dig, with the modern street hovering above the enormous complex, its red dirt floor dotted with Corinthian pillars in various states of preservation. Tourists swarm through the structure like ants, phones at the ready.

"It won't be long," Harper says, reading my mind as we reach the entrance. "We only need a few photographs."

"For the book?"

"For the Gram."

"I hate social media."

"Sure, sure," Harper says. "Until twenty-four hours go by and no one praises you or the books."

"I'm not *that* bad."

"Forty-eight, then?"

I stick out my tongue. "If I stopped posting, I doubt anyone would notice."

Harper glances over her shoulder and I follow her gaze.

Connor's twenty feet behind us, snapping pictures on his phone like a tourist, though he lived in Rome for a year.[39]

"Maybe you should ask Connor to do your socials?" Harper says.

"Ha! But wait, you never said, what did Connor do?"

---

[37] Is this foreshadowing? Well, duh.

[38] I wonder if my editor will let me keep these.

[39] He'd been there most of the year before I met him and left when my month came to an end. For the next six months, up until my impending book publication put an end to our relationship, we met for romantic long weekends wherever he was—London, Paris, Athens. It was a heady time until it wasn't.

Her face clouds over. "I don't want to talk about it."

"You know you can tell me—"

"Did I hear my name?" Connor says, taking a couple of long strides toward us.

"Not in a good way," I say.

Connor raises his hand to his chest. "You wound me."

"I wish."

His eyes turn cold. "You don't have to be such an absolute cow about everything."

"*Moo.*"

He grabs my arm, holding me tightly. "Now listen here, Eleanor, I don't know what's gotten into you, but—"

"Take your hand off of her," a voice commands from behind me. "Now."

A shiver runs down my spine. I'd know Oliver's voice anywhere.

What I don't understand is what he's doing here.

"What are *you* going to do about it?" Connor says, spitting out the words as he releases me.

"If you touch her again, I'll kill you."

I really should've read the itinerary.

# TEN YEARS, TEN BOOKS—WHAT'S NEXT FOR ELEANOR DASH?

*By Sophie Rawleigh for*
*The New York Times*

**July 3**

Eleanor Dash, 35, is ten minutes late for our lunch in a cute café in Venice Beach.

When she arrives, she looks like a writer—elegant athleisure wear, hair in a bun, and her nails unmanicured.

"I'm so sorry," she says. "Harper's going to kill me."

Harper is her sister. An unlikely suspect if she ever falls victim to something like one of the characters in her multimillion-selling books.

"No, you're wrong," she says when I point this out. "She'd be the prime suspect. Because of the inheritance."

Over the next hour, we cover the details of her "Wikipedia entry," as she calls it. She and Harper grew up near here in a house their parents bought "back in the '80s, when my mother's parents died." That house "probably costs a jillion dollars now," but back then, it wasn't a trendy neighborhood. Sometimes it was scary growing up there.

"Maybe that's why I'm a writer? Childhood trauma. Check."

Besides the fact that her mother named her after her favorite fictional heroine (Eleanor from "Sense and Sensibility"), Eleanor didn't check off a lot of other boxes on her way to literary fame. She studied marketing at the University of Southern California, which she attended three years late because she was raising her sister after their parents died when she was eighteen and Harper was fifteen.

"I grew up pretty fast after that," she says.

I ask her what that was like. Losing both her parents at once. Having to pivot to taking care of her sister.

"We took care of each other," she says. "But it's not something you ever really recover from. You're never going to be the same person after something like that."

Did she have any specific examples?

"I was going to be an actress—I'd been accepted at Tisch. But I couldn't go. When it was my turn to go to college, it seemed impractical to try something so ephemeral. I mean, you can be a great actress and never book a gig, right?"

Why marketing, then?

"It's what my father did."

So, she wanted to follow in her father's footsteps?

"I didn't know what I wanted. I was kind of living their life. Looking after my sister, living in their house . . ."

Their house is where she takes me after lunch. It's nestled in the "quiet" section of Venice Beach, up against the boardwalk near the Venice Pier, with an incredible view of the Pacific. Eleanor admits to having spent a large portion of her advance for Books Three through Seven on renovating it.

That's how she refers to her books—Book One ("When in Rome"), Book Two, etc. "I don't even know why I do that," she says. "Do people do that with their children?"

We nestle into a comfortable chenille sofa in her living room that looks at the view. "The people-watching alone is worth it. I'm lucky."

That's a theme of our conversation—luck.

It was lucky that when she graduated college she had enough money left from her inheritance to go to Italy for a month before her first job started. Lucky, too, that she met Connor Smith on her first night there, where she began a whirlwind romance that led to her being embroiled in the infamous Giuseppe bank robberies.

For those who aren't true-crime-obsessed, ten years ago, the Giuseppe family (old-school Roman Mafia) worked out an ingenious bank-robbery scheme: rent a building near a bank, dig a tunnel to it, and then strike on a holiday when Rome was occupied.

"Connor was hired by one of the bank's insurance companies to solve the case, and I tagged along. I'd read all of Agatha Christie growing up, and it was kind of like being thrown into one of her books. With a more dashing Hercule Poirot." She laughs, then turns serious.

During the third robbery, the tunnel collapsed, and when it was excavated, a body was found. "At first, they thought he'd died in the collapse. But he was shot."

The victim turned out to be Gianni Giuseppe, one of the many Giuseppe children.

Connor and Eleanor ultimately cracked the case by staking out a building that was near one of the banks that hadn't been hit yet. Twenty million euros were recovered and Connor collected a finder's fee of 10 percent. Antonio Giuseppe, Gianni's father, went to prison, and one of his henchmen was convicted of Gianni's murder.

"It was an intoxicating experience," she says. "Italy, the danger, and falling in love for the first time. You know what first love is like . . ." She trails off and looks out at the ocean. "What's that thing they say? When you fly too high, the crash is that much worse?"

It's not an expression I'm familiar with.

"Oh God. I think I was just quoting myself! That's embarrassing."

When she got back from Italy, she felt compelled to write about her experiences. She wrote the first draft in three months of "coffee-fueled insanity," as she called it, and changed most of the names and enough of the details to make a unique mystery and to "protect the guilty," she said. "Except for Connor. He was so larger-than-life, I had to leave him in. And the rest, as they say, is history." She laughs, then shudders, her focus pulled to the window.

Outside, a homeless man is talking to the sky. Eleanor excuses herself and goes to talk to the man, who, it becomes immediately apparent, she knows. She gives him some money and he leaves. When she comes back inside, she's bemused. "It looks like I arranged that on purpose."

I ask her if she did. "No. But it would be a good cover, wouldn't it?"

What would she want to be covering up?

"Oh, this and that. Nobody's perfect. Me least of all."

She sits back down, distracted. She gets up in her head, she explains, the downside of being a writer. Which she wasn't ever supposed to be. "Harper's the writer. I'm just a hack."

A hack who got an agent and a large book deal in record time, who's gone on to sell ten million books, I point out.

"Yes, well, that's what I meant about luck. There are so many better writers than me. Take Oliver Forrest . . . His new book is a masterpiece. It's called 'One for the Show' and it's going to win all the awards."

And all the book sales?

"Those things aren't linked, unfortunately. But I hope so."

This is where a journalist is supposed to ask if the rumors about her and Forrest are true. That they dated for several years and then broke up suddenly a few years ago.

But something in her eyes stops me.

Instead, I ask her what she's got in store for us next.

"You'll have to read to find out," she says, then laughs and shows me out.

# CHAPTER 5

## Death Among the Ruins

Oliver steps past me to make his threat against Connor a reality, and I can see Connor choosing what to do like there's a thought bubble above his head with multiple-choice questions.

Throw up his fists, or smile casually and toss the whole thing off?

He chooses the second just as Harper moves between them, her arms forming a T, her palms pointing at each of them.

"Stop," she says, with a force of command that surprises me and them, too.

The men make eye contact over her head. They've wanted to hit each other for *years*, and it's a minor miracle that it hasn't happened yet.

"Oli," I say, my voice a warning, but softer than Harper's.

"What?"

"He's not worth it."

He glances at me now, and it's like a sucker punch.

It's been three years since we broke up, but I don't think being around him will ever get any easier. Certainly not when he's standing five feet from me in an open-collared shirt with the sleeves rolled up enough to show off his tanned arms and the ropey muscles underneath. Not when his dark brown hair is curling in the heat and making him look boyish, though his fortieth birthday is just around the corner.

My hero.

Or he once was.

"Please?"

Oliver hitches a breath, then lets it out slowly. His hands come down and Connor relaxes in response.

"You're right," Oliver says, "he isn't," then stalks away.

I watch his back, the way his muscles move under his shirt, the way that one curl folds lazily onto his neck, and my feet carry me after him against my will.

I've only been in love with two men in my life: Connor and Oliver. At twenty-five, I fell hard for Connor, and when we broke up less than a year later, that was a hard landing, too. Oliver was the one who put me back together when I was twenty-eight. We met when everything on the outside looked like a dream life, but everything on the inside was a complete mess. We had four good years, and then I fucked it up.

That's not a surprise, right? You're getting to know me by now.

"Oli, wait."

He slows only slightly, but it's enough for me to catch up.

We're on the edge of a stone staircase leading farther down into the Forum, an old fountain in front of us, the mosaic tiles surrounding it covered in red dust.

"What, El?" he says, his voice full of the gravel of disappointment.

I stop. It's a good question. What do I want from him?

"What are you doing here?"

"In the Forum?"

"You know what I mean."

He blows out a breath, pushing up the curls on his forehead.

I hate how my brain catalogs everything about him, from the creases around his eyes to the touch of sunburn on the bridge of his nose and down to his lips—full, pink, kissable.

And yes, okay, I know. I *know.*

My inner narration about Oliver sounds like a romance novel.

I can't turn it off.

"Touring my book,"[40] he says, "same as you."

I drag my eyes away from his mouth. "What do you mean?"

"Our publisher saw fit, in its infinite wisdom, to put me, you, and *that* man on the same tour."

"Oh, I—"

"Thought they'd arranged this all for you?"

"No, I . . . You know I don't read itineraries."

He smiles, almost, at this. "You prefer to be surprised."

"I do."

"Did you know *he* was going to be here?"

"He's everywhere."

His smile drops. "And whose fault is that?"

"The reading public."

"Try again."

"Oli, I'm sorry. You know I am. I've said it a million times."

"And now it's a million and one."

"Does it make a difference?"

He looks at me now, really looks at me, and it's hard for me not to turn away, not to wither under the weight of his gaze, out here in the blazing sun.

"I want it to," he says.

Some of the tension in my body releases. "That's something."

"We're going to be together for the next ten days, so . . ."

"It's only eight, now."

Shut up, El. Just *shut up.*

"You're editing me?"

"No, sorry," I say. "It just slipped out."

He nods briefly, then looks past me to where Harper is walking slowly around the complex with Connor. "I hate that guy."

---

[40] Oliver also writes detective fiction, but his novels are much more literary. As I joked once, I get the sales and he gets the awards. I mentioned we broke up, right?

"Me too."

His eyes track back to mine. "Do you?"

"I wish I'd never met him. Or never written about him. Or both."

"Then you wouldn't be here."

"Or know you. It's the central paradox of my life."

He laughs now, a good sound, the best sound. "I'm part of the central paradox of your life?"

"You didn't know?"

"I'm flattered."

"I should tell you, then, that my life is a mess."

He laughs again, then puts his hands into his pockets. "You really didn't know I'd be here? I thought Harper would've warned you."

"She knows better."

"Would've skipped it, hmmm?"

"Honestly? I don't know. The last time . . . well, the last time took a lot out of me."

He doesn't say anything, and maybe that means it took a lot out of him, too.

The last time we were together was at the Salon du Livre in Montreal two years ago. We'd sat in a booth for hours signing books. For the first time in a long time, Connor wasn't there, because he'd gotten a "better offer," as he put it, which turned out to be some screenwriters' conference in New Mexico. It had been a relief to do an event without him, and Oliver and I had spent hours joking about the questions the readers always asked.

But then, in the lobby bar, I'd had one too many drinks and kissed him. He'd kissed me back for long enough to make my knees go weak, then held my wrists firmly and moved my hands away from his face, and said, "That's all over now."

Then he left me sitting there while the bartender gave me a sad, knowing smile.[41]

---

[41] Bartending is the <u>weirdest</u> job ever. Fight me.

I'd hidden in my hotel room for the rest of the Salon and made a vow that I was never going to see Oliver again. And now here he is, looking devastatingly handsome and acting like he might regret the way he ended our last encounter as much as I did.

"It was hard for me, too," he says.

I search the ground. There aren't any answers in this ancient dust. "Maybe . . . we could get a drink and talk?"

"About?"

"*One for the Show.* I read it." I lift my head now to catch his reaction. He looks pleased but wary.

As for me? I've never been able to control my face. If I'm ever interrogated, any competent police officer will see right through me.[42]

"You said so in the *New York Times* profile," Oliver says.

"That's out already?"

"This morning. You really think it's a masterpiece?"

"Oli, come on. I wouldn't lie about that."

I've lied about too many other things, only some of which Oliver knows about.[43]

"Thank you."

We stare at each other, the air pregnant with our thoughts. I'm not used to this kind of silence between us. When we first met, all we could do was talk, talk, talk, our words tripping over one another, no thought left unexpressed. It felt like I'd met the part of me that was missing, and I couldn't imagine anything that could pull us apart.

"Am I awful in that profile?" I ask. "I felt like I was a crazy person that day."

"It's fine."

"Ouch," I say and repeat Connor's gesture from earlier, moving my hand to the space over my heart.

---

[42] Come on, you <u>know</u> this is foreshadowing, right?

[43] Yes, I'll tell you, I promise. I just need to find the right chapter.

"I'm sorry."

"It's okay. You're being honest. I appreciate that."

That hated silence again as the tourists mingle around, no one paying us attention. What do we look like to them? Old friends, old enemies, old lovers? We've been that, and more, and now we're nothing but memories.

"I'm ending the series," I say, surprising myself. "The Vacation Mysteries. Book Ten is going to be the last."

"Why?"

"Because it's time. Past time."

"How are you going to do it?"

"I'm going to kill him."

He throws his head back and laughs.

"I mean it, I'm going to. If someone doesn't beat me to the punch."

"What does that—"

A *scream* pierces the day and our heads swivel toward it in unison.

"Harper!" I shout, searching around me in panic. She's gone and so is Connor. My heart starts to pound, and my gut tightens in fear.

If I put Harper in danger by not taking Connor seriously, I'm never going to be able to live with myself.

"Helllppp!" someone calls and then that *scream* again, high-pitched and keening.

Oliver grabs my hand, wrenching me off the spot. "This way," he says. "Come on!"

We break into a sprint as the scream reaches a peak and then, in a way that's somehow worse, stops.

# CHAPTER 6
## Death Takes a Holiday

When we find Harper near Trajan's Column, my heart feels like it might explode.

She's hunched over on the ground, tangled up with another woman, and all I can think is that I can't even breathe without her. My knees buckle and Oliver catches me before I fall.

"Harper!" I shout as I go down.

She turns and rights herself. "I'm okay. Just a bit scuffed."

Oliver sets me back on my feet, then takes a step away from me. I feel like I'm going to start crying, and I'm not sure what's making me so emotional. Harper's okay, and the shock of seeing Oliver has worn off.

Those screams, though.

They're going to be hard to forget.

"Why were you screaming?"

"I wasn't, it was . . ." She motions to the ground, where the other woman rises slowly and starts to dust herself off. I realize she's not a stranger. She's—

"Allison," Connor says, pulling up beside us, slightly out of breath. "I'd know that shriek anywhere."

Allison Smith, née Rogers. Connor's ex-wife.

Oh, did I not mention her?

Yeah, neither did Connor.

I found out about her right after we'd completed the negotiations—if you can call them that—over *When in Rome*'s publication and Connor's take of my advance. We were meeting with our then publicist, Libby. She was confirming the details of his bio, and that's when I learned he was married.

I should've seen that coming, right? A guy who'd extort his girlfriend isn't someone to be trusted. But it was a shock anyway. And super embarrassing. Libby, who was all of twenty-two, kept asking me if I was okay. But she also hadn't taken me aside to give me a heads-up.

I'm sure she dined out on that story for *months*.

Connor hadn't bothered to deny it. If you can believe it—and why wouldn't you, given everything I've told you about him?—he'd laughed when I confronted him. I "knew what he was," apparently, which I'd demonstrated by capturing him so perfectly in *When in Rome*. A wife shouldn't come as a surprise.

"What are you doing here, Alli?" Connor asks now, his hands on his hips.

"Getting accosted while minding my own business."

She's wearing a light caramel shift dress that's too fancy for this bowl of relics. Petite, with wide-set brown eyes[44]—it was never hard for me to understand why Connor was drawn to her. Besides being beautiful, she's smart *and* kind. We aren't close, for obvious reasons, but every time I've been around her, she's been nothing but nice, though she has every reason to hate me. They divorced after *When in Rome* came out. She'd ended up writing a tell-all about Connor—*The Man Behind the Book*—and we'd had to do more than one event together because Connor has created a constellation of authors in his wake.

The Vacation Mysteries Extended Universe, they call it. Like we're superheroes getting spin-off movies after we've saved the world.

"Is this *your* thing?" I ask Connor.

---

[44] Think Thandiwe Newton and you'll be in the right ballpark.

He shakes his head in annoyance. "I don't know."

"What do you mean?" Oliver asks. "What's 'his thing'?"

Connor shakes his head again, a warning this time.

"He thinks someone's trying to kill him," Harper says.

"Wait, what?" Allison and Oliver say together.

"That's what *I* said."

"You promised not to tell."

"No," Harper says. "Eleanor did."

"Just tell us what happened," I say. "So we can figure out what's going on."

"We were walking back there," Harper says, pointing over our shoulders. "And then, out of nowhere, this woman ran past us and knocked Connor over. Then she stole my purse."

"And the screaming?"

"I'm getting there," Harper says. There's a small trickle of blood running down her forehead. "I ran after her. I came around the corner and I saw a woman holding my purse. I yelled at her to stop, and then I . . ."

"You tackled me," Allison says matter-of-factly. "I thought I was being mugged. That's why I screamed."

Harper's embarrassed. "You had my purse."

"This?" she says, holding up a Birkin-style bag.

Or maybe it's a real Birkin. I've never cared about handbags.

"It looks just like mine. I'm sorry."

Allison pats her on the shoulder. "Sounds like an honest mistake."

"Are you okay, Harper?" I ask.

She touches the blood with her finger. It's already drying in the heat. "Yeah, I'm fine."

I search in my purse for something to wipe it away, but Oliver gets there first with a handkerchief, like some guy from a '50s movie. She uses it to wipe the blood off, then returns it to him. He tucks it into his pocket, folding the stain away.

"Are you okay, Alli?" Connor asks.

"I'm fine."

"Did anyone get a look at the thief?"

"Italian?" Connor says.

"I don't think she was Italian," Harper says. "She had an American accent. North American, anyway."

"What did she say?"

"I'd rather not say."

She must've used the C-word. It's the only one that makes Harper this uncomfortable.

"Was that it? Just a curse word?"

Harper and Connor nod.

"That's kind of unusual, an American thief in Rome," Oliver says.

"It's not *that* unusual," I say.

"Regardless, we should call the police, and file a report."

"No," Connor says. "I don't want that."

"It's not just your decision," I say. "And why not?"

"You know why not."

"Is someone going to fill me in?" Oliver asks.

"He doesn't want the police to know someone is trying to kill him," I say.

"Why?"

Connor crosses his arms. "It's none of their business."

"So, you'll just let them keep trying until they succeed?" I ask. "What could go wrong?"

"I thought you didn't want to be involved?"

"Couldn't it have been a mugging?" Allison says. "Rome is notorious for petty thefts."

"I agree," Oliver says. "That's the most likely explanation."

Connor looks around the half circle of us, then blows out a breath. "Forget it. All of you. Thanks so much for your concern." He starts to leave, then stops next to Harper. "I'm sorry you got hurt, Harper. That was never my intention."

She nods at him but says nothing as we watch him walk away.

"That's probably my cue to leave also," Allison says.

"You're sure you're okay?" I ask.

She gives me a bright smile. "I've come back from worse than this."

She means me, right?

Me and Connor. All those headlines ... Those stupid stories I'd told about falling head over heels with him before I knew about her. It was a story made for TMZ, like we were royals behaving badly, and not just an author, a private detective, and his long-suffering wife.

"I'll walk you back, Allison," Oliver says. "If you two are okay on your own?"

"Yes, of course," I say. "Thanks for your help."

"Not at all. I'll see you at dinner."

I close my eyes briefly. Dinner. Something else I should've seen coming. "Great."

Oliver and Allison leave. I watch them for a moment, then turn my attention back to Harper. "Do you need to have that cut looked at?"

"I think it was just a nick."

"What was in your purse?"

"My wallet and credit cards. The usual."

"My cards?"

"Yes."

"Shit."

"It's fine, I'll call the office. They'll take care of it."

"We should call the police."

"For a purse snatching? There's no point."

I sigh. "Let's go back to the hotel."

"What about Aperol spritz o'clock?"

"We'll have them by the pool."

"Okay, sounds good."

I search around me for the path out of here, and then I find it—a small sign that says EXIT. "Say, did you know Allison was going to be here?"

"Of course. It was all—"

"In the itinerary. I get it."

"Someday you'll learn."

"But not today."

Back at the hotel, Harper and I go to our adjoining rooms to get cleaned up, then meet on the pool deck. It's on the roof, closer to the sun, but big off-white umbrellas guard comfortable canvas deck chairs, and there's a personable man behind the bar.

As I settle into a lounger with my drink, I finally peruse the itinerary on my phone.

**Day 1 (July 1)—** Flight from Los Angeles to Rome

**Day 2 (July 2)—** Arrival in Rome; check-in at the hotel; visit the Vatican

**Day 3 (July 3)—** Free morning; afternoon, Colosseum/Forum tour; dinner at El Campinari (all parties)

**Day 4 (July 4)—** Bus to Sorrento; tour of Pompeii and lunch with BookFace Ladies; transport to hotel in Sorrento; group dinner at hotel in Sorrento

**Day 5 (July 5)—** Boat tour to Capri and surroundings; lunch in Anacapri; return to Sorrento; free evening

**Day 6 (July 6)—** Sorrento to Amalfi Coast, with stops in Amalfi, Positano, and Ravello

**Day 7 (July 7)—** Free day in Sorrento

**Day 8 (July 8)—** Private transfer to Maiori; book signing; group dinner

**Day 9 (July 9)—** Salerno Literary Festival

**Day 10 (July 10)—** Train to Rome; free night in Rome

**Day 11 (July 11)—** Private transfer to airport; flight to LA

It's July 3, so we're already on Day 3, but what the hell does "all parties" mean?

I scroll down, and there it is, buried at the bottom.

## ATTENDEES

**Eleanor Dash**

**Harper Dash**

**Connor Smith**

**Oliver Forrest**

**Allison Smith**

**Guy Charles**

**Abishek Botha**

**Emily Ma**

Oy. That's quite a list.

Oliver and Allison I know. And given that it's a tenth-anniversary tour for *When in Rome* and the whole "extended universe" theme they've been pushing the last couple of years,[45] it shouldn't be any surprise that Guy Charles is here either. He was Connor's business partner before I came along, but Connor's notoriety after *When in Rome* was published killed their business. It's hard to be a private detective when you're famous.

"So what's a Guy to do?" Guy had asked me more than once.

---

[45] I actually attended a meeting to discuss the possibility of action figures. I shit you not.

Well, *this guy*—he always tapped himself in the chest at this point—was going to write about it.

*The Guy Behind the Man in Rome* was about his years with Connor doing the "real" detective work while Connor took the bows. Mostly, I think he just bashed information out of people. In the superhero version of the Vacation Mysteries, Guy is the Hulk.[46]

Maybe *he's* the one trying to kill Connor?

Hmmm. I'll have to chew on that for a bit.

Next up is Abishek Botha. He goes by the name Shek (pronounced "Shake," like the ice-cream-based drink, though he isn't sweet). He's another mystery author, but he doesn't have anything to do with the Vacation Mysteries series. We have the same publisher, though, and he did get into some shady deal over a screenplay with Connor a few years back that I never got the details of. I thought I'd heard that he was retiring, but I don't pay that much attention to the *Publishers Lunch* gossip mill.[47]

Me, Harper, Oliver, Allison, Guy, and Abishek. If I was making a suspect list for who might want to kill Connor, it would probably look something like this.

That leaves only the last name on the list. How does she fit in?

"Who's Emily Ma?" I ask Harper as I motion to the waiter to bring me another spritz. The first one went down too easily.

Harper tips her sunglasses down. She's wearing a white one-piece that has one strap on her left shoulder. As per usual, she turned multiple heads

---

[46] I'd be kind of into this action figure, to be honest. I've always had a thing for the Hulk. Or maybe that's just a thing for Mark Ruffalo.

[47] A daily newsletter put out by Publishers Marketplace that contains information about the latest book deals, personnel switches, and scandals in publishing. The book-deal section is meant to destroy your faith in humanity, I mean publishing. Every author I know claims they don't read it, just like they don't read their reviews.

when we walked onto the pool deck. I, on the other hand, am doing a good impression of Jennifer Coolidge in *The White Lotus* with my large straw hat and shapeless beach coverup.

"Come on," Harper says, "you've heard of her."

"I have?"

"Remember when you were complaining about those TikTok books?"

"'Complaining' is a strong word."

"Uh-huh."

I make a hurry-up motion with my hand. "And?"

"That's her."

"She's the one blowing up on TikTok?"

"One of them."

"How did she get on this tour?"

Harper's mouth turns down. "You're not going to like it."

"Tell me."

"She's here for juice."

"For what?"

Harper pushes her glasses back up. "You know, hype. She's big in Italy."

I feel a pout forming. "I'm big in Italy."

"Not like this. She's already in her tenth printing."

That's a lot. "When did her book come out?"

"Two months ago."

"Wow."

"Yeah, wow."

The waiter brings my spritz, the large glass glistening in the sun as condensation beads on the side. I give it a twirl with my finger, then gulp half of it down. I know I should be careful, but it's so hot, and too many things have happened today.

I deserve this. This, and one more maybe.

"I hear she's super ambitious," Harper says, reaching for her drink. It's a vodka and soda, and she's taking small sips, making it last. She even drinks better than I do, but this, for once, is something I can't envy.

"Nothing wrong with that."

"Yeah, but . . ."

"Just tell me."

"I read her book on the plane. The plot is basically *When in Rome.* The man is different than Connor, and it's set on the Amalfi Coast, but everything else is the same. Even the twist."

"She stole my twist? And no one else has noticed this?"

Harper shrugs. "A few online reviewers, but your book came out ten years ago. It's a different audience. People who don't . . ."

"Read me."

"Yeah." She frowns. "There's more."

"Okay."

"She has a second book coming out next year."

"Let me guess, she stole the plot from *Murder in Nice?*"

"Close. *Gibraltar Is for Dying.*"

"Clever, skipping around like that." I lean back in my chair and close my eyes against the sun.[48, 49] "So she's stealing my plots and she's here because . . . what? They weren't selling enough tickets for my events at the Salerno Literary Festival?"

"That's my guess."

"Fantastic."

"Maybe you can call her on it? Head her off at the pass?"

I grab my glass. It feels good to wave it around dramatically. "It doesn't matter. I'm out of the game anyway."

---

[48] In case you're wondering, I can't sue her for this. Plots aren't protected by copyright, only execution. So long as she used different words, settings, and character names and characteristics, she can steal all the plots she wants.

[49] Once again, I'm not a lawyer. Don't take my advice on anything.

"You are?"

"I'm going to be."

"How?"

I drain the rest of my drink, then clunk the glass down on the table for emphasis. "If someone doesn't do it for me, I'm going to kill Connor myself."

Elevator Pitch: Charming, ne'er-do-well private detective Connor Smith has one last case to crack—his own. Will he solve his murder before it happens, or is he destined to become his first unsolved case?

WHO?

· Connor Smith. Obv.

WHAT?

· Maybe like Agatha offed Poirot. Poison? No. Something complicated with a gun on a string? Grr. Check.

WHERE?

· Amalfi Coast. Pick a specific town on the tour. Be on the lookout for something good, but not crowded.
· There are too many people around all the time, esp. in summer.
· Consider setting it in the fall. But who goes on vacation in the fall??

WHEN?

▪ ASAP. The body's supposed to drop in the first chapter, but since it's Conner, probably have to keep him around for a while. Ugh. Maybe the whole book? Whatever.
· The important thing is that he's *dead by THE END*.

WHY?

▪ Motive #1: Cecilia Crane is sick of being second fiddle to Connor and takes matters into her own hands (thin—do better).

HOW?

· "Therein is the thing by which we'll kill our King." —Shakespeare, probably.

# CHAPTER 7

## A Walk to Remember

Connor's not the only one I kept my writing from.

I never told Harper I was writing *When in Rome* either.

It was hard keeping the secret, but it felt necessary. Ever since we were kids, Harper wanted to be a writer. No, she *was* a writer. She wrote short stories and poems and even a novel, all before she graduated high school. It was her senior superlative—she was the girl most likely to write a *New York Times* bestseller.

That was Harper, not *me*. I was, to put it bluntly, the family fuckup. The girl who didn't try hard enough in school because I got good enough grades to get by.

I mean, why bother studying when there were better things to do?

I don't remember what those "better things" were right now, but you get the picture. I was the one my parents shook their heads over, wondering what they were going to do with me. "Why can't you be more like Harper?" they'd ask when they found me doing something bad, lazy, or incomprehensible to them. "Harper would never . . ."

Sometimes it made me hate her, but that wasn't her fault.

Sometimes I hated them, too.

Then they died in a senseless accident, hit by a car while they were crossing an intersection near our house. The driver had pulled an all-nighter and fallen asleep at the wheel. My parents were on their way to their anniversary dinner. I was home "babysitting" Harper, though she wasn't a baby, she'd always say with a pout.

She was the one who answered the door when the cops came to tell us. She called my name, once, in a kind of primal scream, and when I got to the foyer, I knew. I just knew.

Everything was different after that.

I had to be an adult if we wanted to stay together. So that's what I did. I became *in loco parentis*, childhood gone overnight.

One night, a few weeks after they died, we were sleeping in their bed, hiding under the covers, scared of the sounds the palm trees were making as they scratched against the side of the house in the Santa Ana wind. I was trying to soothe Harper, and myself, too, to be honest, and we decided to come up with a code, a word that only we'd understand.

We chose "pineapple" because we both hated it, even though it was Mom and Dad's favorite fruit. We agreed: If one of us said that word, then the other had to stop whatever she was doing and put the pineappler first.

It was a simple rule. One I knew I'd violated by writing *When in Rome*. So I hid it. I hid it until I couldn't hide it anymore.

No, wait. That's not true.

The truth is I hid it until I couldn't do anything about it. Until I couldn't take it back.

The book had started as a simple exercise—trying to make sense of what I'd seen and heard and *done*. Trying to get it all down straight. Harper was away in Iowa getting her MFA, and I was alone in the house for the first time. I was supposed to start an entry-level marketing job at my dad's company after I got back from my trip, but I never turned up. Instead, I sat at my mother's old laptop and wrote twelve hours a day, barely stopping for meals.

When I finished it, I showed it to my best friend, Emma, because it felt odd just putting it in a drawer after everything I'd poured into it.

Emma's an actress who's represented by a big agency, and without asking my permission, she showed it to her agent. Then her agent showed it to a colleague on the book side of their business. When Stephanie called me to offer representation, I didn't even understand what she was saying at first. But then she started raving about Connor, and I got it.

She'd fallen in love just like I had.

It all happened quickly after that. The book sold at auction in what publishing calls a "major deal," and how was I going to say no to that? I didn't have a job and I'd spent the last of my inheritance on Italy. The house was paid off when my parents died, but there were still property taxes and running costs. All this to say, I needed the money.

But I also *wanted* my book to be seen and read. I thought it was good. And all the excitement around it felt good, too. So right before the advance reader copies were sent out, I took Harper to our favorite restaurant on Abbot Kinney, ordered all our comfort foods, and told her. I watched her face react to the news as realization hit that I'd done it.

I'd stolen her dream.

"Pineapple," she said when I'd told her the half of it.

And then, for the first time, I broke our pact. I didn't stop. Instead, I shook my head and said I was sorry and made a bunch of empty promises about how it would be good for both of us.

But she knew better because, like I've told you before, she's always been the smart one.

I'd stolen her dream, and that meant she couldn't get it back.

That was the first time I realized I'm not as nice a person as I thought.

Not a nice person at all.

"This is a famous restaurant, right?" I say to Harper when we meet in the lobby at eight. I've changed into a sparkly dress and strappy sandals, and my hair is still damp from the pool because it was too hot to blow it out, even with the air-conditioning turned up on full.

Harper tut-tuts at my question like I'm a bad child. She's wearing a pale green dress that accentuates her slender figure, and her hair is in soft, silky waves to her shoulders.

"What?" I say. "I read the itinerary, I swear."

"It has two Michelin stars."

"Is that a lot?"

"It's not a book review. One star is impressive, and three is the best."

"I hope so. Because if someone tagged me in a two-star review,[50] I'd commit a homicide."

"News flash, it happens every day."

"That's why you're the only one allowed to check what I'm tagged in."

She tugs on my sleeve. "Come on, let's go."

"We're walking?"

"It's only a few blocks."

I look down at my impractical heels. I don't usually care about shoes, but I'm having dinner with Oliver. My dress is my nicest—a dark blue shimmery number with colorful flowers—and I put on the only pair of Jimmy Choos I have, black and slinky. "You should've warned me."

"You want me to get you some flip-flops?"

"Distract me by updating me on everyone else that's going to be at this shindig."

We leave the hotel. It's still hot, but bearable now that the sun's gone down. There are lights in the dark green umbrella stone pine trees that line the street, and the air smells like lemons and garlic.

"I thought you read the itinerary?" Harper says.

"I did. I meant, give me the goss."

"The goss? Okay, Grandma." She laughs. "Well, Guy's going to be there. Nothing new to report about him that I know of. Emily, Oliver, and Shek."

---

[50] Never do this. In fact, never tag an author in any review less than four stars (out of five). You're entitled to your opinion, of course. We just don't want to hear that you think our book sucked. Or that they were "meh." That one's the worst.

"That asshole."

"Be nice."

"Why? He's refused to blurb me a million times, and his review of *Highland Killing* in the *New York Times* called it 'derivative.'"[51]

"Amazing how good your memory is when it has to do with insults."

"Yeah, yeah." I almost trip on the sidewalk, then right myself. "I should've worn something else."

"You look nice."

"You too."

She smiles, but she's terrible at taking compliments. "Anyway, I hear Shek's about to get dropped by your publisher, so maybe you can muster some sympathy."

Last I checked, Shek had sold twenty million books over the course of his career. Was no one safe in this industry?[52]

"Really?"

"His last two books tanked."

"So how'd he get on this tour?"

"He still has some suction in certain quarters."

"Right." I sigh. This dinner's going to be painful. "Anything else?"

"There's always Connor."

"The 'victim.'"

"You don't believe him?" Harper says.

"I believe that he got himself involved in something shady, for sure, but murder?"

We pass a group of men in their mid-twenties.

---

[51] Despite popular theories to the contrary, blurbs on books aren't paid for. Instead, authors have to <u>beg</u> other writers to read their work in draft form and hopefully provide something quote-worthy in time for it to go on the dust jacket. Okay, maybe "beg" is a strong word, but asking people for this kind of favor always feels gross, even if you do the same thing for them. Even worse? When they don't turn the blurb in.

[52] Short answer: No. Maybe Stephen King, but that's it.

"*Ils sont jolis,*" one of them says in a Parisian accent. Tourists like us.

"*Je baiserais la grande,*" his uncouth friend replies, clearly referring to Harper since I'm two inches shorter than her. Not like us, then.

"*J'ai compris,*" I say to them, letting them know I understood their desire to debase my sister.

Harper's face is aflame. "Leave it," she says.

"Why? They're assholes."

"*Ah, les Americaines,*" the uncouth one says. He's tall and gangly, like he hasn't stopped growing yet.

"Shove it, jerk."

One of his friends puts his hand on the skinny one's shoulder, muttering something about being late for their reservation. He lets himself be pulled away, but not before he throws out a last "*C'était un compliment!*"

"Compliments are something people appreciate!" I shout back.

"El, please stop."

"Shouldn't have downed that second spritz, I guess."

"You mean fourth?"

"You're counting my drinks now?"

She puts her hands up. "Hey, I'm not the enemy."

"I know. Sorry."

"I guess it's better if you get it out before dinner." Harper tugs at my sleeve. "Why have you been so distracted all day?"

"Besides the obvious? I want to end the series."

"You weren't joking at the pool?"

"No. It's time."

Harper stops walking. "Wow, okay. How are you going to do it?"

"Not sure yet, but Connor's going to die. Maybe the person who solves the murder will be the new protagonist."

"That's not what the publisher wants."

"I know. But thanks to Connor and ten years of busting my ass, it doesn't matter."

"Don't you want to keep writing?"

"Yes, but not at the price of my sanity. Not anymore."

"Is it so bad?"

"You know it is." I blow out a long breath. "Are you ever going to tell me what he did?"

She starts walking again, looking straight ahead. "He just . . . He was being difficult. Complaining about the size of his hotel room, and that he didn't get turn-down service. Stupid things."

"You want me to talk to him?"

"No, I . . ." Harper hugs herself even though it's not cold. "Doesn't the idea of doing this scare you? He's dangerous, El."

"He's a petulant man-baby who's had his way for far too long."

"But he did some crooked things before you met him."

"And since then, too. So much so that he thinks it's worth killing over. But what are you saying? You think if I kill off Book Connor, he's going to hurt me?"

"He might."

"Harper, no. He'll pout and he'll threaten, but that's it. This book is the last on my contract, and he can't force me to write another. He'll realize that eventually, and then he'll be out of our lives for good."

We arrive at the entrance to the restaurant.

"And you're truly not concerned about the consequences?"

"I worry about everything. But if you had to lay a bet on who'd end up dead at the end of this, your money should be on Connor."

"Should I be worried?" Connor says behind us, making me jump in my Jimmy Choos.

"Connor! You scared me." My heart is beating at a frantic pace, pushing hard against my rib cage.

"My apologies." He's wearing a perfectly cut black suit with a light blue tie that matches his eyes. He looks like he stepped out of a magazine shoot, and—

Wait. Stop. *No.*

Your heart's racing out of *fear*, you moron, because he startled you. You do *not* have unresolved feelings for Connor.

"How long were you behind us?" I ask, trying to steady my voice.

Connor gives me a deep stare. I feel like I'm being x-rayed with his eyes.

Can he tell that I put on my sexy underwear?

Not for him, obviously. And not for Oliver either, though a girl can dream.

"Why? Did you say something you didn't want me to hear?"

"I don't have anything to hide from you."

"Oh?"

I pull in a deep breath. "Can we not? Please?"

Maybe it's the "please" that does it, but Connor softens. "I wanted to . . . About earlier. I do need your help, Eleanor. This afternoon proved it."

"That was a mugging."

"I don't think so."

"So, let me get this straight. Someone's trying to kill you, and instead of doing that, they pushed you to the ground and stole Harper's purse?"

He makes a low growl in his throat. "You're not asking the right question."

"What's the right question?"

"What did they want that was *in* Harper's purse?"

Ugh. I hate it when he's right.

"Okay, say that's what was behind the mugging. There wasn't anything about Connor in your purse, was there, Harper?"

"Ahem, well . . ." Harper says. "I realized earlier . . ."

"What?"

"I have a master key. To our rooms. Mine, yours, Connor's."

"How did you get that?"

"I always have one."

"So, the thief can get into my room?" Connor says. "Fantastic."

"But wait," I say. "Those cards are blank, right?"

I fish in my purse and pull out my room card. I'd noticed it earlier. It doesn't have the hotel's name on it. It's just a shiny black card with a silver logo.

"See, there are no identifying marks other than the logo. Which, frankly, looks like the logo of a million hotels. They won't know where you're staying."

"I also had a full paper itinerary with all our hotel details."

That stupid itinerary again. The bane of my existence.

"So, they know what hotel we're staying at and have a key to all our rooms, Connor's included?"

"Looks like it."

I work a spot on my lip. "But wait, that still wouldn't mean they know which room Connor's in. Were our room allocations on the document?"

"No, I only got that once we arrived."

"Okay, good. And the hotel's pretty big, six floors at least. They can't try *all* the doors. That would draw too much attention."

"They wouldn't have to, though," Connor says. "They know what floor I'm staying on."

"How?"

"Because the person trying to kill me is on this tour."

# CHAPTER 8

## No One at This Table Is Innocent

"What does *that* mean?" I ask as a frisson of anxiety works its way up my spine.

I wish he'd stop doling out tidbits of information like he's narrating one of the Vacation Mysteries.

It's so annoying when an author does that, right?

"Care to explain, Connor?" Harper says.

"It has to be someone in Italy. With what happened at the Vatican, and then again today."

"But I didn't know the woman who took my purse," Harper says.

Connor makes an annoyed gesture with his hand. "She's working with someone else, clearly."

"Someone on this tour?" I ask. "Who wants you dead?"

"Isn't that what we've been talking about?"

Harper and I share a glance.

It is what *we* were talking about before he came up behind us, but I'm pretty sure he didn't hear that part of the conversation.

At least I hope not.

I might be impulsive, but I know better than to drop that information on Connor without any prior warning. I'm going to have to find a way to cushion the blow.

Hmmm. I never realized how many common expressions are related to death and violence until I started thinking about killing Connor.

Does everyone have murder on their mind?

"You think it's one of the BookFace Ladies?" I ask. "I could see Crazy Cathy doing something like that."

"I doubt it."

"Because they all love you."

"Because how would they have gotten on the tour?" he counters.

"They could've entered the contest," Harper says. "It would be a good cover."

"But they couldn't guarantee they'd get in," I say. "Depending on that would be a risk. Plus, then why try to kill him in California?"

Harper shrugs. "That didn't work. Plan B, I guess."

"But that was only a couple of weeks ago. Not enough time to get on this tour unless—"

"Can you two stop talking about me like I'm not here?"

"You interrupted a good point," I say.

"What?"

"That you're right."

"How's that?"

"If they wanted to kill you in Italy, or if that was their plan B, then they'd have to know in advance that they were going to be on it. When was the tour announced again, Harper?"

"Six months ago."

"And the BookFace contest?"

"Three months, but the winners were only announced last week. You had to guarantee you'd be available on the tour dates to enter. A couple of the winners couldn't make it, so they went to the alternates."

"Is that how Cathy got on?"

"Marta never called me back."

"That's annoying." I think it over. "So, yeah, Connor, you're right.

I mean, if someone *is* attempting to murder you, which I still think is unlikely, then they're probably one of us."

He gives me a satisfied smile. "As I was trying to tell you—"

"Connor! There you are, darling." A young woman floats up and plants a kiss on Connor's cheek. "Am I late?"

He wipes the worried look off his face and kisses her back. "Not at all, not at all. We were just finishing up. Let's go in, shall we?"

He takes her by the hand and leads her into the restaurant, leaving Harper and me momentarily speechless.

"Did he . . . bring a date to a dinner with someone he thinks is trying to kill him?" I say.

"Looks like."

"That man."

"He has flair, you have to give him that."

Let me set the scene.

The restaurant is a delight—old stone walls, high ceilings, and a glass-enclosed kitchen where you can watch the chefs at work. The tuxe-doed maître d' takes us to a private room on the backside of the rectangular kitchen, where there's a long table laid with what looks like enough courses to serve a king.

There are only two empty seats, and one of them is next to Connor. I take that one so Harper doesn't have to, and she sits to my right. Oliver is across from me, in between a woman who must be Emily on his right and Allison on his left. Shek[53] is at the head of the table because Shek thinks *he's* the king, and Guy's at the other end.

Connor's guest is on the other side of him—a Canadian girl whom he introduces as Isabella Joseph. He claims, under cross-examination from Shek, to have met her on the plane over here.

I don't know why I say "claim." It's entirely believable that he'd meet

---

[53] Shek and Ben Kingsley (né Krishna Bhanji) look like they were separated at birth.

someone on an airplane and invite her to join him for dinner with a bunch of strangers.

As Alanis Morissette says, I oughta know.

Isabella is twenty-five,[54] and this is her first trip to Europe. First trip anywhere, she says, then giggles. She's gorgeous, with thick red hair and startling green eyes.[55] Her dress is short and sparkly, more for clubbing than this staid dinner.

Though maybe it's not so staid after all.

If Connor's right, one of us is plotting to kill him. Maybe tonight.

I look around at everyone's faces—Oliver and Allison, Shek and Guy,[56] Emily and Harper. Does someone here want Connor dead?

I mean, obviously, yes. Like in an Agatha Christie novel, we all have our motives. But it's a long way from motive to action. Take me, for example. I've wanted to off Connor for months[57] and I've barely put pen to paper,[58] let alone come up with an elaborate plan to do so.

And why in Italy? Why the first attempt in California? What's the motive? Some financial scheme, he'd said, which could exclude a couple of people.

Guy, Allison, and I have financial ties to him, but the rest of them?

No way Oliver would ever give him money, and I can't see Shek doing it either, not after that whole fight they had when Connor was supposed to act as his consultant on some script Shek had written.[59]

---

[54] Which tracks with Connor's usual dating range.

[55] Think Rachelle Lefevre, who is ALSO Canadian.

[56] Dave Bautista will play him in the TV show.

[57] Okay, years. Which are <u>made</u> of months.

[58] I'm way behind on my deadline. I was supposed to turn in my book <u>months</u> ago so it could come out this year, but I've been suffering from writer's block. It was part of the reason I agreed to come on this tour—to recapture some of the magic that propelled me the first time.

[59] *The Silhouette and the Black Saloon.* Logline: A private detective known as the Silhouette, because of his light touch, is hired to discover who's trying to sabotage the Black Saloon, an underground New York institution that caters to the city's richest and most depraved. <u>Shocking</u> that it didn't get made.

Emily doesn't even know Connor, so that's her out. He did something to Harper—something I still have to ferret out—but Harper isn't violent. She's too placid, if anything.

Which leaves . . . *me.*

And what kind of writer would I be if all the clues led to me being the most likely suspect?

The waiter arrives and takes our drink orders, then explains that they'll be taking us through an entire Italian menu—*primi, secondi,* etc.— but with their takes on it.

"Just bring me some carabinieri," Shek says, already into his second glass of house red. The top of his half-bald head is shining under the overhead lighting, and his cheeks are tinged with red. He got here "directly on time," he announced when Harper and I arrived, then looked pointedly at his watch.

"He means carbonara," I say to the waiter, not sure why I'm explaining for him.

Shek has one of those bellies that protrudes from his body like he's pregnant, so I think he knows what kind of pasta he likes.

"He thinks it's funny."

"Uh, yes, miss. We don't have that on the menu . . ."

"What? Your fancy chef can't whip some up? For the amount we're paying . . ."

I hold up a hand. "You're not paying for anything, Shek. Just go with the flow, all right? It'll be a cultural experience."

His face flushes a darker red, and he mumbles something about "not needing any cultural experiences, thank you very much."

I tell the waiter he can bring things out at whatever speed they planned, and to do the full wine pairing as well. If I have to sit through this three-hour meal, then I might as well get good and shit-faced.

Connor orders a Negroni, his signature drink. He told me once, in a vulnerable moment, that wine makes him feel jittery, and he can't drink anything in the Champagne family at all.

How sad.

"How many courses is it?" Emily asks, sipping from her glass of Prosecco. She speaks with the flat accent of a Manhattanite, and she's wearing a black cocktail dress that shows off the cut of her collarbones. She's in her late twenties, very thin, and her thick black hair is in a blunt cut at her shoulders. She looks more like a model than an author.[60]

At least my kind of author. No wonder everyone always thinks Harper's the famous one.

"Not sure," I say. "Ten, maybe?"

"Ten!"

"They'll be small. Don't eat it if you don't want to."

She turns up her nose, and I feel a twinge of sympathy. You can only be that thin through genetics or starving yourself, and I'm guessing she's chosen the second.

"Congratulations on all of your success," I say, raising my glass. I catch a startled look from Oliver,[61] who's been quiet since I sat down. "Here's to you and your book. May you stay on the list for as long as possible."

"Oh . . . um, thank you. Yeah, it's been a whirlwind. But you know what that's like." She looks at Connor as she says this, but he's busy talking to the Canadian girl. Isabel? No, Isabella.

"You should enjoy it while it lasts. It can all go away in an instant."

Emily puts her glass down carefully. "That won't happen to me."

"That so?"

"I won't let it."

"Well, good luck with that." I look at Oliver now. He's wearing a dark blue suit without a tie, and his white dress shirt brings out the tan on his face. He's always cleaned up nicely.[62]

---

[60] Like Lana Condor but without the giggle.

[61] I just realized I haven't given you a celebrity image for Oliver. Maybe I won't. Maybe he's just Oliver, suitably handsome and the object of all my desires.

[62] Kidding! He's a slightly older Jonathan Bailey, in Season 2 of *Bridgerton*, of course, sans the period costume, though he'd look great in a pair of breeches.

"Have you read her book, Oli? You might like it."

"Oh?" The side of his mouth is twitching.

"Isn't *When in Rome* your favorite book of mine?"

"Ohmygod! You wrote *When in Rome?*" Isabella says. "My mom *loves* that book."

"Thanks."

"No, like, seriously. She's ob-sessed. She has all your first editions in this little nook . . . *Connor!* Why didn't you tell me who Eleanor was." She gives him a playful whack on his shoulder. "My mom is going to freak when I tell her I met you. Can we get a selfie?"

Before I can say anything, she's up and out of her chair, pressing her face next to mine. She smells like hotel soap and an aftershave I'd recognize anywhere—Connor's.

She holds the phone out from us, raises it, and snaps a picture. She checks it on her phone. "Perfect. I'm texting her now. She's going to *die*."

See what I mean about the violent metaphors?

Once you notice, they're *everywhere*.

"I can sign something for you if you like. For her."

"Maybe at the signing in a couple of days?" She plops down in her seat as she sends a text.

"You're coming to that?"

"Connor invited me."

"You didn't have your own plans?"

"She did," Connor says. "But she changed them."

I try to think of something cutting to say but come up empty.

Instead, I angle my body away from him so his arm doesn't brush against mine, a move that doesn't get past Oliver. I look away from him and go back to perusing my suspects.

Harper's talking to Guy about the Colosseum, and Emily's staring at me over the rim of her glass, trying to make out what I meant by the *When in Rome* comment, I assume.

Did she honestly think I wouldn't notice that she stole my plot?

I mean, I didn't, but I would've if I'd ever read her book.

I drain my glass as the waiters enter with the first course.

"What's this?" Shek asks, poking his fork around the dish with a look of disgust.

"Grilled octopus and artichokes, sir, with olive oil."

"Oh, no," Isabella says. "We can't eat octopus."

"Why not?" I ask.

"Because they're so intelligent," Emily says. "It's like eating a human."

"Surely not exactly like eating a human," Oliver says, and Allison snorts into her glass. Unlike most of the people at this table, she seems to be thoroughly enjoying herself.

I wonder how she does it.

No way I'd spend time with someone who slept with my husband, no matter how innocently.

Emily pushes her plate away. "Well, I won't eat it."

"Wait!" Isabella says, pointing her fork at Emily. "I know who you are! You're Emily. @EmilyBooks!"

"Yes, that's right."

"Your book is, like, everywhere."

"Thank you."

"I haven't read it yet. But I will."

Emily gives her a tight smile. "Okay."

"I'm not much of a reader. But I do want to write a book one day."

Oliver catches my eye. "Ten minutes," he says.

"A land speed record."

"What does that mean?" Emily says.

"It's just this game we, uh, used to play. How long it takes before someone tells us that they've always wanted to write a book."

"She didn't say it to you, though," Emily says. "She said it to me."

"Now, now, Emily," Connor says. "Play nice."

A look passes between them, and Emily narrows her eyes, then turns her head.

Holy shit.

They *have* met before.

The plot thickens.[63]

"My God, Connor," Allison says with a laugh. "Is there any female at this table you haven't slept with?"

He looks at each of us slowly as if he's considering it. "No."

"Is this necessary?" Oliver says.

"I don't see what the problem is. Allison asked a question, and I answered it."

"Can't we just enjoy the meal?" I say.

"This?" Shek says pointing to his food. "It isn't even pasta."

I let out a long sigh, then stand up and tap my glass until I have everyone's attention, like I'm about to make a toast at a wedding. "What's wrong with all of you? We're in an amazing restaurant, and the kitchen staff is staring at us because we're complaining like a bunch of babies. Do you know how many people would *kill* to be in our position?"

*Boom!* There it is again.

I clear my throat. "If you don't want to be here, go home. If you stay, then enjoy the meal, drink the wine, and try to make the best of it."

There's an odd silence after I finish speaking. I can hear the kitchen behind me, the clink of metal, the hiss of liquid as it hits a hot pan. Then Oliver raises his hands and starts to clap.

A small smattering of applause follows. Harper, Isabella, and, surprisingly, Guy join in. Then it stops, and I sit down feeling foolish.

But my little speech seems to have had the desired effect. Everyone finishes their first course, while Guy regales us with a story about an old case involving a widow who killed her husband for the insurance money.

We're almost having *fun* when there's a commotion just outside the room.

"But I'm invited!" a voice that I think I recognize says.

---

[63] I've always wanted to write that.

"Signora, the table is full. If you will just come with me."

"No, I won't . . ." There's the sound of a scuffle, and then Cathy stumbles into the room. She's lost the BookFace T-shirt and is wearing a black cocktail dress. She almost looks like she belongs at the table except for the wild look in her eyes. "You didn't wait for me," she says accusingly.

Harper stands quickly and walks to her side. "Cathy, I'm sorry, but this portion of the tour is only for the authors."

"You're not an author."

Harper flinches, and I stand. "She most certainly is."

Cathy barely looks at me as she scans the room. Her eyes stop on Isabella. "Who is she?"

"She's my guest," Connor says.

"She's in my seat."

"No," I say, my voice more assured than I feel. "Cathy, we've talked about this. You know you have to stay at least a hundred feet away from me."

Her eyes swing back to me. She has this discomfiting way of staring at you without blinking. "But I was invited. I can show you the email."

Oliver stands and walks to her. "Why don't we find you a table in the restaurant? Here, come with me."

He does it so neatly that she's out of the room as quickly as she entered. The waiter apologizes for the disturbance and fills our glasses with the next wine pairing. Oliver comes back a few minutes later and says that she's been set up at a quiet table in the front of the restaurant.

"How did she know we'd be here?" Connor asks.

"She must've gotten a copy of the itinerary somehow," Harper says.

"From your purse?" Connor says with a hint of alarm.

"Was she the one who mugged you?" Allison asks.

"No," Harper says firmly. "It wasn't her. Maybe the publicist screwed up. I've been trying to reach her . . . I'll get to the bottom of this."

"Aren't there supposed to be more courses?" Shek asks, unconcerned. The tip of his nose is red, and I'm glad it's not my job to make sure he gets back to the hotel tonight.

I signal to the waiter, and in a moment, he and a colleague bring out a delicate piece of fish in a white wine emulsion with fried capers and lemon. It's the best thing I've ever tasted, and I try to savor it despite the company and the interruption from Cathy. Tomorrow, I'm going to make sure she's off this tour, but for now, I take a sip of the excellent wine, then put the last piece of fish on my fork.

I want to relish this moment of peace, the delicate flavors, the fine wine.

That's my mistake, though, letting my guard down.

Because it's only an instant later that I stop being able to breathe.

And now, for the first time on this trip, I'm truly *scared*.

# CHAPTER 9

## It Tolls for Thee

The thing no one tells you about dying is that your life doesn't flash before your eyes like you're watching a movie. There's no white light enveloping you while bucolic scenes scroll by—you on a bike with your dad, you at the park with your mom, your first kiss, first time, the last time you felt truly happy. Not when you can't breathe.

Instead, your life closes in like a pinhole camera, tighter and tighter as you try to cough up the small bone that's lodged in your airway. Your hands go up reflexively to your throat like you're trying to choke yourself out, and all you can think is *not like this* as fear floods through your body.

But it doesn't end like this. Not this time.

Because Oliver is the hero of this chapter.

Right before it feels like I'm going to pass out, he bounds around the table and grabs me from behind, his hands on my solar plexus. Then he pushes in and up until the bone dislodges, and *poof*, I can breathe again.

I take in three slow, ragged breaths, and the camera lens widens.

The entire cast is standing in front of me.

—Harper with tears on her cheeks.

—Allison and Emily clinging to each other in shock.

—Guy standing at the ready to do *something*—who knows what.

—Shek with his phone to his ear, trying to explain to the emergency operator in broken Italian that I'm not going to die after all.

—Connor and Isabella standing hand in hand with expressions I can't read. Connor's might be relief, but it might also be joy; I don't want to spend too much time thinking about it.

And finally, Oliver, whose hands are around my waist, my back pressed against him. It feels so familiar to be in his arms that it dissipates the fear and makes it feel like a memory.

"I can't believe that worked," Isabella says, with wide-eyed wonder.

"Thank God for Oliver," I say, but I shouldn't have said anything at all, because his hands loosen and then he moves away from me.

I shiver and hug myself. I almost died. I was just about to die, but Oliver saved me.

All this talk of Connor's death, and it was *my* life that ended up on the line.

That tracks.

"You're okay?" Oliver says, stepping in front of me. His dark eyes are unreadable, but the tone of his voice is one I know—a mix of dread and hope.

"I'll live. Thank you."

He pats me on the shoulder, then rounds the table back to his seat. His chair was toppled over in his rush to get to me, and he picks it up and rights it.

If only we could be put back together so easily.

That's a pipe dream, but his action is a clue to the others, and they disperse to their seats as I sit down.

"What's the next course? Not fish, I hope," Allison says as she smooths out her napkin, and everyone laughs.

Shek raises his glass. "Told you we should've stuck with pasta."

"Pasta's coming," Guy says. "That's guaranteed."

I feel a rustling next to me. Connor is inspecting his plate, poking around it with his fork.

"What are you doing?"

"Checking for evidence."

"Of what?"

He lowers his voice. "You know what."

"You think that fish bone was meant for you?"

"You *are* sitting next to me."

I feel that quiver again, the one telling me that there might be real danger here.

But no, that's impossible, because—

"You can't kill someone with a fish bone."

"Weren't you the one about to die?"

I raise my hand to my throat. "Not on purpose, I meant. It was an accident."

"There have been too many of those. The car, the Vatican, the mugging, *you*. Come on, you must see it?"

And the thing is, I do. I see where he's coming from, even if I can't make it add up to attempted murder. But I'm also sick of it.

I almost lost my life, and now I have to listen to how it was probably his fault?

Fuck this.

I throw my napkin down. "I think I'm done."

"Weren't you the one saying that we should enjoy the dinner?" Allison says dryly.

"Yes, well, since I'm the one that almost died, I think it's my prerogative to call it quits." I stand. "Feel free to finish without me. I'll see you all tomorrow."

I don't wait for anyone to respond; I just push my chair back and go.

I take the path around the kitchen into the main section of the restaurant, scanning the room for Cathy because she's the last person I need to see right now. It's full: couples at tables, families fighting over the bread baskets, laughter, smiles of pleasure. As I walk through it, I feel apart from it, and maybe it's just the lingering effect of almost dying, but it feels like more than that.

Because—what if Connor is right?

What if the next attempt on his life is successful?

What *then*?

"Hey," Harper says, "wait up."

She catches up with me at the door, and we exit together. Outside, in the still air, the paintbrush trees reach toward an inky, starless sky.

I still feel winded and sick.

And then Oliver walks out the door.

"Hi," I say.

"Hi."

"You didn't have to leave because of me."

"I know. I wanted to."

"Why?"

"Because I . . . It didn't seem right, just acting normal, after what happened."

I feel the same way. That's always been the good and bad about us—how similarly we think about so many things. I've missed it, our connection. I wish I knew how to get it back. I wish I could believe that his interest now isn't only because he had to save my life.

"Where to?" Harper asks.

"Hotel?"

"Mind if I walk with you?" Oliver says.

"Of course."

"You do?"

"No, I meant, of course, join us."

Harper squeezes my hand. "I forgot my phone. You go ahead, I'll catch up." She releases her grip, then disappears into the restaurant.

Now we're alone.

"You believe that?" Oliver asks, watching her go.

"Not for a second." I rub my midsection gently. It feels like there's going to be a bruise.

"You sure you're all right?"

I look up at him. He's so handsome in the half-light from the streetlamp. I want to reach up and brush one of his curls away, but that would be a mistake.

Because what if he flinches?

What if he moves away before I can even touch him?

The possibilities for humiliation are endless.

I close my hands into fists at my sides. "Thank you, Oli, for saving me."

"I wasn't going to watch you die."

"I know, but thank you anyway."

He smiles gently. "You want to get a cab to the hotel?"

"No . . . I know this is going to sound crazy, but I think I'm hungry."

He tips his head back and laughs. "You know what, me too."

"Should we get something to eat?"

"You think it's safe?"

"I think the chance of me almost choking to death twice in one night is pretty low."

"Good point."

"There's a place around the corner. Harper and I had lunch there yesterday."

He holds out his hand. "Lead the way."

I walk ahead of him. It only takes a minute to get there, and before we enter, I text Harper to let her know where I am.

"You still love pasta?" I ask him over my shoulder as I pull open the door.

"Who doesn't love pasta?"

Good question. Only, before this trip, I hadn't eaten pasta in two years. It was hard to do it in LA, surrounded by model/actresses and menus full of arugula salads and steamed fish. That first plate of pasta I had yesterday was like a sexual experience.

"Every diet plan ever."

He makes a face. "You don't need to be on a diet."

"You're sweet."

I step to the woman behind the check-in counter and raise two fingers. She says something in quick, flowing Italian, then leads us to a cozy table in the corner with a white tablecloth and an actual candle flickering in a small votive glass.

We order a bottle of the house red, and she hands us each a menu. There are four main courses on it—the four Roman pastas[64]—plus salad and dessert.

Oliver puts down the menu and glances around. Half the tables are full—a mix of tourists and locals, by the looks of them. It feels cozy and romantic.

Maybe I should've picked somewhere else.

Oh, I definitely should have.

"Nice place," he says.

"Harper found it."

He smiles. "What would you do without her?"

"Excellent question. Though I think I'm about to find out."

"Oh?"

I sigh. "After this trip, I think she's done."

"With what?"

"Being my assistant. This life. I think I am, too."

A waiter comes to the table—his apron crisp and his white hair thin—and I order the *amatriciana*. Oliver gets the same and a Caesar salad to share. The waiter pours us each a large glass of wine from a decanter, then leaves.

Oliver raises his glass and clinks it against mine. Our eyes lock in the candlelight, and that inner monologue starts up again.

Only this time it's got sense memories attached.

—How soft his lips were when he used to kiss me.

—The way his fingers felt as they traced slow circles on my skin.

---

[64] They are *pasta alla gricia*, made with guanciale, Pecorino cheese, and black pepper; *pasta amatriciana*, a sauce made up of crushed tomatoes, guanciale, Pecorino, and onions; *cacio e pepe*, a creamy sauce made of Pecorino, black pepper, and extra-starchy pasta water; and carbonara, made with egg, Pecorino, and crispy pork belly. I'm getting hungry just thinking about it.

—The way it felt when I fell in love with him. How it was wonderful and terrifying all at once, because Connor had broken my heart and betrayed my trust.

I didn't think I could survive that again.

Turns out I could. Knowledge I'd rather not have.

Oliver tastes his wine and smiles. "Can I be honest?"

"Of course."

"This is better than that fancy restaurant wine."

I taste mine. It's rich and light at the same time. "Right?"

"So what did you mean, before? About you being done, too?"

"With the Vacation Mysteries. The next book is going to be the last."

"Why?"

I lift my eyes to his. They're a deep brown, and I've always gotten lost in them.

"Because I want Connor out of my life. Once and for all."

The waiter arrives with our food. He places the salad in the middle with a pair of tongs, and sets our pasta dishes before us along with some delectable-looking bread dripping in olive oil and rosemary. We thank him, and then he leaves.

"He'll never be out of your life," Oliver says, reaching for a piece of bread.

"He will. When I kill him, he'll be gone."

Oliver nearly chokes. "What did you say?"

"I'm killing him off."

"Oh, I thought . . ."

I twirl my fork in the pasta. "That I was going to murder him for real? The thought had occurred."

I take a bite, and the pasta is everything I hoped it would be—the umami of the tomato and the spicy guanciale mixing perfectly.

"*I've* fantasized about it," Oliver says.

"You're not the only one, according to him, but him dead in the book should be enough for my purposes."

"He really thinks someone's trying to kill him?"

"Apparently."

"Why?"

"He's been short on details . . ."

"So unlike him."

"Yes, that's the only thing that makes me think it might be real."

"Hmmm," Oliver says. "And you ending the series—you think he's going to let you get away with it?"

"Harper said something similar, but what can he do?"

"You know I hate the man, but he's resourceful, I'll give him that."

"He can't make me write about him."

"Have you spoken to Stephanie or Vicki?"

Vicki is my editor. "No, not yet."

"They're not going to be happy."

"I know."

"What if they won't publish you again?"

"I'm okay with that."

His mouth twists. "Really?"

"I'm fine financially . . . and let's be honest, a final installment where Connor dies will probably sell like gangbusters."

"You so sure they'll agree to publish it?"

This stops me. It hasn't occurred to me that they might turn the manuscript down. "Maybe not. I'll have to see once I write it."

He spears a crouton. "So, how are you going to do it?"

"Not sure yet."

"If you need help . . ."

I catch his eye. "We're talking about in the book, right?"

"Literary murder. Not literal murder."

"Exactly."

He takes a beat, then smiles. "Well, I, for one, can't wait to read all about it."

### AMALFI MADE ME DO IT—OUTLINE

- Poirot died from a heart condition complicated by not taking his pills. That probably won't work. Think of something better.

WHY?
- Motive #2: The ex-wife. Too obvious? Red herring?
- Motive #3: The ex-business partner. Also obvious. But a good red herring?

WHERE?
- Dinner gathering of all the suspects?
- It was *on the itinerary*, so someone could easily plan it. (Ha!)
- Poison in the soup? Could write a super graphic description of his death. THAT would be FUN.

TO DO
- RESEARCH death by poisoning. ERASE search history.
- FIND MORE SUSPECTS—this should be easy.
- TELL AGENT/PUBLISHER—ugh.

Correct quote: "The play's the thing / Wherein I'll catch the conscience of the king."—Hamlet, Act 5, Scene 2

# CHAPTER 10

## Death Comes at the End

When dinner's over, we're both tired, so we walk back to the hotel.

We're all staying at the same one, on the same floor, and I think briefly about that master key floating around out there, the one that was in Harper's purse. I meant to ask her to tell the hotel to cancel it and get another, but the thought slipped my mind.

I'm sure it's fine, though.[65] Harper's always on those sorts of things.

Besides, I'm not the target. If there even *is* a target.

And Connor can take care of himself.

We ride the elevator in silence, the air thick between us, my feet killing from the stupid shoes I never should've worn. Harper texted me while we were at the restaurant asking for an update, but I didn't feel like putting a label on it, so I sent back a devil emoji and didn't wait for her reply.

The door *dings!* on the third floor and we step out.

"How did I not know you were staying here?" I ask.

"You never were that much into the details."

"You sound like Harper."

"She's a smart cookie."

"She is." I take a left toward my door, which is second from the end;

---

[65] Spoiler alert: It's not going to be fine.

Connor is in the last room at this end, and Harper's to the right of me. I don't know which room is Oliver's, and that's probably a good thing.

Because it *sounds* romantic to knock on someone's door in the middle of the night, and then kiss them silently after they open it and tumble into bed together, but the reality is that Oliver's more likely to sleep through the knock because he's a deep sleeper.

Which leaves me in some sexy underwear[66] in the hallway, feeling foolish.

Not that this exact scenario has happened or anything.

I just have an overactive imagination.

"Harper always has good ideas," I say. "When I'm stuck with a plot."

"Is she still writing?"

"I don't think so."

"That's a shame."

We pass Harper's door and now we're in front of mine.

"Maybe it's a good thing," I say. "If it was making her miserable."

"Was it?"

"Not being published certainly was."

Oliver meets my eyes, and a beat of something passes between us. Old feelings, new.

How are you supposed to tell the difference?

"Your career can't help."

I nod slowly. "She thinks I stole her spot."

"That's not how it works."[67]

"I know that, and she knows that, but . . ."

"What does she think about you ending the series?"

"I'm not sure she believes me."

"Why not?"

---

[66] The underwear I put on was <u>not</u> for Oliver.

[67] There is a finite number of publishing spots every year, though. So, it kind of <u>is</u> how it works.

"I hardly believe it myself. I'm determined, though. By the time *Amalfi Made Me Do It* is over, Connor will be dead."

"Amen."

The door to Connor's room swings open, and there he is, shirtless and angry. His hair is mussed and—there's no un-crass way of saying this—he smells like sex.

"So, *you're* the one who wants to kill me?" Connor says. "I should've known."

Oliver steps back like I might be contagious. "His room is next to yours?"

Connor smirks. "That's right, mate. And we've got adjoining doors."

"I didn't ask for that! And it's bolted, you asshole."

"Now, now, Eleanor. You know better than to speak to me like that."

"Do *not* talk to her that way."

"I'll talk to her as I please. *She's* the one plotting my demise, after all."

"It's a fictional murder, for Christ's sake. In the next book. I was going to tell you."

His eyes narrow. "You were going to *tell* me you're cutting me out of the series I helped launch? How kind of you."

"I wrote the books, and you've benefitted handsomely. But it's time, Connor. It's time for them to end."

"Time for *me* to end, you mean."

"For the last time, no one's trying to kill you."

"Is that so?" He reaches into his pocket and pulls out his phone. "How do you explain this, then?"

I take the phone. It's a news article in Italian. "*Pedone ucciso in incidente stradale*," it says. But I don't read Italian, even though I'd promised myself I'd learn before I came on this trip.[68]

"What does this mean?"

---

[68] I tried doing Duolingo, but I think some French is the limit of my language skills.

He takes the phone back and scrolls down until he gets to a photograph of a man in his mid-thirties. "*This* is the guy who pulled me out of the way of the bus outside the Vatican."

"And?"

"He's dead."

"What?" Oliver says.

A door opens down the hall, and Shek pokes his head out. "Will you all keep your voices down? Some of us are trying to sleep."

"I'll speak as loud as I damn well please."

Another door opens—Emily's this time. She's wearing a long blue silk robe, tied elegantly at the waist. "What the hell is going on? Do you know what time I have to get up in the morning?"

"The same time as everyone, young lady," Shek says.

"Because it takes you an hour to put those three wisps of hair into place."

"I'll have you know—"

Guy emerges from his room with a drink in his hand, in his undershirt and boxers. "Shall I get my gun to tame you beasts?"

"You have a gun?" Allison says, poking her head out of her room. "Why?"

"I need the protection."

"How did you get it into the country?"

"I have my ways."

"I wouldn't believe him," Connor says. "He likes to be dramatic for effect."

"You *both* do that," Allison says.

Guy rattles the ice in his drink. "Don't tempt me, Connor."

Connor scoffs. "Oh, please, just do it already, then. Enough with the cat and mouse."

"What are you talking about?" Shek asks.

"He thinks someone's trying to kill him," I say to the potential suspects.

"Someone *is*."

"I can't believe I'm saying this," Oliver says. "But why?"

"I don't have to tell *you* anything."

"You think it's Guy, Connor?" I ask. "Is that what you're saying?"

He looks down the hall. We're all here but Harper. "It could be any one of you."

I sigh. "Well, now they've been warned. So, if anyone here was thinking of killing Connor, he's on to you, okay?"

"You think this is a joke?"

"I've told you once already about speaking to her that way. I won't repeat myself again."

"Oh, Oliver, please. If you cared so much for the way anyone speaks to Eleanor, you wouldn't be hanging around outside her door. You'd have been inside five minutes ago."

I put a hand on Oliver's arm. "Don't take the bait. It's not worth it. He's not worth it."

"That's right, sweetheart. I'm not."

"You should go to bed," Oliver says slowly to Connor. "We all should."

Connor leans against the doorjamb and swings his door open wider. Isabella's sitting up in the bed behind him, a sheet drawn up to her naked shoulders.

"Some of us were already in bed," Connor says. "Care to join us?"

"Yuck. No."

Connor's eyes flash with anger. "You were happy enough to do it before."

"That's my cue to leave," Oliver says.

"No, wait." I hold on to his arm. "Just stop it, Connor. Go away."

"That's what you want, isn't it?" He looks past me down the hall. "That's what you all want."

"What I want is to get to sleep," Shek says. "Or, rather, back to sleep."

"That's what I've been saying," Emily says.

"Have you got someone new in there, Connor?" Allison asks with a laugh in her voice. "Or hasn't that girl seen through you yet?"

"Took you ten years."

"And who knows how much longer it would've taken me if I didn't have Eleanor to thank."

"Catfight," Guy says.

"Shut up, Guy!"

"So sensitive. I'll leave you to it, then." Guy throws back his drink and disappears into his room. His door shuts with a thick *thud*.

"All right, everyone," I say. "Show's over. I'll see you on the bus tomorrow."

"We're not going on one of those *coaches*, are we?" Emily says. "With the tourists?"

"They're called the BookFace Ladies, and yes. Didn't you read the itinerary?"

"Of course I did. It's why I didn't show up to the Colosseum."

"Don't want to hang out with the hoi polloi?"

"They're *your* fans," she says, then turns on her heel and flounces into her room.

Allison shrugs her shoulders at me, and I turn back to Oliver. "I'll see you in the morning?"

"You sure?"

"Yes. Thank you." I kiss him on the cheek. He doesn't pull away, and I have the satisfaction of hearing Connor's door click shut behind me. "Good night."

I take out my key card and open my door as quickly as possible. I don't want to watch Oliver walk away from me.

My door shuts, and I lean against it, listening to the sounds in the hall. They're muffled, but I can hear the other doors closing, one by one.

What a shit show.[69] I'm glad Harper missed it.

---

[69] I want to know the origin of this expression, but I'm afraid to google it.

But where is Harper?

I feel a frisson of unease.

I walk to the adjoining door between our rooms and open it slowly. Her room is dark, and she's in bed, um, *sleeping like the dead.*

But no, I'm being silly. It's Connor who's the target, not Harper.

I close the door quietly and check my texts.

*I'm in for the night,* she wrote hours ago. *Taking a pill so I can get some sleep. I'll wake you at six.*

I let out a sigh of relief. Good for her. She deserves a good night's sleep.

So do I.

I pull off my clothes, then crawl into the big, empty bed and pull up the covers. I can already feel myself starting to slip away. I'm exhausted by the wine and the emotions I've stuffed down.

Did Connor just say that the person who saved him outside the Vatican was dead? I should probably look into that, but it'll have to be tomorrow.

More important, did *I* almost die today?

Jesus.

A person can only take so much, and I've almost reached my limit.

Maybe that's why I nearly choked to death.

"Up and at 'em!" Harper peels back the curtains to let the sunlight in.

I roll away from the light and pull the blanket up over my head. "Morning is a terrible idea. Why haven't we fixed that yet?"

"You should've taken a pill."

"You know I don't like to do that."

"Worked wonders for me."

I lower the blanket. Harper's happy and rested. She's wearing a T-shirt and a pair of blue flowered shorts that show off her lean legs.

"I'm glad. Though you did miss quite the scene last night."

"You and Oliver?"

"I wish. No, Connor and, well, everybody."

"Speaking of which, I have to make sure he's up. When I get back, you'd better be in the shower."

I check the time. It's six thirty. "Is this bus really at seven, or did you lie to me to get me up on time?"

"It's at seven thirty. But we're meeting it around the corner, so you'll have enough time if you get a move on."

"You might want to take a stroll down the hallway and hit everyone's door. No one but you seems to have gotten much sleep last night."

"Good idea." She hesitates. "You've got five minutes."

"Yes, yes."

Harper leaves, and I listen to her work her way down the hall, starting at the far end. Her raps are sharp, and she repeats that phrase—"up and at 'em"—in a clear, ringing voice. I can't hear the responses, though she giggles at one of them, probably Allison's, by the distance, but maybe Oliver's.

There's a pause while she skips her room and mine, and then I hear it, the final rap.

"Connor! Let's go. Time to get up."

Silence.

"Connor! Please acknowledge! We're more than happy for you to miss the bus!"

Good for her.

"Connor! I'm opening the door. You'd better not be naked in there!"

I hear Connor's door push back and then the air's pierced with a single *scream.*

And then again.

I jump out of bed and race for the door. I trip over one of my shoes and slam my hands against the floor.

I push myself up and fling open my door.

Harper is crumpled in a ball on the ground in front of Connor's room with a room key lying next to her.

"What happened?" I crouch down and pull her to me as I look past her.

Connor's lying on his bed, half naked, on his back, his eyes staring fixedly at the ceiling.

Dead.

Ah, *shit*.

# CHAPTER 11

## Greatly Exaggerated

Oliver rushes past me and grabs Connor by the shoulders while my heart shudders in my chest.

I should've taken Connor seriously.

All those events—the car, the push into traffic, the threats, the purse snatching, maybe even the fish bone—they were all there in front of me.

Someone on this tour has killed Connor. Which means police, questions, suspicions, the past dragged up *again*.

On the other hand, this does solve a big problem for me—*No.*

I'm not like that. I'm not.

"Is he dead?" I ask, my voice nearly unrecognizable.

Oliver leans over his face, seeing if he can feel a breath on his cheek. Then Oliver grabs his wrist, checking for a pulse, and he must not find one because he's positioning Connor to start CPR when Connor suddenly sits up, very much alive.

Not even remotely dead.

That motherfucker.

"Get off me!" Connor says and gives Oliver a shove that sends him tumbling to the floor.

Oliver reaches his hands back to stop himself, but it's not enough. He skids across the hard tile and then comes to a stop several feet away.

"You're alive," I say to Connor as I haul Harper to her feet. Her whole body's shaking. "He's alive, Harper. The fucker's alive."

"As you see." Connor swings his legs around and places his bare feet on the floor. He's wearing pajama bottoms, but no shirt. He looks down at Oliver. "You all right, mate?"

Oliver glares at him.

"What the hell just happened?" Guy says, the first after Oliver to arrive. His question is echoed by the others as they pile up behind him like they've been spat out of a clown car.

"Who screamed this time?"

"Is someone hurt?"

"What's happening?"

"Why is Oliver on the floor?"

Connor starts to laugh.

"What's so funny?" I say.

"You should see yourselves. And that scream. Harper, I'm impressed. Almost as good as Allison's yesterday."

"This was some kind of joke?" Harper says.

"It was a wake-up call." He turns to me. "The way your heart's feeling right now? How panicked you are? That's how you'll be feeling all the time if you kill me."

"You should do it," Guy says from behind me. "I'll even help you."

"You hear that? The whole reason he has a career is because of me, and he wants to do away with me."

"I think that's on you, *mate*," Oliver says.

"Can someone fill me in?" Allison asks.

"He faked his death," I say. "That's why Harper was screaming."

Everyone starts speaking at once, a cacophony of "what the hells" and "you must be jokings," and some words that aren't fit to print.[70]

---

[70] I mean, I <u>would</u> print them if it were up to me, but there's a segment of the reading public that gives one-star reviews for language, though I probably sailed past that barrier when I took the Lord's name in vain in the first chapter. Oh, well.

Thank God we have the whole floor. Any outside guests would be asking for a refund.

"Where is she?" Oliver asks Connor with a hard edge to his voice.

"Who?"

"Isabella. Wasn't she here last night?"

Connor laughs again. "Jealous?"

"Absolutely not."

"Then why do you care?"

"I want to make sure she's all right. Given everything."

Connor scowls, then smooths out his features. He hasn't charmed a thousand women by letting people know what he thought about them. "Come out, love."

The bathroom door opens, and Isabella steps out dressed in creamy linen pants and a sleeveless shirt covered in pink flowers. Her red hair's in two braids, and she looks all of eighteen. "Here I am. Safe and sound."

Oliver growls, then stands and checks himself for injuries. He seems fine, though I suspect his pride is more than a little injured.

"You went along with this?" I ask.

"Seemed harmless."

"Piece of advice—nothing he does is harmless."

She shrugs, unconcerned. Which is on her at this point, I guess. I have bigger fish to fry.

"Why did you do it, Connor? The real reason."

"I thought I'd beat whoever's trying to kill me to the punch."

"You wanted to smoke them out?"

He nods slowly.

"And?"

"I've narrowed down my suspects." He stares at Guy. "You're number one."

"Should I be flattered?"

"You should consider yourself warned."

"Care to share with the class?" I say.

Connor blows out a breath. "What do you care? You want me dead anyway."

"Not *actually* dead."

"What's the difference?"

"I exist in print; therefore I am?" Oliver says.

Nailed it.

"Regardless," I say, "that was ridiculous and cruel, Connor. You should apologize."

"To you?"

"To *Harper*."

Connor's eyes are as mocking as his voice. "You want me to apologize, Harper?"

"I don't want anything from you," she says. Her color is high, but she seems more in control. "We've wasted enough time on this. Everyone needs to be on the bus by seven thirty. Let's get a move on."

"Feel free to miss it," I say to Connor.

"You wish."

I put my back to him. Everyone else is still standing there, watching us like we're an episode of *Love Is Blind*. "Let's go, Harper."

We push through the crowd as Connor calls after us. "You'll regret this, Eleanor. You'll see."

He's got that right, anyway.

I already do.

I take a quick shower while Harper finishes packing, trying to rinse off the film of unease that Connor's stunt created, but it's no use. Because someone *is* trying to kill Connor.

I believe it now. Not because I saw anything on the faces of the others on this tour—I'm not a human lie detector, and neither is he.[71]

---

[71] I met one, once, when I was researching a book. She claimed she could tell if someone was lying with 99 percent accuracy. I tested her and she failed. <u>That</u> was fun.

No, it's Connor's actions. Faking his own death smacks of desperation, and that's not something he usually traffics in. He must truly believe he's in danger from one of us. Which means there's something, maybe more than one thing, he hasn't told me yet.

Damn it. This is always how people die in murder mysteries.

They hold back a crucial piece of information that could help identify the killer.

"Eleanor!"

"Coming!"

We make it to the bus with a few minutes to spare.

It's one of those fifty-person coaches, black and sleek with tinted windows and two exhaust pipes in the front that look like horns. Inside, the seats are covered in a plush red material, and there's a bathroom in the back. The air smells like disinfectant and maybe slightly like pee, and I pop a piece of gum into my mouth to distract myself.

I wish I'd had time to grab some breakfast to soak up some of the alcohol that's stuck in my system, but there's a stop in about an hour at a pasticceria, Harper says, so I'll get my fill of empty calories then.

The bus is full of BookFace Ladies, who wave to me excitedly as I pass. Or maybe it's Harper that they're waving to. After this morning's debacle, I could not look further from my author photo if I tried.[72]

Today's T-shirt is a BookFace of *Murder in Nice*. I wonder if they have shirts for every day of this trip.

And oh! I get it—ten days, ten years since the first book . . .

I'm a tourist in my own life.

---

[72] My author photos are so <u>weird</u>. You think you know your face, and then you get a blowout and makeup applied and they use all these filters, and suddenly you look like one of the Kardashian sisters or those women in TikTok makeup tutorials. No wonder no one ever recognizes me. Not that I <u>want</u> to be recognized.

Only there isn't a Book Ten. Not yet. Which is my fault or Connor's fault or maybe both of us together.

I shudder as I pass Cathy, who's waving at me in greeting.

"What is she *still* doing here?" I hiss to Harper.

"I can't just kick her off. There could be liability issues."

I close my eyes for a moment. "At least keep her away from me."

"I'm doing my best."

I catch her hand. "I know you are. I'm feeling off because of everything that happened this morning."

"You don't have to take it out on me."

"I'm sorry."

We walk farther up the aisle until we find two empty seats together. I swing my purse into the mesh rack above and sit down next to Harper. We're wearing a variation of the same outfit—light linen shorts and cute T-shirts with practical walking shoes she sourced for us.

It's selfish to even think about it, but I really will be lost without her.

I wish she'd rip off the Band-Aid, though, and just tell me.

Because the suspense is . . . wait for it . . . *killing* me.

I watch the door as the other authors trickle on one by one, no one sitting together except for Connor and Isabella. They take a row across the aisle from us. Connor shoots me a look, then wraps his arm around her and they start to kiss.

Because what's a better way to distract yourself from your imminent murder than to suck face with a beautiful girl, am I right?

I turn away in disgust. I can't believe Isabella's staying on this trip after this morning, but she clearly doesn't make the best choices.

And okay, *okay*, I made the same choice when I was her age.

Like, exactly the same one.

I shouldn't judge. But judgment's kind of my thing, and it's a hard function to turn off.[73] Maybe when I get back to LA I'll go to one of those personal-improvement groups the creatives in my neighborhood are trying to get me to join.

"Not the sex-cult one,"[74] they always say, like that's going to alleviate my concerns about joining some other kind of cult.

"It's about two hours to Pompeii," Harper says.

"What?"

"That's how long you'll have to be on the bus in total."

"Okay."

"Is that not what you were worried about?"

I start to laugh because even though Harper is as close to me as a person can be, she can't see into the labyrinth of my mind.

I wish I couldn't either.[75]

"Honestly?" I say. "I was thinking about maybe joining a cult when I got home."

"What?"

"It feels easier, you know? Let someone else make all my decisions for me. Since I keep making terrible ones myself."

"Tell me you're joking."

"Sort of?"

"El, no."

I try to stretch out my legs, but there's not enough room. "I wouldn't give them my money."

"You're screwing with me."

"I'm not Connor."

Her face falls, but before I can say anything, Sylvie comes up the

---

[73] I feel like the footnotes are <u>extra</u> judgy. But they're probably going to get axed in editorial so I'm going for it.

[74] NXIVM—what a dumb name for a cult. And that Keith? He was <u>so</u> creepy.

[75] You get to, though. That's what the footnotes are really about.

stairs dressed in another flowing mix of skirt and long-sleeved kaftan and grabs the mic from a stand next to the driver. "How is everyone this morning? Another day, another tour, yes? Ah, there are my BookFace Ladies. And Miss Eleanor, the reason we are all here.[76] *Buongiorno!*"

I can feel twenty-eight pairs of eyes on me as I raise my hand and wave.

Is that disappointment I see on their faces?

If only I could hide my face with a book.

"Did you enjoy your time in Roma, Miss Eleanor?"

"Yes, thank you."

"*Eccellente.* Now, we are going to visit Pompeii, an ancient site where there was a big explosion, yes?"

"I mean . . ." I mutter under my breath.

Harper stuffs a fist into her mouth.

"So relax and we will be there in a matter of hours. And don't worry, there will be a break in one hour. You can get an espresso, a little cake. I will explain more about the tour to you then. *Andiamo!*" She gestures to the bus driver to start the bus, and the engine roars to life.

"Where did they find this woman?" I ask Harper.

"No idea. But I'll let Marta know she's a mess. If she ever gets back to me, that is."

The bus pulls onto the road, and I feel a beat of panic that Oliver didn't make it. I search the other seats, but there he is, up in front, one row back from Sylvie. Somehow, he got on without me noticing.

Is that progress or just sad?[77]

"El?"

"Yeah?"

"Is someone really trying to kill Connor?"

"I think so." I take out my phone and google the news article Connor showed me last night. "What do you think of this?"

---

[76] This turns out to be true in more ways than one.
[77] Rhetorical question.

Harper reads my screen. "What does it mean?"

"Connor told me that this is the guy who pulled him out of traffic at the Vatican."

"Why's he in the paper?"

"He's dead."

"Oh my God."

"Yeah." I put my phone away. I put the article through Google Translate earlier when I was getting ready. There are minimal details. His name was Davide Bianchi. He was a schoolteacher. Married. No kids. One of Rome's many road victims. There's no mention of him saving anyone the day before.

"You think it's connected?" Harper says.

"It's a pretty big coincidence."

"Maybe he saw something?"

"Maybe." I get the same feeling I had last night, like someone is walking over my grave. But I'm not the target. Connor is. "What if it's one of them?" I motion vaguely to the rest of the bus.

"They'd be pretty stupid to do it now, after he announced it to everyone."

"Murder's always stupid."

She frowns. "So, it's not you?"

Um, *what?*

"You don't think that, do you?"

"Not really, but . . ."

"I have a motive."

"Don't you?"

"I'm not the only one."

She purses her lips. "You're the only one talking about it openly."

"The book stuff? That's fake. I'd never be able to kill someone in real life, no matter how much I hated them."

"Okay."

"Hey, now, come on," I say, trying to lighten the sting of Harper thinking I could be capable of murder. "You know I couldn't plan something like that on my own. I'd have to have you help me at a minimum."

"You'd make me an accessory?"

"*An Accessory to Murder.* That's a good title."[78]

She smiles slightly.

"You don't really think I'm capable of that, do you?"

She looks into my eyes, and it's like looking at myself in a retouched photo. "No."

I take her hand. It's cold despite the heat. "Harper, please tell me what's going on."

"I don't—"

"No more of this 'after' bullshit. Please. Just tell me."

She tugs her hand away and looks out the window. We're rolling past a huge white marble building with a massive bronze man on horseback outside of it. The sky above it is a crisp blue, though the heat is shimmering. The wonders of Rome.

"I don't know what I'm doing with my life," Harper says.

"Join the club."

"No. Don't do that. Don't minimize what I'm going through."

"I'm sorry."

"I just . . . I know you don't get it, okay? But I don't know who I am."

"You're an amazing, smart, awesome person."

"I'm a thirty-two-year-old who works for her famous sister. Anyone could do this job."

"That's not true. And you're a writer."

She looks at me. Tears are brimming in her eyes. "Connor doesn't think so."

"What are you talking about?"

---

[78] And already the title of at least one book according to Amazon. Also suggested in my search: "murder accessories." I did not click on that link, but I really, really wanted to. Nothing stopping <u>you</u> from doing it.

"I let him read my book."

"What?"

"I know you said you'd read the new draft, but you were busy with your deadline, and . . . I wanted a fresh perspective."

"I'm sorry it took me so long, but Connor? Seriously? He doesn't know the first thing about writing."

"You're wrong, El. He did creative writing in college. And his notes were good. They were devastating but accurate. He was pointing out all the things everyone always does with my stuff. You know what they say. Competent execution, but ultimately not something anyone ever falls in love with."

I bite the inside of my cheek.

This is, unfortunately, *exactly* what my editor said about Harper's book. And my agent, too, though I've never told Harper I gave her the manuscript. And when I finally read it, I could see what they meant, which was the worst feeling in the world. I couldn't bring myself to tell Harper about any of it, which is why she thinks I haven't read it yet.

Sometimes it's kinder to lie.

"You can't let one person's opinion affect you that much. Especially not Connor's."

"It's not just him. It's what everyone thinks. Even you."

"That's not true—"

"Don't, okay? Just don't. I tried. I wrote the best novel I could, and it got rejected everywhere. Over and over."

"You know I'd change that if I could. But this . . . That's been true for a while now. What changed?"

"You know."

"I don't."

"Honestly, El? Sometimes you're so . . . You have what I want, and you're just going to throw it away?"

My throat feels tight. "You know why I have to do it."

"Do I? Yeah, Connor's annoying. I have to deal with him more than you do. But if you end the series, do you think you're going to get away from him? There's going to be a million think pieces, and pressure from the publisher, and the fans won't even believe he's dead."

"But that will die down, and then I'll be free."

"Free of what?"

I bite the inside of my cheek and taste blood. "They don't want me unless I write about him. That's a cage."

"Looks pretty gilded to me."

"We're supposed to be talking about you, not me."

"There is no me without you, don't you get it? That's the problem."

I sing a line from that Taylor Swift song "Anti-Hero," about me being the problem.

"Please don't make light of this."

"I'm sorry, I just . . . You don't feel that way, do you?" We stare at each other, and I can hear my heart pounding loudly in my ears. "Oh my God, you do."

"It's complicated, El. We're complicated."

"I know I stole your dream. I didn't mean to."

"But you did."

"I wish I could take it back."

"You don't."

My heart feels like it's breaking. "I'm not sure what to say."

"It doesn't matter."

"It does matter. You matter. You matter to me."

Harper looks at me for a long beat and then she says, "Pineapple."

We don't say anything else after that.

- Maybe there's more than one death? The first one is a fake-out that distracts everyone, and then, when Connor does die, everyone will be surprised.

WHY?
- Motive #4: The recently cast-off lover? Connor's a cad. But do you murder a cad for breaking up with you?
- Motive #5: The cuckolded man? Connor could easily push him to the brink. He has a way of getting under your skin, needling you. It's what makes him effective as a detective. And if the other guy thought his old love still had feelings for Connor . . . If he still had feelings . . .

WHERE?
- Maybe Pompeii?
- Something ironic about killing him where so many people died.

TO DO
- RESEARCH POMPEII—Is there some historical analogy I can make? Some theme that can be woven in? This should be epic.
- TELL AGENT/PUBLISHER—If I write it enough times, will it happen without me doing it?

NB: Holmes died when Moriarty pushed him off a cliff. Lots of cliffs in Amalfi . . .

# CHAPTER 12

## Kaboom!

**Pompeii**

After our stop at the pasticceria, where I ate a sinful cannoli with a cream filling that was so rich it could produce an instant heart attack, the coach pulls into an overlook at the Bay of Naples. We file out for ten minutes of photographs, and it's breathtaking. The red-roofed houses climbing the cliffside, and the water a deep blue that almost matches the sky. In the distance, the Island of Capri is shrouded in a set of misty clouds that makes it look blurry.

The BookFace Ladies ooh and aah, we all take photographs on our phones, and then we are back in the coach. As much as I don't want to talk to him, I have some questions for Connor, so I ask Isabella if she minds giving us a minute. She exchanges a glance with Connor, then shrugs and takes my seat next to Harper.

"What do you want?" Connor says.

"We need to talk. Tell me more about this pedestrian."

"Which one?"

"The one you claim pulled you out of traffic and is now dead. Davide something. What happened exactly?"

"I already told you. I was pushed into traffic, and he grabbed me at the last minute and pulled me away from an oncoming bus."

"Did you talk to him afterward?"

"Briefly. To thank him."

"Did you ask him if saw anything?"

"He said he didn't, he just saw me flailing."

"But the killer wouldn't know that necessarily, not if he saw you talking." I think it through. "Did you get his number?"

"Yes, he gave it to me. He said to call him if I ended up going to the police."

"Which you didn't do."

He shakes his head.

"It could be a coincidence that he got killed the next day."

"Come on, Eleanor, you don't believe that."

"Okay, you're right, I don't. He must've seen who pushed you."

"It's the only explanation."

I shudder. "This is scary, Connor. Killing a bystander like that—that's hard-core."

"Oh, now she cares."

I cross my arms. "You want my help or not?"

"Yes."

"Then stop being an asshole."

He smirks. "You did say it was my default setting."

I grit my teeth. "Is that all? Everything you know?"

"Yes."

I don't believe him, but I've had enough of Connor for a while, so I take a seat by myself and decide to try and work for the rest of the journey.

I have a murder to plot, after all.

I've got to get on that.

Our lunch is at a tourist trap in Pompeii with fake frescoes on the wall and a view of Mount Vesuvius in the distance. The pizza is mediocre, which seems like a crime given where we are, and the restaurant isn't air-conditioned. I'm too scared to look up the exact temperature, but I don't need to see the number on the dial to know it's hot.

Climate-change hot.

Old-people-die-in-this-weather hot.

I can't believe we're about to tour a massive archeological site in the full midday sun. It sounds like a recipe for disaster. But that's what this whole trip is, isn't it?

Six more days after this and it will all be over. Maybe before then. One can hope.

One can *pray*.

In the meantime, I wish I had a hat. I'm sure I do—I was wearing it yesterday, wasn't I?—but I'm guessing it's in Harper's bag and I can't bring myself to ask her for it.

She's eating lunch with Oliver and Guy, while I'm stuck with Shek and Allison, with the rest of our group spread out in the open-air restaurant full of faux Corinthian columns and sweating BookFace Ladies.

Connor and Isabelle are at a table by themselves on the edge of the room. He's sitting with his back to the wall, and every time I look over, he's scanning the other tables like he's waiting for someone to knife him.

It must be hard to relax while you're waiting for death.

Even if you're Connor Smith.

I'm having trouble relaxing myself. The conversation with Harper on the bus didn't help. Because even though the rational part of me knows Harper doesn't think I'm trying to off Connor, the fact that she'd even ask is emblematic of the problem between us.

*I'm* the bad thing that happened in Harper's life.

"After all these years," Shek says, penetrating my thoughts. "After all these books, they're going to drop me? It's outrageous. It's age discrimination. I should sue."

"That must be so hard for you, Shek," Allison says with a compassion I can only admire. If I'd been through what she has, I'd be a rageaholic.

I have to ask her what her secret is.

Edibles, maybe?

"I'm sorry, Shek—" I say.

"No." He pauses to drink down some of the massive beer he ordered, which he had to pay extra for because this lunch *didn't* come with alcohol, despite Harper's assurances. "This is as much your fault as theirs."

"What?"

"They took my marketing budget for *The Empty Post* and gave it to you."[79]

"I don't think it's quite that linear . . ."

He puts his empty mug down with a *thunk*. "It's exactly what I was told. Apparently, the book before didn't sell as much as planned so they 'shifted resources' to make it a success. *Passed Out in Paris*, or whatever."

"*Passed Away in Paris.*"[80]

"No wonder it didn't sell, with that title."

I stare down at my plate. He's right. *Passed Away in Paris* wasn't my best work, and the title didn't help. I'd written it right after I saw Oliver at the Salon du Livre, so I wasn't in a great state of mind, and the lackluster reviews had translated into lackluster sales. There had been an all-hands meeting in New York when the marketing ramped up for *Drowned in Porto*, and they told me they were putting a major push behind it.

And yep, they did say they were "diverting resources" to help do that, and you know what? I didn't think about who it would impact. I was just happy they were doing it.

"Still probably not Eleanor's fault," Allison says. "She doesn't make these decisions."

Shek grunts, then raises his hand to the waiter to bring another beer.

"No," I say. "I . . . I'm sorry, Shek. They did tell me they were doing that. Not whose budget they were using, but I did know. I should've asked."

"Typical."

"What did you expect her to do?" Allison says. "Turn it down? Would you have done that? And what about all *your* fat advances over the years?

---

[79] Who is titling Shek's books? AI?

[80] Okay, okay, mine aren't much better.

Wasn't that money 'taken away' from someone else? Or a lot of someone elses?"

Shek splutters as the waiter brings him his beer. Then he stands and takes it with him to another table without saying a word.

"You told him," I say to Allison.

"Men never like to hear the truth."

"Amen."

She smiles, then looks away.

Does she hate me? I feel like she hates me.

"Anyway," I say, clearing my throat to try to break the tension. "I am sorry about what's happening to him."

"You're only as good as your last book." She sounds like she's speaking from experience.

I'm not sure how many copies Allison's book sold. It's not polite to ask.[81] Besides, this is the first real conversation we've ever had.[82] And here she is, defending me to Shek, despite everything I've done to her.

"Did you want to publish another book?"

"It's the only reason I wrote that tell-all in the first place. It was a two-book deal—they were supposed to publish my novel afterward, but because the memoir didn't sell well,[83] they canceled it."

"Ah, hell, I'm sorry."

"Thanks."

"You seem so calm about it."

"I don't find anger productive."

---

[81] You can, however, look it up on BookScan, which authors don't usually have access to except for their own books. Not usually.

[82] I know her basic biography, though. She was a fledgling actress when she met Connor and followed him to Europe when—I'm guessing here—America got too hot for him. She'd acted in a few BBC dramas in minor roles and one French slasher film. For the last ten years, she's done one guest spot a year on a network procedural. And yes, I am very familiar with her IMDb page.

[83] It was ten thousand copies, okay? Not terrible but not amazing.

"I think it's fueled half my life. According to my therapist, anyway."

It's true. That's what she'd said the one time I went to therapy.

Dr. McGill had come highly recommended, but all she'd done was listen to me vent about Connor for fifty minutes, and then she'd told me that I seemed like a "very angry person" and that I should work on "forgiving and forgetting" if I wanted any chance at happiness.

Honestly? That was the advice I paid $250 for?

I mean, would *you* forgive someone who'd tricked you into a relationship while he was a married man, and then blackmailed you for ten years?

Is forgiveness even possible?

Ugh, maybe Harper's right.

I do have the best motive for killing Connor.

"Time for the tour of Pompeii, yes?" Sylvie says, clapping her hands to get our attention. "I hope you enjoyed this delicious pizza." She rubs her stomach like she's just had the best meal of her life. "It will be hot, so please take one of the water bottles with you that we will be giving out at the entrance. We don't want anyone dying on us, no?"[84]

Once we've collected our waters, Sylvie takes us into Pompeii proper, tossing about historical tidbits that are her signature mix of truth and invention.

There are too many names for me to retain—the Villa of Mysteries, the Villa of Diomedes, the Vesuvius Gate, the House of the Faun—and maybe she's making these names up, or maybe they're real. I don't care at this point. I only want to get to the *après* tour, where I can drown my anxiety in alcohol and try to solve the mystery of my own life.

"This heat is going to kill me,"[85] Allison says as we huff our way up a set of stone stairs to get to the city itself. The sun's high in the clear blue sky, and the air is thick with pine and dust. The mountains in the distance are hazy. The stark pyramid of Mount Vesuvius sticks out,

---

[84] Seriously. Death is <u>everywhere</u>.

[85] I'm going to stop pointing these out.

though, and I shiver thinking about what it must've been like to live here, so close to its angry plume of ash.

"It's a killer,"[86] I say.

"Death on the mind, is it?"

"Hard not to with what happened this morning."

"That was a stunt." She laughs. "Connor just loves attention."

He's walking ahead of us, hand in hand with Isabella. Unlike the rest of us, he seems unaffected by the heat. His thick hair is still perfect, and there aren't any sweat stains on the back of his shirt.

I almost tell her that Connor's not making it up, then stop myself. She's a suspect, after all. The less I tell her, the better to ferret out the killer among us.[87]

"You don't want him gone?" I ask. "After everything he did to you?"

She stops. "Everything you *both* did to me, you mean?"

"I deserve that."

"You do."

"Do you want me dead?"

"I don't want anyone dead. Well, maybe a politician or two. But not Connor. That would be bad for me."

"How so?"

"He's got five more years of alimony payments." She laughs again. "Is that crass?"

"I'm sure it's less than you deserve."

"Nope, I got everything I wanted. I have a very good lawyer."

"Good for you."

I hadn't paid too much attention to the details of their divorce. Not

---

[86] Really, this is the <u>last</u> time.

[87] I <u>am</u> going to point out here, though, that I was remarkably casual at this point in the investigation. I can't really explain it other than the fact that I still had doubts about the veracity of what Connor was telling me. Why else would I be so cavalier with my own safety?

her side of it, anyway. I was living on my side of it, which helped, I'll be honest, sell a lot of copies of *When in Rome*.[88]

THE SCANDALOUS DIVORCE BEHIND THE BESTSELLER.

That was one of the *nice* headlines.

I was called a whore, a home-wrecker, and many words I won't repeat here.

Of course Connor was simply a charming rogue, a cad, a heart-breaker.

To the day I die, I'll never understand why we let men control the way women get spoken about.

"What if I kill him off in the books?" I ask.

"So long as he can keep making his payments, I don't care."

That makes sense. But wait.

Connor still hasn't told me who invested in whatever it was, but maybe he was being deliberately misleading. Maybe it isn't about someone who lost money because of him, but someone who might suffer if he doesn't have resources anymore?

But if that is the case, why would he go on a tour with Allison? Though it wasn't until he was already *on* the tour that he realized his brakes failing might not have been due to bad maintenance. Because of what happened at the Vatican.

"Did you go on the Vatican tour?" I ask Allison.

"That's a random switch of topics."

"My brain works that way sometimes."

"I skipped it, why?"

"Connor thinks someone tried to push him into traffic there. I wondered if you might've seen anything."

Allison looks at me like she doesn't believe what I'm saying.

I pull out the water bottle Sylvie handed to me to break eye contact.

---

[88] I told you it's crass to talk about book sales.

I should stop trying to play detective. Because—and I can't believe I'm saying this—I think I'm *bad* at it. I'm certainly not as subtle as I should be.

And that person who crashes around in books, asking everyone all the questions?

That's the person who ends up as the second victim.

"Welcome to Pompeii," Sylvie says, holding her arms out wide. "We will be seeing many wonders today, many streets, and many graves. Because this is the final resting place of thousands of Pompeiians, my friends. Twelve thousand people were living here when Mount Vesuvius exploded." She points to the rectangular mountain behind her.

"I thought only two thousand people were still in town?" Harper says. She's standing next to Emily and the two of them look thick as thieves.

"Where did you hear this?"

"It's called Google?" Emily says, waving her phone. "Maybe you've heard of it?"

"Now, Emily, no need to be like that," Connor says.

Emily clamps her jaw shut.

"Please go ahead," Connor says to Sylvie. "This is all fascinating."

"Thank you, Mr. Smith. I am a fan. A very big fan."

He smiles and moves his hand in a circular motion, inviting her to continue.

"The city of Pompeii was buried under the ash from the volcano. The excavations started in modern times and many wonders were uncovered. It was like a photograph of life. The bread was in the oven, the tables were set, the paintings were on the walls. It is from here that we know the most about the Roman way of life. Now, let us explore and you can see why over two million people come here every year."

She leads us through the gates, and the BookFace Ladies fan out and start snapping photos on their phones.

It is impressive. A large town laid out with cobbled streets on a grid. You can even see the grooves from the chariots carved into the stone. The house walls are mostly intact, though most of the roofs are gone.

I don't need to use my imagination to see what life must've been like here.

Right up until it stopped.

"In here, my friends!"

Sylvie leads us into a house—a mansion, even by today's standards. Emily's in front of me with Harper. Her face is still set in a sour expression.

"Do you know anything about that?" I say to Allison. "Emily and Connor?"

"Connor has a way of zeroing in on the next best thing."

"I've noticed that."

Allison raises a shoulder. "I heard he met her at Books by the Banks in Cincinnati."

"She slept with him?"

"I assume."

"That's too bad."

"Lots of people have made that mistake."

"Right . . ." I stop. Despite the undercurrent of tension, it's been nice talking to Allison today.

And okay, yes, maybe I'm also considering her as a suspect, but I do feel sorry for what I did to her, even though she seems fine with it.

I mean, not *fine with it*, fine with it, but what that therapist said. She's let go and moved on, and she certainly seems happier than me.

I should acknowledge that. I should try to be a better person and take responsibility for some of the mistakes I've made.

For once in my life.

"I've never apologized to you, Allison. I wanted to say I'm sorry. For Connor. For all of it."

"You didn't know about me," she says in a way that might be a question or a statement.

"I didn't. There's no way I would've done anything with Connor if I knew he was married. I'm not a cheater."

"Are you sure?"

Oh God. Does she know about that?

"You never checked him out," Allison continues. "If you'd googled him, you would've known he was married."

"I was young and caught up. The minute I found out about you, I ended things."

That plus the blackmail were enough to put an end to me and Connor.

Then again, I've never really asked myself if the wife alone would've been enough.

I mean, probably. Otherwise, I'd be a total monster.

"The sexual relationship, maybe," Allison says, "but you've kept him in your life. You keep writing about him."

I look down at the mosaic floor below us. It's an intricate key pattern that must've taken hours and hours to lay. "That's a long story."

One that she might know . . . I've never asked, and I don't want to now.

"I'm sure."

"I *am* sorry, Allison. And I'm not asking you to forgive me. I just wanted you to know that I wish it hadn't happened."

"Okay," she says, and for the first time, I see through her bubble of happiness to something else underneath.

Something dark.

See, Dr. McGill? It doesn't work. Forgiveness is a myth.

Besides, what am I doing trying to convince a woman whose husband I slept with and who might be trying to kill him that I'm a good person?

Because I'm not. Obviously.

"Come this way, my friends! We are about to see some erotic art."

Allison bursts out laughing, and it's like the sky has cleared, even though it's been sunny this whole time. "Did she just say 'erotic art,' or am I hearing things?"

"I heard it, too," I say.

"Dear God."

"Can we escape, you think?"

"Doubtful."

"After you, then."

We follow Sylvie into a building that she tells us was a house of prostitution. And sure enough, there are erotic frescoes on the walls, lifelike and not leaving much to the imagination.

"We are lucky we can still see this," Sylvie says. "The early explorers, they were, how do you say, *prudes*? One of the best frescoes of the god Priapus; his penis was too big, so they covered it in plaster."

A woman next to us slaps her hands over her six-year-old's ears. "There are children present!"

"You are in Italy, signora. We treat everyone like grown-ups."

The woman huffs and hauls her kid away. Allison's shoulders are shaking from laughter as she follows Sylvie and the others through the door while I stand in front of the fresco, trying to settle my thoughts.

"It's hot, isn't it?" Connor hisses on my neck.

He doesn't mean the temperature.

And I know it's a cliche, but sometimes those are based on reality, because my skin starts to crawl like there are ants on it.

"Just go away," I say with as much force as I can.

"You'd like that, wouldn't you? Then you'd be free of what we did. That's what you think, isn't it?"

It's exactly what I think.

No. Amendment.

It's what I know.

"No one's trying to kill you, Connor," I say with a conviction I don't feel.

He speaks against my neck again, and the hairs on my arms stand straight up.

"Just wait," he says. "You'll see."

# CHAPTER 13

## A Victimless Crime

Okay, confession time. Given that Connor basically spilled the beans back there, I might as well fill you in.[89]

I mean, you've probably already guessed it, right? The *real* reason Connor has such a hold over me? No? Well, that crime I helped him solve? The robberies that were shaking up Rome? The *murder*?

Connor planned it.

Hold up, hold up, hold *up*.

I thought he solved the robberies, you say?

Yeah, me too.

But after we'd gone to the police with our evidence and the remainder of the Giuseppe crew was arrested in the act, Connor and I had gone out to celebrate, and we'd gotten sloppy drunk. We went back to his room and you can imagine what happened next.[90]

It was wonderful. He was wonderful, we were wonderful together, and I was exhilarated, thrilled, on cloud nine. Every cliché you can think of, and probably some you can't.

Then I woke up.

---

[89] Consider this a footnote promise kept.

[90] There was this thing he used to do with his tongue—chef's kiss.

A couple of hours after we fell asleep, my eyes popped awake. I felt restless and undone. Unfinished. That must've been the reason I started searching through our stack of evidence in the living room of our suite while Connor slept in the bedroom. The surveillance photos and maps and things we'd accumulated over the previous weeks.

Something was bugging me.

Something wouldn't leave me alone.

And then it hit me.

How did he know to stake out the building where they'd caught the robbers? And why was he so sure that particular bank was the next one on the list? There were dozens of banks in Rome. Probably hundreds. It's a close-packed city. Every bank is surrounded by buildings that could be purchased and used to tunnel underground. But Connor had zeroed in on this one. He'd had some explanation about how it was the most likely target, that there was a pattern to the heists, and to be honest, I hadn't asked too many questions.

But during that middle of the night, as I stood over a map with the robberies marked on it with little colored pushpins, I could see that there was no pattern at all.

What did that mean? If there wasn't a pattern, how did Connor know where the next robbery was going to take place? There was only one explanation.

He had to have something to do with it.

But what?

I tried to puzzle that out for hours, thinking back through our conversations, what he'd told me about himself. He was a private detective, he'd said, for expats and people who got into trouble on vacation, but mostly he worked as a consultant.

I'd assumed for the police and insurance companies, but had he said that?

He *was* working with an insurance company on this case. I'd been in one of the meetings with men in tight, tailored suits and sophisticated accents in a glass-walled conference room. And when we'd gone to the carabinieri, he'd known the chief inspector, but their relationship hadn't been warm. Instead, Inspector Tucci had been suspicious, it seemed, wary. It had taken some convincing for him to look at our evidence, and then, until the criminals were in custody and more evidence was found connecting them to the murder, he didn't believe it was true.

Why?

Consultant of what?

Oh, shit. What if he was a consulting *criminal?*

What if *he* was the one who'd planned the robberies, and that's how he knew where the next one would be?

But no. That couldn't be. It was late and I was making things up. I was asking questions when I didn't have to. The mystery had been solved, the bad guys were going to jail, and that was that. This would all seem ridiculous in the morning.

I was sure of it.

I was about to crawl back into bed when a notification flashed on Connor's phone.

I don't know what it was that made me look. I wasn't someone who read my boyfriend's messages—not until then, anyway. But that night I did. Because it wasn't a text; it was a Signal message.

I'd always felt weird about Signal. Connor had suggested we use it when we met, and I didn't question it at first, but eventually, it started to make me uneasy, like a hangnail I couldn't get rid of. Why were we using a communication method favored by cheaters and politicians who didn't want their official communications to show up on government servers?

What did we have to hide?

He'd smoothed that concern away like he'd ironed out so many things since we met.

—How he became a detective and what he'd done before that.

—Where he'd grown up.

—Where he lived when he wasn't being put up in a hotel.

—What he saw in me.

I'd believed all his vague answers and had tried to live in the moment like he'd suggested. But that night, with too many questions swirling in my head, the doubts came rushing back.

Most of all, I wanted to know: Who was Signaling him in the middle of the night?

I checked the bedroom. He was still sleeping. I knew the code to his phone because he'd been casual about using it in front of me. Trusting. He never thought I'd look through his phone. Why would he?

But I did. And there it was, all laid out in his Signal messages. The man who was writing him—someone named Gianelli, a minor figure in the Giuseppe family—wanted his cut of the finder's fee. He was insisting they meet in the morning. And the more I read, the more I saw that I was right. Connor *had* planned the whole thing. It was his idea to rob the banks, and he'd decided which banks to hit, and how. He'd worked it all out for them. And as far as I could tell, the surveillance we'd done was to make sure they were following his plan.

I sat there in shock for an hour, my robe cinched tight.

What I couldn't figure out was why he'd turned on them. Why he'd involved me. Or what I was going to do about it.

But that shouldn't have been a mystery to me, or to you either at this point.

I sat there afraid in the hotel room for hours, waiting for dawn to come, trying to decide if I should confront him or just leave without looking back, but I couldn't make myself go to the door. Connor found me asleep in a chair, his phone clutched in my hand, and knew that I'd discovered his plan.

He had an explanation for everything. He'd turned on them after a member of the team had murdered Gianni because they thought his loyalty was in question. That had never been part of the plan. They were bad people and had to be stopped, and if he got the police off his own back, built up some goodwill, and got a finder's fee out of it, well, then that was just his good fortune, wasn't it?

*Our* good fortune.

Robbing a bank was a "victimless crime," he said. The insurance companies came in and made it all better, and no real person lost their money.

It all sounds like bullshit now, but then?

It made sense to me.

I mean, had he done anything *that* wrong?

Okay, yes, he had, but he wasn't a murderer. He hadn't robbed the banks, exactly, just given the robbers a good idea of how to do it. Was that so different from someone who wrote a heist movie for Hollywood that inspired a real robbery?

This is an actual example he used as he talked me out of going to the police.

He had others. I don't remember them now.

I just remember the feeling of his lips against my ear, the way he made me feel inside.

A victimless crime, he said.

Only that wasn't true. There was a victim. Someone *had* lost his life.

He brushed that away, too. Gianni Giuseppe was a violent member of a criminal family. His life expectancy wasn't anything to write home about. He'd been the author of his own demise.

Does it even matter what Connor said?

It only matters what I did.

I didn't turn him in.

And then, despite everything, despite all of it, I'd written *When in Rome.*

It started as a way for me to try to make sense of what happened. To get my story straight. Not just with myself, but if the police ever came knocking. I didn't need Connor to tell me that I was now an accessory after the fact to those crimes. Maybe I'd even helped facilitate them.

So I wrote and wrote and wrote. I shaped the narrative in a way that made it possible to live with. I left out the real solution, the Connor of it all, and made him the hero. I did such a good job of convincing myself of our innocence that I forgot our guilt.

Which Connor made clear to me in New York when he learned about the book.

He stayed up all night reading the manuscript, and then he came to me with a proposal. I'd give him the cut he wanted. And if I didn't? Well, then he'd let the carabinieri know that I was an accessory. That I'd hidden material evidence.

"And don't think you can turn me in and get away scot-free," he'd said. "I've planned for that." I couldn't take him down without taking myself down, too.

Mutually assured destruction, he'd called it.

Or maybe only I'd be destroyed because Connor wasn't stupid. He'd manipulate the evidence, he assured me, to make it seem like *I* was the one who had planned the heists, not him. So, I was going to comply, wasn't I? I was going to do what he asked. Because if I didn't, there'd be consequences.

And how did I know that *he* wasn't the one who'd killed Gianni?

That was the part I couldn't forget. The coldness in his eyes when he suggested that he might've taken Gianni's life.

I believed him.

I agreed to his terms.

I was scared and foolish and vain and stupid. I paid and I wrote and I smiled for the cameras. I kept my nose to the grindstone for ten years because I was afraid of what I'd find if I looked up.

But then I did. And here's the thing Connor hasn't figured out yet.

There's a statute of limitations for robbery and obstruction of justice in Italy.[91] I discovered it when I was doing research for *Amalfi Made Me Do It*.[92] What that means is, even if Connor tells the carabinieri what I did, they can't prosecute me.

So I'm free to get rid of him.

There's nothing he can do about it.[93]

---

[91] It's a complicated formula that boils down to this: The time limit to prosecute a crime is equal to the jail time attached to that crime, with the exception of crimes where the punishment is life imprisonment.

[92] My original concept for the book was that Connor would return to Italy for the first time in ten years and get involved in something related to the next generation of Giuseppes. I was trying to figure out if Connor could discover something new about the original crime, and that's how I stumbled onto the limitation periods.

[93] Ha ha ha. I'm an idiot.

# CHAPTER 14

## It's Murder on the Med

**Sorrento**

We finish the tour of Pompeii without any further incident, and then we say goodbye to the BookFace Ladies. They climb back into the bus to be taken to their resort while we're sent to our hotel in private cars.

Cathy—who's been keeping her distance all day—gives Isabella a hard stare when she climbs into a car with Connor. Whether it's because she thinks she deserves a luxury ride or because she wants to cozy up to Connor, I'm not sure. Like most of the book's fans, she thinks the sun shines out of Connor's butt, although she's always been more fixated on me than him. If that's about to change, I'm not going to stop it.

I get into a car with Harper, hoping that the ice has thawed between us, but it hasn't. It's as cold as the air-conditioning, and I don't know what to do.

"Harper, will you please talk to me?"

She glances at me. "What were you talking to Allison about?"

"I was apologizing."

"You were?"

"No need to sound so surprised."

The car moves off the highway and onto a two-lane road that looks like it's headed toward the Med. In a moment, the car takes a sharp turn, and now we're driving along the edge of a cliff that goes down at least a thousand feet into rocks and crashing water.

"Wow," I say, "that's beautiful." But it's also kind of terrifying.

We're both transfixed. We're driving toward a town built into the cliff. The buildings are colorful, and the streets are tiered, surrounded by lemon trees. The water below is that blue you only seem to see in photographs, but here it is, *real*.

"It is," Harper says.

"We're lucky. I am."

"I'm surprised to hear you say it."

"I don't say it enough. I don't do a lot of things."

"Such as?"

"Tell you how much I appreciate you. How important you are to me. How I couldn't have done any of this without you."

She smiles sadly. "You did do it without me."

"I am sorry about that. And maybe you're right. Maybe I wouldn't change it, but I can be sorry about it anyway. I can be sorry about what it did to you."

"Are you?"

"Yes, of course. That's what I'm trying to say."

The car takes another sharp turn and Harper grips the handhold on the door like it might fly open and take her with it.

I reach out to steady her. "It's okay, we're safe."

She's a bit green around the edges. She's never been good in cars, and we're both afraid of heights. "I know."

"No, Harper, I mean it. You'll be okay, we'll be okay."

Her eyes connect with mine and I feel a rush of relief. It's still there. The love between us, impossible to shake.

We'll be okay. No matter what.

"How can you be so sure?"

"Because we've been through worse than this. Mom and Dad . . . We're a success story, Harper. You and me against the world."

"Then why do you want to change it? Just because of Connor? What's the point of that? Look where we are right now. He gave us that."

"What do you mean?"

"I think you should keep writing the series."

"What? Why?"

"Because we have a good life. I know you think I should be doing something else. I feel your judgment, okay? But I'm happy being in your shadow. That's what I was going to tell you when we got home. I'm not going to try to write anymore. No more torturing myself at five in the morning, tweeting about how I'm starting some new manuscript. I'm sick of it."

"It's your life, Harper, do what you want."

"But that's the problem, don't you see? Your book life—it's not only yours. It's the way *both* of us make a living."

"So, what? I have to keep writing something I don't want to just to make you happy?"

"I didn't say that."

"But it's kind of what you mean, right? Just keep everyone happy. Dance, monkey, dance."

"Give me a break, El. This is exactly the problem."

"What?"

"You *like* writing those books. You like meeting fans and talking about your writing process and being funny on stage and the money and the accolades and all of it."

"But what about Connor?"

"So, he's annoying."

"He's more than that."

"Whatever. Ignore him. Shut him out of your life."

Harper thinks this is possible because she doesn't know the truth. I've never told it to anyone.

"It's not that easy."

"But it's not going to kill you, is it?"

And what can I say to that?

Death is all around us. That's the only thing I know for sure.

Our hotel in Sorrento is a bright yellow building with a white trim nestled into a rock face at the top of a cliff that looks down into the sea. All of the rooms have individual stone balconies overlooking the water, and this time, we're not all on the same floor.

I make sure to ask this at the front desk as we check in.

With everything that's happened, I feel like I need to know where Connor is at all times.

"Just wait," Connor said. "I'll see."

What does that mean? And what about Harper's prediction that it's not going to kill me to keep writing about him? He's someone's target right now. Being around him is dangerous.

Because if there's one thing I know, it's that when there's a murderer on the loose, it's not only the intended victim at risk. The wrong person dies all the time.[94]

So, no matter what Harper thinks, I need to be free of him.

And why is she so sure I can't write something else? That my only worth as a writer is connected to Connor? It's something I've suspected for a long time but have never confronted her about. But the truth is, Harper thinks I'm not that great a writer.

She's intimated as much before. Not directly, but it's there in her comments about how so many *New York Times* bestsellers are mediocre. How quickly I write, while it takes her forever. That the way to get mass appeal is to be average.

Average. Average.

She thinks I'm average.

That word bounces around in my head because she's probably right. I don't write beautiful sentences about the way the world quiets down

---

[94] This might be a clue. It might also be a warning.

when the snow falls. I've never remarked on the way a leaf in autumn is a different thing entirely from one in a lush summer. I keep it pithy and page-turny and mysterious. I build tension through clue drops at the ends of chapters.[95]

I line up the suspects, then make them each seem plausible in turn.

It may not be pretty, but it gets the job done.

I mean, can ten million people be wrong?[96]

Of course they can. I told you I have imposter syndrome, didn't I? And now my sister is confirming it. I'm not good; I'm just *lucky*.

That's what I told that reporter from the *New York Times* for the profile I can't bring myself to read. I know I'm going to come off sounding like an asshole, and I've already got enough people telling me that I am one.

I take the elevator to my floor and walk to the door to my suite. Like always, it's adjoining Harper's, but Connor is a floor above me, which feels like a relief.

I fish around in my purse for the key I just deposited in there and pull it out. Only it isn't in the paper case for this hotel, and when I look at it, I realize it's the key from the hotel in Rome we left this morning. Black with a silver logo.

But wait, I gave my key to Harper when she collected them from all of us in the lobby so she could check us out.

Oh, *shit*. Is this what I think it is? The missing master key?

I never asked Harper if she'd replaced the other one. But she must have. That's how she got Connor's door open this morning and discovered his prank. She used a master key. It was there on the floor at her feet where she'd crumbled to the ground.

But what's this one doing in my purse? Is it the new one or the old one?

---

[95] You've probably noticed this.

[96] Does this constitute talking about my book sales? In my defense, it's right there on the front cover.

I feel a frisson of fear, then push it away. Harper must've dropped it in there this morning in all the rush to get on the bus. Our bags and purses were next to one another in the lobby. Besides, it's not the key to any rooms in this hotel. If the mugging was connected to all of this, whoever was behind it didn't end up using the key.

I fish around in my purse again and find the key to my room. I make a mental note to ask Harper to keep a sharp eye on her master key and go inside.

The walls are cream, and the sun is flooding in from the balcony. I put my bag down and open the doors, letting the warm sea breeze caress my face. The view is breathtaking, with the sea below and Capri visible in the misty distance. We're supposed to go there tomorrow on a boat, but all I want to do right now is sleep.

"Hey, Eleanor!"

I look down at the veranda. Shek and Guy are sitting at a table with Emily, drinking Aperol spritzes. The glasses are glowing in the sun like luminous jewels.

See, Harper. I *can* write flowery phrases.

I just choose not to.

"Come join us!" Guy says, unusually gregarious.

I shouldn't.

I should lie down and take the nap my body's asking for, but doing what I should has never been my MO.

"Give me ten minutes!"

I rinse my face off in the sink and change into a loose-fitting white cotton dress, then head to the veranda.

It's large and made of sandstone with a wrought iron railing on the edge of the cliff that's capped in more stone. There's a steep set of stairs on the left that lead down to the town below. Twenty black bistro tables with red tablecloths and bright yellow umbrellas are scattered around.

Shek, Guy, and Emily are the only ones out here. Sensible people are probably taking a siesta, or whatever the Italian equivalent is.

The word comes back to me: *"riposo."* That's what Connor used to call our afternoon sessions in bed.[97] I shudder at the thought and take the fourth seat at the table.

"Excellent decision, Eleanor," Guy says. He's dressed in black, his thick arms bulging out of his T-shirt. "Best view in Sorrento." He motions toward the sea dotted with sailboats and superyachts. It's beautiful. Overwhelming, almost.

"We're lucky to be here."

"That's directed at me, I suppose," Shek says. He's wearing a linen kaftan that looks incredibly comfortable, and his head is covered with a straw hat.

"Not everything is about you, Shek," Emily says. Like me, she's dressed in white and looks delicate and intelligent, and I get it now.

She threatens me.

You probably already figured that out.

Because I'm average, in more ways than one.

"I was talking about myself," I say. "I don't always appreciate what I have and where I am. I want to change that."

"Deep thoughts for an afternoon," Guy says.

"True."

"Don't worry," Emily says, touching my hand. "Connor won't appear till dinner."

"He's otherwise occupied," Shek says with emotion. Probably envy.

"Can we talk about something else? How does one get a cocktail, for instance?"

"She'll be here in a minute."

---

[97] I can't think of anything quippy to write about that. He knew what he was doing. Let's leave it at that.

Sure enough, a waitress approaches the table with four lemon spritzes on a tray moments later.

"We ordered one for you," Emily says.

"Thank you."

"Keep these coming," Shek says to the waitress, "every ten to twelve minutes."

"Yes, sir."

She leaves and silence descends.

"Do we have nothing to talk about but him?" I ask.

"Seems like," Emily says.

"That's pathetic."

Shek looks at me over the rim of his glass. "Are you truly going to end the Vacation series?"

Did I tell Shek that? I don't think so. But they're probably all talking about me when I'm not around.

I know that sounds egotistical.

I only meant that it's what I'd do.

"Why do you care?" I ask. I take a sip of my drink, and it's even better than a classic spritz.[98] Where has this been all of my life?

"Because it's a big deal," Shek says. "And a mistake."

"I guess that's my decision."

"Take it from me. You don't want to upset the apple cart."

"I agree," Guy says. "And Connor can be dangerous when cornered."

"Why does everyone keep telling me that?"

"Because it's true."

"What's he going to do, kill me?" I say this in jest, but it doesn't sound like a joke.

---

[98] A classic spritz is made with Aperol, Prosecco, soda water, and an orange slice. A lemon spritz is three parts Prosecco, two parts limoncello, and one part soda water, finished with a sprig of mint. And oh, yes! There _is_ a gelato version of this, too.

"You know he's in big financial trouble?" Guy says.

"He mentioned something about it but wouldn't tell me the details."

Except for the blackmail. But I'll keep that detail to myself for now. Just in case.

Guy smirks. "He was deep into crypto. Lost most of his money when one of those markets crashed."

"Seriously?"

"Happened about six months ago."

That tracks with Connor's story on the timing, but not with the cover-up part. Or maybe it does. Didn't they catch one of those crypto bros in the Bahamas with hardly any money left? Is that what Connor did? Help one of those guys hide his Ponzi scheme takings?

"How do you know that?"

"I keep tabs on him."

That's interesting.

"Why?" Emily asks.

"Keep your enemies close and your friends closer," Guy says.

"That's not how the saying goes," Shek says.

"Well, it should."

Emily tosses her head. "I only invest in blue-chip stocks."

"Good for you, honey," Guy says. "But Connor, sorry to inform you, is a little rough around the edges. Always looking for a get-rich-quick scheme. You know what I'm talking about, Eleanor."

I stare into my glass.

"You invested in something with Connor?" Emily asks.

"No, he's not . . . He just means how I first met Connor. He wanted to solve the robberies to get the finder's fee. It wasn't altruistic."

"That's not how it was in the book."

"So you *have* read it."

Emily tucks her chin in. "Hasn't everyone?"

"That's not what she means," Shek says.

"What then?"

"Didn't you hear her last night? She thinks you stole her plot."

"I didn't do that."

I clear my throat. "A young woman on vacation in Italy gets embroiled in a string of high-profile robberies along with the dashing man she met on her first night of vacation . . ."

"You're quoting my dust jacket to me?"

"I'm quoting *my* dust jacket. But thanks for telling on yourself."

"Catfight," Shek breathes, his excitement palpable.

"Is this whole table full of plagiarists?" I ask. "No wonder you're getting canceled, Shek. You're stealing material from Guy now."

"Oh, screw off," Shek says.

"Isn't that what you girls did with Connor?" Guy says, finishing his drink.

Emily and I stare at each other, and though we're both angry, we can't help it—we start to laugh. Me first, then her. In a minute we're hunched over the table, holding on to ourselves to keep from falling on the ground.

"Did he call you 'darling'?" Emily asks, gasping for air.

"Yes! And that thing where he forgets his wallet all the time?"

"All the time. Oh, and the nuts? Why is he always eating nuts?"

"For the protein!"

"Oh my God, yes."

The waitress comes back with a tray full of drinks. Shek looks at his watch. "That was fourteen minutes."

"*Mi scuse, senore.*"

"Should we warn Isabella?" I say, getting some control of myself.

"You think she'd listen?"

"I wouldn't have."

"I did try to warn you," Guy says. "More than once."[99]

"You did. Thank you, Guy."

---

[99] I met Guy a few days after I met Connor. He told me to walk away and not look back, but it was already too late for me.

"I'm warning you again."

My laughter cuts off, and I feel that chill down my spine. "You think he's dangerous?"[100]

"Look at what he did this morning."

"He was being an idiot."

"Aren't *you* the one who almost died yesterday?"

My hand goes up to my neck. It feels like the bone is still in place. "So I let him blackmail me for life?"

"Blackmail?" Emily says.

"Oh, um, I'm speaking metaphorically."

"Okay," she says, but not like she believes me.

"He made some trouble for me with the publisher about his name being used in *When in Rome*."

"But that's fair use."

"They didn't want to take the risk."

"You paid him off? That was stupid."

"I'm aware."

"You'd have done the same thing," Shek says. "We all would. If we saw our dream slipping away, there's no telling what we'd do."

"What are you going to do, Shek?" I ask.

"I didn't put my money in crypto, so I'll be all right." He raises his glass. "Maybe I'll give self-publishing a try. Or I'll just stop writing."

"Can you do that?"

"Stop getting up at four A.M. every day? You're damn right."

"Worrying about whether they're going to accept your manuscript," I counter.

"Worrying about the first reviews," Emily says.

I shiver. "Goodreads."

---

[100] I long ago decided that Connor hadn't killed Gianni. He was with me when that death happened, so it was impossible. I should've realized that at the time, but I was a bit distracted by the whole blackmail thing.

Emily takes a large gulp of her drink. "Goodreads is the worst."[101]

We start to laugh again, but it's not free like before. Instead, I feel uneasy, like someone's staring at me, that creepy-crawly feeling of eyes boring into my neck. And when I turn around, the feeling's confirmed. Connor's standing there, close enough to hear everything we've said, and he's got that smile on his face, one I know too well.

It's the one he used when he was explaining to me how it was all going to work ten years ago. How much I was going to pay, and what would happen if I didn't.

Then Connor cocks his finger in a pretend gun and pulls the trigger.

The fake bullet lands right between my eyes.

---

[101] Also known as MeanReads among authors, it's a site that lets people review books they haven't even read.

### AMALFI MADE ME DO IT—OUTLINE

I'm a bit too drunk to write this properly, but I think I've solved it: It's making Connor *think* that someone's trying to kill him that kills him. The stress, the looking over his shoulder. The PARANOIA.

It could make you do stupid things. The way you can make a relationship end if that's what you're worried about. There's a word for it.

"Manifestation." So . . .

HOW:

- Make Connor so crazy with worry that he's going to die that he does. It just . . . manifests.
- Ah, shit. That's not going to work.

TO DO:

- Work on this outline when not drunk.

Actual quote: "Keep your friends close, and your enemies closer." —Sun Tzu, *The Art of War*
Good advice.

# CHAPTER 15

## 39 Steps

With Connor's fake bullet between my eyes, I go back to my room and spend ten minutes in the shower trying once again to wash away the feeling that I'm missing something.

It's been a very odd forty-eight hours.

It felt like everything was in place before I came to Italy. After too many months of casting around for a plot, I finally had a plan for Book Ten, even if it wasn't fully formed. But that didn't bother me. I'm a pantser, not a plotter[102]—in writing and in life, too. I like to wing it. I like not always knowing what's going to happen. It's why I went to Italy in the first place. After spending seven years living my parents' life, giving up on my dreams, I wanted to come back to myself. I wanted something just for me.

I wanted to go back to being that irresponsible girl I was until the day my parents died. The girl they shook their head over. The girl they didn't know what they were going to do with.

I got what I asked for. That and much more.

After everything with Connor, I was changed again. I wasn't the girl

---

[102] In other words, I write without knowing precisely what's going to happen next. Apparently, Stephen King does this, too, though I've always had trouble believing that. Hmmm, that's the second time I've mentioned him. Jealous much, Eleanor?

I was at eighteen, but I wasn't the twenty-five-year-old me either. I was some in-between person who suddenly had all these opportunities I never imagined for myself. I lived that life for ten years—the good, the bad, the doubt, the fears, the loss, the love, and the loss of that love. I was managing. I was good, mostly. But I had to go and upset the apple cart.

Was it really about Connor?

Because, if I'm being honest, when I found out about the statute of limitations, when I realized I was *free*, that Connor didn't have a hold over me anymore, my first reaction was *fear*.

What was I without him?

I was terrified to find out.

But then I thought about the other fault lines in my life—those hadn't felt like choices. My parents' death certainly wasn't. Even Italy and Connor and the book—those had never felt like choices. Because I didn't choose to have Connor betray me and break my tender heart. To be blackmailed by him and have him force me to do what he wanted.

But this. *This.*

I could walk away on my terms. So that's what I was going to do. It was scary, but it was all going to work out. I was going to *manifest* it.

I should've known you can't manifest your life. The decisions you make aren't binding on other people. Proof positive: I'm in a fight with Harper, and Connor's very much still here.

And then there's Oliver.

Oliver, whose heart *I* broke when we were having a rough patch and were on a break.

No. That's not true.

We weren't on a break. We'd only fought. And I blew it up into some big dramatic thing because I'm a moron, and then I went on a book tour with Connor and spent too much time drinking and commiserating with him at the bar. The next thing I knew, I was waking up in his bed.

But no, that's a lie, too.

I'm a liar.

Have you figured that out yet?[103]

I tell people what they want to hear so they'll like me.

So here's the truth—if you want to believe the truth of a liar.

I picked the fight with Oliver on purpose. I was in too deep. I was so in love with him that it made what I felt for Connor seem like a minor crush. It scared me, and I needed a way out. Because I couldn't let myself get hurt like that again.

I just couldn't.

So I did the one thing I knew Oliver would never forgive me for. He'd told me more than once how much he hated that Connor and I had been together, how it made him jealous.

I used that. I chose a path with no way out.

Because I'm a liar and a coward and an all-around bad person.

I told you that in the beginning.

And if you think I didn't, then you weren't paying attention.


Dinner's painful, and I can't hear a word.

It's on the veranda, which is now full of other patrons, and there's music being piped in over the speakers. I'm sitting at the head of the table this time, and Oliver's at the other end. The music's so loud I couldn't talk to Allison to the left of me or Shek to the right even if I wanted to, which I don't.

Instead, I drink. I ask the waiter to bring me my own bottle of wine, and no one notices. I keep trying to make eye contact with Oliver, but he's talking to Harper, and it feels like he's studiously avoiding looking my way.

It's my tour, but I'm not the center of attention. Which is probably what I deserve. It occurs to me that almost everyone around this table has as much reason to hate me as Connor. I've betrayed so many of them in big and small ways that my death at one of their hands wouldn't come as a surprise.

And isn't that perfect irony—that if I'm the one to die, my suspect list and Connor's would line up perfectly?

---

[103] I might not be a plotter, but I've left a lot of clues about this.

You'd have thought someone planned it that way.[104]

So I drink, and the only person who seems to notice I'm here is Connor. He's sitting in the middle of the table, wrapped up in Isabella, but he keeps shooting me looks and, once, his signature fake gun that again has a bigger impact on me than it should.

Is it a warning or just a stupid gimmick meant to make me feel like I should be looking over my shoulder?

*Just wait. I'll see.*

I wait.

I drink.

When we get to dessert, I push my plate away and stumble to the edge of the veranda. It overlooks the cliff and the beautiful sea, and I can feel its pull. I'm not going to do it, but it does cross my mind that my life would be so much easier if it was over.

I read once that most people who commit suicide only spend five minutes thinking about it before they do it. It's not some long-term plan, but the impulse of a moment, with the opportunity at hand. I never understood it before, but as I stand here and imagine what the rocks below might do to my body, I get it now.

You make a quick decision and then that's it.

There are no more decisions to make.

"Don't jump," Oliver says gently, resting his arms on the stone next to me. He's wearing a white shirt and his face is tanned from our day in the sun. He's so appealing I want to wrap myself in his arms and—

Oh God, is this why I came to stand here? Was I trying to draw him to me?

I mean, obviously I was. And it worked.

I am the *worst*.

"I won't."

His eyes are troubled. "But you were thinking about it."

---

[104] It's me, hi, I'm the plotter, it's me.

"How do you know that?"

"You were talking out loud again."

"That's embarrassing."

He smiles. "It's one of your more charming characteristics."

"Why, thank you." I run my hands over the smooth stone of the wall. "What did I say?"

"'One little jump . . .'"

"I wasn't being serious."

"I hope not." He sighs and adjusts his body. He's closer to me now, the fabric of his shirt touching my arm. It's hard to concentrate.

"What was making you think about it?"

"The usual."

"Life, et cetera."

"Pretty much. Which makes me a fucking brat. I mean, look at this place. I have no right to complain." I sweep my hand out in front of me, taking the setting sun over the Med, that clear blue water, the sailboats with their white sails, and the megayachts. The cliff face full of multi-colored buildings built long before we were born. That scent of lemon and olive in the air. The warm breeze on my face as the sun sets on the horizon. The stone steps below us, winding down and down and down.

"Everyone's allowed to complain sometimes," Oliver says.

"Sure."

"You want to talk about it?"

"Not really."

We watch the brilliant orange sunset for a minute as it sinks into the sea, our arms touching. It feels like something's happening between us, but that's probably just wishful thinking.

It's magic hour, and this feels magical.

So that tracks.

But magical thinking is dangerous. It means you miss things. That you don't see danger coming.

I shudder, then turn my attention to a man climbing the stairs toward us from the town below. He's red in the face, but he keeps going up steadily. I admire his determination. I would've crapped out three flights ago.

"Happy Fourth of July, by the way," Oliver says.

"Is it the Fourth?"

"All day."

"I guess that's not something they celebrate here."

"Probably not."

"I sound like a stupid American," I say.

"You're not stupid."

"I've been feeling pretty stupid lately."

"Why?"

I hug myself, wrapping my arms tight. "I screwed everything up. Me and you, me and Harper."

"What happened with Harper?"

"She was telling you about it at dinner, wasn't she?"

He nods slightly. "Some."

"You two were always good friends."

"We both loved you."

A lump forms in my throat. He used the past tense. Not just for him, but for her.

Is this what it feels like when your heart is breaking? Like you can't breathe?

Like you never knew how to do it?

"Harper will come around," Oliver says.

"And you?"

He turns toward me. The setting sun is reflecting in his eyes, giving them an orange cast. "I came on this trip, didn't I?"

"You didn't have to?"

"I'm a grown man, El. I only do the things I want."

I work through what this means. Oliver *always* reads the packet. He knew this was my tour, and he came anyway. He sought me out. He—

Okay, El, slow your roll.

It's not like he's down on one knee.

"I'm glad you decided to come."

"Me too, mostly."

"Mostly?"

"There are a few things I'd change."

Connor, he means. The one constant between us. But I don't want to talk about Connor right now. I want to forget he even exists. I want it to be me and Oliver against this encroaching night.

I lean against him. It feels nice to stand like this and *not* talk. To watch the sunset like a normal couple would on a romantic vacation in Italy. The way it would've been between us if I hadn't gotten scared and we'd never been apart.

"Do you think that guy's having a heart attack?" Oliver says, pointing to the man I was watching earlier.

"He'll be all right. And if not, you're always here to save him."

"I'm not a hero, El."

I put my hand on his. He doesn't pull back. He doesn't pull *back*. "You saved me yesterday."

"Anyone would've done that."

"But you're the one that did."

He stares at me like he's trying to puzzle out the code we're speaking. We always used to know what the other meant; there wasn't any need for interpretation.

"You don't need me," he says eventually.

Tears sting my eyes. "I do. It's been terrible without you."

"Terrible, huh?"

He twines his fingers through mine. His touch feels overwhelming—warm and familiar, but somehow new.

"Oliver, I—"

"Sun's almost set," he says.

"On us?"

"It's not a metaphor. Look."

I turn toward the water and watch as the last of the sun drops below the horizon. And then, like it was coordinated, an enormous *BOOM!* sounds over our heads and the sky fills with a shatter of colorful stars.

"Fireworks?" I say. "Did you do this?"

"I wish . . . I guess it's for the Fourth, after all."

There's another explosion, and the other guests start to gather around us, pushing up against the railing to watch the fireworks splinter over the water.

"They do it every year," someone says near me, and I'm not sure who it is. I'm still holding on to Oliver, but it feels like he's being pulled away from me by the crowd.

The explosions come like rapid fire: *Boom! Boom! Boom!*

The crowd surges forward, and Oliver's hand slips through my fingers.

I look for him, but now I'm being pushed toward the top of the stairs as the crowd multiplies. We're all here: Harper and Shek. Allison and Emily. Oliver and Guy. Connor and Isabella. Everyone's in twos but me, and the crowd is still pushing against my back.

I feel unsteady. I try to call out, to tell them to *step back!* But it's too loud for anyone to hear me over the *oohs* and *aahs* and pointing fingers at the sky.

*Boom! Boom! Boom!*

And then it hits me.

Fireworks, a distraction, a crowd, those stairs that go down and down and down. One firm hand to the back, and it would be hard to tell who was responsible.

It would be impossible.

The only problem is, *I'm* the one losing my footing. Not Connor.

Then I feel it—a hand on the small of my back, pushing me to the edge, and then a hard shove.

And now I'm falling, and all I can think is: Maybe I'm the one who dies in this story after all.

# CHAPTER 16

## Life After Death

This is it, I think as I tumble out into space. This is the end.

And yeah, I know, I know—my almost-dead dialogue sucks.

Is this truly going to be my last thought? Editing myself as I tumble into—

A frantic hand catches the fabric of my dress and pulls me back. I'm not on solid ground; I'm floating in someone's arms with my heart on fire, ready to explode.

"I've got you, El. I've got you."

It's Oliver. It's always Oliver.

Damn it.

"Can you speak?"

"I . . . I think so."

He lowers me gently to the ground. My feet touch the cement, and my legs give way underneath me.

"I've got you," Oliver says again, and he doesn't let me fall because it's Oliver and he'd never let me fall, not even if he were the one who wanted me gone.

Because my God, my God. Someone wants to kill me.

Someone tried to kill me.

What. The. *Fuck*.

"Thank you," I say, trying to steady myself.

My back is to him, his arms around me like they were last night when he saved me the first time. I press against him, hoping his solidity will seep into me, and take several long, slow breaths.

I turn around slowly as the rest of the world comes back into focus. There's still a crowd around us, the fireworks exploding above.

*Boom! Boom! Boom!*

Everyone's faces are turned up to the sky, lit up by the lights. Blue, red, gold.

I scan them quickly—those I know and those I don't. No one seems like they just tried to push me off the edge. No one looks *guilty*.

No one's looking at me at all, except for Oliver.

His dark eyes are clouded with concern, the fireworks reflecting in them like this is some scene from a movie. And I know what's supposed to happen now. We're supposed to move closer and closer together as the music swells until we end up in a clinch.

That's how I'd write it, anyway.

But instead, he takes a step back and lets me go, and I'm on my own, just like I've always been.[105]

"You saved me, again."

"What happened?"

"Someone pushed me."

"What?" Oliver looks around at the crush of the crowd. "Who?"

"I don't know. I felt a hand on my back. You saw what happened next."

He puts his hands on my shoulders, pulling me closer. And maybe we will kiss now, only I think if we do, if he shows me any more tenderness, I'm going to burst into tears, and that's not how I want our first kiss in years to go.

"Are you sure?" he says, and he's so close to me I can feel his breath

---

[105] I was listening to Tay-Tay while I wrote this. Can you tell?

on my lips. "Maybe it was the crowd. Everyone pressing toward the railing to watch the fireworks?"

Moment's over, I guess.

"No," I say, taking a step back, away from his arms, away from the temptation. "I felt it."

"You've had a lot to drink."

"You're monitoring my drinking?"

"I was only paying attention."

He was watching me, he means. In a good way, he means. This should melt my cold heart, but instead, it makes me mad. "You don't need to do that. I'm fine on my own."

"Clearly not."

There's another rapid series of booms, building to a crescendo. It's so loud, I'm not sure he's going to be able to hear me, but I say it anyway. "What do you care?"

But he does hear me. It's right there in his face like I've slapped him.

And I did. My words were a blow, one I meant to deliver. Because it's easier to push him away than to hold him close. I proved that to myself once before, and here I am proving it all over again. I can use both hands, too, and end us once and for all.

"You really mean that, don't you?" he says.

I don't say anything, and that's what convinces him. Because I always take the opportunity to have the last word if I can unless I'm using silence for emphasis.[106, 107]

"Next time, I'll let you fall, then."

Ouch. Oliver can use words like swords, too.

I watch him turn and start to push his way through the crowd.

---

[106] Not my best characteristic, but can you blame a writer?

[107] Given how this is going, my last words will probably be in a footnote.

The fireworks are over now, just like us, and it's only a moment before he's gone.

Maybe for good.

I let the crowd disperse, feeling stupid and scared and still drunk, but not quite drunk enough. It's fully dark now, the sea black and glittering in the moonlight.

"There you are, El," Harper says. "I've been looking for you all over."

"Here I am."

"What happened?"

"What do you mean?"

"You're crying."

I reach up to my face and find tears. "Oh ... Someone tried to kill me."

"*What?*"

"During the fireworks. They tried to push me down the stairs."

"Oh my God. Are you okay?"

"Oliver saved me."

She wraps her arms around me. They're not the arms I want right now, but they're much better than nothing. "Connor. You. What's happening?"

"I don't know."

"You didn't see who it was?"

"No, I just felt a hand on my back ... I ... I'm such an idiot."

Harper hugs me tight, then releases me. "It's not your fault."

I almost laugh. "First of all, yeah, obviously it is. If someone wants me dead, I've clearly done something to piss them off."

"What's your second point?"

"Huh?"

"You said 'first of all.'"

"The second thing is, I'm an idiot."

"Why?"

"Because I told Oliver to get lost."

Harper leans her forehead against mine. "Oh, El. You silly girl."

I pull away. "Is that supposed to help?"

"Sorry. What should we do? Call the police?"

"Why would we call the police?" Connor asks, pulling up next to me with Isabella on his arm.

"God, Connor, not now!"

"Someone's calling the police?" Shek says, popping his head out from behind them.

The rest of the suspects—I mean, other people on this tour—start to circle us, closing in.

"Eleanor wants to," Isabella says.

"What?"

"Why?"

"What happened?"

I raise my hands over my ears to try to block them out. They're like the fireworks, a boom, boom, boom of distraction. I can't figure out what I need to do with everyone looking at me like I'm crazy and should be locked away somewhere. But just like the last time I almost died, when I nearly choked on that fish bone, I don't have to stand here and take it. I can be like Oliver and walk away. I can banish myself from my own life.

So I do it.

And the fact that everyone follows me like lemmings, well, that might be predictable, but sometimes predictable things happen in life.

In books, too.


We end up in the hotel library. I didn't know this hotel had a library, but when I got inside the building with the rest of them trailing behind me, I didn't feel like leading them to my room, so I took a left in the lobby and ended up in here, a room lined with books and cushy red velvet sofas.

I sit down on one near a roaring fire, and even though it's still a million degrees outside, the heat feels good. I'm shivering and feel feverish.

I must be in shock.

Well, obviously.

"What happened, Eleanor?" Allison asks sitting on the arm of the couch in front of me. She's dressed in a flowing chiffon number that looks like something a movie star would've worn to the Oscars in the 1950s. It looks amazing on her, and I feel a flash of jealousy.

So, I've come out of my second near-death experience with my personality intact.

Good to know.

"Someone tried to push me down the stairs during the fireworks."

A murmur of shock travels through the room like a wave.

"Did you see who did it?" Guy asks, and I can't help but wonder if his voice sounds nervous.

Because he's a suspect, right? They all are.

Did I say that already? I feel like I did, but my brain's not working quite right.

"No, they were behind me."

"Are you sure it was deliberate?" Shek asks. "There were a lot of people out there. Everyone was trying to get a better view, but as I informed the *very* rude girl who pushed me aside, the fireworks were above us, and there was no need to vie for a better spot."

"Shek makes a good point. Maybe you were only *jostled*." Connor's eyes are twinkling with something, which is never a good thing.

But I know what he's saying. Because it's what I said to him about what happened in Rome outside the Vatican. That being pushed around in a crowd isn't evidence of anything.

"I . . . I'm not sure."

"How can you not be sure?" Emily asks.

"It felt like someone pushed me. Maybe it wasn't deliberate?"

But even as I say it, I don't believe it. There have been too many almost-deaths on this trip, both real and faked. I don't believe everything happens for a reason, and there *are* coincidences, but not this many.

Which means that someone's trying to kill me *and* Connor.

But who?

I hug myself and angle my body toward the fire. It feels like I'm never going to get warm.

"I think someone pushed her," Oliver says, stepping into the room. We make eye contact, briefly, then turn away. He's still mad, and I still feel stupid.

That is what I wanted, wasn't it?

"Why do you think that?" Allison asks.

"I saw it happen. She didn't just stumble . . . I barely caught her."

I start to tremble, feeling that floating feeling I had right before he gripped the fabric of my dress. What would've happened to me if he hadn't been there? Would I have tumbled down those stairs like a stone, spinning? What parts of me would've been broken?

"We should call the police, then," Allison says.

"The carbonara?" Shek says. "Is that necessary?"

"Carabinieri," Harper says. "And yes. If someone tried to kill El, then we need to call them."

"No," Connor says. "We can't do that."

"I'm not putting Eleanor's life in danger just because *you* did something illegal," Oliver says. "And since this is your fault, you don't get a say."

"My fault?"

"Do you think someone mistook Eleanor for you?"

"Of course not, old boy."

"Then think it through, *old boy.*"

Everyone catches up at the same time. "Someone tried to kill Eleanor," Emily says.

"Isn't that what I've been saying?"

"Someone wants to kill Connor *and* Eleanor?" Allison says.

"Or just Eleanor," Shek mutters.

"Excuse me?" I say.

"Why would anyone want to kill Eleanor?" Oliver says, and I love him for it.

And though I assume he meant this as a rhetorical question, the silence is, well, *telling*.

"Harper might," Guy says eventually.

"What?" That might be me or it might be Harper. Our voices are very alike, and I'm not in my right mind.

"You said it yourself in that *NYT* piece. Doesn't she inherit everything if you die?"

"You said that?" Harper says as two spots of color bloom on her cheeks.

"She called you the prime suspect, I believe."

"Harper, you know how flustered I get when I do those things. I just babble."

"And accuse me of wanting you dead?"

"It wasn't like that. Read it, you'll see. I was joking."

"Freudian slip," Isabella says.

I shoot her a look. She doesn't belong here and she should stay out of it.

"No. That's not what it was at all."

"It makes sense, though," Connor says. "Harper hates me and stands to inherit a lot of money if you die. And if we both die, together, here in Italy on the tenth-anniversary tour, then . . ." He moves his hands in a dramatic way, tracing large circles in the air. ". . . Imagine the book sales."

"Shut up, Connor. Will you? For once." I take a deep breath. No one's reacting to the news that my own sister might want me dead with surprise. Only Harper is standing there, shaking her head slowly, like she can't believe what's happening.

"Night's over," I say.

"What about the police?" Shek asks.

"No, forget it. No one saw anything, right?"

Once again, the silence is telling.

"That's what I thought. So what's the point?"

There's none. I've dealt with the carabinieri before. They treated me with about as much respect as you'd expect, i.e., none. And that was when we had solid evidence of a crime. When Connor was known to them. Who knows what the local officers are like? I'm going to assume they've never heard of Connor or me, and aren't going to take some drunk semi-famous tourist claiming that a member of her own entourage wants her dead very seriously.

I stand and sweep my arms in a mimic of Connor's gesture from earlier. "Thanks for coming to my TED Talk."

I turn as dramatically as I can and try to flounce out of the room because I've always wanted to do that, but instead of leaving in a trail of perfume and stunned faces, I stumble into a low table and smack my shin in the worst way possible. I stifle a scream.

"You okay, El?" Oliver asks.

"I'll see you in the morning," I say without looking back.

The morning.

What are we doing tomorrow? Oh, right. The boat to Capri. Won't that be fun?[108]

I finally make it out of the library, then try to remember where my room is. I fish around in my purse for my key—which I've miraculously somehow *not* lost throughout this clown show of an evening—and pull it out. But once again, it's not my room key; it's that master key I found earlier. How did it make it into my bag? The only person who was in my room yesterday morning was Harper, but—

No. *No.* I'm not doing this. I'm not going to add up the evidence that Harper might want to kill me.

I'm going to my room and to my bed and I'm going to sleep, and tomorrow, when the day is fresh and the alcohol has cleared from my system, I'll figure out what's going on.

I press the button for the elevator and get inside when the doors

---

[108] I mean, no, right? No fun is going to be had on that boat.

open. I lean my back against the glass wall, avoiding my reflection because I don't want to see what I look like right now.

"Hold the door!"

I don't follow instructions, but Oliver makes it onto the elevator anyway. He squeezes through the opening and the doors clunk closed behind him.

"Shouldn't the doors open when you pass through like that?" he says.

"Defective, I guess."

"Dangerous."

This whole trip is dangerous.

And me and him being in an elevator together, even for a minute?

That's the most dangerous of all.

"I'm sorry," I say.

"About?"

"What I said on the veranda after you saved me. I . . . I was being a brat."

He rubs at the stubble on his chin. "You almost died."

"Is that my excuse now? I almost died; therefore I can act like a jerk to the people I care most about?"

"I'm one of those people?"

"Well, duh."

He laughs out loud. "Well, good."

Our eyes lock as the elevator door pings and the doors slide open. "This is my stop."

"Mine, too."

We exit, our arms brushing as we walk down the hall. I have a strong feeling of déjà vu, like we're reliving last night, only this time two things are different: Connor's room is on another floor, and someone wants me dead.

Maybe that was true yesterday, too, but I didn't know it.

I still can't absorb it.

I stop in front of my room. The air feels pregnant with our thoughts, but what does that mean, exactly? So many expressions we use without thinking about it.

"Give me your key," Oliver says.

"Why?"

He gives me a look that says not to ask, so I dip my hand into my purse and take out the right key this time. He takes it from my hand—did his fingers linger for a moment too long?—and opens my door.

He steps inside and starts to look around. He crouches down and checks under the bed.

Great. I want to sleep with him and he wants to search my room. So romantic.

"What are you doing?"

"Making sure it's safe."

"What if it's you I have to be worried about?"

Oh, bravo, El. That will bring him running right to you.

But it does. Not running but walking toward me in slow motion.

What was in that wine, anyway? Oh, alcohol. Right, right.

"You do."

"I do?"

He stops when he's inches from me and the air shifts. I've felt this energy before, and it always—

Wait, wait, wait. No spoilers.

Not even for me.

His hand goes to my face and touches my cheek gently. "Do you think you'll be all right in here?"

"I'll lock the door."

"And throw away the key . . ."

Oh, no. These are the lyrics to this song we made up years ago, a dance we'd do, swaying. Like a call-and-response in a musical. *I'll lock the door / And throw away the key. / I'll keep you safe / Stay close to me. / I'll love you the most / No, that's me. Just lock the door / And stay here with me.*[109]

---

[109] Yep, we were cheesy like that. Deal with it.

I stare into his eyes. They're supposed to be the windows to the soul, but I've never understood what that means either. All I see is myself, and then Oliver's lips are on mine and I can't think anymore.

I don't want to.

*Bang!*

I freeze, unsure of what's happening because my brain is so muddled from the day and the proximity to Oliver, and were we just kissing?

"What was that?" I ask.

Oliver looks at the ceiling. "Sounds like someone dropped something up there."

"Connor."

His mouth turns down. "You know where his room is?"

"Only as a precaution."

"Against ending up there?"

"What? No!" I take a step back. "You don't really think that, do you?"

He wipes his hand over his face. "I don't know what to think, El."

"I don't want anyone but you," I say. "But you have to forgive me, Oliver. Can you?"

"I'm not sure."

Ah, hell. Why did I have to go and ask that?

"Okay."

"I'm sorry."

"You have nothing to apologize for."

"You'll be all right in here?"

"I will."

"I'll be two doors down if you need anything."

"Okay, thanks."

He stares at me for a second more, then leaves, gone before I have time to call him back.

I lock the door after him and put a chair under the door handle for good measure. I take off my dress and put on a soft T-shirt and climb into the big, lonely bed.

I'm not sure I'll be able to sleep, but it turns out that almost dying on a daily basis is a good sedative.

Or maybe it's the alcohol.[110]

---

[110] It's probably the alcohol.

# CHAPTER 17
## Spreading like Rabbits

**Capri**

The morning breaks with Harper's familiar knock at the door, but this time, I don't need her to wake me up. I started awake an hour ago, my head throbbing and my mouth dry. I should've done something about both—Tylenol, a large glass of water—but instead, I stared at the ceiling, waiting for the events of yesterday to make sense.

Waiting for the fear to dissipate.

Because that's what I feel this morning. Behind the hangover and the exhaustion—I'm terrified.

Someone's trying to *kill* me. Someone on this tour, someone I know. But who? Who's been sitting across from me at the dinner table for the last two nights wishing I'd disappear?

Have I made Harper's life so miserable?

Is it Allison—pretending to be my friend, but looking for an opening to get rid of me once and for all?

Shek, because I got his marketing budget?

Emily, because I'm the competition in her way, the one who might reveal where she's getting her killer plots?

Guy, for some reason of his own, buried inside and chewing at him for years?

Is it Oliver?

I might've understood it of him if it had happened three years ago. I'll never forget the look on his face when I told him I'd been unfaithful with Connor. It was like I was tearing his heart out with my bare hands, and all he kept saying was "Why did you tell me?"[III]

He'd wanted me to lie. He didn't want me to put my burden on him. He wanted to live in a fantasy where I was a good person and he didn't make a mistake loving me.

People have killed for less.

Harper, Allison, Shek, Emily, Guy, Oliver. Their faces circle through my brain and chew at my gut, like a roulette wheel where I'm waiting for the ball to drop and land on the lucky winner.

Or maybe all of them are in on it, like in *Murder on the Orient Express* and all its pale imitations, and I've missed the whispered conversations, the clues hidden in what I thought were meaningless words.

How do I get it to stop?

How do I reverse course?

Because I know one thing: My life isn't perfect, but I don't want to die.

"Hello, hello, my writing friends!" Sylvie chirps from the dock in Sorrento.

After a nearly silent breakfast, we walked down the steps that almost killed me last night separately, a single file with Harper as our camp leader bringing us to the edge of the glistening sea.

Most of us have backpacks on, packed with boat shoes and towels, and a change of clothes for after we dip in the sea, and the only people with smiles on their faces are Connor and Isabella.

Because nothing brings Connor down, apparently.

Not even the thought of my murder.

---

[III] An excellent question for another day, or another book. Not sure yet.

Though maybe that's the source of his happiness? Were the attempts on his life a smokescreen for the attempts on mine?

What does it say about my life that the possibility of Connor wanting me dead is the last thing to occur to me? If I were writing this, he'd be the prime suspect.

Sylvie waves her hand toward the water behind us. She's wearing a bright red linen tunic, and her hair is tossing in the breeze. "Today we are going to Capri, one of the most beautiful islands in the Mediterranean. Also, the one with the most famous people visiting every year. Recently, these visitors have included my girls Beyoncé, RiRi, and J.Lo—they all love themselves some Capri."

"Did she just say, 'my girl Beyoncé'?" I ask Harper.

Harper's arms are crossed over a light blue T-shirt with a sailboat decal on it. "Nothing surprises me anymore with this woman."

"We're not paying her enough."

"I thought you wanted to get her fired?"

"Nah, she's growing on me."

"Like a fungus."

I touch the tip of my nose with my right index finger and point the other at Harper. "Ding, ding, ding."

She laughs, and it feels like the ice is breaking between us.

"For the record," she says, "I'm not trying to kill you."

"I know, baby girl."

"You haven't called me that since we were kids."

Since before our parents died, she means, and maybe she's right. We tucked so many things about them away because it was easier, but maybe that was a mistake.

When your life is on the line, you start to question everything.

"Remember how you used to call me El-nor, like I was an elf in *Lord of the Rings*?"

"Your ears did stick out."

"It is time to get on the boat! *Andiamo!*"

Harper rolls her eyes. "She wants us to get on the boat."

"We better get on, then," I say.

Her smile turns into a frown. "Do you think it's safe?"

The sky above us is clear and cloudless. "The weather looks good."

"No, I meant for you. What if . . . What if someone tries something on the boat?"

"In front of all these witnesses?"

"There were plenty of witnesses last night."

"No," I say, "there weren't."

She bites her lip. "Just be careful, okay?"

"I will."

"And maybe . . ."

"Don't drink?"

"I didn't say it."

"I can feel your thoughts."

"Ooh, do they hurt?"

"They won't kill me."

Harper shakes her head slowly.

"Don't worry. I'm taking this seriously."

And I am. Deadly seriously.

"So you'll do what I said?"

"I'll be careful, I promise." I lean in. "But just in case, keep an eye on me, okay?"

"Do I have to keep an eye on Connor?"

"Let's not go too far."

We get in the boat. It's a twenty-five-footer, white, with a Mediterranean-blue tarp covering the captain's seat. Our captain is a local in a black cap, with tanned arms and a weathered face, whom Sylvie introduces as Marco.

He starts the motor and sets the boat toward the Island of Capri. On the way out of the marina, we pass a large boat containing the BookFace

Ladies. Their shirts are a bright lime green today, but I can't tell what book they've got on them. They wave to us enthusiastically as we pass them, all except for Cathy, who's got her arms crossed and seems to be wishing that our boat would sink.

Oh! Maybe *she's* the one who pushed me last night?

But wait. No. The BookFace Ladies aren't staying at our hotel. They get the three-star accommodation while we get luxury with a side of attempted murder.

"The ride to Capri is twenty minutes," Sylvie says. "We are not going to land until lunchtime, though. Because we are going to be visiting many caves today, my friends."

"The Blue Grotto, of course," Shek says.

We're sitting in a semicircle on the white PVC benches in the full sun. But out here on the water, with the breeze and the waves, it feels bearable. I'm sitting between Harper and Allison. Connor and Isabella are ensconced on the small aft seat, while Shek, Guy, Oliver, and Emily sit across from us. Sylvie's standing in the middle with her back to Captain Marco, her hands flowing as she gets into her lecture.

"The Blue Grotto is very famous," Sylvie says, "but we are not going there."

"Why not?" Emily asks. She's got a white beach cover-up on over a skimpy black bikini and is wearing a wide straw hat and oversized sunglasses that hide her eyes. Against the backdrop of the sea, she looks like she's posing for her next book cover.

Or plotting her next murder?

"The Mafia," Sylvie says.

"Huh?"

"Italian organized crime," Connor says. His long legs are extended out, and he looks totally relaxed, almost bored.

I've learned from experience that this is when he's at his most dangerous, like a wild cat yawning right before it strikes.

"I understand the word," Emily says tartly, "just not the connection."

"They *run* the Blue Grotto. It has been a big problem for the last twenty years . . . They came to Napoli first, to control the garbage trucks. But now they are in Capri also, and any money you spend at the Grotto, it goes to them, the Giuseppe family, so we stay away from them, yes?"

"The Giuseppe family?" Connor says, less casually now. He exchanges a look with Guy, and then me. "The same one as from Rome?"

"A branch of the tree," Sylvie says. "When the capo went to jail, there was a . . . *guerra per il territorio*—a war over the territory? Some things were divided up, and the losers came to Napoli. You have heard of them?"

"I thought they all went to jail?" I say.

Shit. Is *that* the answer to this mystery? It's not someone on this tour, but someone else in Italy who has a reason to want me and Connor dead?

"The *capo*, yes," Sylvie says, "but the Mafia, they are like rabbits. They breed quickly, and suddenly they are everywhere."

"Weren't you the one who sent him to jail?" Shek says, pointing to me. "Oh? *Come?*"

"Pretty sure that was the police," Oliver says, and I'm grateful. He's still willing to defend me, despite everything. Maybe there's hope for us yet.

He won't make eye contact with me, though.

That's probably too much to ask after last night.

"What does Oliver mean?" Emily asks. "Eleanor put someone in jail?"

"*When in Rome,*" Allison says. "The Mafia family that planned the robberies they solved, that was the Giuseppe family."

Was it just me, or did Allison look at Connor when she said the word "planned"?

Oh, wait, you can't actually see us. Not yet, anyway.[112]

"I do not understand," Sylvie says. "You wrote a book about the Giuseppe family?"

---

[112] When this gets made into a television series, Allison will pause here and give Connor a look.

"No, not really. I . . . We, Connor and I, helped to discover who was robbing the banks. For the insurance company. And then when the murder happened . . . Anyway, I wrote about it. Not them, exactly, but a fictionalized version. That was my first book." Why am I so badly spoken today? I clear my throat and try to do better. "*When in Rome.* Like the BookFace Ladies had on their T-shirts at the Colosseum?"

"Ah, yes! Your novel *famoso.*"

"Haven't read it?" Emily says under her breath.

"I do not read books," Sylvie says. "I like watching books."

"How can you . . ."

"Like *The White Lotus.* You have seen this show, yes?"

"That wasn't a book."

"No?"

"No."

"Ah, well, I make a mistake."

I can feel Harper shaking next to me as she raises her fist to stuff it into her mouth. One good thing about Sylvie: She's bound to distract you from anything serious going on in your life.

"What happened to them?" Emily asks. "The robbers?"

"Murderers, you mean. Still in jail, last time I checked," Connor says. "And rightly so."

"Agreed," I say, shuddering despite the sun. The principals are all still in jail. That's them out, then. Which tracks. The first attempt on Connor's life happened in California. It wouldn't make sense for them to try to kill him there a few weeks before he was coming to Italy.

That's a relief. I only met Gianni Giuseppe once before he was killed, and briefly, but there was no mistaking the menace he presented. It was the first time I was ever scared by a person, truly terrified, and all he did was say "hello" and kiss my hand.

"If you do the crime, you do the time—that is what you Americans like to say, yes?" Sylvie looks around us expectantly, but no one comes to her rescue. She doesn't seem to mind. Instead, she smiles at us in that beatific way she has. "In America, there are so many prisons, I have read. So many people in jail."

"Well," Emily starts, "that's because of systematic racism and—"

Allison puts up her hand. "Good Lord, not today. Let's enjoy the view and save the lecture for later."

"I would've thought that . . ."

Allison stares at Emily hard enough to make her thoughts run dry. "And I would've thought *you'd* be the last person to stereotype me."

Shek takes his hat off and starts to fan his face, while Guy leans forward like he'll miss part of the exchange.

I point to him and Guy. "If one of you says 'catfight,' I will throw you in the water myself."

"I wouldn't dream of it, Eleanor," Shek says. "Repeating myself? Never."

"So much for solidarity," Emily says.

Allison gives her a big smile. "You'll survive all right on your own."

Guy looks back and forth between them. "That's it? How disappointing."

"Honestly, Guy?"

"I'm sorry, Sylvie," Oliver says. "You didn't sign on to manage a kindergarten."

Emily's mouth purses, and my own neck starts to burn. Oliver's right. We're a bunch of bickering idiots. No wonder all we're good for is writing made-up stories.

"Which cave are we going to, Sylvie," Isabella asks, clearly trying to change the subject, "if not the Blue Grotto?"

"It is right around this cove," Sylvie says, pointing ahead. "We will be there in a moment."

The boat leaps through the surf as we approach the shoreline, then throttles down. Captain Marco turns and starts to follow the coast. As we come around a corner, three massive superyachts come into view. They're anchored near an opening in the rocks, and the water is dotted with people swimming and holding on to pool noodles. One of the yachts is called *Sorry* and is flying a Canadian flag.[113]

"We will anchor here for one hour," Sylvie says as Marco cuts the engine. "You can swim, enjoy the view, or take some sun. There is also a cooler with some drinks."

She busies herself by opening the door to the hold down below and pulling out the pool noodles and a cooler.

"Are you going in the water?" Harper asks me.

"God, yes. I've been wanting to get in the sea since we got here." I swim in the ocean all the time at home, even in the winter. Harper thinks I'm nuts, but it helps keep me sane-ish.

"Do you think it's safe?"

"I keep telling you I'm a good swimmer."

"But away from the boat . . ."

I stand and take off my shorts and T-shirt. I'm wearing a tankini underneath. My body's a bit softer than the last time Oliver saw it without clothes on, and I like how this suit holds in my middle and pushes up my boobs.

Not that I spent ten minutes in the mirror thinking about it after I dragged my ass out of bed or anything.[114]

"What are you worried about?"

"Well, duh, you dying?"

I bend down and kiss her on the forehead. "I'll be fine! Even better if you come, too. Be my bodyguard."

"What's all this?" Allison asks. She's stripped off her sundress, and her perfect body is encased in a red bikini that leaves just enough to the imagination. I wish I had her confidence and her abs.

"Harper's worried about my safety."

"As she should be. And you too, Eleanor."

---

[113] Have you noticed how Canadians apologize for everything?

[114] It might've been twenty. I have a lot of angles to check.

Is that a warning tone in her voice?

I wish I didn't feel like I had to parse everything everyone says to me for clues.[115]

"I'll be careful."

"You're not worried?"

I stretch my hands above my head. "I am, but I don't want to be. You can't live your life like that. Wondering if someone's trying to kill you all the time? Look at where we are right now. Look at how beautiful it is."

I twirl around, taking in the 360-degree view. I flash past the others' faces—Connor, Isabella, Oliver, Guy, Emily, Shek, Harper, and Allison on a carousel like they were in my mind this morning—and try to ignore the quizzical looks they're giving me.

"You understand, don't you, Allison?"

"I do."

"Swim?"

"Absolutely."

"You can swim right to the cave and even inside," Sylvie says. "The noodles are helpful for that."

"We're noodle-free, right, Eleanor?" Allison says, taking my hand.

I take hers and squeeze it. "Yes."

"Ready?"

She doesn't wait for me to agree; instead, she runs toward the back of the boat with my hand in hers, tugging me along, then lets go as she gets to the seat where Connor and Isabella are sitting. She climbs onto the back of the boat in two graceful leaps, then dives into the ocean. I follow after her without thinking and almost slip on the seat as I climb past Connor.

"Hey! Watch where you step!"

I banish the thought of what I might've just stepped on and launch

---

[115] You're doing that, too, though, right?

myself into the water. I hit it with a *smack*, but it feels glorious anyway. I surface to the sound of Allison laughing.

"I think you stepped on Connor's balls."

"I've been wanting to do that."

"Dreams do come true, then. Let's go." She starts to swim toward the mouth of the cave with easy strokes, and I follow after her. She's fast and strong and reaches it before me, but she stops and waits, treading water until I catch up.

It isn't wide enough for a boat, and the water inside is that pure, crystalline blue that never comes out right in photographs unless you have a specialized camera. There are stalactites hanging down from the ceiling.

"Wow," I say as I hear splashing behind me.

I turn. It's Shek.

"You swim fast."

"I'll take that as a compliment." He motions toward the cave. "Are you going in?"

I look back at the boat. The rest of our crew is getting out of the boat slowly, climbing down the ladder, holding on to pool noodles. Oliver's already in the water, but he's the only one.

"Should we wait for the others?"

"You're not afraid, are you?"

Allison splashes at the water. "Of course she isn't."

I look into Allison's open, sunny face and feel a chill go through me. She dared me to come here with her, and now we're separated from the group.

I get a weird flash of her holding my head underwater, my legs kicking in struggle. It doesn't take that long for someone to drown if they're not used to holding their breath. In under a minute, it could all be over.

"I . . ."

"You *are* scared. Wow."

"It's not that, I just—"

"Eleanor, if I wanted to kill you, I would've done it a long time ago."

"I'm sorry."

She shrugs. "Your loss."

She turns and does a little dive into the water, her body folding into itself, and then her feet come up straight behind her and she disappears.

I watch the rippling water, feeling mean. Allison's right; it doesn't make any sense for her to want to kill me, and wasn't I just saying this would be a stupid place to do it? I need to be on my toes, but I don't need to be making accusations I can't support—

Wait. Where's Allison?

She's been under too long.

Oh, shit. Oh, *no*.

I never should have let my guard down.

# CHAPTER 18

## The Medicinal Properties of Pee

"Help!" I yell and start to swim in a panic toward where Allison went under. Shek is behind me, like a shadow.

I get there right as Allison surfaces with a grimace on her face.

And then she starts yelling bloody murder.

"What is it? Allison, are you okay?"

"A jellyfish," she yells. "I got stung!"

"Try to hold still," Shek says. "That thrashing can't help."

Allison grits her teeth and steadies herself, but the pain is written all over her face.

Oliver swims up next to me, his hair wet, water clinging to his shoulders.[116] "What's happening?"

"She was stung by a jellyfish," I say. "Be careful."

It seems to occur to Shek for the first time that if Allison got stung, he could, too. He starts to glide away from us slowly on his back, his hands making small movements at his sides.

Coward.

---

[116] I <u>told</u> you I can't help describing him in romance-novel terms. If I could turn it off, I would.

Meanwhile, Oliver swims around Allison and slips his arms under her armpits. "Try to stay still. I'll swim you back to the boat."

Allison nods calmly, but she has tears streaming down her face. Oliver turns her around and starts to swim backward, passing Shek with a few powerful kicks. The swimmers from the other boats have kept their distance, forming a loose semicircle around the mouth of the cave, and the rest of our party have reversed course and climbed back into the boat. Everything looks so calm, but my heart is thundering and I feel short of breath.

Another almost-death. Another woman who needed to be saved by Oliver.

What was I just saying about coincidences?[117]

I turn back toward the cave and search the water, waiting for it to clear. When it does, all I see is my legs, making slow circles as I tread water. I'm not sure what I was expecting to find, but then it hits me, like it must've occurred to Shek, that I might not see the jellyfish until it's too late. So, I start to swim away from the cave, passing the silent group of red-shouldered tourists bobbing on their pool noodles.

"Be careful," I tell them. "There are jellyfish in the water."

A man with a thick thatch of gray hair says in a slightly imperious manner, "There aren't any jellyfish in the Med."

My heart starts to hammer again as I swim away from him. Is that right? It's easy enough to look up. But why would Allison lie? Her screams and tears were real. What would she have to gain by faking that?

I shake the thought away as I watch Oliver and Connor bring Allison up into the boat as Shek watches.

"You planning on helping?" I say as I pull up next to him.

---

[117] I tried to understand probability theory once—a theory that's meant to quantify random events and see if it's possible to predict the future—but it made my brain hurt. All I know is that a coin is supposed to have a fifty-fifty chance of landing on heads or tails in theory, but that's not what actually happens when a person tosses a coin over and over again.

"They seem to have everything well in hand."

I roll my eyes as I pass him. Is it wrong to think that it makes more sense for someone to want Shek dead than me?[118]

I grip the ladder and haul myself up, happy that Oliver's already in the boat and can't see how inelegant I am as I climb up the ladder.

"What are you doing?" Allison says as I stand on the deck.

"Just hold still," Connor says with his back to me.

I walk toward my bag so I can get my towel.

"Don't do it."

I have a better angle now. Connor's in the middle of undoing the belt on his shorts.

"Stop, Connor, you perv!"

His face is crimson. "I'm going to pee on her leg to stop the stinging. Urine has medicinal properties in these situations."

"You are *not* doing that," Allison says from the bench, gritting her teeth. There's a red welt on her leg and I instantly feel better. She's not making it up. Something *did* sting her.

Which sucks, of course, and must hurt like hell, but in the grand scheme of things, it's better than it being an invention.

Better for me, I mean.

I am the *worst*.

"Do your pants up, Connor, for once in your life," Oliver says.

Harper starts to giggle. She's sitting where I left her when I went in the water with Emily and Isabella. Isabella hides her laugh behind her hand. Maybe there's trouble in paradise? If she's already at the laugh-at-Connor stage, she's smarter than I've given her credit for.

"There must be something we can do that doesn't involve the medicinal properties of pee," Emily says. "Sylvie?"

We turn toward the upper deck, where Sylvie is consulting with Cap-

---

[118] Yes, yes, rhetorical question.

tain Marco. He jumps down onto our deck with a small white box in his hand with a Red Cross on it.

"I have some salve that will help," he says with almost no Italian accent. He crouches down by Allison and opens the box, then takes out a small container and opens it. "Does someone have a cloth?"

"I do," Oliver says. He picks up his discarded shorts and pulls out a pristine handkerchief with his initials on it, like the one he used on Harper the other day. It occurs to me now that it's part of the set I gave him for his birthday four years ago. So he didn't throw all of me away. "This do?"

Captain Marco takes it, then applies a clear, goopy concoction to Allison's leg as she winces. "This will numb the area and heal the skin," he says. "I will give you the container. Apply every four hours."

"Thank you."

"Perhaps we will go to Capri a bit early?" Sylvie says. "There is a clinic there."

Allison leans back against the cushions. "I think I'll stay on the boat. Is there somewhere I can take a nap?"

"There is a small cabin below deck," Captain Marco says. "You can rest there."

I wrap my towel around me and run my hands through my hair. Then I tap Oliver on the arm to get his attention. "You saved the day, again."

He stands and turns. I try not to stare at his naked chest. Instead, I pick a point on his face, a single freckle that wasn't there yesterday.

"I don't think she was in any danger of dying."

"Only in danger of getting peed on by Connor."

Oliver starts to laugh. "Do you think he was really going to do it?"

"Nothing surprises me with him anymore."

"Excuse me," Connor says. "But this is no laughing matter."

Isabella hides her smile again. I might actually like the girl in different circumstances.

"Allison's going to survive," Oliver says, getting control of himself. "She'll be all right."

"Thanks to you, I suppose."

"Thanks to most jellyfish not being deadly."

Shek emerges at the top of the ladder and takes in the scene in a lackadaisical way. "I say, have you noticed that this trip is cursed?"[119]

An hour later, we're on a small bus to Anacapri. The BookFace Ladies have been up there since this morning, Harper tells me—joy!—and I'm sitting next to Connor, which, for once, is intentional.

When we got off the boat in Capri, I regretted it immediately. Out on the water, it was lovely and cool. But the town of Capri is cramped and crowded, full of tourists and loud buses honking at the people who are crazy enough to rent mopeds at the height of the tourist season.[120]

Sylvie shepherded us onto a series of minibuses and told us she'd meet us at the top for lunch at another local restaurant with a fantastic view. Based on my experience in Pompeii, I wanted to skip the lunch, but Harper reminded me that I'm contractually obligated to be there.[121]

In the meantime, it was time to get serious about figuring out what the hell is going on. So, I let Oliver get on the bus in front of me, then basically pushed Isabella on after him and watched the doors close. Then I grabbed Connor by the hand and hauled him onto the next bus while he sputtered in protest.

"What did you do that for?" Connor asks as we take a seat on a small two-seater bench that leaves us way too close together for comfort.

"Because it's time to tell me the rest of it."

---

[119] Ooh, business idea! Instead of those mystery tours, what about one where someone is fake trying to kill you the whole time? Would that be fun? Hmmm. The insurance might be hard to get. More research needed on this, I think.

[120] If you wanted to kill someone, suggest they rent a moped in Capri in July. The odds will be in your favor that you'll never see them again.

[121] I really need to start reading the things people put in front of me.

"Rest of what?"

"Who is it, Connor? Who's trying to kill you?"

"I don't know."

"Yes, you do. That investment you made. You need to come clean."

Connor looks around. There's no one on this bus that we know. "Why?"

"Because someone *is* trying to kill both of us, and I want to know who."

"Maybe it doesn't have anything to do with that. Not if you're a target, too."

"You're questioning that?"

"No, I—"

"Just tell me already."

Connor sighs as the bus starts to climb a twisty, narrow road. I'm next to the window, and the barrier between us and oblivion is a low rock wall.

Maybe it wasn't the best idea for the both of us to get on the same bus.

"Last year, I made an investment in a cryptocurrency company."

"I thought you were smarter than that."

"Excuse me?"

"Everyone knows that's a scam."

"Oh, everyone does now?"

"Any financial product that has celebrities hocking it is suspect.[122] I mean, are there Federal Reserve ads with Julia Roberts insisting that the dollar is a great investment in the future?"

"No need to be so condescending, Eleanor. Especially since it's your fault."

"My fault?"

"The royalties from the Vacation Mysteries series are diminishing at a precipitous rate."

---

[122] Like those reverse mortgage ads. Those things are a total scam! Don't do that.

"I . . . They are?"

"You haven't noticed? That figures."

I haven't. Harper takes care of my finances.[123] But why wouldn't she tell me about this? "We're talking about me, not you."

"Fine. Well, they are. And I have a big monthly nut,[124] and I needed to diversify to protect my assets."

"But crypto? Why gamble like that?"

He smiles in a way I know he thinks is charming. "I've always been a risk-taker. You know that . . . Anyway, part of my, um, deal with them was that I encourage others to invest."

"Your deal?"

"My endorsement deal."

"You were a celebrity endorser?"

His face sets. "No need to sound quite so surprised."

"Okay, fine. Sorry. How did you do it? I don't remember seeing the TV spot."

"It was a more personal approach."

"Like what? Meetings?"

"No, I . . . sent out a newsletter."

"You have a newsletter?"[125]

Wait, wait, wait. Is *Connor* blushing?

"I, uh, I've been building one for a while."

"Building how?"

"Adding people to it here and there."

"How come I don't get it?"

He shoots me a look. "You unsubscribed."

---

[123] I know, okay, I *know.*

[124] Seriously, who talks like this?

[125] I have one, too, because my publisher insists on it, but Harper writes it and I don't pay much attention to what's in there. I think right now I'm recommending the new season of *Only Murders in the Building* and fielding questions on whether any future season of *Bridgerton* will live up to #Kanthony's season. My bet's on no.

"I . . . what?"[126]

He crosses his arms and looks away.

"Why do you have a mailing list, Connor?"

"If you must know, I've been writing a book."

Plot twist!

"Like a memoir?"

"Like a novel."

Um, *what?*

My brain starts to whir, and then I remember. "Harper mentioned something about you studying creative writing in college—is that true?"

"Yes. I have an MFA."

"You have an MFA."

"No need to repeat me."

I give myself a shake, trying to make sense of the information I've received in the last minute. "I'm sorry, I just . . . Whenever I asked you anything about your past, you'd always change the subject."

He gives me an appraising look. "Is that why you were with me? Because you were interested in my past?"

Now it's my turn to blush. "I . . . What kind of novel?"

"It's a rom-com."

"A *what?*"

"A romantic comedy."

Don't laugh, El. Do. Not. Laugh.

"Is it being published?"

"It's not finished yet." He sighs. "But if you must know, I'm planning on polishing it this fall and then taking it out to agents."

"What . . . what's it about?"

"It's called *Spare Parts*. A Mr. Fix-It who lives in a seaside town ends

---

[126] Yes, Harper reads my author email, too. Save your judgment for the murderer.

up on a date with a woman who's come home to nurse her ailing father after she bids on him in a charity auction."

!!![127]

He looks at me. "Are you all right, Eleanor?"

"I'm processing." My brain is skipping like our DVD player used to do when we were on a bumpy car ride with my parents. "Okay, so, you sent out the crypto offer to your newsletter—who took you up on it?"

"I don't know."

"How can you not know?"

"That's the whole point of blockchain;[128] it's anonymous."

"The better to defraud people."

"It's not built for fraud. I . . . Forget it."

I put my hand on his arm. "You must know something more than that. Why else would you be so sure that the person who's trying to kill you is on the tour?"

"They're all on the newsletter."

"And?"

"I believe Shek invested."

"Based on?"

"Things he's said to me over the last couple of months."

I stare at him. I've never been able to tell when he's lying. I mean, obviously. But Shek? I'd always thought he was an open book.

I think back to our conversation on the veranda yesterday and pluck something out of the fog of alcohol. "But wait, yesterday he said he didn't invest in crypto. Though that confirms that he did know about it."

"I wouldn't believe anything Shek says."

The bus jolts, and I look out the window. We're halfway up the hill now, and the views are breathtaking but also dizzying. I should've taken the aisle seat.

---

[127] OMG. It's probably going to sell a million copies!
[128] Whatever the fuck that is.

I turn away and refocus on Connor. "Okay, so, Shek."

"Maybe. I'm not sure. Guy, potentially, though he'd deny it, too."

"And what happened? It crashed?"

"It did."

"And you were involved in that?"

"No, I . . . I helped the CEO leave the country."

"To the Bahamas?"

"What? No. Only idiots try to hide in countries with extradition treaties with the US. He's somewhere he won't be found."

"How would anyone know you helped him?"

"People know my skill set, and . . ." Connor rubs at his chin. "I got the idea from one of Shek's books."

"Which book?"

"*Cage the Snake.*"[129]

"So, you lost all of Shek's money, then stole his book idea to cover it up?"

"From Shek's perspective? Yes."

"So it's *Shek* who's trying to kill us? Why didn't you tell me this before?"

"Because I wasn't sure. I'm still not. If money's the motive, it could be any one of them."

"Wait, not anyone. I doubt Oliver's on your mailing list."

His eyes go dark. "He unsubscribed, too."

---

[129] *Cage the Snake?* <u>Who</u> titles these things? For real.

### AMALFI MADE ME DO IT—OUTLINE

WHY?

- The woman Connor based his book on didn't give her permission, and she's killing him out of revenge?
- Turnaround is fair play.

HOW?

- Are jellyfish poisonous? There must be maps of where they're likely to be found, right?
- Research anti-poisons—I mean antidotes.

Confession: It's way less fun to plan Connor's murder when someone's trying to kill him for real.

# CHAPTER 19

## Lights Out

Lunch turns out to be a pleasant surprise. The pizza is delicious, with gooey fresh mozzarella that bubbles around bright green basil. When I bite into a piece, it's one of the best things I've ever tasted, that perfect mix of tomato and cheese, and my God, I'd eat nothing but this crust if I wouldn't end up needing a new wardrobe.

The BookFace Ladies are happy. Now that they're up close, I can see that their T-shirt today has their *Death on the Thames* BookFaces. I avoid Cathy but say hi to some of the others after I polish off an entire pizza by myself and sign a few books. I'm distracted, though, searching out Shek in the crowd, wondering if he's truly dangerous or just another one of Connor's victims.

He's sitting at a table with Harper and Emily. He's holding court about something, and they keep making faces at each other that he doesn't notice. I feel a tug of jealousy. What can Harper and Emily have in common? And how did they get so close so quickly?

But that's a stupid way to think. Harper needs friends and a life outside of me. I should be encouraging that. Even if the source of their bonding is their current unhappiness with yours truly.

"Can I talk to you for a minute?" Oliver asks, tapping me on the shoulder.

"Yeah, of course."

I follow him out onto the veranda that juts out over the cliff, but not to the railing. "Careful, Oli. Don't get so close."

Oliver smiles. "Still afraid of heights?"

"Definitely. Plus, someone *is* trying to kill me, so . . ."

"That's what I want to talk to you about."

"Did you learn something?"

"I'm not sure . . . Do you think what happened to Allison today was an accident?"

"I thought that at first, but now I'm not so sure."

"Maybe someone was in on it with Captain Marco? If that area is prone to jellyfish . . ."

"I . . ." I think back to this morning. How I felt like Shek and Allison had goaded me into the cave. Or was that just Shek? "Did you notice Shek acting oddly?"

"More than usual?"

"Yeah, listen to this." I fill him in on what Connor's told me. The dead pedestrian, Davide. His investment in crypto, and Shek's potential involvement, and how he stole Shek's idea to cover it up.

"Yikes," Oliver says.

"Yeah."

"How would Shek know that he stole his plot?"

"Good point. Connor didn't say."

"That man and his secrets."

I stare out at the water. I think I can see our boat down at the dock. Is Allison in danger as she sleeps below deck?

No. Everyone loves Allison. Even Connor, though I doubt he'd admit it.

"Does it all fit together?" Oliver asks. "When did Shek arrive in Rome?"

"He wasn't on my flight. I think he came from New York."

"So he could've been at the Vatican?"

"We'd have to check. But he wouldn't need to have been there . . . if he's working with someone else . . ."

I think about Davide, the innocent bystander. Killing Connor I can understand, but a stranger? Could Shek do that?

Then again, he's a man who's spent his life writing about clever murders. That does something to a person. Reveals something about them, too.[130]

"Does he know anything about cars?" I ask.

"Doesn't he famously have a classic car collection?"

"Oh, he was on an episode of the show Leno does, right?"

"That rings a bell. Has he been in LA recently?"

I pull out my phone and google Shek. He has an Instagram account that appears quite active. I navigate to it and check his posts. There's one from our trip—the street where the restaurant was, and—oh! "Look, he *was* at the Vatican. Two days ago."

Oliver takes my phone and scrolls down. "And in LA. He had an event there. When did the car thing happen?"

"I'm not sure. A couple of weeks ago, Connor said."

"We need a timeline."

I take my notebook out of my purse, flipping past the pages of my outline for *Amalfi Made Me Do It.*

*June X—Connor's car*

*July 2—Vatican attempt*

*July 3—Connor's savior killed*

---

[130] And me, of course. You think I started out this way?

*July 4—Eleanor attempt*

*July 5—Jellyfish?*

"Where was Shek during the day on the third?" I ask. "He wasn't at the Colosseum or the Forum."

"Only the dinner." Oliver looks at his Instagram again. "Nothing here."

"What about Twitter? Didn't he get in some flame war with someone on there recently?"

"You know I don't follow all that stuff."

I take my phone from him and go to my Twitter app. I search for Shek and find him. Turns out, he's been posting a regular travel log of our trip, tweeting every couple of hours. On July 3, he visited a bunch of sites in Rome—the Trevi Fountain, the Spanish Steps, and a restaurant near the Colosseum. I show the tweets to Oliver.

"Where did that guy get killed?" Oliver asks.

"Near the Pantheon . . . Check this out." I point to one of Shek's tweets. On July 3 at 2:42 P.M., he tweeted, *The Pagan gods would be pleased*, along with a photo from inside the Pantheon. "He was there."

"That was before we were in the Forum."

"Yes. Our Colosseum tour was at two."

Oliver thinks it over. "And we were in the Forum around three thirty."

"So, enough time to get from one location to the other if he's working with whoever mugged Harper."

"Right. But why would he signal his location? Why tweet at all?"

I tap my pen against the notebook. "Maybe he thinks he's creating an alibi? Or it's a way to cover up his phone signal? An explanation of why he'd be in the area if anyone went looking?"

"That's smart," Oliver says. "Do things near tourist sites when you're a tourist . . ."

"What is it?"

Oliver takes my phone and types something. He reads for a moment, then his face pales. "I thought so . . . That's what the murderer does in *Tourist Trap*."[131, 132]

"You've read Shek?"

"You haven't?"

"I mean . . ." I check the timeline. "So he was everywhere he needed to be. And he was on the balcony last night. Everyone was . . ."

"And today? How could he know about the jellyfish?"

I take my phone back and google "Mediterranean jellyfish." *Pelagia noctiluca* comes up as the first hit, the most venomous jellyfish in the Mediterranean. "The Med is full of them, apparently. I bet there are maps of places to avoid, even."

"Are they deadly?"

"I'm sure the worst ones can be in large doses. But maybe he's just trying to keep us off balance?"

"Why?"

"I don't know."

"More importantly, why would Shek want to kill you? Because Connor, I get . . ."

"I got his marketing budget."

"People don't kill people because their books aren't selling."

I cock my head to the side. "I don't know about that. Does logic apply to killers?"[133]

Capri itself is a trip of dualities. The beautiful boat ride was ended by the stinging jellyfish. The island was picturesque from the water but choked with people and noise when we get to shore. The views were breathtaking at the top, but the bus ride was scary.

---

[131] Another one of Shek's masterpieces.

[132] Is my sarcasm translating through these? Just wanted to make sure.

[133] I don't know if you've noticed, but I leave space for the jokes to land.

And then there's the whole someone's-trying-to-kill-me thing.

No, not someone, *Shek.*

That's a hard one to wrap my head around. Thinking some unnamed person is trying to kill you is one thing, but settling on a perpetrator is something else. Even if it's someone I don't much like, I *know* him.

It wasn't always like this between Shek and me.

I remember when I met him for the first time nine years ago. It was at Killer Nashville, which is not a conference for murderers, but for those that write about them.

I was a newbie, one book out, nervous about my first author talk, and sitting at the bar nursing a glass of something when he told me I was in his seat. He was wearing a three-piece suit and a black felt fedora, and didn't I know this was Noir at the Bar?[134] Didn't I know that he always sat at this very corner of every Noir at the Bar, whether it was at ThrillerFest, or Bouchercon, or Left Coast Crime?[135] Who did I think I was just sitting there not waiting my turn, not standing in a line I didn't know existed?

He didn't say all of these things out loud.

Some of them were subtext, but I could read it loud and clear.

If a murder had happened that night, he would've been the victim, because he was the one barreling through the crowd, full of bravado, creating antipathy wherever he went.

I know this because I didn't challenge him for my seat. Instead, I moved to a corner spot, right next to the wall, and watched the other participants, my new colleagues, mostly men, regale one another with stories. One man with a thick Irish accent even stood on the bar and recited Keats.

It was a lot.

---

[134] This is a real thing. I didn't make it up.

[135] More mystery-writer conventions, which are just opportunities to boast about how you're, uh, killing it.

And to be honest,[136] I felt like I should be taking notes the whole time because who'd believe me if I didn't have some kind of evidence?

Eventually, I went to bed and woke up with a hangover, wondering if the hotel was going to be clogged with police and wannabe detectives who thought they could be helpful.

But Shek didn't die that night. Instead, he showed up for our panel with shades on and a better attitude and spent a patient ten minutes beforehand explaining to me how to answer questions. And then he gave me a compliment. He'd read *When in Rome*, and I was a *fresh voice*, he said. I was going places. I was going to be a star. Wait, I already was.

I went to bed that night feeling like I'd made a friend, and he *had* been friendly for a while. We'd trade emails sometimes or have lunch when our paths crossed at conferences. He felt like an ally in a business where it's sometimes hard to make friends when you start out on top.[137] And that's how it was between us right up until he hired Connor to work on a screenplay.

I never got the full story of what happened; I only know it ended badly and Shek somehow blamed me. And because I was used to that by now, people blaming me for bringing Connor into their lives, I didn't push to get the full story.

But now, on the minibus back down the mountain, seated next to Oliver, I wish I had.

If Shek wants me dead, I'd like to know what I'm supposed to have done besides take his marketing budget. Because only a lunatic would kill someone over marketing dollars. And whoever planned all this is too methodical for that.

---

[136] A lawyer once told me that if someone on the stand prefaced what they were about to say with "to be honest," this was a massive red flag. But I am telling you the truth.

[137] Because my first book was an instant *New York Times* bestseller, I was told by more than one person that I didn't really know what publishing was. It's only about failure, apparently, and disappointment. "You'll see," said one helpful person with an expectant expression like she couldn't wait for that day to come.

But Shek is methodical.

He's a plotter.[138]

It says so right there on his website under "Writing Tips."

"You all right?" Oliver asks as the bus drives too fast for my liking down the hill. I'm in the aisle seat this time, but I can still see disaster coming.

"In the circumstances."

He smiles at me, then takes my right hand and holds it on his lap, our fingers intertwined. "I don't know if we have enough to go to the police."

"I know."

"You're thinking we should investigate."

"That's stupid, right?"

"It makes sense."

"It's how people get killed in my novels."

He smiles. "Mine, too."

"One question too many. One action. Confronting the killer. Bashing around like they've got an invisibility suit on."

"All part of the genre."

I watch our hands together. I don't want to let his hand go, but we're almost at the bottom and it's going to end sometime. "But in real life . . . I don't think I'm very good at it."

"We've come this far. We have the timeline, the Instagram photos, the tweets."

"I should screenshot all those."

"Good idea."

I make no move to do so.

"Not now?" Oliver asks.

"My hand is occupied."

---

[138] I saw one of his outlines, once. Unlike my scratches and questions and research notes, it was a sixty-page document that was essentially a rough first draft of his novel.

He looks down at our hands like he didn't know he was doing it, and I curse myself. Why do I always have to state the obvious?

Why can't I leave well enough alone?

"You can do it on the boat," he says, and my body flushes.

He doesn't want to let go either.

I'm taking that metaphor for the win.

"Shek will be on the boat," I say.

"He will. It's just hard to believe that he's . . . I mean, he's Shek."

"The man who famously brought his cat to the Anthonys[139] because it would be too lonely if he left it alone."

"I forgot about that."

"He's a complicated guy."

"I guess we all are."

He nods slowly. "We should be sure it's him before we say anything."

"How can we be sure?"

"We need more evidence."

"We can't just wait till he succeeds in killing someone."

"No, I know, I . . . Let's just keep our eyes peeled. We can reconvene tonight."

That word—"tonight"—hangs there like a promise as the bus pulls to a stop and the other passengers start to shuffle out. Oliver and I are locked in, though. Maybe both of us want to say something and can't quite manage it.

Or maybe we both know that once we leave this bus, nothing good lies ahead.[140]

Back on the boat, Allison has recovered and enjoyed her day reading a beat-up old paperback of one of Shek's books—*natch*—she found below deck and sleeping in the sun.

---

[139] An award I've never won and I'm not mad about that <u>at all</u>.

[140] By now you knew this footnote was coming, right?

Apparently, Captain Marco caught some fish and cooked it right there in butter, garlic, and wine, and it was "divine."

And against the odds, everyone seems happy, busy chatting and filling us in on how they spent the afternoon.

Isabella gushes about the views from Anacapri and shows off a cute scarf she bought in one of the shops while Connor beams at her indulgently.

Emily and Harper tell us about the hot men they'd met at a bar, where it's clear they consumed several double somethings by the way they're giggling.

Shek and Guy spar good-naturedly over something that happened today back in the States,[141, 142] and Sylvie tells us that Marco's going to take a slow ride back to Capri so that he times it right with the sunset. Apparently, the sunset in Sorrento is "So romantic, yes? In the meantime, I have a surprise for you!"

She bends down, and then stands, brandishing a bottle of Champagne. "Thanks to Eleanor and her team, we will be sipping on Champagne[143] as we watch the sun set."

This news is received generally well—this isn't a teetotaling crowd, and any grumbling is probably because she seems to have only one bottle with her, which isn't enough for the numbers who'll want to imbibe.

Oblivious, Sylvie pulls out some plastic Champagne flutes and a tray and asks Isabella to help her. They busy themselves pouring out the glasses, making the pours even[144] while we chatter about the reckless drivers on mopeds that our buses almost hit on more than one occasion.

Isabella starts to pass the glasses around—Emily, Harper, then Allison, me, and Oliver. When she gets to Connor, he waves a hand at it, and before she can ask why, Shek picks up his glass and holds it aloft. "We should toast."

---

[141] Who cares about the details; you're not here for my political views.
[142] If you are here for those, I share them on Twitter.
[143] Fine, it's Prosecco. My books sales are <u>declining</u>.
[144] It's a half glass, by my calculation.

"To what?" Guy asks.

"Life."

"Live long and prosper?" I say.

"No *Star Trek*, you nerd," Harper teases me, and I stick out my tongue in response.

"To life," Oliver says holding his glass up and looking at me.

"To life," everyone repeats as they raise their glasses and drink.

"You don't want to toast, Connor?" Isabella says in a teasing voice.

"Connor doesn't like Champagne," Allison drawls. "Everyone knows that."

And it's true—everyone does know that, but not the *killer*, obviously, because oh, shit!

Shek, who downed Connor's glass, and then his own for good measure before I'd finished my first mouthful, is foaming at the mouth and clutching at his neck.

He falls to the boat deck making a strangling sound, and it's all over before anyone can do anything but stare.

Shek is dead.

Actually, totally dead.

And this time it's for real.[145]

---

[145] Fool me once and all that—amiright?

# CHAPTER 20

## I'm a Pantser, Not a Plotter

**Sorrento**

We don't take the slow way back to watch the sunset.

Instead, after checking for a pulse to ensure that Shek had shuffled off this mortal coil, even though he's pale and has a dead-eyed stare fixed at the sky, Captain Marco and Oliver carry Shek's body below deck, while Sylvie calls the local police to tell them what happened, and the rest of us sit frozen, our Champagne flutes discarded at our feet, the remnants of our drinks mixed in with the salt water we tracked in earlier when we went swimming.

If I were writing this scene, I'd say that a deathly silence enveloped us, but I'm not sure that's quite right. I think there are at least two of us who are contemplating life instead. Our lives, and how we're still here despite numerous attempts to push us out of frame.

Or maybe that's all of us, because it doesn't take a genius to figure out that Shek drank Connor's Champagne, and caught the sentence someone tried to mete out to him. It could've been any of us who took that glass and swallowed that poison and spent their last moments on earth suffocating and in pain while a bunch of people stood around and did nothing.

But it's hard not to be grateful for the little things when you watch someone die in front of you.

So we're silent as the boat beats against the waves, and when we pull into the dock, there are blue cars with white stripes and police lights, and a black van without windows to greet us. The local police take our names and the basic information about the tour from Sylvie, and then two officers from the *polizia provinciale* escort us off the boat. The young *capitano*, who looks like he's about Emily's age and has a rash of acne along his chin, tells us we'll be escorted back to our hotel for questioning, but we'll have to wait until the senior officer—the *ispettore capo*—arrives from Naples.

At least I think that's what he says. As I mentioned, I never completed the Duolingo course I meant to do before this trip.

And yes, in case you were wondering, I *can* make jokes at a time like this.

I keep these thoughts inside, though, as we climb into the white van that will take us up the hill to our hotel.

Harper sits next to me. She hasn't said a word since Shek hit the deck, just hugged herself like she used to do when she was a kid and something was frightening her. I put my arm around her shoulder, and she rests her head on mine.

*It'll be okay*, I want to say, but how can I?

Because now there's no doubt at all: The murderer is one of us.

When we get back to the hotel, the officer escorts us to the library.[146]

I'm not sure why, but we end up in the same chairs and positions we were yesterday.

I'm on the couch to the right of the roaring fire, still perversely necessary because they've got the air on high, and Harper's sitting next to me. Oliver is seated across from us with Allison and Emily, and Connor is standing behind a wing chair with Isabella sitting in front of him. The

---

[146] Because of course he does. Where else would you gather all the suspects?

other wing chair is empty because that was Shek's chair, and when Guy went to sit in it, everyone glared at him. Instead, he's standing by the fireplace, holding his hands out to it like they need to be warmed from a blizzard.

A police officer is stationed outside the door, and we've been told not to dispose of anything on our person. He hasn't told us not to talk to one another, though, which seems like a mistake.[147]

"Well," Allison says after we've been staring at one another for several minutes, "don't everyone all talk at once."

Nervous laughter spreads through the room; then Guy speaks. "You really did it, didn't you, Connor?"

"Did what?"

"Pissed someone off enough that they wanted you dead."

Connor speaks through clenched teeth. "I thought we'd established that *days* ago."

"You expect me to believe everything you say?"

"Is this helpful?" Oliver asks. "Someone is trying to kill both Eleanor and Connor, and now Shek is dead."

"I agree," Emily says. "We need to do something."

"What?" I ask.

She waves at me and Oliver. "Solve it. Haven't you written, like, a million mysteries between the two of you?"

"It's not the same in real life."

"It can't be that different. And Connor and Guy are private detectives. Or is everything in *When in Rome* fake?"

"They're more like . . . consultants," I say.

---

[147] I'll let you in on a little secret. Despite the fact that I've written nine murder mysteries, I don't know much about police procedure. Research is boring, and even when you do it, it's often so different from what's shown on TV that there's no point in being accurate. Anyway, it's fiction!

Connor raises a finger to his lip, then quickly lowers it. But he doesn't have to worry. I'm not about to spill my secrets or his.[148, 149]

"But yes, they solved some crimes."

"Including a murder."

"Yes," I say, "but . . ."

Allison shifts in her seat. "I agree with Emily. It's obviously one of us, and I, for one, am not looking forward to leaving my fate in the hands of the local police."

"Why not?"

"Look at what happened to that girl. The one they thought was involved in the sex-crime killing of her roommate? Only it turned out she barely even knew her."

"Amanda Knox?"

"Yes. Her. She spent years in jail before she was exonerated. And did you see that documentary about it? That policeman thought he was Inspector Clouseau. It was ridiculous."

"She has a point," Oliver says. "They're already violating basic police procedure by leaving us all here together to get our stories straight."[150]

"You think we can figure it out before the inspector gets here?"

"It doesn't hurt to try. We know each other better than the police ever will. We were witnesses to what happened. And we do have some skills in this department."

"Yes," Allison agrees. "You can plot it all out just like in one of your books."

"I'm a pantser, not a plotter," I say.

"What does that mean?" Guy says.

"She writes by the seat of her pants and makes it up as she goes

---

[148] That'll come later. Because secrets in novels are like Chekhov's gun—they go off by the third act.

[149] If you're wondering, we're deep in the second act now.

[150] Will it surprise you that Oliver does the research? No, right?

along," Harper says, finally coming out of her shock long enough to speak.

"I mean, I have a general idea of where it's going when I start writing. I know the killer, for instance, and the main twists, but yeah."

"Why is this relevant?" Connor asks.

"I'm just explaining my process . . ." I stop myself. Who cares how I write a book? It's not relevant to solving Shek's murder. "We need to make a timeline. If we write down who was where when, we might be able to figure out who did it."

"That's a good idea."

I take out my notebook, the one I used this afternoon with Oliver when we made our timeline for Shek. Oliver catches my eye, and we both realize at the same time that if Shek's dead, then he probably wasn't the one who tried to kill Connor or me.

But what about the evidence we'd uncovered? Was it just a coincidence that he'd been on the scene when the other attempts had taken place? Hadn't I just established that the law of coincidences was that there were more than you thought, but not as many as this?

So, no, it wasn't a coincidence that Shek was around when the attempts took place, but that doesn't mean that he was behind them.

"We can use this," I say, waving the notebook.

"It would be helpful to have somewhere that we could all see," Allison says. "Like an easel or a—"

"Whiteboard," Oliver and I say together.

It's this joke we used to make when we watched cop shows. At some point, the suspects were always going to go up on a whiteboard. Maybe sometimes there'd be string involved in tying the pieces together. But are real crimes ever solved that way? Crazy people have whiteboards, too, only we call them "crazy walls" and act like they're different.

"I think I saw something like that," Isabella says.

She jumps up from her seat and walks to the corner of the room, where there's a folded screen in bright colors with a flower design on it cornering off the room. She returns with a large easel with white butcher paper on it and several colored markers.

"Where did that come from?" Oliver asks.

"The guy at the front desk said there was some kind of conference here before us? I noticed it yesterday and asked." She puts it near the fireplace so we all have a view. "Shall I write? I have good handwriting."

I look around the room. This is usually the point in movies where someone with a guilty conscience gives it away with a look or a resistance to the process. But no one looks any different from usual, and everyone seems to think this is a good idea.

You see what I mean about reality versus fiction?

"We need to know where everyone was at the key times," Oliver says.

Isabella makes a series of boxes with our names in them.

| Eleanor | Connor | Oliver | Harper | Guy | Allison | Emily |
|---------|--------|--------|--------|-----|---------|-------|

"What about your name?" Guy says.

"Don't be daft, Guy," Connor says. "She doesn't have anything to do with this."

"I'm happy to include me if you like." She adds her name to the list.

| Eleanor | Connor | Oliver | Harper | Guy | Allison | Emily | Isabella |
|---------|--------|--------|--------|-----|---------|-------|----------|

"What now?" Isabella says, tapping the board.

"We need some more squares down the left," Oliver says.[151] "And then under everyone's names."

Isabella adds the boxes. "What do I put in the left-hand boxes?"

---

[151] He showed me the matrix he makes for his books once, and I buried my head in shame.

"Motive, means, opportunity."

She writes it down.

| | Eleanor | Connor | Oliver | Harper | Guy | Allison | Emily | Isabella |
|---|---|---|---|---|---|---|---|---|
| Motive | | | | | | | | |
| Means | | | | | | | | |
| Oppo | | | | | | | | |

"What's the difference between means and opportunity?" Allison says. "I never get that one right."

"Opportunity is whether they have a chance of doing the act," Oliver says. "Means is whether they're capable of doing it."

"Like, if someone was shot," I add, "did they have access to a gun, and did they have the ability to shoot the gun."

"Mr. Green in the library with a knife."

"Exactly."

"Well," Emily says, "we know what the means are, don't we? Shek was poisoned by his drink."

"Right," I say, thinking back to the glasses on the tray, arranged in a half circle just like we were. But then Connor turned his glass down, and Shek grabbed it before anyone could stop him. "That was supposed to be Connor's glass."

"That's one thing the killer got wrong," Allison says. "Connor hates Champagne."

"You're right, I do."

"Did everyone know that except for me?" Isabella asks.

There's a chorus of yeses.

"You didn't pour it, though," I say. "Sylvie did." I look around. "Where is Sylvie, anyway?"

"I heard the police say they'd question her separately," Isabella says, "and Captain Marco, too."

"You understand Italian?" I ask.

"I did Duolingo before I came on this trip."

Of course she did. "Good for you."

"You think the police think that Marco and Sylvie were in on it?" Allison asks.

"That doesn't make any sense," Connor says. "I've never met Sylvie before this tour, and Marco only today. And neither of them was there for the other incidents."

"I agree with Connor," I say.

"But Sylvie poured the Champagne," Emily says. "She had the best opportunity."

"And she wouldn't have known that Connor doesn't like Champagne," Harper adds.

"It wasn't them," Connor says.

"How do you explain it, then?" Oliver says.

Connor works his jaw, like he's trying to decide what to say.

"Now's not the time to hold back, Connor," I say. "Someone is already dead. Two people, in fact."

"Two?" Guy says.

I explain about the man outside the Vatican, and the information is received with a sobering silence. Because you can make sense of one murder, but two?

"What did you want to say before, Connor?"

"Yes, well, Allison said I didn't like Champagne when I didn't take the glass. Which conveniently provides an alibi for everyone but Marco, Sylvie, and Isabella."

"Why is it convenient?" Isabella asks. "Oh, you think someone is framing me?"

"That's ridiculous," Allison says.

"Is it?" Connor says.

"Who's supposed to be the one doing the framing?"

Connor just stares at her.

Allison stares back. "This is why police interrogate people separately. So they can find out what people *actually* know without spoiling it."

"You suddenly know so much about police procedure?"

"It's common sense," Allison says. "But if we must play this stupid game, then we're better off filling in the motive boxes. Because we *all* had the opportunity."

"Not all of us," Connor says. "*You* were the one who stayed back on the boat. You had plenty of time to put poison in that bottle."

"I didn't even know there was a bottle."

"Easy enough to say that now."

"It was *your* girlfriend who gave out the glasses."

"I did that in front of everyone," Isabella says. "You all saw me."

"Well, I didn't touch the glasses. And if it was in the bottle, then we'd all be dead, wouldn't we?"

"You didn't drink any, I noticed," Connor says. "And we wouldn't all be rich if I died."

He walks to the board and takes the pen from Isabella's hand. He turns his back on us and starts to write. When he's done, the board looks like this:

| | Eleanor | Connor | Oliver | Harper | Guy | Allison | Emily | Isabella |
|---|---|---|---|---|---|---|---|---|
| **Motive** | | | | | | $$ | | |
| **Means** | | | | | | Poison | | |
| **Oppo** | | | | | | Botany Mechanic | | |

"You're going to have to decipher this for the rest of us, Connor," Oliver says. "What does botany have to do with any of it?"

"Allison did a minor in botany when she was studying acting. When we first got together, she was doing this whole unit on poisons."

Allison looks unperturbed. "You remember? I'm flattered."

"Please, I was worried for myself."

"Didn't keep you away."

"I think everyone in this room knows I don't always make the best decisions."

Allison stares at him with an amused glint in her eye. Or maybe she's gloating?

"She was always saying back then that there were poisons all around us. All you had to do was know where to look."

"We don't even know what killed Shek," I say.

"Mark my words, it will be something she could've made once she got here that looks innocuous."

"So you think I brought a beaker and a Bunsen burner with me?" Allison drawls.

"I know what I know. And I bet that jellyfish was only a diversion."

"Now I stung myself with a jellyfish on purpose?"

"You needed a reason to stay on the boat."

"Couldn't I have simply feigned seasickness? Why go to the trouble of something so elaborate?"

"You always did have a flair for the dramatic."

"As I think we've already established, that's *you*."

I listen to the ping-pong of their conversation while staring at the columns and rows on the easel. There's a lot more information that could be filled out, but for now, I want to understand what Connor's getting at. "What does 'mechanic' mean?"

He glances at me. "Allison's father was a car mechanic. He taught Allison everything about cars when she was a kid."

"So, she'd know how to cut your brakes."

"Anyone can google that on the internet," Allison says.

"How do *you* know?"

"Because you can google anything on the internet."

"It still would take some expertise to do it so that it didn't give out right away, though ... What about the attempt on my life? And the second attempt on yours?" I think back to last night. All that wine in my system. The booms of the fireworks. The hand on my back. "I don't know if it was a man that pushed me. But I don't remember Allison being near me on the veranda."

"I saw her outside the Vatican," Connor says. "Half an hour before I almost died. And we were all near you on the veranda. You were just too wrapped up in Oliver to notice."

Oh my God. We'd had an audience for that? That's embarrassing.

Oliver coughs discreetly. "What about the accomplice?"

"Which accomplice?" Guy asks.

"The one who mugged Harper."

Harper stirs next to me. "Oh!"

"What is it?"

"Remember after I tackled Allison? She said she had the same bag as me. But maybe it *was* her, and I chased after the right person."

My eyes go wide. I'd forgotten about that. I *am* bad at this.

"That's ridiculous," Allison says. "I didn't steal your purse. I *do* have the same bag. I can show it to you if you like. And you would've recognized me."

"We've only met a few times ..."

"*Connor* would've recognized me."

"I'm not sure ..." Harper stares at her, like she's trying to remember back. "If you were wearing sunglasses and a wig and a hat ... It all happened very quickly."

"Where would I have put those?"

"In your bag. My bag. It's big."

"And the clothes I was wearing?"

"Maybe you had another layer on and you ditched it."

"What am I, Houdini?"

"No," Connor says, "you're just very motivated."

"Motivated by what?"

"Revenge, obviously."

"I already got my revenge. It's right there in our divorce settlement."

"Exactly." Connor taps where he wrote the "$$." "This is about money."

"What do you mean, Connor?" Oliver asks. "Did she invest in crypto?"

"Crypto?" Allison says. "That was real? Your newsletter wasn't hacked?"

"You knew about the newsletter?" I ask. "Did everyone?"

Everyone but Oliver nods slowly.

"Harper, did you unsubscribe me?"

"Of course. You never look at that email address anyway."

"Why didn't you tell me about it?"

"I—"

"Um," Connor says. "Excuse me? We're in the middle of something here."

"We were talking about the money," Emily says. "Please go on. This is all fascinating."

"Taking notes for your next novel?" I ask.

"You're the one who uses real-life situations."

"And you'll just wait until it's published, *then* crib it."

"Honestly?"

"Sorry, Connor," I say. "Go ahead."

"Yes, thank you. As I was saying . . . If I die," Connor says, "then Allison will benefit."

"How?"

"Her remaining alimony will become due in a lump sum payment, and I have to maintain life insurance to cover the payout."

Allison doesn't say anything, just looks at Connor like a slightly proud parent for figuring this all out on his own instead of stumbling around in his usual fashion.

"Is that true, Allison?" Oliver asks.

"About the insurance? That might be in the divorce settlement. My lawyer took care of that."

"Your very good lawyer," I say, remembering our earlier conversation. "And the payout? It's due if he dies?"

"Yes."

"Has he been making his payments?"

"Until now."

"But he's in financial trouble, and my book sales are declining . . ."

"What do your declining book sales have to do with anything?" Isabella asks.

"I get a percentage of her sales," Connor says. "Since she uses my name."

My face burns, and I don't make eye contact with Oliver or Harper. I've never told either of them this.

"Yes, yes," Allison says, "all of that *would* give me an excellent reason to kill Connor, wouldn't it? Except for two things."

Why is it always *two* things?[152]

"What?"

"I didn't do it."

"No, you killed Shek instead," Emily says. "He didn't deserve that."

"You have no idea what he deserved."

"What's the second thing, Allison?" I ask.

She looks at me frankly. "I have no motive to kill *you*."

"You must hate me, though. For the affair?"

"A hate I've waited ten years to do something about? Please."

I sigh. She's right. And there's the rub. When I look at the board, I

---

[152] Apropos of almost nothing, *Tell Me Three Things*, by Julie Buxbaum, is an excellent read.

come up against the same thing. No one has a motive to kill me *and* Connor. Not now, anyway. Not so many years after our crimes.

"I'm sure there's some explanation,"[153] Connor says.

"So no cuffs quite yet?" Allison says. "Though you did like to play a bit rough, didn't you?"

Connor's eyes narrow, and he's about to say something when the lock on the door to the library squeaks.

We all turn expectantly toward the door. It opens, and a man walks through.

I suck in my breath, feeling like I've been put in a time machine.

"Not *you*," Connor says.

And for once, I can't help but agree with him.

---

[153] Spoiler alert: There is.

# CHAPTER 21

## Inspector Tucci, I Presume

The man who walks through the door is Inspector Tucci.

Who's he, you ask?

Close readers of whatever this is will find the name familiar. That's because it's the name of the inspector Connor and I took our evidence to ten years ago. The one who didn't like Connor. Who didn't believe us to start out with. And who was pissed at us even once it turned out that everything we told him was true.[154]

Back then, Inspector Tucci was a rising star in Rome's police department. What he's doing in Naples is anyone's guess. But given the expression on his face[155, 156] as he surveys the room, then lands on me, then Connor, we're about to find out.

"Mr. Smith," he says in nearly perfect English with a slight British accent to it. I think he studied in the UK, or maybe he did an exchange

---

[154] Okay, not everything, obviously. But all the essentials that were needed to convict the Giuseppe family and put Gianni's murderer behind bars.

[155] I wish I could tell you that Inspector Tucci doesn't look like Stanley Tucci, but I'd be lying. They could be brothers. The Tucci genes are strong.

[156] I have no evidence that Inspector Tucci and Stanley Tucci are related. They just look like they are.

with Scotland Yard. It's not like policemen's résumés are just out there on the internet. "And Ms. Dash. Together again."

"Inspector Tucci," I say, mustering a smile. "How nice to see you."

Connor shoots me a look, but then smothers it and holds out his hand. "Small world."

Inspector Tucci looks at Connor's hand like it's a snake. "It is not, as you say, a small world, but a cruel one."

"Yes, I . . . It's terrible what happened to Shek . . ."

But Inspector Tucci's not looking at Connor anymore. Instead, he walks past him and toward the easel near the fireplace with our theorizing on it. Isabella steps aside, capping the pen she's been using, and Inspector Tucci stands in front of it for a long moment, then takes a photo of it with his phone. Then he turns to face us, taking us in one by one while we wait for him to say something.

Anything.

I believe this is what they call a pregnant silence.[157]

Inspector Tucci's dark eyes stop on the small table next to the couch I'm sitting on. He walks toward it and picks up my notebook. "Does this belong to someone here?"

I feel the need to put up my hand like I've been called on in class but squash it. "Yes, it's mine."

He pockets it in his blazer. He isn't wearing a uniform, and he didn't in Rome either. Back then, he was always well tailored, but now he's a bit rumpled, and his suit has that shine to it that clothes get when they've been dry-cleaned one too many times. Inspector Tucci has come down in the world.[158]

"What are you—?"

---

[157] Also known as a pregnant pause—a moment where everyone is waiting for something.

[158] Cousin Stanley, on the other hand, is doing pretty well for himself. He had that cooking show on CNN and a viral cocktail during the pandemic. He's not quite the internet's daddy, but certainly its hot uncle.

"All of you will turn in your bags and the items in your pockets to Officer Salvo, and then I will bring you in for individual questioning."

"Do you know what happened to Shek?" Emily asks.

"Mr. Botha? He is dead."[159]

"Yes, we know that, Tucci, but how?"

Inspector Tucci gives Connor a cold glare. "It is *Inspector* Tucci. And I do not have to answer your questions." He turns back to the rest of us. "You will stay here while your rooms are searched."

"Don't you need a warrant?" Guy asks. He and Inspector Tucci also met once or twice back in the day and had a grudging respect for each other.

"This is Italy, not America."[160]

"And if we don't agree?" Connor asks.

"Is there some reason why you don't want your person or room searched, Mr. Smith?"

Connor works his jaw. "Of course not."

"Then we will not have a problem."

"Oh, but I do have a problem. I know why you're in Naples. You got reassigned there, didn't you, after you failed to solve the Giuseppe robberies on your own?"

Inspector Tucci doesn't say anything, just continues to stare at Connor with enmity.

"You should recuse yourself from the case."

"Pardon me?"

"You can't investigate this," Connor says. "I'm the intended victim. You have as much reason to want me dead as any of them. Maybe more than some. You're biased."

---

[159] Inspector Tucci likes stating the obvious. It's one of his interrogation techniques.

[160] Turns out we should have googled that because you <u>do</u> need a search warrant to conduct a search in Italy, just like in America. In our defense, we were scared, and Shek had just died right in front of us.

"That is ridiculous. As ridiculous as your assumptions generally are. I do not hate you. I have a beautiful life in Naples. The ocean is warm, the pizza is delicious, and the cases are generally easy to solve, as I'm sure this one will prove to be." He looks to the easel. "Who is Allison?"

This time, Allison does raise her hand. "That's me."

"Allison . . . ?"

"Smith."

Inspector Tucci glances at Connor and then back to Allison. "How unfortunate."

Allison laughs. "Don't pity me. I divorced him long ago."

Inspector Tucci's eyes flit in my direction.

"Yes, that's right. It was her fault. Hers and Connor's."

I sink into the couch, feeling a wave of shame. Oliver hasn't said anything in a while, and while I want to catch his eye, this isn't the moment.

Allison laughs again. "Don't look like that, Eleanor. I forgive you."

"And me?" Connor asks.

"Let's not take things too far, shall we?"

"I see you are as good at creating enemies as you always were," Inspector Tucci says.

Connor places his hands on his hips. "This is exactly what I'm talking about. You can't be on this case."

"But I am." He extends a hand. "Mrs. Smith, please come with me."

"It's Ms. Smith, now."

"My apologies."

She tilts her head down in acknowledgment. "What do you want to speak to me for?"

"Since your party seems to think that you are responsible for this tragedy, I will question you first."

"You got all that from this?" Isabella says. "I'm impressed."

"Don't be," Connor says. "You don't have to talk to him, Allison, if you don't want to."

"Oh, now you care about my well-being?"

"I—"

"Forget it, Connor. I can take care of myself." She gives a little shrug and follows Inspector Tucci out of the room.

The police officer who's been guarding the door, whose name I've already forgotten (I told you I was bad at this), comes in with a notepad and takes our names and basic details. Then he collects everyone's backpacks and bags, and gets us to turn out our pockets. He also takes our phones, labeling each with our name. He gives no indication of when we'll get them back.

Then he leaves with our things, and we're alone again with our thoughts.

"Maybe we should keep working on this?" Harper says, pointing to the easel.

"I'm game," Emily says.

"But it's not a game," Oliver says. "Shek is dead."

"You don't need to remind me," Emily says. "We all saw it happen."

"If that's the case, then, did you see anything useful?"

She cocks her head to the side. "I've been thinking . . . Everyone was standing around, holding their glasses. It's a small deck. We were all near one another. Someone could've slipped the poison into Shek's glass after he took it off the tray."

I think it through. "But then that would mean Connor wasn't the intended victim."

"Yep."

"Why would someone want to kill Shek?" Isabella asks.

Emily shrugs. "I'm sure the police will figure it out."

Connor scoffs. "That man is barely a detective."

"Surprising you don't get along better, then, isn't it?" Guy says.

"Really, Guy? You're so smart? Then tell me why someone would want to kill me, Eleanor, *and* Shek? Explain it to me like I'm five."

"I don't think this is helping," Oliver says. "We should leave all this to the professionals."

"I agree," I say. "We're not getting anywhere."

"We got Allison somewhere," Harper says. "Right into the hot seat."

I lean against her. "Maybe she did it?"

"You don't believe that, do you?"

"No, but my instincts are for shit. That's pretty well established."

"Then we should keep on with this," Harper says. "We can't let Allison suffer for something she didn't do."

I look at the easel. "But the problem is, clearing Allison means making one of us the suspect."

"I didn't think of that."

"It's okay. Solving a murder is fun on paper, but not so much when it's someone you knew."

"None of this is *okay*," Harper says, looking around the room slowly. "Shek's dead and one of us did it."

We don't talk after that. Instead, we sit there, waiting for our turn to be interrogated, each of us lost in our own thoughts.[161]

I think about someone going through my things, running their hands in my suitcase, flipping through my notebook, seeing what shows and books I've downloaded on my Kindle.[162] It feels like judgment, but I'm the one judging myself.

An hour goes by, and then Inspector Tucci returns with Allison.

It's my turn now, he says, and this time no one makes a move to discourage me from talking to him.

Harper gives my hand a squeeze, and Oliver watches me leave the room,[163] but no one else seems to be paying much attention. They're all too wrapped up in their own fears.

---

[161] Though I'm pretty sure Oliver is still trying to work out who did it. He keeps getting up and standing in front of the easel, then walking away.

[162] I'm reading the Bridgerton books, by the way. For research, obvi.

[163] Yes, I look back to check.

I remember someone telling me once that everyone has something to hide and it's always at the forefront of their mind when they're being interrogated, whether it's related to the crime or not. So the first time a question comes anywhere near the subject you're afraid of, out the secret comes.

This is somehow related to why people confess to crimes they didn't commit, though I'm not entirely sure how. All I know is I'm supposed to let Inspector Tucci finish his questions before I say anything, and only answer what's asked.

In other words, be the opposite of how I usually am.

He takes me to a small conference room on the other side of the reception. There's one big window, a square table, and a couple of comfortable chairs around it. A small black recording device is in the middle of the table.

Inspector Tucci sits and indicates that I should sit across from him. "Ms. Dash, it is a pleasure to see you again."

"Is it?"

He frowns. "I see that you have not changed."

"What does that mean?"

"Still hostile to the authorities. Still keeping company with Connor Smith."

"That's only because of the book tour."

"Ah, yes. *When in Roma*," he says. "I have read this book."

I sit in my chair. "Good read?"

He raises his eyebrows. "A lot of facts have been rearranged. And this inspector character. He's me, yes?"

"It's fiction."

"He's described exactly like me."

"Are you going to sue me?"

"No, Ms. Dash. Italians are not so quick to go to the courts as you Americans."

"Okay."

"You've had much success with this book."[164]

"Yes."

"A whole series, many millions of copies sold?"

"That's what it says on the cover."

"And Mr. Smith, he's the hero in all of these books."

"I'd say more that Cecilia Crane is the hero. Connor's the sidekick."

"Regardless, they go together. They are, how do you say, the backbone of the series."

"Yes."

"But you are sick of Mr. Smith."

"In the book or in life?"

"Both, I think."

"We've had our differences. As you know, Connor can be . . . a lot."

He taps the table with his fingers. "But you're still romantically involved?"

"No."

"Since when?"

It sounds like he already knows the answer. Which he might. But how? The only person I ever told about that was Oliver, and Tucci hasn't talked to him yet.

Unless Allison knows? Maybe *that's* why she wanted to kill us? Because she still has feelings for Connor?

That doesn't feel right, but what do I know.

In the meantime, I have to answer the inspector's question.

When in doubt, go with the truth.

"We had a dalliance a few years ago. It didn't mean anything."

---

[164] This is another trick people use in interrogation. They make statements instead of asking questions, and you're supposed to agree. According to my research, I'm supposed to stay silent until he asks me a question, but I don't think that's going to fly here.

"But this is the reason your relationship with Mr. Oliver Forrest ended, correct?"

"Correct."

"You dated for four years, I believe."

I've counted out the minutes and days, but if I recite them now, I'm going to seem pathetic.

"That's right."

"You must have been upset."

"I was, yes."

"And Mr. Forrest, too?"

"Yes, of course."

"You perhaps both blamed Mr. Smith for this occurrence?"

He's not getting me to fall for that. "No, Inspector Tucci. I was an adult who made a bad decision. Oliver was upset at me, and so was I. It wasn't Connor's fault."

"No? The man generally has some part in it."

"I was upset at the situation. But that was three years ago. It's in the past."

"For Mr. Forrest as well?"

I'm not falling for this either.[165] "You'll have to ask Oliver how he felt."

"I will. But you resented Mr. Smith. You have for a long time, maybe."

"We're not friends."

"You felt trapped with him. That you, perhaps, had to write about him?"

"He's the main character in my books, as you pointed out."

"Books you didn't want to write anymore?"

Goddamn it, Allison. Couldn't you throw suspicion off of yourself without putting it on me?

"I'm on the last book of my contract."

"Ah, yes. *Amalfi Made Me Do It.*" Something flashes in his hand. It's my

---

[165] If you're ever interrogated, never speculate. You can thank me later.

notebook. *My* notebook, where I've been outlining *Amalfi Made Me Do It.* The book where I kill Connor off.

Shit.

"I was thinking of ending the series, yes."

"By killing Mr. Smith?"

"Yes."

He flips open the notebook. "And you contemplated many ways for him to die? You enjoyed this, perhaps."

"It's an outline. For the book. It's how I figure out the plot. I write down questions and suggestions, and eventually the story comes together."

"And one of the things you contemplated was poison."

"I thought of a lot of things. But those are just ideas. Not anything I did."

"No?"

"No." I pause, trying to remember what I wrote in there. This is why I hate outlining. I never remember what I write and end up taking the story in an entirely different direction anyway.[166] "Didn't Allison tell you that someone is trying to kill me *and* Connor?"

"She did say that, yes."

"So, then you know that I'm not the one who tried to kill Connor."

"I do not know that at all. What Ms. Smith told me was conjecture. Suggestions that could have been planted by you."

"What do you mean?"

He opens up his hands and lays them palms up on the table. Nothing to see here. "What is the evidence that someone is trying to kill you?"

"Someone pushed me down the stairs last night."

"You could have, how you say, staged that."

---

[166] It's also boring, and takes away the fun of discovering what's going to happen as I write it. I'm the first reader of my books, even when it comes out of my brain. Pretty cool, right? But I should be paying attention to this conversation. More later.

"Ask Oliver. Mr. Forrest. He saw me . . . He saved me . . ."

Inspector Tucci watches me as my words die in my mouth. "Ms. Dash, I will speak with Mr. Forrest, but in the meantime, what I have to deal with are facts."

"What are the facts, according to you?"

He holds up his index finger. "Fact one: You have a tumultuous relationship with Mr. Smith. Fact two: You are outlining how to make him disappear from your life. Fact three: Mr. Smith knows about this and is unhappy. Fact four: Someone has been trying to kill Mr. Smith and may have gone so far as to kill another person to cover up that crime. Fact five: A master room key was stolen from your sister's purse, a master room key which we found in *your* room."

"I don't know how that got there. I just found it yesterday."

"That is a convenient excuse."

"It's the truth."

"I deal in facts, as I said, not what you decide the truth is."

"What about the fact that I didn't try to kill Connor?"

He ignores me and moves on to the fingers on his second hand. "Fact six: One of the methods you contemplated using on Mr. Smith was poison. Fact seven: Mr. Botha died of poisoning after consuming a glass of Champagne that was meant for Mr. Smith—"

"It was Prosecco."

Shut up, El.

"Excuse me?"

"I'm sorry. It was nothing." I try to regulate my breathing. "But wait. I knew Connor didn't drink Champagne. I would never have tried to poison him that way."

"That is not a defense."

"Am I on trial?"

"You might be, Ms. Dash."

I swallow down my fear. "I didn't try to kill Connor."

"Then how do you explain this?" He holds up a small needle

attached to a plastic disk with a loop on it, like one of those candy en-gagement rings I used to love when I was little.

"What is that?"

"Mr. Botha wasn't poisoned with the Champagne."

"What?"

"He was poisoned with this. Injected into the back, like so." He positions the device between his fingers, then makes a stabbing motion. "You see, it is quick, over in the blink of an eye. No one would notice."

My mind is a tilt-a-whirl. "I . . . *Shek* was the intended victim?"

"Yes."

"Why?"

"I was hoping you could illuminate me on that."

"I don't know why anyone would want to kill Shek."

"Perhaps he saw you do something in the last few days. I see from your notebook that he was near the Vatican when the attempt was made on Mr. Smith's life."

"But I wasn't there. I mean, I was, but I didn't push Connor into traffic."

"That remains to be seen."

"No, speak to Harper. She was with me that whole day."

"Harper, your sister?"

"Yes."

"She would naturally provide you with an alibi."

I shake my head. "No, she's not a liar."

That's me. *I'm* the liar. "Why would I be trying to solve the case if I knew who did it all along?"

"Cover."

"Cover for what?"

"For this," he says, holding up the ring again.

"I've never seen that in my life."

"I'm very surprised to hear it, given that it was found in your backpack."

## AMALFI MADE ME DO IT—OUTLINE

I don't think I can write this book anymore.

# CHAPTER 22

## Guilty Until Proven Innocent

"I didn't kill Shek," I say to Inspector Tucci, but the effort it takes to say it makes it sound unconvincing, even to me.

He folds his hands on the table next to the ring-like device that was apparently used to kill him. There's a bit of condensation on the plastic evidence bag it was placed in, like it was wet before it went in there.

"You can say that all you like, but the evidence states the contrary."

I point to the bag. "Even if it was found in my things, I promise that I've never seen it before."

"I'm sure its origins will come to light in time."

He means he thinks he's going to discover where I purchased it or how I made it.

But here's the thing: If I did do this—and I'm not saying I did—I wouldn't be stupid enough to leave evidence of it just lying around for anyone to find.

"Anyone could've put it in my backpack," I say.

He makes a dismissive gesture. "A convenient excuse, which you have used before. The key card, the backpack . . . Is that the best you can do?"

My fear is being replaced by rage.

At the unfairness.

At the condescension.

At the blow to my ego.

Take your pick.

It all mixes together, and now I'm going to say something I've been told never to say. "I'd like to speak to a lawyer."[167, 168]

"In due time, I'm sure you will consult one, Ms. Dash."

"No, now. This interview is over."

He smiles at me in a way that makes my blood boil. "Ah, but you do not get to decide this, Ms. Dash. Again, this is not the American cinema. We do things differently here."[169, 170]

"I don't have to speak to you."

"Again, wrong. But that is all well and good. I have enough."

"Enough for what?"

"To obtain, in your terms, a warrant for your arrest."

My mouth goes dry, but there's no water for me to drink, or air left for me to breathe. "A warrant?"

"For your arrest. I will speak to the local magistrate and return with it in the morning."

"This can't be happening."

He stares at me with pity. "But it is, Ms. Dash. And not like in one of your stories where some convoluted explanation will appear to save you."

"You mean, the truth?"

"The truth is usually simple and very straightforward. There isn't some big reveal or mystery to unlock. People behave in predictable ways."

"This is exactly why you didn't solve the Giuseppe robberies."

---

[167] It makes you seem guilty. If you don't want to talk to the police, you just tell them no at the beginning. You don't answer their questions until they get to a difficult one and then ask for counsel.

[168] Once again, I'm not an attorney. I just write mystery novels for a living.

[169] You guessed it, right? They don't. The rules are basically the same for America and Italy—you have to tell the suspect that they have the right to counsel and give them an opportunity to consult one.

[170] All of which begs the question: Why was Inspector Tucci lying to us? Was he simply corrupt, or was there something else going on? Too soon to tell.

"Ah, but I did."

"No, you didn't."

He stares at me, trying to process what I'm telling him. "What could you possibly mean?"

I stare back. This is the only power I have. The secrets I know. It's the only chip I have to play. "I'm not going to tell you. But you *did* miss something all those years ago, something crucial. And now it's too late for you to do anything about it."

Something flickers behind his eyes, and I know that I've done what I could.

I've created a doubt. Whether it's reasonable or not is for another day.

But what about you?

Do *you* think I did it?[171]

When Inspector Tucci and I are finished with our staring contest, we return to the library.

It's late now, my stomach is rumbling because despite the shock—and is that . . . *sadness* at Shek's death? I think it is—my body needs to be fed at regular intervals.

Everyone is pretty much where we left them. The easel has no more clues written on it. Oliver's pacing by the window, the inky sea reflecting the moon. Harper's opened a book, but I can tell she's not reading it. Isabella and Connor are ensconced on a settee, intertwined, but not engaging with each other directly. Isabella's head is on his shoulder, and he's staring at the easel like it might contain the meaning of life. Allison and Emily and Guy are standing by the fireplace talking in low voices about Lord knows what.

---

[171] This is not a confession, but it's highly unlikely that I'd be writing this if I did. Though . . . I do write about my experiences. I change a few details to cover the *guilty*, but the clues are still there.

Inspector Tucci claps his hands to get everyone's attention.

They turn to him, but Oliver makes eye contact with me, a question in his raised eyebrows. I shake my head in a warning, but how am I supposed to convey what's happening?

I'm going to go to jail for a murder I didn't commit.

If I survive that long.

Inspector Tucci clears his throat. "I am here to inform you that I will be seeking an arrest warrant for Mr. Botha's murder."

"Allison?" Connor says with grim certainty.

"No." He pauses. "Ms. Eleanor Dash."

Harper's hand flies to her mouth, but it's Oliver who speaks. "That's ridiculous."

"Be that as it may, it is where the evidence leads."

"What evidence?"

"I do not need to disclose that to you. This is not some parlor game we are playing. A man is dead. I owe my duty to him."

"Well, well, well," Connor says, smirking at me. "I didn't think you had it in you."

"Shut up, Connor," Harper says. "Just shut up. For once in your life."

"Good for you, Harper," Allison says. "Though I doubt he'll listen."

"There must be some mistake," Oliver says, searching out my face again. "Whatever you think the evidence shows . . . I know Eleanor isn't behind this. I saw someone try to kill her with my own eyes."

"Who?" Inspector Tucci asks.

"I don't . . . It was dark, the fireworks were flashing, but she *was* pushed."

"Or she made it look that way to elicit your sympathy and cover her intentions."

Oliver opens his mouth to say something, then stops.

Is that doubt I see on his face?

Of course it is.

He knows I'm not to be trusted with his heart. Why would he trust me about anything else?

"This is the problem," Inspector Tucci says. "You think that you are able to solve this crime by yourselves, and you cannot. You must leave this to the professionals."

"Ha," Connor says. "Because that worked so well the last time."

Inspector Tucci glares at him. "I do not think you understand, Mr. Smith. There is a murderer among you. Seeking them out"—he points to the easel—"is a bad idea."

"Why don't you just take Eleanor into custody, and then that will be that?" Guy asks.

"It does not work like that here. I must go to the magistrate first."[172]

"You still have doubts," Oliver guesses. "You're not sure Eleanor did it, so you want to cover your tracks. Make it someone else's decision."

"I do not have to explain myself to you."

"But I'm right, aren't I? It's because of what Connor said before—you were demoted ten years ago and I bet if you screw up again you'll be out."

Inspector Tucci works his jaw. "As I said before, you need to leave the investigating to the police. If you do not, you might stumble on something you shouldn't and provoke a reaction." He looks at me at this point and it's not subtle. He thinks I'm dangerous. That they should be afraid of me. "Ms. Dash may not be acting alone. Be careful. Lock your doors tonight."

"What about the rest of us?" Harper asks. She is surprisingly calm for someone whose sister was just accused of murder. But maybe I'd react the same way because I'd know it wasn't true.

I mean, it can't be true.

"What do you mean?" Inspector Tucci asks.

---

[172] Again with the lies and half-truths, Inspector Tucci?

"You said you'd question all of us. Don't you need to do that to be sure that you're right?"

"Events have surpassed . . . But we will question all of you in the morning. I will return with my colleagues then. Be safe."

He shoots one last glance at me, then leaves, taking the police officer with him.

The door is open; we aren't locked in here. I feel trapped nonetheless.

Because this has to be a joke, right?

But no one's laughing. No, instead, everyone's looking at me in a way that I understand. They think I'm guilty, even though they haven't even heard the evidence against me.

"Did you do it?" Isabella asks.

"Of course she didn't," Harper says. "Right, Eleanor?"

"I didn't kill Shek."

Ugh, that wasn't convincing *at all*.

"I didn't kill him." There, I put my back into it that time.

"Hmmm," Guy says, walking toward the easel. He picks up the discarded marker. It hovers on the square next to my name with the word "motive" in it. "Eleanor definitely had a motive to kill Connor."

"Give me a break," I say. "We all have one of those."

"You wanted him out of your life."

"On paper. Not in reality."

"I know you're not that naive. Connor wasn't going to just disappear because you wrote him out of your book series."

"And what about the blackmail?" Emily says. "That's a good motive."

"Are you saying that Eleanor blackmailed Connor and then tried to kill him, because that's nonsense," Harper says.

"No, no, not *that* blackmail," Emily says. "The one Connor did with Eleanor. With her book deal."

Ah, *shit*. When did I tell her that?

Oh, right. Yesterday. The lemon spritzes that came every ten to twelve minutes.[173, 174]

Oliver and Harper look at me with questions in their eyes.

I've never told either of them about the blackmail or even that I was paying Connor at all. I never showed Harper my contracts—I just told her that the lawyers took care of it, and she handled the money once it was received. And Oliver, well, Oliver hated Connor on sight. Telling him anything about it would've made it worse.

So I kept my secret.

But secrets don't keep; they rot until their stench makes them impossible to ignore.

"Connor's blackmailing you?" Harper says.

"I . . . Yes. I have to pay him twenty percent of my royalties."

"Since when?"

"Since the beginning. I mean, it was ten percent then. But you get the idea."

"How did I not know this?"

I shake my head in shame. "I didn't want anyone to know."[175]

*I'm sorry*, I mouth at Harper and Oliver, but who knows if it will get through.

"How does Emily know about it?" Oliver asks.

"She told us yesterday," Emily says. "Didn't she, Guy?"

---

[173] Has anyone researched alcohol as an interrogation technique?

[174] Of course they have. *That* was a rabbit hole. Fascinating, though. TL; DR: the majority of suspects are under the influence when they're interrogated and are more subject to police influence as a result.

[175] I've never let Harper look at my royalty statements. She has access to the online portal where some, but not all, sales are reported, so she knows about my sales trends, but never the gritty details like how much I'm paid per book. Things were already so weird between us, I didn't think the details would help. But I also didn't want her to see that annotation about the consultant fee. Because, as I've told you more than once, Harper's the smart one.

"It wasn't my fault," I say. "I was under the influence of too many spritzes."

"Is that going to be your defense for the murder, too?" Isabella asks.

Oliver raises his hand to cut off whatever stupid thing I was going to say. "What happens if Connor dies? Do you have to keep paying?"

"I'm not sure. Maybe it goes to his estate?"

I look at Allison. Is she Connor's heir? I've never asked Connor if has a will, but if he does, I assume that he wrote her out of it when they got divorced.

But then again, Connor's never been someone who's up on his paperwork.

Speaking of Connor . . . he isn't saying anything. And a silent Connor is a Connor you need to keep your eyes on.

"Maybe for the old royalties, but not on a new deal, right?" Emily asks. "If you sell another book series, then it will be clean."

"Eleanor wouldn't kill someone for money," Harper says. "She has enough of it to last a lifetime."

"Does she? That expensive house in Venice Beach?" Guy says. "And her book sales are declining, I hear."

"That was our parents' house. And even with the declining sales, we're fine."

"It's you, isn't it?" Connor says, shaking himself into action. "You did it."

"I did not."

"Come on, El. You've been angry ever since that night at Bouchercon."

Oliver's head snaps up.

Bouchercon, the scene of a different crime.

The place where I killed our relationship.

"You wanted me dead," Connor continues. "But most of all, you wanted me scared. Maybe you thought I'd be happy to give up my payments if my life was on the line."

"That's ridiculous. If I wanted to kill you, I would've done it years ago."

"That's *everyone's* excuse," Allison drawls. "I thought you'd be more original."

Connor stares at me. "You didn't have the guts then. But you're different now."

I want to deny it, but this is one of the first true things that Connor's said about me in a long time. I do feel different now. I'm just not sure when that change happened.

"Did you blackmail her?" Oliver asks Connor.

"Call it what you will."

He turns to me. "But why, El?"

"I couldn't publish the book if I didn't. It was his name . . . him."

"I don't buy it," Oliver says. "You could've easily changed his name in the book and enough details to keep him out of it. There has to be something more."

I look at him. The pain on his face is like a punch.

A sucker punch, and I fall for it.

"He was behind the robberies."

"Eleanor!" Connor warns.

I don't listen to Connor. I've listened to him long enough.

"He planned them. He wasn't behind the murder, but he planned the robberies with the Giuseppe family. I found out when we were still in Italy, but I didn't tell the police. He convinced me not to."

"I don't get it," Emily says. "How did that make you vulnerable to blackmail?"

"Because you were an accessory after the fact," Oliver says.

"Yes."

"You should stop talking, Eleanor," Guy says. "Wouldn't want to incriminate yourself any further."

"It doesn't matter, Guy."

"That's an odd thing to say in your position."

"It's past the statute of limitations. Even if I confessed to Inspector Tucci, they can't do anything about it now. And that's why Connor's theory doesn't make sense. I don't have to submit to his blackmail anymore. That's why I was okay killing him off in the series. He doesn't have a hold over me."

"When did you realize this?" Oliver asks.

"A couple of months ago. I was doing some research for the book and I stumbled across it. That's when I knew I could write him out of the series."

"But you came on this tour."

"The publisher insisted. And I thought, why not? One last tour. It wasn't going to, well . . ."

"Kill you?" Oliver says.

"Yes."

"But that means . . ." Allison says, "that it's someone else here. Doesn't it?"

"I don't know. Shek is dead. He *was* poisoned . . ." I stop. Should I tell them what Inspector Tucci told me about him being the intended victim? He didn't tell me to keep it to myself. Fuck it. "Shek wasn't poisoned with the Champagne."

"What?" Harper says. "He wasn't?"

"No, apparently it was some . . . I don't know what you call it. This needle attached to this device that could be concealed in your hand. All someone had to do was tap him with it."

"But he started to choke right after he drank it."

"That could be a coincidence. We don't even know when he was poisoned. It might've been something that was slow-acting."

"Inspector Tucci told you this?" Oliver asks.

"About the device, yes."

"Do they know when it was administered?"

"He didn't say. I assume they won't have the lab results back till later."

"But how did he know, then?"

"They found the device."

"Where?"

I look at the floor. "In my backpack."

"So that's why..." Oliver says.

"Yes."

"Anyone could have planted it there," Isabella says.

"That's what I said."

"I don't think so." Harper stands and walks to the easel. She turns the paper over and picks up a marker. She draws the hull of a boat and then starts filling it in with *X*'s.

x—Captain Marco

x—Eleanor x—Connor x—Shek

x—Harper x—Isabella x—Oliver

x—Emily x—Guy x—Allison

x—Sylvie

"What are you doing?" Guy asks.

"Trying to figure out who could've poisoned Shek."

"Inspector Tucci told us not to do this," Allison says.

"So," Harper says, ignoring her. "Connor, Isabella, and Oliver all had access."

"But it could've happened at any time," I point out.

"Not any time, surely," Connor says.

"Any time since we got on the boat after Capri," I say.

"You don't know that."

"You should hope that's the case, or it's you in the hot seat."

Connor's eyes narrow. "Why would *I* want to kill Shek?"

"Because he was blackmailing you..."

We stare at each other, the energy in the room charged.

"I think Inspector Tucci was right," Allison says. "This is dangerous. Us throwing accusations around. Someone's going to stumble on the truth, and then what?"

"Maybe that's what Shek did . . ." Harper says.

"That gossip?" Connor says. "He'd never keep it to himself."

"I think Allison's right, El," Harper says, putting down the marker. "It's late. We should eat and then go to bed."

"Separate?" Emily asks. "That's always when bad things happen in situations like this."

"Shek died when we were together," I say. "I'll take my chances."

"I don't leave anything to chance," Guy says. He turns and reaches into the bookshelf, moving a book aside and pulling out a gun.

"What the . . ." Harper says.

"I didn't want it confiscated in the search."

"So we have a murderer among us, and you have a gun," Connor says.

"*I'm* not the killer."

"Why not?" Allison says. "You have just as much reason to kill Connor as anyone. And you must've been in on those robberies. You were a team back then. Thick as *thieves*."

"This is the first time I'm hearing about it."

"I find that extremely hard to believe."

"Enough," Harper says. "Enough. Guy's had the gun the entire time and he hasn't done anything with it. Let's just stick to the plan and get out of this room. Okay?"

She looks around at all of us, waiting for our buy-in. Eventually, it's Isabella who comes to our rescue.

"Is the dining room still open?" Isabella asks. "I'm starving."

# Breaking the Fourth Wall

Okay, so, let's take a little break here and bring you into this.

That's right—it's your turn to solve it.

Why?

Because we've reached the third act of this thing.

What's that, you ask? Well, in a classic three-act structure (which applies to most books and movies), the first act is the setup (generally the first third of the book); the second act is the main engine of the story (middle third), where the protagonist (that's me) faces multiple obstacles and dangers (hello, someone tried to kill me!); and the third act is where the main story and all of its subplots get resolved.

The third act also includes the climax of the book—where everything gets *super* tense as all the threads the author has been doling out intertwine and then, *boom!* The central question of the novel is resolved and the remaining characters can go about their new lives armed with the knowledge they've acquired over the course of the book about themselves and their relationships.

Ideally, the main character grows, changes, and emerges in a better place.

That's how it's supposed to work, anyway.

I'm not making any promises about growing *or* changing.

Anyway, to recap. In Act 1 (Chapter 1 to Chapter 10) you met the protagonist (again me) and the antagonist (Connor), and learned that while I was planning on killing him off in my next book, someone was planning on killing him off for real. You also learned about tensions with my sister, Harper, and my messy relationship with my ex, Oliver, and met all the other potential suspects (Guy, Allison, Emily, Shek, Isabella) and got some insight into why they might want Connor dead. Then Connor faked his own death for stupid reasons that didn't accomplish what he wanted, but someone else died—Davide, the Good Samaritan. You didn't meet him, but we can pour one out for him anyway.

In Act 2 (Chapter 11 to Chapter 22), the plot thickened. Some big secrets were revealed (Connor was behind the Giuseppe robberies; I knew about it and did nothing), and oh, fantastic, someone is trying to kill me, too, for reasons that I'm sure will be made clear eventually.[176] Oliver and I decided that Shek was behind all of it, but then Shek died. Connor accused Allison of being responsible, and she was looking pretty good for it until the police arrived and another bombshell dropped that makes me, apparently, responsible for all of it, and I'm just waiting to get arrested in the morning.

Which brings us to Act 3 (Chapter 23 to Chapter 29).

What do you have to look forward to?

A couple things.

1.  Shek's murderer will be revealed.
2.  You'll learn whether someone *was* trying to kill Connor.
3.  Ditto for whether someone was trying to kill me.
4.  There are going to be some tense moments. It's called a *climax* after all.[177]

---

[176] Yes, I promise.

[177] And yeah, maybe the double entendre is intentional. I mean, of course it is.

5.   There's probably going to be another attempt on someone's life. If I'm being honest, another body might drop.

6.   A bunch of secrets are going to come out.[178]

Why am I telling you all this?

First of all, it's fun seeing behind the curtain, isn't it?

But second, I think it's time for you to play along.

Yep, that's right! *You* get to solve this!

How? Well, you have everything you need to know right now. I'll even give you a clue.

I mean, more than the clues I've already given you, which have been a lot, I promise.

So it's time for you to get to work. I'm not going to be the only one figuring this out here, right? You're going to put some effort in, too?

Excellent.

Okay, look at the next page. Your clue is waiting for you.

---

[178] Wait, what? There are more secrets? Of course there are. I may be a pantser, but I have a plotter's soul.

CLUE: I'M NOT GOING TO GET ARRESTED.[179]

---

[179] Okay, maybe technically this isn't a clue, but more of a foreshadowing of something that's going to happen, which <u>is</u> a clue, I promise. One more hint: The clue is in the <u>why</u> I don't get arrested.

# CHAPTER 23

## The Last Supper

"Hey, El, wait up," Harper calls after me as I drift toward the dining room.

I stop and wait for her to catch up. She looks like she's in shock, and I'm hit hard by the realization that she's a mirror of me. I open my arms wide and she walks into them. Before hers have even closed around me, I feel the tears start to fall. She hugs me close and I hug her back, and we stand there like that, two sisters who don't have anyone else in the world, holding on for dear life.

I don't know how to make the tears stop, so I grasp for the only thing I can think of.

"Pineapple," I say, and I can feel Harper's smile against my hair, even as her tears stain my shoulder.

She pulls back. "I'll say."

I wipe my tears away with the back of my hand. "What's happening?"

"I'm so scared," she says.

"Me too."

"You sure? Back there in the library you seemed, I don't know, not that bothered."

"I think I'm in shock." I expel a slow breath. "Shek is dead."

"Yeah."

"Fuck. That was horrible."

"For Shek, too."

"Yes, for Shek, too, obviously."

"I don't want you to go to jail, El."

"Thanks, baby sis."

She smiles thinly. "What do we do now?"

"I don't know."

"Food?"

"Yeah, fuck it, let's eat."

We walk to hotel's dining room. Everyone has spread out at various tables already.

Connor, Isabella, and Guy are at one table near the bank of windows that look out on the Med. Allison and Emily are at another in the middle of the room, near a family with unruly children. That leaves Oliver's table, which I don't want to sit at, but I don't *not* want to sit at if you catch my meaning.

The choice is taken out of my hands when Harper leads me right to him.

It feels like so much of this trip has been about that between us—one of us tugging the other into something she doesn't want to do. That hasn't worked out well for either of us so far, and given the whole humiliating reveal that I knew Connor had planned the robberies and did nothing about it, that I let myself be blackmailed by him, well, it doesn't feel like anything good's going to come of this meal either.

But maybe I'm wrong about that.

Why not? I've been wrong about everything else up to now.[180]

At least this table is near the door, which seems like a good idea.

This feels like an evening where I might need to make a quick exit.

"Take a seat," Oliver says as he shakes out his white linen napkin and places it on his lap. "The menu looks delicious."

"It can't be better than lunch," I say. "I wanted to marry that pizza."

Harper laughs, and it eases some of the tension. I look at the menu

---

[180] This is pretty much true if you're working on the solution. Almost everything, but not quite.

that's on top of my place setting, printed on a thick piece of cream paper in silver leaf. They have Caesar salad and something called lemon pasta, which sounds incredible. I decide to order that, and though I want a million lemon spritzes to go with it, I'm going to hold off.

I mean, the last time someone had a drink near me, he ended up dead.

Oh! Harper told me not to drink on the boat. Does that mean . . . No. *No.* My sister is not a murderer.[181, 182]

Right?

I watch her while she peruses the menu, and nothing seems amiss. Not more than it is with all of us. Shek's death is weighing on us, but maybe not as much as it should.

Does that make us terrible or just human?

The waiter comes to take our orders, and then it's just the three of us. There's a nervous pit in the bottom of my stomach that I can't shake. Is this my last night of freedom? It can't be. But that's how everyone must feel in this kind of situation. Like they're in a movie where someone will run in at the last minute and put a stop to all of this.

That can happen anytime, universe.

"This won't be your last supper," Oliver says, tipping his glass of red wine at me.

"How did you read my mind?"

He lifts the corner of his mouth. "Practice."

I smile at him, but his being nice to me doesn't help.

I guess we can be pen pals or something while I'm in jail.

Assuming Italian jails let you have pen pals?

"You told me before that Inspector Tucci was a bit of a bozo," Harper says. "The magistrate must know that."

"I don't . . . Can we talk about something else?"

---

[181] Though *My Sister, the Murderer* would make a good title. Oh, wait, someone took that already. *My Sister, the Serial Killer.* That title is, well, *killer.*

[182] The book is killer, too. Highly recommend.

"Sure." Harper smiles at me sympathetically. "Can I ask you something, though?"

"Yes."

"Why didn't you tell me about Connor?"

Oliver nods. "I have the same question."

I glance toward the door, but there's no escaping this.

"I was embarrassed."

"Why?" Harper says.

"Isn't it obvious? I was an idiot. I knew what Connor was and I wrote about him anyway. I kept him in my life."

"You were twenty-five."

"Is that an excuse?"

"It might be," Oliver says. "We've all done stupid things, especially when we were younger."

But I wasn't *that* young when I did the stupidest thing.

"How did you figure it out?" Harper says. "Did Connor tell you?"

"No, I put the clues together . . . and he played it all down when I confronted him. So a bunch of criminals went to jail, so what? So a bad man got killed by one of his associates . . . It all sounds so stupid now. But then, I don't know, I wanted to believe him."

"You were in love," Oliver says.

I try not to flinch. "I was in something. But I'm not even sure that was it . . . I . . . That's why I wrote the book, I think. To justify it to myself."

"And then he read it?"

"Before it came out. And he had all these demands, and the publishing house wanted me to cave and . . . I should've just shelved the book. If I'd done that, everything would be different."

"We wouldn't be here now," Oliver says.

Is that regret I hear in his voice or relief?

"I know. But Shek would be alive."

"You can't blame yourself for that."

"Why not? Inspector Tucci thinks I'm responsible."

Harper shakes her head. "But you're not, I know you're not."

"Thank you for saying that."

"I don't think you did it either, for the record," Oliver says.

"For the record, I appreciate it."

Our eyes lock across the table, the way they always seem to, and I can hear that rising music in my head. Maybe it's that Taylor Swift line about being saved by a perfect kiss, maybe not, but something, and it's just the two of us at the table, Harper receding outside of our bubble.

Then he looks away, and just as quickly the moment is gone.

And I'm back in a room with someone who wants to kill me, and it occurs to me that all of the evidence that Inspector Tucci referred to—the key, the device that killed Shek—means more than my guilt.

It means someone is trying to frame me for his murder.[183]

But who?

After dinner, which is delicious and filling in the best way, we go to our rooms.

There's no awkward silence in the elevator, just me, Harper, and Oliver playing over the day in our minds. We separate without discussion, and mindful of the fact that I'm not the killer, that Guy has a gun, and Shek is definitely dead, I double-lock my door and put a chair under the handle for good measure. I also stole a knife from the table, slipping it into my pocket, and while it's dull, it's better than nothing. I put it under my pillow, and since the police still have our phones, I take out my iPad and put on something I've watched before to try to lull myself to sleep.[184]

After thirty minutes of tossing and turning, I wish I'd asked Harper for a sleeping pill, but on second thought, being drugged seems like a bad idea in the circumstances.

---

[183] Maybe this occurred to you a while ago. If so, congratulations, you <u>may</u> be suited to become a mystery author.

[184] Okay, fine, it's *Bridgerton*, Season 2. Episode 4 is my favorite. If you know, you know.

If someone comes to kill me tonight, I want to have my wits about me.

But what I want most is sleep, which feels like it's going to be a permanent stranger, particularly given the noises coming from above.

Coming from Connor's room.[185] But mostly I hear Isabella.

They're going at it hot and heavy, and this is the last thing I need to be listening to. I stuff a pillow over my head, but that doesn't erase the squeaking bed and the grunts and moans that are all too familiar.

And okay, I confess. It still has an effect on me. Connor was a good lover. He had skills, ones I've tried hard to forget. But you can't tell your body what to react to.

It doesn't help that this might be my last night of freedom.

Do I want to spend it listening to someone else's raucous love life?

No, I do not.

I get up quickly and slip on my robe. I don't stop to check my hair or what I look like, because if I do, I'm going to stop myself altogether, and I don't want to do that. Instead, I pull the chair away from my door, unlock it, and walk into the hall. I close my door behind me carefully; I don't want to wake Harper, who's a light sleeper.

I pass her door silently and stop in front of Oliver's.

This is a terrible idea. I'm going to get rejected. He might not even hear my knock because he's a deep sleeper and rarely wakes to a noise. And isn't this the exact scenario I envisioned the other night?

And now I'm making it happen.

I am a glutton for punishment.

I knock sharply once, then wait a second and knock again.

It's an old signal that we had for each other—I don't even remember why we invented it. Something about when we were kids and you'd call a friend twice to get past parent screening? Or did I read that in a book once? I—

The door opens. Oliver's standing there in boxers and a T-shirt, his

---

[185] To let you know where we all are: Harper, Oliver, Allison, and I are on the same floor. Above us are Connor and Isabella, Guy, Emily, and Shek's empty room.

hair rumpled, his eyes tired, but he wasn't asleep. I know because when he wakes up, his eyes are half closed for at least ten min—

"El?"

"Yeah."

"Everything okay?"

"No," I say, then stop myself from saying anything more.

There have been too many words today.

Instead, I launch myself at Oliver like I'm Kate in the church after Anthony and Edwina's failed wedding,[186] and it happens just like that as my lips crash into Oliver's. There's a minute of hesitation on his part where I think he's going to push me away, and then his arms are around me pulling me closer, closer, closer, and he tugs me into his room and the door snaps shuts behind us, and any memories of Connor are erased in an instant because that's what Oliver does to me.

When we're together, there's nothing but us.

And it's scary. It's terrifying.

But I'm not going to let go this time.

I'm going to hold on with everything I've got.[187]

Hours later (ahem), we're tangled up together in Oliver's bed. My head is on his chest and I can feel his heart beating in time with mine. He's stroking my hair slowly, and we still haven't said anything.[188]

It's perfect, this moment, but everything perfect comes to an end.

I should know.

Sometimes it's easier to be the one to end it.

"Hi," I say, looking up at him.

"Hi," he says back, then kisses me. "That was . . . unexpected."

---

[186] Yes, I've watched Season 2 more times than I want to admit, okay? Sue me.

[187] Were you hoping for more details here? Little secret: Writing love scenes is hard and embarrassing.

[188] I mean, there were words exchanged during, but I'm not writing them down.

"Unexpectedly good?"

"What do you think?"

I smile at him, then expel a long breath. "I'm getting arrested in a couple of hours."

"No, you're not," Oliver says, sitting up a little. "I made a call after I got back to my room."

"A call?"

"To our publisher."

"Oh God."

"You should've done it."

"It didn't even occur to me."

He brushes his nose against mine. "I figured. Anyway, after she calmed down, Vicki said she was going to get you a lawyer. She sent me an email confirmation an hour later. They'll be here at eight A.M. And Tucci was lying to us."

"About what?"

"All of it. Police procedure, whether he needed a warrant. Nothing any of us said to him will be useful. The case will get thrown out."

"How can you be sure?"

"They're going to hire the best. They don't want their golden goose in jail for a crime she didn't commit. And Shek dying on their tour. None of this is good, and they want to clean it up quickly and quietly."

"I didn't even think of that. What if this gets into the press?"

"Shek's death definitely will, but no one's picked it up yet, thankfully. They're going to put out a statement tomorrow after we get the lay of the land from the lawyer."

"Really?"

"Yes."

"But what about . . . I mean, doesn't my contract have a morality clause? They could cancel me for all of this."

"They can't cancel you for being falsely accused of murder."

I'm not so sure about that, but I'm touched and relieved that he's made the effort. If I have to sacrifice a book deal to avoid time in an Italian jail, I'll make that bargain.

"Thank you, Oli."

"Of course."

"It doesn't solve the problem, though."

"Us?"

"For once, that's not what I meant."

"What, then?"

"Who killed Shek?"

He frowns. "I don't know."

"We have to figure it out before something else happens."

He pulls me closer. "I'm not going to let anything happen to you."

"I don't want anything to happen to anyone else either," I say as a shiver goes through me.

Shit, shit, *shit*.

Remember how I told you I was magic earlier? Not actual magic, but how sometimes I have these premonitions about things that are about to happen or words people are about to say?

I'm having one of those right now, only it's visual this time.

A flash of someone creeping along the hall with a gun in their hand.

And then, *bang!*

*Bang!*

It goes from premonition to reality before I have time to prepare myself.

# CHAPTER 24

## Things That Go Bump in the Night

"Those were gunshots!" I say, springing out of bed and searching frantically for my clothes. There isn't much to find—a T-shirt, my robe, underwear—but it's dark in here and I don't remember where they fell.

"Wait," Oliver says. "Eleanor, it's not safe."

I find my underwear and put it on, struggling on unsteady legs. "But it was on this floor! What if Harper is . . ." My throat closes and I can't get the words out. I sink to the ground.

He swings his legs around and picks up the bedside phone as I hear a door close with a thick *thud*. It sounds like it's next door, but it's hard to tell.

"I'm calling the front desk. They'll call the police."

"And what, we just wait?"

"We have to. Someone's wandering around with a gun. It's not time to play the hero."

"Call them. Please."

Oliver dials reception. "*Ciao. Questo è Oliver Forrest.* I'm in room 206. I just heard gunshots. *Sì, due. Per favore, chiami subito la polizia.*" He listens for a moment. "*Grazie. Sì.*"

He hangs up. "They said to stay in our room. They're calling the police."

I hug my knees to my chest. The carpeting is scratchy beneath me. "I can't just . . . I—"

I stop because there are footsteps in the hall, maybe on the stairs, and some above us, too. Heavy footfalls.

"Is that upstairs?" I ask.

"It's hard to tell. But it doesn't . . . I'm sure those shots woke everyone up."

"But then they'll come out of their rooms . . ."

Oliver steps off the bed and pulls me up next to him, then wraps his arms around me. "I know this sounds terrible, but there's nothing we can do. We have to wait. It's too dangerous."

I lean back against him, wanting him to be right. But every fiber in my body is telling me to move my feet and get out of this room.

I listen to the noises around me. Everything seems heightened, ominous. The footsteps up and down, a murmur of voices, and then—a *scream*. Again.

"It's Harper!"

I wrench myself away from Oliver and grab my robe off the floor, throwing it on as I open the door. She screams again, and it sounds like death to me, but I have to charge toward it anyway.

When I'm in the hall, I realize the screams are coming from *inside* my room. I fish in my bathrobe pocket for my key and fumble to open the door as quickly as I can. It takes two tries to scan the key right, but then the lights turn to green and I wrench open the door.

Harper's on the floor, in the threshold of the connecting door, a dim light illuminating her from behind. She's staring fixedly at my bed, which is just a dark shape in the half-light.

But as my eyes adjust, it looks like someone is lying there. A large lump covered by the comforter.

I feel sick. Is it possible that someone . . . Wait, no. It's just the way I left my pillows when I left the room to go to Oliver's.

I rush to Harper and wrap my arms around her. "I'm here. I'm okay."

"Eleanor?"

"Yes, I'm fine. It wasn't me." I hold her tearstained cheek to mine. Her lashes tickle my face.

"Someone . . . shot you."

"No, no, they didn't. I'm okay. I'm right here."

She pulls away, scanning my face. Her eyes are large and frightened. "I didn't see. I couldn't get the door open . . ."

"It's okay, Harper. It's okay. I'm here. No one's hurt."

The light snaps on. I look back over my shoulder. Oliver's surveying the room in his boxers, his hands on his hips. I follow his gaze back to my bed. There are two bullet holes in the covers, and a gun wrapped in a cloth on the floor.

Oh my God.

Someone was shooting at *me*.

I feel bile rise up my throat and I choke it down.

"What happened?" Allison says from behind Oliver. She's wearing the same green flowing robe she was wearing the other night, and I have a flash of that scene from *Murder on the Orient Express*—a bright robe with a dragon on it. But there's nothing on the back of Allison's robe and my mind is playing tricks on me.

"Someone tried to kill Eleanor," Oliver says.

"What?"

She looks from me and Harper to the obvious holes in my bed to the gun that's lying on the floor. She takes a step forward. "Is that—"

"Don't touch that," Oliver says. "It's evidence."

She takes a step closer anyway. "Is that Guy's gun?"

"I don't—"

"It must be," Guy says, arriving fully dressed—black pants, black T-shirt, like a villain. "Mine's missing."

"Missing?" Oliver says. "Since when?"

"I had it when I went to sleep," Guy says. "It was on the nightstand next to my bed."

"Can you tell if that's it?"

Guy walks into the room and stands over the gun. I turn my body away from Harper, still holding her close so I can watch him. My hands are shaking.

Guy crouches down, getting close to the gun. "It's mine. But Oliver ... It's got *your* handkerchief around it."

"What?"

Oliver walks to Guy with Allison right behind. They form a little triangle around the weapon, staring at it.

I haul Harper up to her feet. She's steadier now, and we walk together toward them.

They widen the circle so we can see, too. Guy's right. His gun is wrapped in a white handkerchief that has Oliver's initials on it.

And also a drop of blood.

The next thirty minutes are a blur.

Hotel security arrives and secures the room.

They usher us out and tell us that the police will be arriving shortly. Without discussion, Harper, Oliver, Guy, Allison, and I go downstairs to the library and are soon joined by Emily, who says she didn't hear the shots, but was awoken by the commotion.

It's after six now, the sun rising across the water, and someone is nice enough to bring us tea and some Italian pastries, and it all feels so civilized except for the riot in my brain.

If I hadn't gotten up and gone to Oliver's room, I'd be dead right now. Dead.

*Finito.*

I can't make any jokes about that.

Would I even know what had happened? Would I be watching all this unfold like some movie I couldn't reach through? Or would I be in some black oblivion, nothing, all that's left of me on a page somewhere?

I've never thought about death this much before, despite what I do for a living.

The people who die in my books aren't real. They're pieces of a puzzle I've invented. It always surprises me when fans speak to me as if they're alive.

But now that I'm in the middle of my own murder investigation, I wish I'd shown more compassion to the people I killed on the page. Because even if you're a liar and a bad person, dying before your time isn't something I'd wish on anyone.

"Did you want some tea, Eleanor?" Oliver asks me.

I blink against the light. It feels like I'm coming out of a fog, but it's still there, right in front of me.

"Yes, thank you."

Harper squeezes my hand, and I realize that we're back on our couch. The easel with our Allison accusations is still here, all the other squares blank, a series of missed opportunities.

Oliver hands me a cup of tea and I take a sip. It's full of sugar and cream, and the English know what they're about, thinking tea is the cure for everything, because a couple of sips and I do start to feel better.

All things considered.

"Well, we know one thing," Allison says sitting on the settee across from me. "Eleanor didn't kill Shek."

"She could've shot at her own bed," Emily says next to her.

"No," Oliver says, standing behind them. "She was in my room when the shots occurred."

I can feel everyone's eyes staring at me, but I'm not embarrassed. The only good thing to happen last night was me and Oliver.

"Yes. We were together."

Harper squeezes my hand again, a show of approval. "So that leaves you two out of it."

"How did they get your gun, Guy?" I ask. "I thought you always slept with one eye open?"

He shakes his head like he's trying to clear it. "I think I was drugged."

"Drugged? Come on. How many glasses of wine did you have at dinner?"

"Several, I admit. But this feels like more than that." He taps the side of his head. "It feels like a sleeping pill."

My eyes dart to Harper's and then away.

"How could you have taken a sleeping pill without knowing it?" Allison asks.

"Someone could've dosed me over dinner," Guy says. "We were all there in the dining room. Easy enough to intercept a glass going to my table. And if I recall, a few of you came to talk to us at various points. It would be the work of a moment."

"Okay, maybe," Oliver says. "But wouldn't you taste it when you drank it?"

"Depends on what they used. But I know when I've been drugged."

I'm going to leave that there.

No point in asking him about the *other* times he's been drugged.

"But how did they get into Eleanor's room?" Allison says. "Those doors lock automatically when you close them."

"The key," Harper says in a small voice. "The *master* key."

"You still have a master key?" I say.

Her hands flutter by her sides. "They gave it to me when we checked in."

"What do you mean?" Emily asks. "You have a key to everyone's room?"

"I always have one."

"Why?"

Harper shakes her head slowly. "I don't know . . . I never questioned it. The first tour we did, they gave me one because the master booking was in my name, and it seemed easier. With packing Eleanor's things and . . ." She looks at me with an apology in her eyes, and I'm not sure what she's excusing herself for. "Anyway, every time we go on tour, I have one."

"I get it for Eleanor's room, but why the rest of us?"

"I don't know."

Emily crosses her arms over her chest. She's in a cute romper, her hair in a messy ponytail. She looks younger and more vulnerable than I've seen her since we met. "You expect us to believe that someone just gave you a key to all of our rooms without your asking for it?"

This doesn't extend to her tone, obviously.

"What are you implying, Emily?" I ask.

"Seems pretty clear to me."

"Why don't you make it clear for the room?"

"That's how they got the gun. With the master room key."

Allison nods slowly. "And then that handkerchief around the gun. That's yours, right, Oliver? You gave one to me yesterday for the salve, but it didn't have that stain on it."

"What stain?" Harper asks.

"There was a bloodstain on . . . Oh! The ruins. When Harper tackled me . . . She cut her head and she used your handkerchief to wipe the blood."

"I took that back," Oliver says. "I put it in my laundry bag to clean when I got back to the States."

"Are you sure?"

His brow creases, and though I have a distinct memory of him taking the handkerchief back and putting it in his pocket, now I'm not sure either. "I can check."

"I'm sure the police will do that," Emily says.

"Where's the master room key now?" Allison asks Harper.

Harper pats herself down, like she might find it on her person. "It was in my purse . . ."

Guy holds up his hand and counts off on his fingers. "The room key, the gun, the handkerchief . . ."

"And she has sleeping pills," Emily says.

There are two bright spots of color on Harper's cheeks. "Yes, I have sleeping pills. But I didn't use them to drug anyone. I wasn't even sitting at Guy's table."

"You went to the bathroom, though, and stopped to talk to them," Emily says. "I saw you."

"Wh . . . I . . . I was just returning Isabella's lipstick. She left it in the bathroom."

"What is your problem, Emily?" I say. "Do you honestly think that Harper tried to kill me? Or killed Shek? Or tried to kill Connor?"

Emily shrugs. "Yeah, I *can* kind of believe all of that. She told me that she didn't want you to stop writing your books. That she was mad at you about it. And she inherits everything if you die."

"What about Shek?"

"Shek probably saw something he shouldn't and couldn't keep his big mouth shut," Guy says.

I follow their logic and then reject it. "If Harper wanted me dead, why do it on this tour? We live together. She has plenty of opportunity to do away with me."

"But then she'd be the prime suspect," Guy says. "Whereas here . . ."

"There are plenty of suspects to go around . . ." Allison says. "Isn't that what we've been proving with this?" She points to the easel.

"Okay, I'll give you that. But why would she try to frame me for Shek's death?"

"Someone tried to frame you for Shek's death?" Oliver says.

"That has to be what happened. That device that was used to kill Shek, it was in my backpack, and the other master key was in my purse, the one from Rome. I found it the other day. That's what made the police think I did it. But I didn't. Which means someone is trying to frame me. Why would Harper do that?"

Emily shrugs again. "I'm not saying I have it all worked out. But do I believe she's a viable suspect? Definitely. Means, motive, opportunity. She has all of it. And especially if you aren't going to write anymore, now's the time to strike. When's the next time that she might have this kind of chance?"

"Harper," Allison says, "aren't you going to defend yourself?"

Harper is completely still next to me.

But I know that doesn't mean anything. She's always taken a moment to process.

"See, she doesn't even deny it," Emily says. "And then there's the Connor stuff."

"What Connor stuff?" I say, dread building inside of me.

"Her and Connor."

"There is no her and Connor."

Emily tilts her head to the side. "Not anymore. That's the problem. He broke her heart when he ended their affair."

Wait, *what?*

"Harper, is that true?"

"Why would I make that up? Besides, Connor told me all about it when we hooked up at Books by the Banks. How he'd bedded both sisters." She looks around. "Come on. Remember at dinner a couple of nights ago when Allison asked if he'd slept with every woman at the table and he said yes?"

Ugh. I do remember that. I hadn't thought through what it meant because I didn't want to know.

I still don't.

"I thought you knew," Emily said.

"I hadn't made the connection," I say, but as I say it, I'm not even sure that's true.

I've been worried something was going on between them for a while, all the hints I tried to ignore. The way she was around him, the way he looked at her, those moments between them in the church in Rome. And then . . .

"That's why you let him read your pages," I say to Harper. "That's why you trusted him with your work? Why his opinion meant so much to you?"

She nods her head slowly, coming out of whatever haze she's been in. "I'm sorry."

"What are you apologizing for?"

"For trying to kill you, obviously."

"Shut up, Emily!"

"No! I didn't try to kill anyone. I didn't do that to Shek. I don't know who got Guy's gun or how, or when they got my master key, or any of it."

Emily scoffs, turning to me. "How can you trust her if she didn't even confide in you?"

"That's between us. And you're one to talk. If having your heart broken by Connor is a motive, you probably want to kill him, too. Or was it just some stupid one-night stand that didn't mean anything to you?"

"Shove it."

"That's the best you can come up with? 'Shove it'? No wonder you have to steal plots to get published."

Emily lifts her chin. "The *New York Times* called my book 'brilliant and satisfying with a twist you won't see coming.'"

"So you can't be a murderer if you get an endorsement from the *New York Times*?[189] Come on. I saw you cuddling up to Harper in Pompeii and then again in Capri. Was it all some trick to get her to confide in you? Maybe you were looking for dirt about me? Or maybe . . . You could've taken the room key then. And you also went to Guy's table last night, didn't you?"

I'm bluffing about this last part because I only had eyes for Oliver, but sometimes that's how you get through life.

You take a shot in the dark, and it hits the bull's-eye.

"So what?"

"So, *you* could've spiked Guy's drink. Assuming it was spiked."

---

[189] There's at least one *NYT* bestseller who was a convicted murderer: Anne Perry. She's who that movie *Heavenly Creatures* is based on. I met her once. She was nice, but I couldn't get the fact that she'd killed someone out of my head.

"What does *that* mean?"

I glance at Guy. "We don't have tox results. We only have your word for it. Inspector Tucci was right, we need to stop speculating and go with the facts."

"I grant you that I've thought about killing Connor over the years, but what possible reason could I have for killing you?"

"Cover."

"Please. I'm not a sociopath. And if I did it, no one would even know he was dead. He'd just disappear."

"Sounds like a confession."

"Speaking of disappearing," Oliver says, "where's Connor?"

Oh, shit.

*Connor.*

Somehow in all of this, I forgot about him.

We all did.

I stand. "What if the shots in my room were just a diversion? Something to keep us looking away from Connor long enough for someone to do away with him?"

"You may have a point."

"We should check on him."

I nod to Oliver and we make for the door.

Out in the lobby, the staff are rushing around and the phones are ringing. We're not the only guests in this hotel, and others have been disturbed by our drama. There's a heavyset American man with a deep Southern accent demanding a refund from a harried-looking woman behind the check-in counter.

"What do we do if Connor's dead?" I say to Oliver.

"It'll be okay."

"But they might think we planned it together..."

He puts his hand on my arm. "Don't worry about that now. Come on, let's take the stairs."

We walk toward the grand staircase that winds down into the lobby.

And there he is, walking down the stairs arm in arm with Isabella, looking refreshed.

"What's all the commotion?" Connor asks. "Why are you dressed like that?"

"You didn't hear? It didn't wake you?"

"I had a wonderful sleep courtesy of Mr. Ambien." He looks around. "Has something happened?"

"Harper tried to kill Eleanor," Guy says behind me. "Welcome to breakfast."

# CHAPTER 25

## Too Many Suspects

Connor and Isabella follow us back to the library after Guy's announcement. It feels like the quieter place to be with all the commotion in the lobby, and Connor uses his charm on one of the waitresses to get her to bring in a more substantial breakfast. Over eggs and toast, Oliver catches Connor and Isabella up on what's happened this morning, while the rest of us listen like we're children in grade school who've been told that if one of us steps out of line, then we're all going to be punished.

Connor takes it in, then turns his gaze to Harper, who's sitting next to me with her hands in her lap.

"It's you?"

"No."

I rub her back, encouraging her.

"I didn't try to kill Eleanor and I didn't try to kill you."

"What evidence do you have for that?"

"I wouldn't have any idea of how to mess with your car, for one."

Connor nods slowly. "But you did have a key to my house."

"I gave that back!"

"You could've easily had a copy made."

My stomach twists. Harper had a key to his house? This was way more serious than I imagined. How long were they involved? And why, why, why didn't she tell me?

But I know the answer to that question. She was ashamed. She thought I'd judge her. Maybe she was even doing it to get back at me subconsciously.

And let's be honest, if she'd told me she was dating Connor, I would've used every trick in my toolbox to break them up.

Harper knows me. So she didn't tell me because she didn't want me to interfere.

She wanted to make that mistake on her own.

"Harper's not a liar. Or a murderer," I say.

Harper leans forward. "I can prove that I didn't do it."

"How?"

"I wasn't at the Vatican when you were pushed. I was with Eleanor the whole day."

"Oh," I say. "That's right. We were together. She couldn't have pushed you."

"And the witness who died the next day? Davide. I was with Eleanor that whole day, too."

Connor sips at his tea slowly. "You could be each other's alibi."

"So now we're in on it together?" I say. "Come on."

He gives me a cold stare. "She does everything else for you. Packs your bags, organizes your life, unsubscribes you from newsletters."

Oh my God, the ego on this man.

"Neither of us tried to murder you, Connor. And what are you saying? Either Harper tried to kill me or we were working together to kill you. You can't have it both ways."

"Right," Oliver says. "And what about Shek? How does *he* fit into all of this?"

"And what's the motive?" I say. "Is it your financial shenanigans, or is it because you're just a disgusting jerk who treats other people's hearts like toys?" I point to Isabella. "You should get out while you can, Isabella. Honestly, I can't believe you're still here."

She doesn't answer me, just gives a shrug with her shoulders while a small smile plays at her mouth.

It occurs to me that she might be enjoying herself. Like she's in a murder mystery come to life. A choose-your-own-adventure where you're a bystander.

But bystanders can catch stray bullets.

"The problem," Allison says, "is there are too many suspects. Everyone on this trip has a motive to kill Connor."

"And Eleanor," he says petulantly, but I don't think anyone agrees with him.

At least, I hope not.

"It's a good point," Oliver says. "Something we haven't thought of before."

"What's that?"

"Who put this tour together? The publisher, I know, but it had to be more specific than that. Who gave them the idea to put all of us on this tour? How did this many people with a reason to kill Connor end up together?"

"That's probably easier than you think."

"Hey!"

"Fine, fine."

"Harper, do you know?" Allison says.

"It wasn't me, if that's what you're asking. Someone in publicity approached me about it. Her name is Marta. She's pretty new. She pitched it to me about six months ago, and mentioned Connor and Allison and Guy, of course, because of the—"

"Vacation Mysteries Extended Universe," I complete.

"Okay, those were obvious choices. But how did Oliver get here? Or Shek? And Emily . . ."

We all look at one another.

"What?" Emily says. "I don't have that kind of pull. I just go where they tell me."

"Who knew about you and Connor?" I ask.

"There were some TikToks," Harper says.

"Excuse me?"

"One of those fan pages . . . You know the one who's always making these relationship-theory videos?"

"What are you talking about?"

Harper rolls her eyes. "I've shown them to you . . . Anyway, there are a couple dozen BookTokers who're obsessed with Connor, and Emily is big on there, too. One of them got some photos of them together and made this whole thing. Here, I'll show you." She reaches into her pocket, then stops. "Oh, I don't have my phone."

"The police still have them," Guy says. "It's rather annoying."

"Hopefully we'll get them back today," I say. "But did you know about this, Emily?"

"There's a lot of stuff on TikTok about me and my book. I can't keep up with all of it."

"What about you, Oliver? How did you end up on the tour?"

"Marta asked me to do it."

"Hmmm . . . Who's Marta again?"

"She's been in the publicity department for about a year, I think?" Harper says. "You met her. When we were in New York last year?"

I think back. New York was a blur of events and signings and TV appearances around the release of my last novel. There was a new woman in publicity who shepherded us through all of it, but I can't put a face on her.

"You should email her and ask," I say to Harper.

"I've been trying to get in touch with her for the last couple of days, actually . . ."

"Why don't you call Vicki when you get your phone back and find out why Marta hasn't been returning your messages?"

"You don't think she's involved in it, do you?"

"I have no idea . . . Connor, do you know her? Did you sleep with her?"

His chin rises. "I met her just like you did last year, and no, I don't sleep with every woman I meet."

"You sure about that?" My eyes flit to Isabella, but she's unconcerned. Must be nice to have that kind of confidence.

"It's *your* tour, Eleanor, not mine."

"What's that supposed to mean?"

"The only certainty was that *you'd* be on it. So maybe we've been looking in the wrong place. Maybe it doesn't have anything to do with me, and I'm the smokescreen to get to *you.*"

"You know," Allison says, "Shek's the only one who's dead. Maybe he was the intended victim."

We all turn and stare at her.

"You mean *we're* the smokescreen?" I say. "But what about the shots at me this morning? That wasn't an accident."

"Hmmm," Allison says, something occurring to her. "Maybe—"

"Maybe you should have listened to me," Inspector Tucci says, striding into the room, "and left all this to the professionals."

Inspector Tucci is, how do you say, *not pleased.*[190]

Not pleased at all.

He'd warned us and what happened? Exactly what he said would happen.

I'm lucky to be alive.

Oliver points out that he was coming here to arrest me, and Inspector Tucci gets a sour look on his face and divides us up into individual interviews with the flotilla of police officers who've arrived with him.

---

[190] There were several sharp, fast words that he issued in Italian, but they went by too fast for me to figure out what they were. Swear words, I assume, which, like in French, are mostly religion-based.

Mine takes place in the same room as yesterday, with the lawyer Oliver arranged for me. I was allowed to get dressed before the questioning, under police escort with my lawyer in the room. Lorenzo Scaperelli is in his mid-thirties and is wearing a light linen suit. He has a firm handshake, dark hair and eyes, and an assured manner about him.

I can talk to the police or not, as is my wish, he says, but there isn't going to be any arrest warrant issued. Scaperelli has already spoken to the magistrate, an "old friend," and explained the issues to him. Inspector Tucci is on thin ice—he should've recused himself, just like Connor suggested—and no one is going to take just his word for it that a world-famous author is gadding about Italy killing people.

I tell Inspector Tucci about last night, that I was with Oliver when the shots rang out. I describe my room to him when I made it there: Harper on the floor in the doorway to her adjoining room, the bullet holes in the bed, the handkerchief wrapped around the gun.

"Did you notice anything else out of place?" Inspector Tucci asks, scratching notes in his notebook. He's dressed like he was yesterday, in a rumpled suit that's seen better days, his hair needing one more turn with the brush.

"No, I . . . I was upset, obviously."

He puts his pencil down and scans my face. "Had you planned to go to Mr. Forrest's room?"

"It was a spontaneous decision."

"Did you tell your sister beforehand?"

"No, like I said. It was the middle of the night. I couldn't sleep because . . ."

"Yes?"

I can feel myself blushing. "I could hear Connor above me with Isabella . . . They were . . ."

"Having relations?"

"Yes."

"What time was this?"

"Around midnight? It, um, went on for a while."

"So you went to Mr. Forrest's room at midnight?"

I glance at Lorenzo, who's sitting next to me. He told me I had two choices: I could refuse to talk at all, or answer everything that was asked of me truthfully. There was no in-between. Since I didn't try to shoot myself, it was probably easiest to speak to Tucci and get it over with, as a refusal could raise suspicions. He'd be minimal in his interference, he told me, and only interject to clarify questions that were unclear or invasive for no reason.

This question is kosher. He nods to me to answer.

"Something like that," I say. "Maybe a bit later. I wasn't paying a lot of attention to the time."

"And then you were with Mr. Forrest the whole time?"

I look at my hands as flashes of last night come back to me. "Yes, um, yes."

"Neither of you left the room at any point?"

"No, I . . . I fell asleep for a bit, and then we, uh, were intimate again."

"Could Mr. Forrest have left while you were sleeping?"

"I don't think so. I'm a light sleeper."

He purses his lips and makes a note. "Did you hear anything before the shots? Anyone walking around?"

"No."

"But you were awake when the shots happened?"

Postcoital but awake. Oliver had woken me with a trail of kisses up my abdomen and we'd had a second go-around. It was quiet and intense and . . . Ahem. That's enough of that.

"Yes. We heard two shots."

"What time was it?"

"Before six. It was starting to get light out."

"And then what?"

"I wanted to go and check what was going on, but Oliver thought it was too dangerous."

"He held you back?"

"Yes."

Inspector Tucci nods his head slowly, and I hate that the look in his eye puts thoughts in my head.

Thoughts like: Was Oliver really worried about something happening, or was he holding me back for some other reason?

But no, that's ridiculous. Oliver wasn't behind any of this, even though Allison was right.

There are too many suspects.

"How long did you wait to go out of the room?"

"A couple of minutes? When Harper started screaming . . . Maybe five minutes?"

"And did you hear anything while you were waiting?"

"Yes, there were footsteps on the stairs and above . . . People moving around who'd heard the shots, I assumed."

"Anything more distinct than that?"

"No, I . . ."

"Yes?"

"I might've heard a door opening and closing?"

"From which direction?"

"I can't remember."

"Your room?"

"It's possible. The person would've had to have gotten out that way."

"If they left."

If they . . . Oh, no, he means Harper. Harper didn't leave.

"Harper didn't do it."

"We shall see. Anything else?" He flips a page in his notebook so that it's blank. "This is the second floor. Your room was at the end of the hall here. And then Harper was next to you, then Mr. Forrest, and then Ms. Smith, yes?"

He writes our name and room numbers on the paper.

*201—Eleanor / 202—Harper / 203—Oliver / 204—Allison*

"Your party was the only one in this section of the hotel."

"So any noise I heard was from one of us?"

"Most likely. Though it is possible that someone could have taken the elevator down from the third floor." He taps the paper. "This is where the elevator is. Did you hear the elevator doors open or close?"

"No, I . . ." I think back. Those doors make a distinct sound opening, and there's a bell that dings. "No. I would have heard if they did."

"All right. And here, next to your room, there is a set of fire stairs."

"An emergency exit, you mean?"

"Yes, that is right."

He marks the spots on the page.

*Fire Exit / 201—Eleanor / 202—Harper / 203—Oliver / 204—Allison / Elevator*

"Where does the fire exit go?" I ask.

"Up to the next floor, and also down to the lobby."

"So it could've been someone on the third floor who came down that way?"

"Yes."

"Connor's up there with Guy and Emily."

"Correct."

"But it could've been someone on my floor, too, or someone else entirely. Someone who came up from the lobby."

"Yes."

"What about . . . Have you spoken to the BookFace Ladies?"

"Who are you referring to?"

"The other women on the tour. The fans. There is one, her name is

Cathy, and she's a bit obsessed with me . . . I got a court order against her in the States."

"Why is this the first time I am hearing about this?"

"Because she seemed too remote . . . They have mostly kept to themselves. They were on a different boat yesterday, for instance, and they're not staying at this hotel."

"But we have just established that someone could have come in from the outside."

"Yes, but how would she know about Guy's gun? And she must've been with the other women when the mugging happened. And she wasn't on the boat."

"If the poison was administered on the boat."

"Do you know when it was administered?"

"The toxicologist has not made that assessment yet. But the poison is not one that acts immediately. There can be a delay depending on various factors."

"Such as?"

"That is not something I can share at this moment."

"Oh, right, but . . ." I let my thought trail away. Why am I trying to convince Inspector Tucci that it can't have been Crazy Cathy?

I mean, it probably isn't her, but it can't hurt to let her get investigated. Let her see how it feels to have your life under someone else's microscope.

"Harper can tell you where they're staying."

"Excellent. Now, did you hear someone walk by your door?"

"Mr. Forrest's door," Lorenzo says.

"Yes, that is what I meant."

"I'm not sure," I say. "I was frightened, and Oliver was trying to soothe me."

Or distract me?

No. Stop it, brain.

Stop it immediately.

"Or the fire door opening and closing?"

I search my memory. There was a *click*. I thought it was a room door, but it could've been the emergency exit.

"Maybe. But what if I'd come out of the room immediately?"

"But you were supposed to be dead."

"I see what you mean. But what if Harper had come through the adjoining door? Or if Oliver or Allison had come out of their rooms?"

"They took a risk."

I think it through. "Maybe it wasn't so risky . . ."

"How so?"

"Harper had been taking sleeping pills because of her jet lag. Connor also took a pill, he said. And Guy thinks he was drugged . . ."

"What's this?"

I explain about Guy saying that someone had spiked his drink last night.

"Hmmm, what about the others?"

"I don't know, you'll have to ask them."

"Perhaps you should take samples from everyone?" Lorenzo suggests. "For testing?"

"Yes, yes." Inspector Tucci taps the notepad. "It would've been the work of a moment . . . The shots, leaving the room and going through the door. If you moved swiftly, no one was going to see."

"And maybe they wore a disguise," I say. "Something to make it harder to recognize them."

"Yes, that is possible. We will search the rooms again."

I look at the layout, imagining the people above. "It could've been anyone."

"Not anyone," he says. "Not you or Mr. Forrest, as you have said."

"No," I say. "Not us."

"And we will speak to the BookFace Ladies, but it is likely not some-one from the outside. The gun, the handkerchief—this was, how you say, an inside job."

I shiver. "Yes."

"Your sister?"

"No, it can't be her."

"Why are you so certain?"

"Besides the fact that I'd know if she wanted to kill me?"

His mouth presses together. "No, Ms. Dash. It is precisely this kind of arrogance that leads to people losing their lives. You do not know what someone else might harbor in their heart. The resentments that build up over time. The injuries from the past that can come back to haunt you."

Why does it sound like he's describing me and Oliver?

No, no, *no*. This is just another form of self-sabotage.

Yes, he knows about cars, and yes, he hates Connor. And okay, yes, he was standing close enough to me on the veranda to save me, which means he could've pushed me, and he knows about poisons because he does the research, but he didn't come on this tour to kill me.

He came *for* me.

He came for *us*.

"Ms. Dash?"

"You were saying about Harper . . . But we live together. I see her all the time. I would know if she wanted to harm me. She's not an actress. She can't hide her emotions like that. And she was there with me outside the Vatican. We're each other's alibis for that attempt. And when that man was killed. Harper and I were together all day that day until after dinner."

"Hmmm."

But I have no idea where Oliver was on the day we went to the Vatican, or during the time between the Forum and dinner. I've never even asked him.

I shake my suspicions away. "You don't believe me?"

"I think there's something at work here that neither of us are seeing at the moment."

He lets that sit there, maybe trying to provoke a reaction, but I won't let him see the doubts in my mind.

I can't.

"One thing *is* clear, though, Inspector Tucci," Lorenzo says. "You will not be arresting my client."

"Yes, yes, you have made that point very clear."

"Are we finished, then?" I ask.

"For the moment. But you must stay in Sorrento."

"What about the rest of the tour?"

"When are you supposed to depart?"

That damn itinerary. I've never been able to keep the details fixed in my mind.

"What's the date?"

"July sixth."

"I'm not sure. I think we're here today."

"All right. Let us return to the library."

"Can I get my phone back?"

"Officer Garza has them there."

I'm taken to the bathroom to provide a urine sample, and then I follow Inspector Tucci through the lobby to the library, where everyone is reassembled and clothed, clutching their just-returned phones like missing limbs.

My eyes go to Oliver. He gives me a smile, one I know well. He's happy to see me, but worried, too.

This is not the smile of a murderer.

It can't be.

Officer Garza hands me my phone, and I hold it to my chest, glad to have it back. I tuck it in my pocket. I'll check my messages later. It's not like there are any emergencies in publishing.[191]

Inspector Tucci claps his hands to get our attention. "Good morning,

---

[191] I mean, there shouldn't be. Despite my sometimes flighty nature, I'm a stickler for deadlines. I've never missed one. But that doesn't mean the schedule doesn't get screwed up in other ways. More than once, I've been given copyedits to review over Christmas, and—but what am I saying? We should get back to the story.

everyone. Here we are again. As you can see, I have not issued an arrest warrant. Yet. But that does not mean that this is not a very serious situation. The most serious, in fact. You did not listen to me, and Ms. Dash almost lost her life last night."

No one says anything.

"It is very important if anyone knows anything of value that they tell me immediately. Do not hold back anything." He looks at each of us slowly. "If any of you saw something in the hall that night, for example . . ."

I follow his gaze as he looks at Harper, Oliver, then Allison in turn.

Is it just my imagination, or do they all look discomfited?

But no. That's just my overactive brain. I may not have a poker face, but that doesn't mean everyone wears their heart on their sleeve.

Besides, if one of them saw anything, they'd say so, wouldn't they?[192]

He looks at Officer Garza. "Has everyone provided a sample?"

"*Sì*. They are being taken to the lab immediately."

Inspector Tucci nods as Allison puts up her hand.

"Yes, Ms. Smith?"

"Couldn't that have been planned all along? Eleanor's almost-death."

"What are you saying?"

"It's not necessarily our fault that this happened . . . If the plan was always to kill Eleanor, it's not because we were investigating that it happened."

"Be that as it may, I have told you before that investigating a murder is dangerous, and you did not listen to me."

"What are we supposed to do, then?" Guy says. "Just sit around and wait like sitting ducks?"

"I do not understand this expression. Regardless, we will be opening an investigation into how you got a gun into the country."

---

[192] Nope, as it turns out. Though I never did figure out why.

"I have all the necessary permits, I assure you."[193]

"We shall see. In the meantime, it was your recklessness in hiding the weapon in the first place that gave the killer the opportunity to use it."

"My personal safety comes first."

"That is so selfish, Guy," Emily says.

"Keep your opinions to yourself."

"Guy has a point, though," Allison says. "Not about the gun, but what are we supposed to do now?"

Sylvie enters the room in swirl of fabric. "Ah, here you all are."

"Oh," Harper says. "The tour."

"What tour?" I ask.

"We're supposed to go to Ravello today. The BookFace Ladies will be there, too."

"Oh good Lord," Connor says. "Surely not."

"Why not?" Allison says. "It would give us something to do rather than sit around theorizing all day wondering which one of us is going next."

"What do you think, Inspector?" I ask. "Are we allowed to leave the hotel?"

He taps his chin, considering. "You would be all together, under supervision . . ."

"So, that's a yes?"

"Perhaps . . . You are only going to Ravello?"

"Sì," Sylvie says. "We have a wine tasting at Wine and Drugs—"

"Wine and what?"

"It is a wine and drug store . . ." Sylvie says.

"The wonders of Italy," Emily says.

"And then lunch in the square."

---

[193] Doubtful, as it turns out. Italy apparently has some of the most restrictive gun laws in Europe. And Guy doesn't strike me as someone who keeps up with paperwork.

"When will you be back at the hotel?" Inspector Tucci asks.

"Five o'clock?"

"All right, yes, you may go."

"I'm out," Connor says.

"No," Inspector Tucci says. "You must all go together. I will send Officer Garza with you. I cannot spare more than one."

"All for one and one for all," Isabella says.

"What's that?"

"Nothing," I say. "We will all go, Inspector."

"We shall have some more answers when you return. The toxicology results, for one."

"Perfect. All of us on a bus, hanging out in a cliffside town in a wine and drug store . . . What could go wrong?"[194]

---

[194] I mean, everything, right? It's <u>one of those books</u>.

## Checking In . . .

Hey, fam!

How's the solution coming?

You figure it out yet?

It's time to get cracking because we're heading into the final reveal here. So, what do you think?

Was it Harper? Sick of Connor and me, and looking for a life of leisure in our Venice Beach house, and enjoying the fruits of my labor?

Was it Allison? For pretty much the same reasons?

What about Oliver? He's hated both of us at some point, Connor especially, but does that amount to murder?

Guy? I bet you have no problem seeing him doing something evil. And you don't know that much about him. There are all kinds of things that I haven't told you about him. That's *suspicious*.

Emily? She had an affair with Connor, and she stole the plot of at least two of my books, so she's sus for sure. But why would she need either of us out of the way? She doesn't need to kill me to steal my book plots. Did Connor break her heart? She did say something way back at the beginning about not letting what had happened to Shek happen to her. Her career isn't going to just slip away, she'd said with a determination that was a bit scary, now that I look back on it.

Do people kill for book sales?

Maybe on TikTok.

Isabella? I can't even think of a motive for her, so that's probably her out.

One of the BookFace Ladies?

Crazy Cathy?

They weren't around at key moments, but it can't be a coincidence that my stalker is on this tour, right?

And what about that girl in publicity, Marta? She put this tour together and now we can't reach her. Is that suspicious or just . . . *publishing*?

Then there's Inspector Tucci. He's a late entry onto the list. Normally you have to meet all the suspects in the first act, or it's not considered fair to the reader. And I might be a liar, but I do believe in being fair. But he *was* mentioned in the first ten chapters, so I'm technically in the clear. What's his motive, though? He probably hates me and Connor for showing him up all those years ago, but enough to put all of this together? Was he in on the Giuseppe murder/robberies somehow? In on it with Connor and then double-crossed? It's never occurred to me before, but anything is possible. Because something *is* going on with that dude.

Either he's totally incompetent or he's in on it somehow.

Maybe they all are.[195]

I wish I didn't have to include Harper or Oliver in this list, though. It breaks my heart to think either of them might be involved. And by "either of them," I mean Oliver. I know Harper didn't do it, but I can't quite get there with Oliver. And the thought that he might've been playing me this whole time in order to distract me long enough to kill me is tearing my heart in two. Even thinking he might've done it feels like a betrayal.

So I'm trying to push the thought of Oliver aside, but I'm not saying *you* need to do that.

He's a viable suspect.

---

[195] Okay, no, because that would be *me* stealing someone else's plot, and I'm not about that.

They all are.

That's the point, right? Too many suspects. Too many motives.

Just don't judge, okay?

Maybe this many people want to kill you, too.

Honestly? If he weren't dead, I'd think Shek was behind it. Shek was the kind of guy who thought in extremes. And you can't get much more extreme than murder. He was also on the brink of losing everything—his livelihood, his pride—and desperate people do desperate things. He thought that was my fault, and part of it definitely was Connor's fault. It all lines up so nicely. Him being in Los Angeles, near the Vatican, all of it.

But Shek is dead,[196] and maybe even the target of all of this. We should examine that possibility more closely. I mean, *you* should.

And then there's me. I should be on your suspect list, too. After all, I've told you I'm a liar—that makes me an unreliable narrator. Maybe this is my version of *The Murder of Roger Ackroyd*.[197]

Did you know that Agatha Christie was super annoyed that people thought that book wasn't fair? She complains about it in her autobiography. All the letters she got, the criticism. If Agatha were alive today, she'd be duking it out with one-star reviewers on Goodreads, I just know it.

Anyway, you should consider everyone, is all I'm saying.

Because maybe I've been looking in the wrong place all along.

But not you, right? You've figured this out?

No?

Either way, pour a drink—a spritz, obvi—and read on. The solution's coming soon.

And as the song goes, there's one last call for alcohol.

---

[196] No, Shek didn't fake his death. That would also be stealing someone else's plot.

[197] If you haven't read it, SPOILER ALERT: The narrator is the killer.

# CHAPTER 26

## Am I About to Get Murdered on a Minibus?

**Ravello**

The only person who talks on the minibus to Ravello is Sylvie.

She's a nonstop fount of half information, chattering out chipper facts about the beautiful towns that dot the coast. Amalfi (my least favorite), Positano (colorful and expensive), and finally, at the top of a cliff, Ravello.

"And now we come to Ravello," she says, talking through a small microphone that looks like a CB radio from the seat next to the driver.

We're all buckled in tight because of the twisty road, but she seems unconcerned, half out of her seat and facing us.

Oliver's in the first row behind the driver with Allison; then it's me and Harper, then Guy and Emily, and Connor and Isabella way in the back.

"Ravello is a resort town set three hundred and sixty-five meters above the Tyrrhenian Sea by the Amalfi Coast and is home to iconic cliffside gardens. The thirteenth-century Moorish-style Villa Rufolo offers far-reaching views from its terraced gardens and hosts indoor and outdoor concerts during the popular summertime Ravello Festival. Villa Cimbrone, a medieval-style estate perched on a steep outcrop, is surrounded by another celebrated garden."[198]

---

[198] Google search result for "Ravello Italy."

"Oh my God," Harper says, nudging my elbow. "She's just reading off the internet now."

She puts her phone screen in front of me. Sylvie's directly quoted from Google without changing a word of the phrasing.[199]

"An impressive feat of memory," I say. "Or she's got her phone in her lap."

"It's weird."

"This whole trip is weird."

Harper pulls a face. "Understatement."

"I know." I put my arm around her shoulder. She feels hot despite the air blowing full blast in the car. "We're okay, right?"

She squeezes me back. "Of course we are."

"Everyone wants me to believe you tried to kill me."

"Everyone wants *me* to believe you faked your own almost-death to frame me."

"What? Who said that?"

"Emily."

I turn my head to steal a glance at her. She's gazing out the window, not paying attention to Sylvie. I mean, no one is, really. What's the point? We can google on our own.

"Ignore her," I say.

"Yeah."

"I'm sorry she betrayed your confidence like that."

"Whatever."

I tap Harper on the chin for emphasis. "No, not 'whatever.' I'm sure that's not how you wanted me to find out about you and ... Connor, for one."

She dips her head way. "Are you mad?"

"No, of course not."

"I don't believe you."

---

[199] So we're clear: I'm not plagiarizing. I cited my source twice.

"I'm more . . . concerned?"

"It was stupid."

I smile at her. "I made the same mistake."

"I thought he was going to be different . . . I know this sounds weird, but we were friends. That's why I let him read my stuff. And then . . ."

"You were feeling vulnerable."

"Yeah."

*How did I not know this,* I want to ask, but there'll be time enough eventually for me to learn all the gory details if I want them.

Ugh, no.

"When did you become friends?"

Harper sighs. "You were busy writing, and LA can be lonely sometimes. So many of the people we grew up with are . . ."

"Different?"

"Married. Or in the business like Emma or . . . I just don't have a lot in common with them."

"And Connor? You have things in common with him?"

"We're both in your orbit, so yeah. We can relate."

Famous adjacent, she means. I know the feeling. I have friends in the business, like my best friend, Emma,[200] and when I'm around her, especially in public, it can be weird. I only get recognized when I'm at an event for one of my books, and usually not even then. But Emma is different. People know who she is and have no compunction about coming up to her in any circumstance, including the bathroom, to tell her how much they love her or get an autograph. People are weird.

I know what it's like to be around someone who sucks all of the oxygen out of the room, is all I'm saying.

"I want better for you than him."

---

[200] No, it's not weird that I'm mentioning her for the first time here. I don't like to name-drop. And I <u>did</u> mention her earlier—you just forgot. Anyway, you'll meet her in the next book.

"Me too."

"So, we really are okay?"

She leans her head against mine and says, "Pineapple."

It's not a rebuke this time; it's a reprieve. So I don't ask her anything more. Instead, I change the subject.

"What do you think she's going to tell us next?" I nod toward Sylvie.

"No idea."

Harper's phone buzzes in my hand.

It's a news alert: "Bestselling author Abishek Botha dies on a yacht in Capri. Death being investigated as possible homicide."

Ah, *hell*.

I'm about to show it to Harper when everyone's phones start to buzz, like plops of rain hitting a metal roof.

That's death, nowadays. It doesn't happen until there's a breaking news alert.

"A yacht?" Connor says from the back. "It was basically a fishing boat."

"Is that really what's important?" I say.

"I need to check TikTok," Emily says. "Does anyone have reception? I can't get it to load."

"I can't imagine anyone on TikTok cares about Shek dying," Allison says.

"I could totally make one of his books blow up right now, though," Emily says. "Oh, that's better." She raises her phone above her face and puts on a fake smile. "POV, I'm here in a minibus in Italy and I just got the news about . . ."

Oliver knocks the phone out of her hand.

"Hey, what are you doing?" Emily says as she retrieves it from the floor.

"We don't need to commodify Shek's death."

"I was *helping* him!"

"There's no him to help anymore."

She scowls as she brushes her phone off. "His estate, whatever."

"Just delete it, Emily," Harper says.

"Fine." She presses a button and puts her phone away. "But what are you saying? No socials?"

"I think that's a good idea for the moment," I say. "We don't want to give Inspector Tucci any reason to take our phones away again."

Emily looks horrified. "I missed two book clubs' Zooms last night, you know."

"You were zooming into book clubs on this tour?"

"What of it?"

I roll my eyes. Not that I thought she was a suspect, but this kind of puts paid to that. Who has the presence of mind to book club and murder at the same time?

Not me, that's for sure.

"Is everyone agreed?" I say, turning in my seat to make eye contact with Connor, Isabella, Guy, and Allison. They nod one by one. "No point in feeding the frenzy. Hopefully, no one knows we were traveling with him yet."

"Easy enough to find out," Isabella says.

"I know, but let's get through the tour today, and then we can decide how to handle it."

"What about the BookFace Ladies?" Harper says. "They're going to know."

"Can you round them up when we get to Ravello and let them know not to say anything? That we won't be taking questions about it? Make sure to tell Cathy specifically. She's always narrating everything on social."

"Okay, good idea."

I scrunch up my face. "Sorry to send you on that kind of errand."

"She's used to it."

"Shut up, Connor!" we both say together.

"And now, here we are in Ravello," Sylvie says as the bus stops on the side of the road. There's half a parking lot and a set of stone steps carved into the rock. The sun is high in the sky and the air is thick with heat like a blanket you can't shrug off. I'm already dreaming of an Aperol spritz or at the very least a Coke Zero.[201]

"This is it?" Connor says.

"No, it is up the stairs. A little journey, but it is worth it."

"Where are the BookFace Ladies?" I ask Harper, shading my eyes with my sunglasses and wishing, once again, for a hat.

"Up there." She points. "In the town square, I think."

"You sure you're okay to do this alone? Inspector Tucci did tell us to stay together."

"Yeah, it's fine. Don't worry. I'll back in a few minutes."

"Meet us at Wine and Drugs," Sylvie says. "It is at the top of the stairs."

"I'm sure I'll need both by then."

She leaves, and Oliver replaces her at my side. I've been keeping my distance since Inspector Tucci stirred up my suspicions during my interrogation. He's given me a couple looks, but I'm hoping he thinks that I'm feeling shy or confused after last night.

Which I am.

I mean, you would be, too, if you half thought you'd slept with someone who was trying to kill you and they'd made you orgasm twice.

"Wine or drugs?" he says with a glint in his eye.

"I should probably stay away from both."

"Given what's happened I tend to agree with you." He reaches out his hand, and I take it, my doubts melting away. A man who looks at me like a snack he can't wait to have can't be plotting to kill me, can he?

Then again, isn't an orgasm also called a *little death*?

Sometimes I hate my brain.

"Ready for the climb?"

---

[201] Wait, have we talked about this yet? No, I don't think so. You can't get a Diet Coke anywhere in Italy, just Coke Zero. It's a poor substitute, and I feel like it's eroding the enamel on my teeth. Can someone tell me what Italians have against Diet Coke?

"The Miley song?"

"What?"

"Never mind."

We head for the stairs. They're steep and twisty, and I'm sweating and out of breath by the time we get to the top of them. I definitely need to get back to my morning swims and throw in a run or two for good measure.

At the top, I turn and look out at the view, which is breathtaking. Unlike in the other towns we passed through, there are a lot of trees in Ravello, and the shade makes a huge difference in the temperature. The water is blue and calm, the sky is clear, and even the tourists seem less frazzled than they did in the hustle of Amalfi.

If someone weren't trying to kill me, I'd say that this was the prettiest spot in all of Italy.

"Here we are, right this way." Sylvie motions to a small shop whose black door is cut into the stone. The sign, WINE AND DRUGS, swings above it. "We will have a delicious wine tasting and then we will have lunch."

We follow her inside, and a shopkeeper in his mid-fifties greets us. The store is lined with bottles of wine, and there are several set out on oak barrels ready for our tasting.

"Where are the drugs?" Guy asks.

"What? Oh, the name," the shopkeeper says. He has a pasta belly and a thick head of salt-and-pepper hair. "There are no drugs."

"No drugs," Guy says.

"No."

"Well, that's bullshit."

Allison pats him on the arm. "Marketing ploy got you down?"

"I believe in truth in advertising."

She tips her head back and laughs. "That's the funniest thing I've heard all day." She points at the shopkeeper. "Please, ignore us. Let us begin the tasting."

I look around at the others. Does anyone really want to drink from some unknown bottle in *this* group? I can't be the only one thinking this.

But apparently I am, because Connor picks up a small glass of red wine and downs it with a flourish.

"I thought you didn't like wine," Isabella says, picking up her own glass.

"That's Champagne," Allison says. "Important distinction."

Isabella wrinkles her nose and tastes her wine. "Oh, this is lovely."

I watch her drink it, and when nothing happens, I pick up a glass.

"I thought we said . . ." Oliver mutters.

"When in Rome, am I right?"[202]

"When in Ravello."

He picks up his glass and we clink them together. Only they're plastic, so the sound they make is unsatisfying.

"Here goes nothing," I say, and tip it into my mouth. The flavors are wonderful, and when nothing happens, I finish the glass and look around. "What's next?"

"Shall we open the next bottle?" the shopkeeper asks.

"Bring it."


An hour later, we're all drunk.

Drunkity drunk, drunk, drunk.

Even Harper. Even Oliver.

This is what happens when you give a bunch of people who fear for their lives and/or are plotting murder unlimited alcohol during the middle of the day before lunch.

Day drinking.

Day murder.

Wait, that's not a thing, is it?

Lord, I hope not.

Some of the wine is delicious, some mediocre, and some it doesn't

---

[202] Yes, I <u>have</u> been saving this until now.

matter given how much we've all had. We're supposed to be spitting it out after we swirl it around and appreciate it, but—and I mean this in the nicest possible way—*fuck that.*

I drink it all down, and so do the others, and I order a bunch of it to be sent to me in Venice (California, not Italy). Harper clucks her tongue at the price, but I tell her that you only live once and you can't take it with you, and she rolls her eyes and laughs and we're into the Champagnes now, so everyone but Connor is giggling.

Even Oliver, even Guy.

Someone's about to say *I love you, man* when Sylvie tells us that our time is up and we need to climb some *more* stairs to the town square to meet the BookFace Ladies for lunch.

There's a chorus of groans, but this is a good idea.

We all need to step away from the drinks and take a beat.

Mostly, we all need food.

So we say our thank-yous to Pietro, the shopkeeper, who's now our best friend, and troop out of the store.

Sylvie tells us to *andiamo!* and we stumble up the stairs. I've got my hand on Oliver, holding on tight, because stairs are not safe for me, even when I'm sober.

But I am not sober—no, sir.

And maybe I'm being an idiot. Oh, I definitely am.

But sometimes you have to throw caution to the wind.

Sometimes you have to live that Instagram slogan like it's meaningful. As if it's not just a way to get likes. Like it might actually change your life if you follow its edict.

Everyone feels it, I can tell. We're all connected in a way we haven't been till now because one of us wants to end some of us.

And that connects people, right?

The murderer and the murderee?

There's a bond there. Murder is a close emotion. Especially when it's planned.

It builds and builds until it's a force that lives inside you.

At least, I assume.

Not like I'd know.

We get to the top and I suck in my breath. It's even more beautiful up here. A wide, circular piazza with bistro tables and benches where you can sit and stare at the view. Farther in, there's a medieval castle (the building Sylvie was quoting Google about), its turret reaching up to the sun.

The air feels cleaner, and maybe that's why my brain clears out, too.

It's like a swift wind blowing in there, and then the solution thunks into place.

I know who's trying to kill me.

I know what their motive is.

I know what I've missed until now.

But I don't have any proof.

Normally, I'd end the chapter right now and let you sit with that banger for a while. But I'm not going to do that this time.

Nope.

Here's what I figured out.

The thing I haven't spent enough time thinking about is why me *and* Connor.

Because it's not about Shek. It never was. He got in the way of someone's plans, and so he was disposed of like yesterday's newspaper.

Anyway. Let's get to the solution, shall we?

Who has a motive to kill both of us? I know I've joked that everyone does, but that's not true. Allison is an old hurt; Oliver, too. I didn't know Emily before this tour, and killing someone to ensure your book sales seems extreme. The only one with a real double motive is Harper, but there's no way.

And that's the problem.

That's the solution.

Someone *isn't* trying to kill both of us.

They're just trying to kill *me*.

I've said it before, but now I know it's the truth. There's no evidence that anyone actually tried to kill Connor. There's only his word for it, and his word is bullshit.

The push at the Vatican, the bystander who saved him, the incident with his car. The man who died in the street could've been anyone, a convenient excuse to pull me in because it's not like he mentioned Davide by name before he died.

And none of what Connor says occurred happened in front of anyone else.

Only *my* almost-deaths did.

Mine and Shek's.

If there's one thing I know after all these years of writing about murders: If the pattern doesn't match, then it should be tossed out. And if you toss out what Connor said happened and you're left with only what we know happened, well, then it's a clearer picture.

It's been Connor, all along.

Connor told me that his life was in danger to distract me. To distract everyone. Because who's going to benefit the most if I die?

*Him.*

A murder mystery author gets murdered on her tenth-anniversary book tour? That's gold.

And Connor's out of gold right now.

He must've found out I was thinking of ending the series. Maybe it was Harper who told him, guessing the truth even though I never said it expressly, or maybe he knew about the statute of limitations, or maybe it was just his instinct.

He's always had good instincts about people.

That's how a con man operates.

So that's who did it.

Who's doing it.

Who isn't finished doing it.

Connor.

The most obvious suspect is usually the best answer in the real world, and sometimes even in books. Then again, sometimes it's just terribly wrong.

Now you can flip the page.

# CHAPTER 27

## So You Solved It, Now What?

It's an odd feeling when you feel like you know something no one else does.

And the thing I know is: Connor is trying to kill me.

I feel it in my bones. And it's weird because it doesn't frighten me like I thought it would. Not like all the harried thoughts of the last few days, the uncertainty, the not knowing.

Now that I know, I feel calm. I only need to decide what I'm going to do about it. How I'm going to go about proving it.

Because what evidence do I have?

None.

And I'm not naive enough to think I can just waltz into the inspector's office (he has an office, right? a cubicle at least) and point some dramatic finger at Connor and he'll be taken away in handcuffs.

I can't expect Connor to confess. That's not his way. Even when I confronted him about his crimes ten years ago, he never quite confessed to anything. It was all innuendo, and "If I did it, then what?" like he was O. J. Simpson.

"Plausible deniability," he'd called it, and even if it wasn't, it felt like it was.

I was naive then, but I'm older and wiser than that now. I know I'm not going to be able to simply sit him down in the library with all the other suspects and lay it out like I'm Hercule Poirot and get some snarling confession out of him.

That's not going to happen.[203]

I'm going to have to find some other way to get the evidence.

Some other way to convince more than myself that I'm right.

And I need to do it before he stops fucking up and kills me for real.

Remember how I said that sometimes I can see things before they happen? Like this morning with the gun?

Well, right now my vision's foggy, but I know, whatever happens, that it's going to be dangerous.

Are you ready?

I am. But I'm also hungry, so we have lunch with the BookFace Ladies in the Piazza del Duomo at a series of bistro tables set up on one side of the plaza. A massive church looms above us, blocking out the sun, and there's a breeze in the air, the scent of lemons and the sea.

I think, despite everything, that I might retire here.

If I live, if I survive this, this is as good a place as any.

Thirty-five isn't too young to retire, right? Not if you're exhausted? Not if you're worn down by life and everything that's happened to you in the last ten years.

No one would judge me.

I can become an expat who speaks bad Italian and buys my food at the local shops, putting my purchases into a basket I sling over my arm. I can get a bicycle and sturdy walking shoes to go up and down these streets and climb down to the Gulf of Salerno and swim my morning laps in the sea.

"You want to retire here, don't you?" Oliver says, sitting next to me. I left the seat open for him, but I wasn't sure if he was going to take the invitation.

---

[203] I mean it. It doesn't happen in the library.

"Why can you always read my mind?"

"I don't know." The skin on the bridge of his nose is peeling, and his freckles are popping. His face is open and kind, and if I'm not getting ahead of myself, I can see love in his eyes.

How could I have thought that he had anything to do with this?

That's what Connor's done with his too many suspects and his pitting us all against one another. Like I put in my outline, but with a twist. It's not just the thought of murder that kills you. It's the thought that some-one you love might be the one to do it.

"I wish I could read your thoughts as clearly," I say.

He leans back and crosses one leg over the other. "I was thinking that retirement doesn't seem so bad, right now."

My heart kicks into another gear. "Retirement with me?"

"Potentially."

"Where would we go?"

"We could go anywhere."

"Not Florida, though," I say.

"Florida is bullshit."

"Florida *is* bullshit."

We grip hands across the table, and I know I should confide in Ol-iver, but I don't. I don't want Connor in this moment. He's been in too many moments between us.[204]

Instead, I open my menu and say, "Do you think anything's good here?"

He laughs and says that it all looks amazing, and we order some *cacio e pepe*, then make idle conversation while I watch the rest of our party.

Harper's sitting with Emily, an uneasy détente. Guy and Sylvie are

---

[204] And let's be honest, if everyone hadn't made a bunch of stupid decisions, me included, this book would've been over long ago.

at a table with the bus driver. And then there are the BookFace Ladies, chattering and taking photographs on their phones. They're subdued, though, tamped down. I wonder why until I hear Cathy tell Susan that she's thinking of going home.

Shek, I realize. They're mourning him.

I should do that, too, more than I have.

A newsletter devoted to him. Or a lecture series. I should read his books and promote them. Emily should do her thing on TikTok.

The man died, after all, because of me.

Wait, wait, wait, hold up. It's not what you think.

I'm not the perpetrator. I'm just the catalyst. So that makes me responsible but not, you know, legally.

Which brings me to Connor, the person who *is* responsible.

He's sitting with Isabella and Allison, surrounded by BookFace Ladies, and I can't help but wonder what's going on at that table.[205, 206, 207]

Connor looks carefree, but Allison's usual sunny demeanor has slipped. She's biting her lower lip, concentrating on something, while Isabella tells a story, gesticulating with her hands for emphasis.[208] Cathy watches them from the table next door, and I wonder once again how she got on this tour. Maybe that was part of Connor's plan. To torture me first with Cathy before he finally did away with me. That might explain her disinterest in me and the shift in her focus to him. Because there's one thing I know about Cathy—no one tells her what to do.

---

[205] If I ever get a superpower, I think I want it to be superhearing. How cool would that be?

[206] Though, on second thought, maybe not. It's bad enough when I get tagged in a bad review. I don't need to hear everything people are saying about me just out of reach. It would be helpful in this context, though. If I survive, I assume I won't need to listen in on potential murderers anymore.

[207] Turns out I'm wrong about this, but that's for another book.

[208] I'm noting here that this is where Allison has figured out what happened.

Our food comes, and the *cacio e pepe* is delectable, creamy, and spicy, with the pasta fresher than fresh. I don't have much appetite, though, with everything going on. I try to make light conversation with Oliver, but it's hard not to feel like there's a target on my back.

That's why I'm sitting on the edge of the group, my eyes on everyone.

No one's sneaking up on *me* at this lunch, I'll tell you.[209]

When the meal's over, I pose for a group photo with the BookFace Ladies in front of the church or cathedral or whatever it is. Then Sylvie leads us to the Villa Rufolo, which is, according to Sylvie and Google, "one of the largest and wealthiest on the Amalfi Coast. Built by the influential Rufolo family in the thirteenth century, it's been the host to Renaissance poets and Neapolitan royalty. It was even the source of inspiration for the composer Wagner."

It's impressive. The architecture is Moorish in origin, with scalloped walls and gardens full of colorful flowers laid out in intricate designs. And soaring above it all is the Torre Maggiore, a medieval tower that has a magnificent 360-degree view of Ravello.

If Sylvie's to be believed, anyway.

Which, I think we can all agree, she shouldn't be.

"Some of you want to climb the tower, yes?" Sylvie asks, pointing up.

"No," Connor says. "Some of us do *not*."

"It is optional. Inside there is a museum and I have bought you all tickets. You can walk in the gardens for the next hour, but if you want the best view in Ravello, then up, up, up you go."

I catch Harper's eye, and she rolls her eyes at me. I shake my head in response. In a few days, we'll be rid of Sylvie, and then all she'll be is a footnote in our lives.[210]

If I last that long.

---

[209] Nope, that happens in the next scene.

[210] Yep, I've been saving that one, too.

I'm repeating myself.

My mind is clouding with too many thoughts. That pure clarity I had an hour ago? It's slipping away. I didn't have anything more to drink with lunch, but all that wine in the morning, that day drinking—as fun as it was—it's still there, swirling around.

I need to feel that clear certainty again so I can make a plan and execute it.

I look up at the tower.

There.

That's where I need to go.

"I'm going to climb," I say to Oliver.

"In this heat?"

"It's not so bad."

He fans himself with his napkin. "Speak for yourself."

"I am."

"Ha ha. But seriously, El. You want me to join you?"

"No, it's . . . I need a moment to think."

He frowns. "Are you sure it's safe?"

"I have my wits about me."

"It's not your wits I'm worried about."

"I know." I reach across the table and kiss him on the cheek. "I'll be okay. No one's going to hurt me here."

"You know that's not true."

He's right. Isolating myself from the group is a bad idea. But I want to do it anyway because I have that feeling like I'm sure you get sometimes, too. When something's on the tip of your brain and it's going to come to you at two in the morning. Or a dream that feels so real when it's happening, but whose details you can't remember an hour after you wake up.

That.

And I know from experience that if I don't give it the time and space to emerge, then it will fade forever, leaving only the memory of having the answer but not the answer itself.[211, 212]

All this to say, I need to get up in that tower before I forget the solution to this case.

"I . . . How about this? Why don't you keep an eye on Connor?"

His brows knit together. "Do you think . . . ?"

"I . . . I don't know, but yes, maybe."

"I'll kill him myself."

"No one needs to be killed. I just need to think it through for a minute, and then we'll go to Inspector Tucci, all right?"

"Okay."

"Walk me to the entrance."

We leave the table and walk through the piazza. The ground is uneven, made up of cobblestones, and the light feels magical, clear, and slightly breezy, with high paintbrush trees providing a canopy.

"Be careful," he says.

"Just watch him," I say. "It'll be all right."

He scans the crowd ahead of us and finds Connor entering the flower garden. He's alone, and I wonder for a moment where Isabella is. Maybe she's finally wised up and left him.

"I'll be over there with him," Oliver says. "But if you need anything, call."

"You won't be able to hear me."

"I meant on the phone." He takes his phone out of his pocket and waves it at me.

"I'm embarrassed to say this, but I don't think I have your number."

"What?"

---

[211] This happens to me all the time when I'm writing. This is why I carry around a notebook. So I can write down words to help me remember what I want the next chapter to be, like: "tower, no air, sees conversation, then googles."

[212] Oops, those are the notes I sent myself about <u>this</u> chapter. I guess you can consider it another clue. Though you've figured this out by now, haven't you?

"I, uh . . . I deleted it."

"Why?"

Come on, Oliver, you're smarter than that.

Or has he forgotten the drunk texts I sent him in the middle of the night begging him to forgive me?

"I needed to before I did anything more to embarrass myself."

"You didn't."

"I did."

"Be that as it may . . ." He takes my phone and puts in my code. The screen unlocks. "Never changed your code?"

"Nope."

"Trusting."

"Yes."

He smiles at me, then sends a quick text. "There you go, you texted me."

"What did I say?"

"You'll have to check to find out." He kisses me quickly. "Be careful, El. I don't want to lose you right after I found you again."

Damn it.

You see? This is why I'm still in love with him.

Anyway.

I watch him walk toward Connor; then I check what he wrote.

*I will never erase this number again.*

I laugh out loud, catching the attention of a couple of the BookFace Ladies. I wave at them and hold my phone over my heart. He's right, I hope.

But that's the future. If I want to get there, I have to solve my past.

So up, up, up I go.

I take a ticket from Sylvie and walk into the bottom of the villa. It's dark inside, the walls made of thick gray stone. There's a museum, like she said, the artifacts and pottery set into illuminated niches and on plinths. It's cooler in here, but airless, too.

But I'm not here for a history lesson.

I need to get up to somewhere I can think.

Which is weird when you think about it because I'm usually afraid of heights, as I've already established.

Maybe it's the fear that clears my mind.

Or maybe it's only a plot device.

Probably the second.

Read on to find out.

I wander through the rooms until I find it—the winding black metal staircase that will take me up to the roof. I don't know how many stairs it is; I only know that my calves are protesting after one flight, and I pass two couples coming down, both red in the face and looking like regret.

I'm full of regret, too, but still I climb.

Finally, when my breath is heavy and thick in my throat, I get to the top. It's worth it.

I walk onto the square top of the turret. The 360-degree view of Ravello is as advertised. The vibrant green mountain behind it; the trees and colorful houses nestled into the cliffside; the winking blue Med. What wasn't mentioned, though, is the hard plexiglass walls that surround the top of the stonework.

Did someone try to end their life up here? Did they succeed? Or is it preventative?

Whatever it is, it's airless and hot, and the opposite of what I was expecting to feel when I got up here.

Because I don't feel free; I feel claustrophobic.

I take a couple of long, slow breaths. I cannot have a panic attack up here. Not that I've ever had a panic attack, but this is what it feels like, right?

Like you can't breathe?

Like your heart might explode?

Or is that a heart attack?

Don't be an idiot, El. You're not having a heart attack because you walked up a couple of stairs.

I move toward one of the walls. There are slits between the plastic, and some air comes through. I gulp at it, trying not to think about how ridiculous I look, like a fish out of a fishbowl, lapping at the drops of water so I can survive.

But it works. My heart calms, my pulse slows, my breathing returns to normal. And I can take in the beauty below. The gardens with their red, yellow, and purple flowers. The sea beyond it. The forest green trees.

No wonder Wagner was inspired.

I'd write a symphony about this place, too, if I could.[213]

I scan the garden to the left. Allison and Isabella are in the courtyard, alone, talking.

Wait, no. They're having an argument, but in hushed, angry tones. Isabella is checking the surroundings, like she's worried about being overheard.

But maybe it's because I'm above them and sound travels upward like heat, that I do hear some of what they're saying.

"I saw you," Allison says.

Isabella shakes her head, but Allison is insistent.

She saw her where? What is she saying?

Where could Allison have seen Isabella that it would matter?

My mind tumbles over like the mechanism of a lock.

*Click, click, click.*

There's only one place where it would matter if Allison saw Isabella.

The hallway outside my room that morning.

Allison's room is on my floor. It stands to reason that the shots would've woken her. Of course they did. And maybe she didn't hesitate to open her door. Maybe she got there fast enough to see a figure running toward the stairwell.

*That* was the door I heard opening.

Not the door to my room, but the one right next door.

---

[213] Or did he write operas? Is there a difference?

Allison's.

She heard the shot, rushed to the door, and saw Isabella.

Isabella, the woman who met Connor five days ago and decided to ditch her plans to follow him around Italy. Isabella, who could easily have slipped out of her and Connor's room if Connor had taken a sleeping pill. Isabella, who was sitting at Guy's table and could've drugged him in a moment.

And wait, wait, *wait!*

Isabella was the one who distributed the wine on the boat. She was near Shek right before he tumbled over, dead. She could've been wearing that device, and tapped him without anyone noticing.

But why?

Why would she want to kill Shek?[214]

Who is Isabella, anyway?

Who would want me *and* Connor dead? What connection do we have?

Then it hits me. Finally. Something that crossed my mind days ago on the boat to Capri that I dismissed.

I've been looking in the present when I should've been looking in the past.

The robberies. The Giuseppe family. He had a daughter, didn't he? The capo—Antonio Giuseppe.

I take out my phone and google it. The signal is weak, and it takes a moment for the results to load. I click a recent article.

Oh! He died in jail. Survived by his five children—Gianni, Marco, Rosa, Marta, and *Isabella.*

Oh my God. Oh my God.

Really? The *Canadian* did it?[215]

---

[214] Means, motive, opportunity. Did you know you don't even have to prove motive to convict someone? But any prosecutor will tell you that if you don't explain the why, no one's going to buy it.

[215] This was my agent's suggestion.

With Marta the publicist?

What. The. *Fuck.*

But wait, there's more! There's a family photo in one of the articles from some gathering fifteen years ago. The capo and his wife surrounded by their children. And I know this woman, despite the years. She has that same blowsy casualness about her, though the photo says her name is Sophia.

"Enjoying the view?" Sylvie says behind me.

Ah, *shit.*

I knew I shouldn't have come up here.

# CHAPTER 28

## Whoops-A-Daisy

There's this scene in *The Princess Bride*—maybe the movie, maybe the book, maybe both[216]—where it comes to a climactic moment in the action, and the scene cuts (I'm almost sure it's in the movie), and we're back with the narrator (Peter Falk) telling a young Fred Savage (long before he was canceled) that the protagonist does not die in this moment.

Fred's taken aback and wants to know why his grandfather's told him that.

Because you looked worried, he says, and I didn't want you to be worried.[217] He wanted his grandson to know that as bad as it was looking for Princess Buttercup and the Man in Black, they were going to survive.

It's a funny, sweet moment that I've always loved, and imitation is the sincerest form of flattery.

So: I do not die in this chapter.

You were looking a little worried, and I wanted you to know that I'm going to be okay.

I mean, you knew that already since you're reading this.

---

[216] Both are genius. If you haven't read the book, go do that. I mean, not right this instant, but as soon as you finish this one.

[217] I'm paraphrasing here for legal reasons.

But I wanted to remind you because I care about you and I didn't want you to worry.

That doesn't mean some bad things aren't about to happen. There's one more death in this book and it's dramatic, if I do say so myself. And I know you're looking at the amount of pages you have left to read or the percentage on your Kindle and I told you before that I'd solved the crime.

Only I was wrong.

But enough about me, for now.

Let's return to the scene of the reveal, shall we?

Just to catch you up, I've overheard a conversation between Isabella and Allison that has led me to make the connection to the Giuseppe family and realize from my Google search that the capo, Anthony Giuseppe, had daughters named Isabella and Marta, and a wife whose real name is something else but who's definitely Sylvie. I'm holding my phone in my hand with the web page up, and Sylvie has just come up behind me and cornered me on the top of a medieval turret in the Italian town of Ravello. That turret is surrounded by plexiglass walls that will make it impossible for anyone to hear me scream.

We are alone.

Dramatic much?

So back to me.

Because oh, no. Oh, *shit.*

Sylvie.

It's Sylvie *and* Isabella.

This whole time.

They were here the whole time, right next to us, on the scene. *They're* the people we never looked at because why would they have a motive to kill us? To kill me?

Isabella even joked about it in the library when she was holding the marker at the easel while we tried to puzzle out the subjects.

She agreed she should be a suspect.

She *laughed* about it, and I missed it.

I really am bad at this.

But right at this moment, I need to keep my wits about me. I need to maintain a poker face, only my poker face is terrible. Everyone always knows exactly what I'm thinking. But Sylvie and I are all alone up here, high up, with nowhere to go but the steep spiral staircase behind her.[218]

"Ms. Eleanor," Sylvie says. "Are you all right?"

"Oh, I . . ." I flex the hand that was holding my phone but realize I've dropped it. "You startled me, is all. And I'm a bit out of breath from that climb up the stairs . . ."

"It is worth it, though, no?"

"Oh, yes. Yes, the view is fantastic. Just like you said."

I bend down and pick up my phone, my heart hammering in my chest. The screen is still open, the results of my Google search visible, face up and pointing toward Sylvie. The name "Giuseppe" seems abnormally large and obvious to my very nervous eye.

I can't let Sylvie see it. I click quickly on the button on the side to shut the screen off, then tuck my phone into my pocket.

Damn it. I shouldn't have put it away. I need to call for help.

Call if you need me, Oliver had said not twenty minutes ago, and then he put that text in my phone so I'd have his number.

I can do this.

"Have you checked out the view?" I say to Sylvie in a voice that sounds unnatural.

"I have seen the view, of course. Many times."

"Oh, right, great." I use my finger in my pocket to unlock my screen, doing the pattern that is my password, a gesture I repeat dozens of time a day. My finger slides to my texts, and I hope I'm clicking on the right part of the screen to call Oliver. Miraculously, I hear that faraway sound of

---

[218] Isn't there a famous book called *The Spiral Staircase*? No, no, that's *The Hidden Staircase*, a Nancy Drew book. But there is a horror movie called *The Spiral Staircase* and maybe I'm caught in it.

an international call and hit the volume button, then cough to cover it. I don't know if Oliver will be able to hear me, but maybe the call is enough.

"You are acting strangely," Sylvie says. Her eyes are staring straight at me, unblinking. And did she always look this menacing, or is that just a product of my imagination?

"Am I? I'm just . . . a bit out of sorts today. You understand."

"Because of the shooting."

"Well, yes." I look around me as if there might miraculously be someone up here besides us two. But no.

There's no magic here.

Only malice.

"It's high up here in the tower," I say, and try to make my voice sound normal. "Did you find it hard to climb the stairs, Sylvie?"

She cocks her head to the side. "It was nothing."

"I think I'm going to go back down."

"No, come, look at the view with me."

She's blocking the door, and how can I get by her without looking like a complete lunatic?

Without giving what I know away?

And oh, shit, shit, *shit*. Did she come up here to kill me?

"I don't feel well."

"Ah, yes, you are afraid of heights, no?"

"How did you know that?"

She smiles the same smile she's been giving me this whole time, only this time, as the kids say, it hits different. There's a glint in her eye that I don't like.

"I know lots of things about you, Ms. Eleanor."

"Oh, ha . . ." I try to laugh it off. "The price of fame, I guess."

"The price . . . Yes. There are prices to pay for things in life."

"I mean, sometimes?"

"Only sometimes?"

"Sometimes people get away with things. And I'm okay with that."

She looks at me, but through me like I'm transparent. Like she's seeing a ghost. "What does that mean?"

"I'm not looking to get anyone into trouble."

She nods slowly. "But you already did this."

"Did what?"

"Got people into trouble. You and Mr. Smith. You ruined a family."

So here we are. She's not hiding anymore, and there's no reason for me to do it either.

She saw my phone. She knows I know who she is.

"I didn't make anyone rob those banks or murder anyone."

"No?"

"They were criminals before I came on the scene."

"You do not understand."

"So, tell me."

She tips her head back and laughs. "No, Miss Eleanor. No. I do not owe you that."

"What are we talking about?"

"I think you know."

"You're a Giuseppe."

She tilts her head down.

"You planned this whole thing. You and Isabella and Marta."

She opens her hands. There's something on her ring finger, inside the palm. It looks like the device that was used on Shek.

I gulp down my fear. "I could scream."

"Ah, but no one would hear you, would they?"

"They might. Oliver knows I am up here."

"And yet he let you come up here alone?"

"I asked him to."

"I do not believe you."

And why should she? It sounds like the kind of lie people tell in movies to escape someone who wants to kill them.

"You don't have to do this."

"You are wrong about that. You took everything from me."

"I'm not the reason your husband went to jail."

"You are."

"I didn't make him commit crimes. I only discovered it after the fact."

"You do not understand. He was a good man. He was providing for his family. But you and Mr. Smith, you wanted the money for yourselves. You went to the police without a thought for who it would hurt. And my Gianni . . . my beautiful boy."

"Connor didn't kill him."

"He would be alive today if they'd never met."

"I'm sorry, but . . ."

But she isn't listening. "And he just gets away with all of it? And you? You become famous because of it? Everything you have, I gave it to you."

"If it's money you want . . ."

"No. I am not some . . . No. Money isn't enough. It will not bring back my husband. It will not bring back my son."

"But he was going to the police, wasn't he? Gianni? That's why he was killed."

"Do not speak of him."

"I . . ."

She takes a step forward. What's taking Oliver so long? Did I even call him? Maybe someone else is listening to this sparkling conversation. Or maybe no one's listening at all.

I'm such an idiot for coming up here.

"Let me go, Sylvie. If you do this . . . you're going to get caught. Inspector Tucci . . . He'll figure out who you are. Who Isabella is . . . He'll put it together."

"That man? Please."

"It's basic police work . . ."

"No one will even be looking at me."

"They will. Oliver will. Harper. They won't just sit still and—"

"You are so certain these people you treat as disposable will come to your rescue? Will care that you are gone? Isabella has told me how they are suspects even in *your* head. Please. Your sister will take the money and your lover will move on, and all that anyone will remember you for are some books that aren't very good."

I mean . . . *ouch*.

"Why take the risk, Sylvie? What if you're wrong?"

She hesitates for a moment, and this is my chance. I think about pushing past her, but how am I going to avoid that needle in her hand? It would be so easy for her to prick me.

So, instead, I bend low and barrel my elbow into her stomach, pushing her out of the way.

It's amazing the strength that adrenaline gives you.

She lets out a strangled cry as she falls to the floor, and I see the device slip off her finger. I kick it away with my foot, watching it tumble down the stairs.

But I've miscalculated because now she has her hand around my ankle. I kick at her again and she releases me. I get to the top of the stairs and grip the railing.

If I'm not careful, I'm going to fall down these very steep stairs. I grip the railing tighter.

And now I can sense Sylvie right behind me, so I turn and duck, and the force that she's using to come after me makes it impossible for her to stop.

She screams as she stumbles past the top step, trying to grab onto the railing, and I watch in sickened horror as she flies into the air, then hits the stairs and tumbles down, down, down until she lands with a terrible *thump* at the bottom.

I fall to my knees as Harper comes into view below me, holding her phone in her hand.

She stares up from Sylvie to me and back again. She takes the stairs two at a time and catches me before I fall.

But the world is going black, the edges creeping in as she wraps her arms around me.

"I've got you," she says.

And then I am gone.

# CHAPTER 29

## I've Got a Lot of Questions About What Happened Here

**Sorrento**

Life feels different when you kill someone.

There's a heaviness to it that wasn't there before, and even if that person deserved it, even if they were trying to kill you in the moment that you killed them.

That *I* killed her. Sylvie.

This isn't a theoretical conversation but something that happened.

Not on paper but IRL, as the kids say.

I don't know if it's something I can ever get over.

Time will tell.

But for now, I have questions.

We all do.

And if this ever gets made into a TV show, this part will be in slow motion.

We'll emerge from the villa one by one, but after the body does, of course.

It will be loaded into a body bag, resting on a stretcher, surrounded by police, and a song will be playing over the shot. Maybe "You're on Your Own, Kid," by Taylor Swift.

Because I always have been.

*   *   *

They've brought us back to the hotel in separate cars.

Me, Harper, Oliver, Connor, and the others. We're all going to be questioned again, but their questions won't be like mine.

Because I killed Sylvie. I did.

And I saw it in their faces when I was led out of the villa—the accusation that this might have been the plan all along.

They stood in a half-moon, watching me, supporting one another.

I'm apart from them now.

It's a distance I don't know how to breach.

Maybe when the truth comes out—when they learn that I was the victim—then it will all be okay.

Then again, maybe not.

Again, time will tell.

For now, my lawyer meets me in the lobby, and we're given an hour alone where I tell him everything that happened. We agree together that I should tell my story to Inspector Tucci, nothing left out, nothing added. I haven't done anything wrong, but someone is dead.

More than one person.

There are questions that need to be asked and answers that need to be given.

So I'm back in the room I was in when Inspector Tucci questioned me. Was that only this morning?

The room feels different. I didn't notice the wallpaper before—a faded print of multicolored peacocks. And the windows full of sunshine. Were there always windows? The light hurts my eyes, and my lawyer closes the blinds when I put my hand up to shade them.

What was I saying? Oh, right. The room. I was trying to describe it, but I can't latch onto the details.

The truth is—I feel drunk. Maybe I still am.

Only I don't think so.

But it feels that way. Like everything is sped up and slowed down and I'm being very careful with my words, though I haven't said any-thing yet.

Maybe if I catalog everything slowly, I'll be able to come to some kind of solution in my mind. A solution for myself.

So:

—My hands are folded on the table.

—It's still daylight outside.

—The air is a bit cold in here.

—Someone offers me coffee, but I don't take it.

—My lawyer is seated to my left, and we're both facing an empty chair, waiting.

I memorize these details like I'll have to write them down later.

Eventually, the door opens and Inspector Tucci walks in with the other officer he was with this morning. Don't ask me to remember his name.

I barely remember my own.

He sits across from me and puts a recording device down on the ta-ble. My lawyer nods. I've forgotten his name, too. Inspector Tucci starts the recording and notes the date and time. He says who's present and then we begin.

"Before I take your statement, Ms. Dash, are there any questions that you have for me?"

"I . . . Yes."

"Please go ahead."

"Is . . . Is Sylvie really dead?"

I know she is, they don't put live people in body bags, but I have to ask anyway. Because that's the kind of day it is. One where even some-thing I witnessed with my own eyes feels made up.

"Yes, her neck snapped on the stairs."

So that was the sound. I feel like throwing up, but I choke it down.

"And Isabella?"

"She's in custody. We apprehended her at the train station in Napoli."

"She was running away?"

"She is not speaking. But yes, that is what we believe."

"And she's Sylvie's daughter?"

"Yes. She had been going by the last name Joseph."

"It is Giuseppe in English," my lawyer says.

"Yes," Inspector Tucci says. "We believe she changed it when she emigrated."

I blink slowly. "To Canada?"

"There were three children who were still underage. They were sent there after the capo went to jail. They had relatives there."

"Do you know where Marta is?"

"We do not. But we have established that she entered the country with Isabella. They were on the same plane."

"The one that Connor was on?"

"And Mr. Abishek, yes."

"How do you know all this if Isabella isn't talking?"

He flips open his notebook. "I was conducting an investigation . . . These facts came to light this afternoon. We were about to alert you when we received the call about the incident in Ravello."

"Marta was working for my publisher. In the publicity department. She was the one who put together the tour."

Inspector Tucci writes this down. "Who can I contact about this?"

I give Inspector Tucci the name and contact information of my editor.

"They didn't hide what they were doing very well," I say.

"I do not think they ever expected anyone to look. But criminals make mistakes all the time. That is how they are caught."

I lean back in my chair. I can feel the hard wood between my shoulder blades. "How long do you think they've been planning this?"

"Since shortly after the capo died. I imagine that his death, how do you say, stirred up all of the feelings again."

"It must have taken a lot of planning. Marta getting the job at my publisher . . . suggesting the tour . . ."

"Yes."

"And they planned all of it together?" I say. "They decided to have someone in the group . . . Isabella."

"I imagine that it was easier than they hoped to get close to Mr. Smith."

"She is a beautiful girl."

"He should not be so trusting."

"Agreed," I say. "And how did they plan to kill us?"

"That is less clear . . . The first attempt on Mr. Smith near the Vatican . . ."

"That was Marta?"

"We assume," Inspector Tucci says.

"And that pedestrian, he saw what happened?"

"Yes, we believe so."

"Who killed him?"

"Marta again, likely, though we have not mapped out all of Isabella's movements."

"She wasn't there at the Colosseum tour . . ." I remind him about our movements that day. The church, the gelato, the Forum. "I didn't meet her until dinner that night."

"We will pull the street camera footage . . . We will find out what happened."

"But she's missing? Marta?"

He makes a notation. "We will find her."

"Should I be worried?"

"I would keep an eye out, yes."

I think through the last few days. All those near-death experiences. "Do you think the jellyfish was on purpose?"

"It is hard to know. It is a known risk in that area. We are also looking for the captain of the boat . . ."

"Maybe they were just trying to torture us?"

"That is possible, yes."

"But the gunshot," I say, "that would have been final."

"Yes. They took a risk given that the police were involved at that point . . . Perhaps they felt like it was their last chance."

I shudder. "To kill me and frame Connor for it?"

This had occurred to me earlier. That's why I thought he had done it. Because that was the plan all along.

"Yes."

"But Allison saw Isabella?"

"She did. It was a stupid decision not to tell us what she had seen. Your life was almost sacrificed for that."

"Isabella drugged Guy earlier on and took the gun? And Connor took an Ambien after they . . ."

"Yes."

"What about the hotel cameras?"

"Disabled."

"By her?"

"Sylvie, perhaps. Maybe Marta . . . We will find all of this out."

"And the blackmail? Blackmailing Connor? That, too?"

"We do not know everything yet, but we will find out who was behind that as well."

I've run out of questions, so he takes my statement.

I take him through my day, remembering it as I go.

I feel better getting it out, like a poison I'm expelling. He listens and asks good questions and doesn't act like he's assuming that I'm making this up to cover some bigger crime.

When I've finished, he tells me that he needs to check in on the others, and leaves.

But not before another warning: I need to stay in the hotel. No more sightseeing for us. Not until they find Marta. Not until they figure all of this out.

I leave in the room in a daze and walk into Oliver's arms. He wraps me up tight and tells me it will all be all right, and this also feels like it's happening in slow motion, like in a montage. Harper is there, too, full of questions, but I can't answer any of them now. I want to sleep for a week, and maybe, tomorrow, in the cold light of day, there will be answers.

So that's what I do.

I go to bed and I try to sleep, but it's fractured. I'm skimming along the surface like sleep is a thin sheet of ice on a lake.

Any minute, I'm going to break through and fall into the cold black water.

And maybe, given everything, I'll never surface.

I do, though. Life, after a fashion, goes on.

I turn the page on a horrible day. Impossibly, I wake up and realize that it's only the seventh of July. I check the tour schedule for some grasp at normality, even though we're not going anywhere. We have a free day in Sorrento.

Is the tour schedule laughing at us?

Maybe.

My phone is a nightmare of notifications and missed calls from "Maybe: New York Times" and "Maybe: CBS News." I have thirty-eight voicemails and hundreds of emails, including panicked ones from my editor and agent. I text them both to let them know I'm okay, that I'll call them when I can, then shut off my phone.

I don't want to talk to anyone about any of this, but I know my immediate punishment is going to involve a day with what's left of our group, and maybe, if I'm very lucky, the BookFace Ladies.

I get up and get dressed. I meet Oliver and Harper in the dining room and eat breakfast. Allison joins us, while Guy, Emily, and Connor sit together at another table. Connor looks deflated and more vulnerable than I've ever seen him. Which shouldn't be a surprise given that he's been sleeping with someone who wanted to murder him.[219]

It's another hot day, the heat shimmering through the windows like a mirage on a hot highway, and I'm glad to be inside.

Under the circumstances.

"El?" Oliver squeezes my hand under the table like we're kids in school with an illicit romance.

"Yeah?"

"You okay?"

"I'm getting there."

Harper shakes out her napkin over a huge plate of food. "I'm strangely starving."

"Death will do that to you."

She gives me a look.

"Think of Irish wakes."

"That's the alcohol."

"Oh, right." I look down at my plate of eggs and bacon and a flaky croissant. I need to eat, but it all tastes like sawdust in my mouth. I try anyway, and we take our time over it because we have nowhere to go.

And we can't help but talk about what happened, some clues popping into our memories like popcorn.

—How I thought that whoever thought it was a good idea to book a tour in Italy in July was a lunatic.

—How Connor said he thought the person who mugged him was Italian.

—How Connor had Davide the pedestrian's number, which meant that Isabella then had it, too, so was able to find him.

—How Marta must've planned for Harper to have the master key.

"But why the mugging? They didn't actually use that key, right?"

---

[219] These girls really went all in on their plan, didn't they?

"Maybe they meant to, and Connor's stupid plan to fake his own death got in the way."

"Hmmm," Oliver says.

"What?"

"They're an odd mix of competence and incompetence, like more than one person was holding the reins."

"There were *three* people holding them. All the Giuseppe women."

"Not all of them. There's one more sister—Rosa."

I shiver. "Let's not think about her, shall we?"

"Hard agree. You know, Sylvie never knew anything about any of the sites we went to," Harper says. "It's so obvious now."

"The way she parroted Google."

"And anyone can visit the catacombs at the Colosseum. I checked last night."

"She must've studied. But not much."

"And why did we just accept Isabella like that? She must've laughed at us so hard."

"And she never said 'sorry.' Not like real Canadians do all the time."

*Pop!*

"Oh my God," I say. "Remember at the dinner, when she said her mother was a huge fan and she had a shrine to me?"

"And you took a selfie?"

"And she sent it to her!"

Harper breaks her croissant in two. "She must've been gloating. Look, Ma, I did it."

"Do you think the part about the shrine is true?"

"Maybe it's like, a set of voodoo dolls."

"Or a stalker's shrine," Oliver says. "Like those creepy ones from the movies."

I shudder again. It's not funny being stalked, though I'm sure I'll see the humor eventually. "They must've arranged for Cathy to come on the trip."

"Why?"

"To torture me. Or to make her the scapegoat. The more suspects around, the better."

"How did they know about her?"

I think about it. "The restraining order. That's public. It must've come up in their research."[220]

"Where is Cathy, anyway?" Oliver asks.

"The BookFace Ladies are under the watchful eye of two police officers at their hotel down the road," Harper says. "They've been told they're not allowed to post anything on social media, but you've already been tagged in a bunch of posts this morning."

"What a shit show." I sigh. "They were trying to frame Connor for my murder."

"How do you reckon?"

"I figured it out before I figured it out."

"What now?"

"All the attempts on his life were when he was alone. Not provable. But mine were public and undeniable."

Oliver nods. "So it would look like he was acting as if it was the both of you who were targets, but it was really just you?"

"Yeah, I think so."

"But what if he'd died?"

I shrug. "Then they'd blame me. One of us in jail, one of us dead. Then no one would look anywhere else. Either way, they'd get rid of us."

"What was going to be your motive, though? How did they know you wanted him dead?"

"They knew he was involved in the robberies, but I left that part

---

[220] Who they hired to conduct that research is a story for another book.

out in the book. They must've assumed I knew about it and made the connection that he was holding it over me." I bite my lip. "Plus, I think they were trying to reverse what he'd done."

"How so?"

This occurred to me late last night. The one thing I'd never asked Connor or got an answer to. "He used me as a shield. All those years ago. That's why he got involved with me, I think. Why he brought me into the investigation. I was his cover."

"Bastard," Oliver says through his teeth.

"He is."

"You don't seem mad at him."

"I know, right? It must be the shock."

We finish breakfast, and then collect in the library like it's a ditch we've driven into.[221]

We go to our usual positions and more things drop out of the memory hole they fell into.

"How did they get us all here?" Allison asks.

"Marta," Harper says. "She was working for the publisher. In the publicity department. She started there last year. She was the one who came up with the idea for the tour."

"Why steal your purse, then?" Emily says. "If not for the itinerary?"

"For the master key."

"Oh, right. That master key. Was that her doing, too?"

"Of course," Harper says.

"Where is she?" Emily asks. "Are they going to catch her?"

"I hope so," I say. "I don't like the thought of her being still out there."

"Same," Connor says.

Oliver bunches his fists. "This is all your fault, Connor. Getting El involved in the first place. Taking up with Isabella."

"I was taken in by a con woman . . ."

---

[221] I'm feeling very *prose-y* today. I'm just pointing it out for, well, <u>reasons</u>.

"Please, Connor," I say. "Just go away."

He doesn't, though, just slumps down in his chair in a way that makes me feel sorry for him.

That'll teach me.

And maybe it does, because it occurs to me that Connor and I, we're the same. I was taken in by him for *his* scheme, and he was taken in by Isabella for hers. It could happen to anyone.

That's what I tell myself.

We spend the morning bandying about theories; then the hotel serves us lunch. We have a choice between *gnocchi alla Sorrentina*[222] and *spaghetti Nerano*[223] with a dessert of *delizia al limone*, a lemon cake with a sweet glaze. I have the spaghetti, and it's creamy and wonderful, and it reminds me of how Shek just wanted a plate of carbonara. Maybe he's eating at an unlimited pasta bar in the Good Place.

I hope so, at least.

I spend the afternoon on the balcony, watching how the light shifts across the water, wishing I were on one of the crisp white boats that dot the harbor. Or maybe Capri when the crowds dissipate. Despite everything, I love this place. I hope it's not ruined now for me, forever.

When we're starting to think about cocktails and dinner, Inspector Tucci comes back.

He's been asking questions today, too, he tells us, and he has some answers. Not from Isabella—she's still not talking—but from the fruits of their investigation, he says, a bit proudly, because he has something to prove.

Some of it we've worked out for ourselves and some of it is news.

---

[222] It's potato gnocchi in a fresh tomato sauce with basil and melted mozzarella from Campania.

[223] Spaghetti, zucchini, parmesan, and basil.

Marco the boat captain is a relative, too, for instance. Sylvie's brother. *Sophia's* brother.

This murder plot was a family affair.

"But what about the blackmail?" I say. "Was that them, too?"

"No, that was Mr. Botha."

"What?" Harper says. "Seriously?"

"How?" Emily says.

"We found an encrypted app on his phone . . ."

"That's how they communicated with me," Connor says. "Whoever was blackmailing me."

"Yes, we found the messages."

Connor puts his hands on his hips. "So Shek was blackmailing me? That's just a coincidence?"

"No," Inspector Tucci says. "It was not."

"I don't follow," I say.

"He was working with them."

"With the Giuseppes?"

"Yes. I understand he lost a significant sum of money in an investment with you, Mr. Smith?"

Connor puffs up his chest. "That is not quite what happened, but he might see it that way."

"How did they know?" I think it through. "Oh, wait, Marta? Marta was his publicist, too?"

"Yes."

"He confided in her?"

"She encouraged the relationship, I believe . . . A young, sympathetic ear."

"See, I'm not the only one who fell for it."

"Shut up, Connor!" It's our chorus now—we all say it together.

"Please go on, Inspector," I say.

"He was upset at Mr. Smith for many reasons," he says. "Once we had access to his phone . . . There was a script that didn't work out, I believe. And then Mr. Smith encouraged him to invest in that crypto-currency scheme. The final straw seemed to be when it all fell apart and Mr. Smith helped the CEO escape . . ."

"I didn't do that—"

"Let him finish, Connor. You're not on trial."

"Not yet," Harper murmurs.

"This is what *he thought* you did, you understand?"

Connor nods.

"And then using the plot of one of his books to cover it up . . ."

"Go on."

"Marta used of all that to get him to participate."

"Did he know about killing me?"

"I think he only wanted to scare Mr. Smith. And to get his money back."

"What did he do?"

"The car brakes, we think . . . if that happened."

Connor scoffs. "It did."

"If it happened," Inspector Tucci repeats, "he might've been in-volved. The messages we found are suspicious but not as clear as the others."

"Wait . . . the car brakes," Allison says. "Didn't he kill someone that way in *Whisper of Iron*?"[224, 225]

We all look at her.

"What?"

"You read that?"

"Didn't everyone?"

No one wants to admit to the sin of reading (or not reading) Shek, so the silence rests there for a moment.

"Is that everything?" I ask.

---

[224] Seriously, who titles these things? I have to know.

[225] Okay, I figured it out. There's this title generator online. That has to be it.

"We might never know all of it," Inspector Tucci says, looking at us like we might have the missing answers.

"Some mysteries are never solved," Oliver says, and I love him for it.

"Yes, that is true. Speaking of which . . . What is this I've heard about you and Mr. Smith being behind the robberies in Roma?"

Uh-oh.[226, 227]

---

[226] All my footnotes are getting cut, aren't they?

[227] I mean, there's over two hundred of them, so I shouldn't be surprised?

# EPILOGUE

## Three Months Later

In the end, I don't kill Connor off.

After he swore up and down to Inspector Tucci that I had nothing to do with the robberies and cut a deal to avoid jail time himself,[228] it felt wrong to do it.

I wouldn't say we're friends now, but being the joint object of assassination attempts *does* bond you.

Besides, I got my publisher to agree to let me start a new series. I'll be doing two books a year, which sounds insane, but I asked for it, so I shouldn't complain.[229]

There's this saying in Hollywood: Do one for them and then one for you. And that's the approach I'm taking.

They haven't found Marta. There's an international warrant for her arrest—one of those Interpol things you see in the movies—so I assume they'll find her eventually. I try not to think about it too much because

---

[228] Turns out that statute of limitations thing doesn't apply to accessory to <u>murder</u>, so if Connor hadn't protected me, then I would've been in serious legal trouble, too.

[229] I probably will, though. Can't change everything about myself all at once.

you can't live like that, looking over your shoulder all the time, waiting for someone to strike.[230]

Isabella is awaiting trial. We'll all have to go back to Italy to testify when it happens, which I'm kind of looking forward to. I mean, it's not like I wanted to be a witness to a real murder, but now that it's happened, I can get something out of the experience. Everything, as they say, is book fodder.[231] Write what you know.

When we got back to the States, Harper and I helped organize Shek's funeral. Even though he was kind of in on the plot to kill me, I don't hold it against him. I don't believe that he wanted me dead, and let's be honest: I 100 percent understand the desire to torture Connor a bit for his crimes.

Yep. Harper's still working for me. The difference is, she doesn't resent me anymore. We're back to how we used to be, and she's given up writing. Maybe she'll go back to it someday, she says. But for now, she's happy helping me out.

Shek's funeral took place in the small town he lived in a couple of hours outside of New York. It was a heavy July day, pregnant with rain, and we stood around the graveside dressed in black and cloaked in silence under black umbrellas. In the end, it was Shek who had the real flair for the dramatic.

It was the first time we were all together again—me, Harper, Oliver, Connor, Allison, Emily, and Guy.

And the BookFace Ladies, of course—let's not forget about them.

They wore black T-shirts with Shek's book covers on them, which I thought was a touching gesture. Apparently, it was Cathy's idea. She reached out, contrite, and confirmed that Marta had invited her to come on the tour. Having been the unwitting accomplice of a murderer seems to have knocked the crazy out of her. I'm not saying we're going to be

---

[230] I should, because we haven't seen the last of Marta.
[231] And the trip will be a tax write-off, so.

BFFs, but I asked my lawyer to lift the restraining order. If she comes to my next book launch, I'm not going to be mad about it.

The funeral was nice and appropriately sad, and at the reception, the executive editor of our publisher announced that three of Shek's books are back on the list. I feel almost certain that he'd be happy to know this, though his life was too big a price to pay even for the top three spots on the *New York Times* bestseller list.

Emily was shy and full of some secret. It was written all over her face, though I never got a chance to ask her what it was. Probably that *she's* signed a three-book deal. I'll find out eventually. I caught her making a TikTok as we walked away from the graveside. Change doesn't always come easy.

Taking a cue from Connor, Allison brought a date to the funeral, a man who looked at her with the reverence I doubt she ever got from Connor. Where did she meet him? That's a story for another day. *No One Was Supposed to Die at this Wedding*, more specifically. Yep—there's a sequel! And a third book in the works, too.[232]

Which brings me to Connor.[233] I was surprised he showed up, to be honest, because it was his fault that Shek was dead. But there he was, a beautiful woman on his arm, and . . .

Okay, okay. He didn't actually bring a date to the funeral. But it was believable that he'd do it, right? You were totally picturing him looking tragic with some dishy blonde on his arm!

Anyway, sometimes people surprise you. Maybe he *has* changed.

Or maybe not.

I've solved enough mysteries for one day. You figure it out.

---

[232] *This Doesn't End Well for Anyone.*

[233] He made some kind of deal with Inspector Tucci. It might have had something to do with dropping the misconduct charges for lying to us about interrogation and search rules.

*   *   *

"What are we doing here, again?" Oliver asks a couple of months later. It's October and he's wearing a tux, bow tie and all. He looks like he could be cast as the next James Bond.[234]

Oh, yeah. He's still around.

We're making a go of it.

I'm not saying it's been easy, but me almost dying a bunch of times clarified Oliver's feelings for me.

He can't live without me, apparently, and obviously the feeling's mutual.

He's in a tux because we're at a black-tie wedding on Catalina Island. My best friend, Emma, got married today. She's taken over the Descanso Beach Club for the weekend—a large white-sided Cape Cod–style building with a series of balconies that stare at the ocean and a coved beach/ marina where you can park your private boat.

It's that kind of wedding.

"I told you a million times. I made this match."

He wraps his arm around my waist. I'm wearing an eggplant bridesmaid dress, and because Emma has excellent taste, I don't hate it. I snuggle into Oliver. His aftershave is fresh, and his eyelashes tickle the skin on my neck. The band is playing Mazzy Star's "Fade into You" and any moment now, Oliver's going to ask me to dance.

"Oh, so you're a matchmaker now?" he says with a grin I can feel against my skin.

"I mean, yeah, kind of."

"Why would you want to get involved in someone else's love life?"

Good question.

And this might seem weird, given the uneven state of my own relationships, but I've always loved weddings. All that love on display. Two

---

[234] Just a suggestion, but Jonathan Bailey would make an <u>excellent</u> James Bond. Google images of him in a tux. Yum.

people facing each other, promising that their love will last through time. Then that first married kiss, sealing the troth, making it clear that forever starts today.

*Forever.*

That's the hope. To do better. To do right. To treasure.

Even—if you kink that way—to obey.

An idea worth preserving, I think. Worth helping come true.

All I'm saying is, there's a reason people are suckers for romance.

"I like putting things together, you know that."

"So, a match is just another mystery to solve?"

"In a way." I catch his hand and twine my fingers through his. Our foreheads are touching now, and it's almost like we're dancing. The sun is setting over the Pacific, the sky outside the windows that amazing orange hue that only lasts for a few minutes. White-sailed boats bob on their moorings, and the air is tinged with the ocean's special brine.[235] "It takes work, you know, finding two people who're right for each other."

He tilts his chin toward me and now we're almost kissing. "Oh, I know."

"Are we going to dance, or what?"

He reaches for my waist without saying anything and pirouettes us onto the dance floor. I laugh, happy, as I tuck my chin on his shoulder. We turn slowly past Emma and her husband, and they look happy, too, as they should.[236]

"Enjoying yourself?" Oliver asks as we navigate past the other dancing couples.

"What's not to enjoy?"

"You seem distracted."

"Oh, I'm just . . . plotting."

"No rest for the wicked."

---

[235] See, Harper? I *can* write flowy things when I feel like it.
[236] More on that later, obviously.

I laugh.

"Every couple I've matched is still together."

This is true.

Until today, that is.

Not that I don't consider today's wedding a success. The ceremony took place, the promises were made, and Emma was beautiful in her white sheath dress that looked simple but cost an astonishing amount. The reception is tasteful and full of glamorous people, and they *will* be together until death parts them.

So, it's not my fault that when I leave Oliver on the dance floor to use the facilities, I find one of the wedding party splayed out on the floor of a supply closet, the cake-cutting knife sticking straight up out of their back like someone tried to serve them up for dessert.

Is it?

Ah, *shit.*

# ACKNOWLEDGMENTS

In the summer of 2022, I knew I needed to make a change in my writing life. I'd been working on a new idea and it wasn't gelling, the way that happens sometimes. Good idea, wrong time, maybe, hard to know. But I was going on vacation to Italy for ten days, and I decided, for once in my life, not to write on vacation. Ha! My brain had other ideas, as it often does. So, as my husband and I were wandering around a *very* hot tour of Pompeii a title came to me: *Every Time I Go on Vacation, Someone Dies*. Maybe it was because I was surrounded by death: Pompeii is a gravesite and that's the reason tourists go there—to see all that frozen life, in death.

Anyway, that title was like a thunderbolt—I knew I had to write it, but what was it about? I'd wanted to write a book about an author whose main character was driving her to murder for a long time, but I had put that idea aside. But it felt like it fit, so I picked it up again and shaped it into this book. I was taking a risk, but in the best kind of way, and I'm so proud of the result. I hope that you've enjoyed it, too!

I didn't get here by myself, though. When I told my agent, Stephanie Kip Rostan, about the title and the idea, she was enthusiastic from the start and guided me along the way with excellent feedback and suggestions, like it should be the Canadian that did it because that's funny. It is!

Thank you so much for believing in me and being up for all of my ideas, because there are too many, I know, but that's just who I am.

Thank you also to my amazing publishing team at Minotaur and Macmillan UK—Catherine Richards, Vicki Mellor, Kelley Ragland, Sarah Melnyk, Allison Ziegler, and Kelly Stone. You have all been so welcoming and enthusiastic and I'm so glad we're doing (at least) three books together! Aperol spritzes for everyone!

Thanks also to Mary Beth Constant for finding my mistakes, to David Rotstein for designing this wonderful cover, and to the team at Levine Greenberg Rostan for selling this book into so many territories.

A special shout-out also to my film and TV management—Rich Green, Brooke Lindley, and Ellen Goldsmith-Vein for helping make all my dreams come true. And to the team at Fox: Charlotte, Brooke, Jillian, and Deborah, for entrusting me with bringing this book to the small screen.

To my tennis ladies, especially Sandra, for keeping me fit and sane.

To my running ladies, especially Janet, for ditto.

To my lady ladies—Tasha, Candice, Sara, and Christie, for always having my back. And to Tanya, for fast texts and random *Twilight* jokes.

Finally, to my husband, David, for agreeing to go to Italy in the first place and for being by my side for thirty years and counting. Good thing I went to that boat dance when I was sixteen.

*Andiamo!*

# ABOUT THE AUTHOR

**Catherine Mack** (she/her) is the pseudonym for a *USA Today* and *Globe & Mail* bestselling author of more than a dozen novels. Her books are approaching two million copies sold worldwide and have been translated into multiple languages, including French, German, and Polish. Television rights to *Every Time I Go on Vacation, Someone Dies* and its sequels sold in a major auction to Fox TV for development into a series, with Mack writing the pilot script. She splits her time between Canada and the United States.

I still can't believe we got so many AH-MAZING quotes for the back cover— and from such great authors too! You didn't bribe them, right?

El, here's the publicist's number in case of an emergency! Marta: 212-555-1279 — Harper

...please don't misplace this note!!!

Ooooh—this new cover sketch is better....BUT on second thought... Can we try something where Connor isn't shown at all? Or maybe just a hint of his presence, like his stupid fedora? He will be livid about his abscence on the cover, but that's an added bonus!